1

Beyond the Wall

Beneath the Dragoneye Moons: Book Four

Selkie Myth

Beneath the Dragoneye Moons

Oathbound Healer
Adventures in the Argo
Ranger's Dawn
Beyond the Wall
Journey to the Center of Pallos
Immortal Moments
Return to Remus

This is a work of fiction, and the views expressed herein are the sole responsibility of the author. Likewise, certain characters, places, and incidents are the product of the author's imagination, and any resemblance to actual persons, living or dead, or actual events or locales, is entirely coincidental.

This story is dedicated to my wonderful wife, Lauren, without whom this wouldn't be possible. Her endless love and support keeps me going.
This story is also dedicated to my beautiful daughter Flora, whose smiles light up my every day.

I would also like to acknowledge my beta readers, who put up with my endless typos, fix my mistakes, and help guide the story, so it can be the best story possible.

I'd like to thank all the other supportive authors and writing communities, and all the kind words they have.

Lastly, I'd like to thank Royal Road. My story and success wouldn't be possible without their website.
Thank you, to each and every one of you.

Chapter 1

A day in the life I

Waking up at the right time was a well-ingrained habit at this point. I woke up, stretched, and looked around my room.

I'd moved back with my parents a year ago, because why not? It had taken them a few months to move, but once they were living in the capital, the villa Night had "gifted" them was huge, so much so that it felt like we were rattling around in it sometimes. It would've been a waste *not* to live there. We were – more like, I was – able to afford to pay someone to help clean the whole place, and it was most certainly a full-time job.

Mom really, *really* appreciated the help. She even had her own little clinic! She was rarely in it though. She took a much more personalized approach, having a small, select group of women that she treated, along with their kids. Having a house in the fancy part of town meant that all of our neighbors were also fancy and rich, giving us automatic social standing, and made up the majority of her clients.

I didn't begrudge her the choice. We all had different priorities. She was healing, she was putting her skills to good use, and she was busy living her best life.

Dad had originally wanted to become one of the guards that worked at Ranger HQ, but I shamelessly put my foot down on it. *No way* was he going to be a regular at my work. That would just be way too weird. And awkward. Dad saluting me as I went to work? Daily?

Nope nope *nope.*

There was some minor potential for grift, corruption, and general nepotism that I wanted to get ahead of to boot. I would never participate, but there was no telling what happened in the background. I wanted no part of it, and the doors were firmly barred.

Having a Sentinel as a kid opened doors for him everywhere though, there was no denying it. He managed to end up as a member of the Praetorian Guard, the elites defending the Senate.

Which was extra-cushy, because the biggest threat to the Senate were loiterers. Dad basically got to walk around with Senators all day, and hear the most *interesting* things.

Which were naturally shared with mom and I. As the Senate saw it, Dad was simply keeping things in the family, and only sharing it with *women* to boot. Whatever. Everyone talked to their spouse. Who cared?

I was a frequent visitor – teacher, really – to Artemis's School of Sorcery and Spellcraft.

As was Julius. I had some sneaking suspicions why Julius was a constant visitor there, but nothing confirmed.

I had absolutely no problems letting Julius know the gossip I'd overheard – which inadvertently gave the Ranger half of Ranger Command a *very good* look into the current inner workings of the Senate. Sure, we were their minions. Sure, we had two Senators on the Ranger Command directly. Didn't mean they always talked with us, and let us know everything that was going on.

Master Spy Elaine. Totally tripped right into the role. Not like I was passing anything super secret or confidential, but Julius seemed to find it interesting, and Night had blessed the activity, and didn't try to find me anything else to do, apart from the marketplace healing.

The *Pastos* incident had been over a year ago, and nobody was letting me forget it.

I was entirely unrepentant. I'd do it again in a heartbeat. Either way, the less that was said about *Pastos* the better.

I had a nice, large, luxurious bed – topped with that fur I'd liberated from the pirates way back when. Forbidden fruit tasted the sweetest, and I slept extra-well on it.

My gear was on an armor stand, along with everything needed to maintain it. I semi-regularly brought it to the Quartermaster – especially when it was damaged – but being my gear, it was my responsibility.

It was my life on the line if something went wrong. Wasn't about to take a risk over something so minor, not when all it took to fix was time.

I nearly got in the habit of taking a trophy every time I was in a major fight, or solved a major problem, but Night had given me a Talking To.

My trophy-collecting ended before it began, and I didn't even buy souvenirs. After Night's little Talking To, I didn't even want a sniff of suspicion that I was doing anything uncouth. Nope. Nu-uhm. No way.

After all was said and done, I was paid *really well,* and my living expenses were fairly minimal. Not only was everything I needed provided for, apart from extra clothes and food, but I was making serious, *serious* money at the marketplace. I gave Autumn a generous allowance, kept increasing my personal hoard of coins, donated some to the general household fund, and even then, I had a bunch leftover.

Which I used on artwork! I had a number of high-quality frescos in my part of the home, along with some paintings, and marble busts.

Of me and my family. I was working on a "Sentinel Series", but I kept a strict budget on how much I spent on artwork each month. It was tempting to blow more, but I had self-control.

For artwork.

I had various little chests and wardrobes for my clothing. I liked mixing it up. Some days were armor days, full on Sentinel Dawn. Other times, I liked wearing some [Pretty] clothes. All depended on my mood, and what was on my plate that day.

I got up, out of bed, and put on my gear. Fancy armor day! No helmet, red cape. I looked quite dashing. I'd considered getting someone with a Wind element class to follow me around and blow air on me. Constant cooling breeze, and permanent cape fluttering.

Too impractical.

I made my way out of my room, smiling as I saw my younger adoptive brother Themis, who was groggily heading to the kitchen as well.

"Themis! Morning! How's it going?" I asked him, all cheerful like.

I got a foul look and a grunt.

Teenagers, I swear. I mean, technically, he wasn't a teenager, not yet, still had another year to go, but moody and untalkative? Oh yeah, he had that down pat. He was going to be a right terror as a teen, unlike me, the model of a cooperative teenager.

Apart from the whole "running away from home and worrying my parents sick" part.

"Training with the guards today?" I asked.

I translated his grunt as "yes".

I considered a few other questions I could ask him, discarded them, and shrugged. Whatever. My poor brother was tragically lost to me, victim of hormones for the next 6-8 years or so. He'd grow up, hopefully realize he was a dickhead like most teenagers, and our relationship would improve.

Wouldn't stop me mercilessly teasing him while I had the chance. Not this morning though.

"Morning mom!" I said, entering the kitchen – a massive affair now, much larger than the cramped little room we called our kitchen back in Aquiliea.

"Elaine! Themis! Good morning!" Mom said, sitting at a table, eating her breakfast.

Themis just grunted. I wasn't the only one getting the grunt-treatment.

"Busy day?" I asked her.

"Oh, you know how it is. One appointment in the morning, two in the afternoon, it's either light or crazy, depending."

Yup. Mom's work being the personalized healer also made her a type of pseudo-therapist, where she listened to all the various problems the rich and powerful had – most of them made up or self-imposed. Like, "The new pillars are simply wonderful, but they clash with the pool aesthetic." I'd seen enough sick and near-death patients from the slums, enough fights and bloody clashes to have absolutely no sympathy whatsoever for those types of problems.

Mom was better than me at that, and she was the sympathetic ear who could cure their physical ailments, which people interpreted as also being able to solve their mental ones to boot. Hey, it worked for her, it worked for them. Who was I to judge.

"Think we'll be able to have lunch together?" I asked her.

Mom tapped her lips thoughtfully.

"I don't think so. Valentina tends to talk *quite* a bit."

I nodded my understanding.

I grabbed some fruit and veggies from the kitchen – mangos and carrots – and walked out the door with them, contentedly munching on them while I made the short trip to Ranger HQ.

"Sentinel." The guards respectfully saluted, while I offered them a cheery wave. I made my way down to the Sentinel meeting room/living room, bumping into Acquisition on the way.

"Acquisition!" I said, happy to see him.

"Dawn." He said, respectfully.

"I'd like my purse back please." I told him, holding my hand out.

"It wasn't me!" He protested.

"Yes, but they installed you as the best thief. You're all the thieves' boss. One of them took my purse, you're the boss, ergo, you took it, and now need to return it!" I said, cheerfully explaining my extremely poor logic to him.

"I don't control them!" He continued to protest.

I just held my hand out and glared. With a sigh, he pulled out *my pouch* and returned it to me.

"Probably half the coins were gone already anyways." He grumbled to me.

"Eh, whatever. I like my pouch. It's got a sun stitched on it, for me!" I told him for what must be the thirtieth time, cheerfully pointing out the sunburst on it. Sunburst for Sentinel, Sunburst for Dawn. It was *perfect.* And mine.

"The fact that every time it gets brought to my attention and I need to get it back makes it a game for the other thieves." Acquisition complained. "More of them target you as a result!"

"Yup." I cheerfully replied. "And I make no effort to stop them. They'll eventually get bored of the game, and hey." I said, tone going from 'excessively cheerful' to 'dead serious' – "It's not *badges* they're trying to steal anymore. Eventually they'll realize that I'm letting them have it, it'll stop being a cool thing to do, and they'll move on."

Acquisition shuddered. His little talk about 'don't steal Sentinel Badges' hadn't hit the mark, and when Sealing's badge had gotten stolen – Night had *words* with the thieves of the town.

Well.

Night had no words. The thieves had quite a few of them, mostly "please spare me" and "Oh gods no". Acquisition got declared the head honcho of thieves, demonstrated his prowess by stealing the clothes off of Senators while they were in session, and demonstrated he should be the boss by *getting away with it.*

I was glad I'd been away on a mission when it happened.

Ocean nodded to us when we arrived, taking our seats. I had a preference for a big fuzzy chair, and I figured the trick to preserving it was throwing a shield around it when a brawl started.

I had a realization *dawn* on me.

Man. It must kinda suck to be Ocean or Hunting. In a normal organization, they'd be groomed to take over leadership one day. Except. The head honcho of the Sentinels, Night, was an immortal vampire. Kinda hard to take over when your boss had been in the job a thousand years, and was aiming to stick with it for at least another thousand.

Everyone trickled in, including, to my minor surprise, Nature. We all sat down, and Night began the morning meeting.

"Well, now that everyone who will be here is here, does anyone have pressing business before we begin Nature's after-action report?" Night asked. Formal. Polite. One step at a time.

Carefully checking things off a checklist perfected hundreds of years ago. He never knew what was coming up, even though I had no doubt he'd heard every message and communication already. Still. It was somewhat disconcerting to hear the *exact same* message and question every single time someone completed a mission.

We looked around at each other, giving subtle shakes of our heads.

"Right. Nature. Please begin." Night said.

"Multiple caravans had been vanishing in the Kadan. Two Ranger teams couldn't locate anything. Went there, started sniffing around. Didn't find anything. Decided against recruiting a bunch of animals to help me look around – the Kadan is just too big. Decided to start joining caravans incognito until something struck. Took three trips until we were attacked. A big sucker of a tree had become a treant, and not only that, but it had a number of other treants under its command."

Nature shuddered.

"Couldn't keep the rest of the convoy alive. Living trees working as a team are *tough,* and my skills couldn't get purchase. They're not trees, they're not animals, I had to do it the *hard* way."

I winced at that mental image. Treants were tricky with Nature's skillset. He had a number of wood-related skills, but against something that actively resisted them? It was almost a counter to his abilities.

Ironically, I would've had an easier time with it. Radiance against wood? Yikes. Too easy. Fire would be even easier.

Nature gave a detailed breakdown of the fight, which consisted mostly of "dodge stuff and slowly chop multiple self-healing trees in half." It sounded incredibly tedious.

"Thoughts on areas of improvement for Nature?" Night asked us.

"Could you have kept multiple animals either on multiple convoys, or scouting up and down the line until you found something, then rushed over when they got a hit?" I asked. "No need to play the 'hit or miss' convoy game that way."

Nature frowned, but nodded at my remark.

"Should've broken the branches first." Brawling said. "You took too long going for a direct kill, before realizing you needed to *whittle* them down first."

I groaned, along with most of the other Sentinels, while looking at Brawling with amazement. I didn't realize he had it in him.

He looked around, and the coin dropped.

"Pun not intended."

Magic had a new trick. Fake rotten fruit materialized in all our hands, and he made it "move" convincingly as we threw it at Brawling. Sadly, it had no heft, no weight – but it was fun anyways.

More analysis, and before long, it was time for training at Ranger Academy. I had a morning class, so I was off, jogging with Ocean down the great tunnel to the Academy. He taught sailing in the morning as well, at a slightly later time. Had a half-dozen mentees that he taught while I taught everyone else medicine.

I gave a quick blast around me with **[Shine]**. Nothing showed up, nothing disappeared. No Magic shenanigans. He'd started avoiding me ever since I got the skill, and applied his own paranoia against him.

After all. I never knew when there was an invisible threat somewhere nearby.

He'd been *incensed* when I used his own logic against him. Out of respect for his own, well-justified, paranoia, I didn't use it during our daily meetings. A truce, of sorts. Both of us protecting ourselves.

I'd heard enough stories of his after-action reports to mentally degrade his "paranoia" down to "completely reasonable caution".

A bonus to **[Shine]**- it made me look *awesome* while it was going. A constant glow around me, and I happily tied it off with **[Persistent Casting]**, to give myself a permanent anti-mirage skill running, without needing to think about it.

And light in the dark.

And I looked *awesome*.

"I'm so glad I don't have any mentees." I said with gusto. I had enough on my plate.

Ocean gave me a sour look.

"Rub it in, why don't you?" He said, no spite in his voice.

"Sure! It's great that I don't have mentees! Fabulous! Fantastic! Wonderful! Brilliant! Great! Thank you so much for getting that one bard to quit!"

"Ok, ok, I get the point." Ocean said, pained. "Please stop rubbing it in now."

I stuck my tongue out at him. He'd literally asked for it.

We made idle small talk as we reached the end of the tunnel leading to Ranger Academy, the tunnel ending in a sprawling, luxurious villa that housed the Trainees that had passed the Hell Months.

Ocean waved to me, and headed over to the docks, where he'd be teaching. No surprise he wanted aquatic-based education.

I got myself ready where I'd be teaching. I'd gotten a dead body of a relatively healthy man procured for me, and I'd annoyed the hell out of the Quartermaster by insisting I was involved with every single step of procurement. There was *no way* I was getting involved in the unethical body acquisition business, not even by turning a blind eye. No. My standards bordered on absurd. Had to be almost completely healthy. Needed a willing family. Needed not a whiff of foul play.

Most of the Trainees were assembled. I had it arranged like an amphitheater, with me in the middle, and rows of Trainees around me, looking down.

"Morning!" I said, bright and cheerful as ever, before jumping into my standard speech. It helped orient me, it helped wake the Trainees up and let them know that yes, it was time to start thinking again. "I wish I was given enough time to teach you enough medicine to be useful. Sadly, I only have time to lightly go over everything once, and pray to all the gods and goddesses that it'll be enough. Get a real healer with you when you travel. It'll save your life."

"Today we're going to review the digestive system." I said, flipping open the Y-shaped cut on the body, grabbing the intestines, and displaying them for everyone. "We previously followed food down the mouth, and into the stomach. Now we're going to follow the path through the small intestine, large intestine, and colon, then review common injuries and emergency remedies."

I paused a moment, letting the more industrious students scribble. I mentally marked three who were basically falling asleep in my class. I had the ability to review my students, and my criteria was real easy – don't sleep in my class.

When it came time for us to solve the giant puzzle of who ended up a Ranger, those three would be on the bottom of my recommendations. End up on the bottom of too many Instructors and Sentinel's lists, and a promotion to Ranger at the end of Academy wasn't in the cards.

It was possible that they'd make it up with extreme strengths in other categories. As I said. I was only one, small piece of the puzzle. Just another cog in the machine.

I gave them a brief – far too brief – lecture and overview on the digestive tract, focusing on common injuries, along with basic management.

"Onions are fairly rare, but if you happen to be in a region with them, make onion soup and drink it. Then carefully smell around the wound. If you smell onion – you're not going to heal naturally. You *must* get to a healer. You will die otherwise, regardless of your vitality stat." I said, hammering the point home.

It was technically possible to naturally heal from an injury that would normally kill someone with enough Vitality, especially when talking about slow injuries like gut wounds. I wasn't about to start sticking that notion in people's head. Before I knew it, people would be telling me about mages with 100 vitality biting the dust, and how I'd said that it'd be "fine".

Rangers tended to be a smart bunch, but exposure to medicine and first aid like I was teaching was a first for many. I was, arguably, literally the leading expert on the subject.

Far too soon, with far too many salient points left, did the gong go off, marking the end of my class. With how much material I needed to cover, an hour a day for almost two years wasn't nearly enough. I could barely handle covering normal pathology, let alone getting into abnormal! Best I could do was a light skim over everything, and pray enough of it stuck when it came to first aid.

I spent a lot of time on injuries and stabilization first aid. It was the critical skill I was trying to impart after all.

I thoroughly washed my hands afterwards, got the body back on ice, to use again later, and with a skip to my step, I headed back to Headquarters. It was one of those mornings where I had an appointment with Albina!

The joy of being a Sentinel. People came to *me,* not the other way around.

"Albina! Good morning!" I cheerfully greeted her as I made it to my "public" space at Ranger HQ.

"Elaine! So glad you're here!" Albina cheerfully gave me a friendly hug. I returned it, flashing **[Phases of the Moon]** through her quickly, making sure she was in peak health, awkwardly trying to not press too hard around her large baby bump.

"Yup! No dire emergency ripping me away this time!" I said, happily taking my seat. "What's up for today?"

"Nothing special! Standard **[Beautician]** session. Nails, hair, makeup, and I've got three outfits for you to try, although I think you've seen one of them before!" Albina happily chirped, awkwardly waddling around me. She was due in about a month, and I was keeping a laser eye on her health. I kept trying to make my way down to her place, so she wouldn't have to walk up here, but she kept beating me here handily, and *insisting* that we do it here.

At a certain point, arguing more would just be condescending, and both her and baby were in perfect health.

I had a sneaking suspicion that her husband had barred her from doing any other work, and the only reason she still saw me was he didn't *dare* tell a Sentinel that her personal **[Beautician]** was no longer available. It'd explain the sudden jump in time and care Albina suddenly had about two months ago.

It was her personal business, and she knew I had a sympathetic ear, and would rain fire down for her if needed.

16

Some careful inquiries got nothing, and I wasn't going to pry too deeply. Not when she seemed genuinely happy, not while she remained healthy.

Albina worked her magic, and all of our time together had been good for her and her levels and classes. She'd gotten a Mirror element class, which let her, well.

Do the most *obvious* Mirror trick for a **[Beautician]**.

"What do you think? Like it?" She asked, a mirror magically appearing in front of me, reflecting myself in it.

I was *way* paler than a woman who was regularly outside should be. A combination of my constant self-healing with **[Phases of the Moon]** and getting half my face burnt off *again* in Massalix didn't lend itself to a tanned complexion.

Or to scars. I'd be so horribly scarred over every inch of my body if it wasn't for magical healing.

Even though I did spend half the summer tanning, trying to level up **[Sun-Kissed]**. A light tan, not a deep tan.

Bright blue eyes, flecked and sparkling with the stars, anchored my face, surrounded by long, slightly wavy light brown hair. The benefit to hanging out with Albina a bunch was I could cut my hair whenever I went on a mission – long hair was hell to maintain on the road – then immediately get it regrown when I got back.

A heart-shaped face contained a happy grin and a cute nose. I looked good, I knew it, and I had **[Pretty]** reinforcing it, and a **[Beautician]** bringing out the best in me, making me look as good as supernaturally possible.

"Thanks! I love it!" I told Albina. "I have no plans for lunch, wanna join me?"

She made a bunch of fussing noises before agreeing.

Life was good.

[Name: Elaine]

[Race: Human]

[Age: 19]

[Mana: 58840/58840]

[Mana Regen: 49245 (+23244.375)]

Stats

[Free Stats: 407]

[Strength: 271]

[Dexterity: 199]

[Vitality: 770]

[Speed: 770]

[Mana: 5884]

[Mana Regeneration: 5635 (+2324.4375)]

[Magic Power: 5121 (+59915.7)]

[Magic Control: 5121 (+59915.7)]

[Class 1: [Constellation of the Healer - Celestial: Lv 256]]

[Celestial Affinity: 256]

[Warmth of the Sun: 215]

[Medicine: 240]

[Center of the Galaxy: 256]

[Phases of the Moon: 256]

[Moonlight: 256]

[Veil of the Aurora: 245]

[Vastness of the Stars: 147]

[Class 2: [Ranger-Mage - Radiance: Lv 215]]

18

[Radiance Affinity: 215]

[Radiance Resistance: 215]

[Radiance Conjuration: 215]

[Shine: 104]

[Sun-Kissed: 165]

[Blaze: 215]

[Talaria: 215]

[Nova: 215]

[Class 3: Locked]

General Skills

[Identify: 151]

[Pristine Memories: 200]

[Pretty: 152]

[Bullet Time: 230]

[Oath of Elaine to Lyra: 234]

[Sentinel's Superiority: 240]

[Persistent Casting: 111]

[Learning: 256]

Chapter 2

A day in the life II

Lunch with Albina was wonderful. We'd grabbed a bite to eat, and were moseying through the streets.

"Could I interest you in a play at the amphitheater?" Albina asked me.

I hesitated a moment. They did have some good stuff right now.

"Sorry, no. I gotta spend time in the market." I said, shaking my head. I felt a little bad for Albina. Still had energy, not a ton to do. Unfortunately, I was also busy, and had things I needed to do.

Albina didn't push, just switched topics and happily told me all about her plans for the baby. Names they'd picked out, a **[Carpenter]** who'd made a crib for them.

"You'll be there, right?" She asked again, nervously.

"I can't promise that." I said, trying to gently let her down. "You know my work."

She looked down, and I patted her shoulder, letting **[Phases of the Moon]** work its magic. I also tried to push **[Warmth of the Sun]**, making it nice and warm.

I was so damn happy that **[Phases of the Moon]** had evolved to handle blood loss when I hit 250.

"Hey, listen, even if I'm not around, ask Markus, or one of the other healers. I know a great **[Midwife]**! They're fantastic! Could even ask my mom for help. Listen. You'll be fine."

I really hoped her husband would let her keep working after the kid. It was a sad reality that babies and kids needed an insane amount of work, and the mom had to do most of it – they were up feeding the kid in the first place, it was "only natural" that they do a bit more than that, and poof! Suddenly, they had no time to keep working a job.

Hence, quite a large number of people being reluctant to take girls on as apprentices. If they were just going to get married, have a kid, and stop working, "what was the point", was their logic.

I *hated* the logic.

I also couldn't deny that having a kid would completely and totally derail my work as Sentinel Dawn, which had sadly kept my attempts at relationships fairly platonic.

I did drag my lunch out just a hair to spend more time with Albina, paid her for the month, tipped her generously, then she was off, back home. I went back to HQ, grabbed my gear – I was still in the fancy outfit Albina had gotten me in – and headed back home.

Totally mis-planned the day. Should've just gone out in a tunic. Now I was hauling my gear around in a bag back home, instead of just tucking a spare tunic in my quarters.

I mean, sure, I could put my gear in my quarters, but I liked having it near me. It was comforting, almost. It helped me sleep better at night.

Whatever. It wasn't like I was on any schedule but my own, once my morning meeting and classes were handled.

It was hilarious how when I went out in the morning, crowds parted before me, and I could get from A to B at basically max speed. In a tunic, without my gear on?

A leaf in the wind, and by wind I mean crowds of people bustling and jostling around. I almost missed the days of being allowed in the grey zone, the part of the road where people with insignificant stats were allowed, mostly so they didn't get crushed by mistake.

Such was life in the city. Fortunately, we were in the rich, wealthy, read: uncrowded part of town, and I got back home without a problem.

"Themis! You around kiddo?" I called out as I wandered through the villa I called home.

No answer. Must still be at guard training. Oh well, not like I wanted him for anything special.

I dropped my gear off, carefully re-arranging it back on the armor stand, wiping off a small amount of dust that I'd gathered throughout the day.

I was *tempted* to stay in all day. I'd gotten a few scrolls from the library, the only reason they'd let them leave the building was I was a Sentinel, but no. I was called.

Not out of duty, but out of my own sense of obligation.

I was *so tempted* to just read a little... but I knew the moment I started reading "a little" the next thing I knew I'd be hearing a call to dinner, and I'd have lost the entire afternoon to reading.

I would know. I'd done it more than once. I wasn't going to have a repeat performance today.

I made my way down to the marketplace, amused by the crowds. I *could* just fly over there, but I was wearing the wrong tunic for it. Plus it was nice to walk sometimes. No more crowds parting! I was practically invisible without my gear, without my badge pinned to my chest. I'd put it in my real pouch, inside my tunic, while leaving my "steal this" pouch on the outside.

Also known as my "annoy Acquisition" pouch.

I slowly made my way through the bustling crowds, eventually making my way to the marketplace where I had my stall.

My daily mango was placed on my stall, untouched even though it was unwatched.

Well, unwatched by me. I already had a bit of a line waiting. The appeal of free medical attention was too much for most people to pass up. And between Autumn, Neptune – my mango hook-up – and the line, well, there were too many eyes on the "unattended" mangos for street urchins to steal.

It didn't stop them from occasionally nabbing it and running. Nobody was super inclined to chase after them, and gratitude only lasted so long. A kid starving on the street didn't care that I'd patched them up two weeks ago if they were going to starve today.

It kinda stung, but I wasn't going to start cracking down on it. I just used it as my daily barometer, a type of omen. Mango present? Good day. No mango? Bad day.

"Elaine! Elaine! You're here! Yes!" Autumn said, jumping down from her seat at the stall next to mine and running over to me.

The beanpole was getting even *taller* than me. I knew I was short, but it still rankled.

"Autumn! You ready?" I asked her, grabbing one of the mangos, and carefully peeling and slicing it with Radiance.

Made the inside a little overcooked at times, but it was worth practicing my control every day. Especially since I'd lost **[Radiance Manipulation]** for **[Shine]**.

Didn't really miss the skill. The only thing I really noticed was I couldn't curve **[Nova]** balls anymore. Radiance was weird that way.

She nodded furiously.

"Alrighty! Let's go!" I said, before settling in to see the first patient of the day.

The man showed us his arm, with more bends in it than normal.

"Alright Autumn, what's the problem here?" I asked her. There was some fancy rule about "not talking with mango in your mouth", but I was the VIP here. Nobody was going to tell me off.

Except Autumn. Maybe. The only respect I got from her was in my ability to teach her how to make mountains of money.

"Broken arm." She promptly said, stating the obvious.

The man being healed blessedly kept his mouth shut. Nobody was a stranger to apprentices, and "Free healing" tended to smooth over a lot of speed bumps.

"Can you fix it?" I asked her.

She hesitated.

"Maybe. I'd try to realign the bones, then use **[Boost Natural Healing]** on it. That *should* hopefully fix the problem." She hedged.

23

"Hopefully?" I said, prodding her. Gotta give my apprentice a hard time. It was how she learned.

It was one of the greatest joys in my life so far when she'd taken – with Neptune's blessing – a Light healer class as her second class when she hit level 64. Literally brought tears of joy to my eyes.

"Rule 4 of medicine. Medicine is an art, not something that can be weighed and measured." She recited.

She'd made up the rules herself. I was so *proud*.

"So can you?" I asked her.

I could see the struggle on her face.

"No." She finally admitted.

"Good call." I said, leaning over and tapping the dude, hitting him with both **[Vastness of the Stars]** then **[Phases of the Moon]**. With a sickening *crunch* his arm realigned.

Autumn held out her hand, staring at the dude with huge, accusing eyes.

"I thought it was free." He grumbled, handing over quite a few coins.

"It is! Thanks for your donation!" Autumn said, whisking away the coins so fast her hand almost blurred, even with my improved vitality. I *swear* she had a skill for that. **[Mine, Mine, they're all Mine!]** or something.

The line continued to shuffle through, Autumn carefully taking and examining each patient one at a time, while I oversaw her work, and healed behind her, making sure whatever the problem was got fully fixed.

She only had Light healing, which meant she was stuck with boosting and restoring, and **[Restoration]** variants were high-level skills which she didn't have yet. The path of being a Light healer was *rough* at the early levels, which is why most healers didn't go down that route.

Which was part of why healers that did manage to not only make it through the early levels, but were lucky enough to get a **[Restoration]** skill, made so much money. There was no price that could be put on getting a hand back, on regrowing a leg.

Didn't stop Autumn from trying. She was going to end up very, *very* wealthy.

Well, her family was.

The line kept going, and the scourge of my existence showed up.

Stalkers.

They made me somewhat nervous. Sure, I could blast them to pieces if they threatened me or Autumn, but they didn't. They just showed up, whispered to each other, and *stared.*

The guard occasionally cleared them out – being a VIP had perks – but they always came back.

Staring at me.

Creepy as fuck.

Being a VIP had downsides to boot.

A *very large* coin purse got placed on my stall.

"Heya! Want to go on a date?" The dude asked, as Autumn whisked it away.

"No, thank you." I said after a moment.

The dude's face fell, as Autumn rubbed her hands in glee. The sign had been her idea, and while I wasn't a fan, it did cut down on unwanted proposals significantly.

Ask Dawn on a date! 800 coins! No refunds. She'll probably turn you down.

I'd insisted on the last part.

Fortunately, he took it with good grace. I'd occasionally given a date a shot, but they'd all been horrible busts so far. A few people got mad due to absolutely terrible reading comprehension, and seemed to think paying to ask was the same as me agreeing.

Autumn was all fire, and took no prisoners.

Like. I hated the sign with a burning, fiery passion, but it was the single best way to get people to bugger off and leave me alone. A "No dates" sign was simply taken as a challenge, and nothing at all was also seen as an open invite.

Next in line was a sort of "non-emergency ambulance". An enterprising set of teenagers had realized that there was a market for picking up someone really old or sick, and carting them over to me. They charged a bit, and we'd had a long talk together, making sure they didn't lie to people, and charge them the full price of a healer, then claim "oh you paid us already, that's the same as paying the healer."

Didn't stop the occasional patient with dementia from causing problems, but all in all, it was a solid service they provided. I didn't have the time and energy to hunt for sick parents holed up in their home – they did. They also provided the transportation, originally on a makeshift gurney, which they'd upgraded.

I didn't know what it was like for them when I didn't show up, but Autumn had laughed herself sick when she tried to tell me what it was like.

I never did get the full story out of her.

The day passed, and we made surprisingly good money for being "free healing". Autumn was practically rubbing her hands in glee. Money, training, experience, *and* levels? Money-grubber paradise.

I glanced at the sun, and saw it was getting a bit lower than I'd like.

"Right. I want to close up." I told Autumn.

"Awww, you sure?" She asked me, giving me the trademark puppy eyes.

"Yes." I firmly told her. "Everyone, start moving!" I called out.

The massively decimated line started moving, and I held my hand out in a "side-five" gesture. As everyone passed, they gave me five, I blasted healing through them, and they moved on.

Downside to being at the back of the line – a much longer wait.

Upside – no Autumn harassing you for coins.

It was only about eight people left in line, and we were done in under a minute.

"Right, now what?" I asked Autumn.

She rolled her eyes at me.

"Already stashed the coins *ages* ago, dunno why you're asking me." She said.

I had a deal with Neptune, where basically he held onto my coins, and got most of them deposited in the right place for me. He took a small cut, and I trusted him not to skim more off the top.

Not when I was his kid's lucky break.

I stretched and made my way through the crowds, to a nice home. I knocked on the door and let myself in.

"Kallisto! Cordelia!" I called out. "I'm here!"

"Elaine! Welcome!" Cordelia said, juggling Flora. "Come, sit! Kallisto just got back, he'll be ready in a minute."

Shame I couldn't give Cordelia a hug, not while she was holding Flora.

I sat down at the dinner table, with a pair of slaves bustling around, getting the last touches ready as Cordelia directed them.

I'd gotten mom and dad to not use any slaves, instead hiring a freeman. The ethics argument didn't sway them that much, but me paying for it did. Cordelia had no such compunctions, and I'd run the argument into the ground ages ago. I stopped bringing it up, to keep the peace. We both knew where we stood on this.

Didn't stop me from trying to convince Kallisto when we were out on missions together though.

"Kallisto!" I happily called out to him, waving.

"Elaine! Glad you could make it!"

Dinner with Kallisto and his family. A wonderful time of day.

"Anything new?" I asked him.

I got a discreet look from him, a quick flash of Ranger hand code which said something along the lines of "yes, ugly."

"Nope! Same old, same old. Guard likes being able to handle most things. I swear sometimes they just send us on busy work so we're not constantly in their hair, reminding them of just how much better we are." He said.

His hand code had sent an entirely different message. He'd been on something so nasty and ugly, he didn't want to mention it in front of his wife and kid. It was his call, and frankly, having occasionally gone on one of his missions as back up – yeah. I got it. Didn't approve, but I got it.

"Guard good!" Flora said, throwing some food.

I'd never thought I'd be using **[Veil]** to defend against this type of attack.

All too soon, dinner ended, and I was heading out of town, to Artemis's School of Sorcery and Spellcraft. It was out of town, but the capital was so darn safe.

Also, it was guarded by Artemis, who rivaled some Sentinels in combat prowess, and had absolutely no problems applying lethal force, much to some ex-burglar's, well...

...Can't exactly experience *chagrin* if you're dead.

"Artemis! Julius! How's it going?" I asked them, making it to the school. A few of the healers I was about to lecture to were hanging around.

"Good! How's your day been?" Artemis asked.

"Same old, same old. Nothing new or exciting." I said. "Oh! Autumn got another level today!"

Artemis grinned at me. She knew the joys of teaching well.

"I look forward to when she joins as a student."

Julius snorted.

"Like the little merchant would ever pay for something she can get for free."

Artemis casually swatted at him, which Julius leaned to avoid without looking.

No – he'd been leaning even before Artemis started moving.

If I didn't know better, I'd swear they acted like an old married couple.

"Here to give your recruiting pitch?" I asked Julius.

"Yes. We need more healers." He turned to Artemis.

"I was lucky enough to get Dawn casting the tie-breaking vote. We can pay any Ranger-Healers more!" Julius said.

I grinned. I'd been particularly happy to be in that meeting. One of the earlier ones.

I didn't mention to him that the Sentinels had a long discussion on it ourselves, and we'd also voted on the measure, privately, which had determined how we would vote.

Hey. We were allowed our secrets.

"Anyways, they're waiting for you." Artemis said.

I happily went into one of the lecture halls, where a good number of healers – mostly apprentices – were waiting for me. I lectured once a week, and it was good for everyone. Artemis's school was exploding in popularity, and everyone in the room was leveling.

Incredibly tiring to work on and prepare a lecture though, but I was doing good. I was making the world a better place, and all it took was hours of my time.

I mean, I had to prep the Ranger's lecture to boot, but that was literally my job, and I was determined to do it well, unlike Sky who just *winged* it.

I probably should be paying attention to Autumn's rule 1 – always get paid – but while I had energy, I was going to keep the lectures up. I was feeling burnout start to creep up now and then, but...

Ok, fine. I'm not sure how much longer I'd be able to keep these up, not without help. I needed to talk with Night, and possibly Command about it. If I started charging, dozens of people would vanish.

"Welcome! Thank you everyone." I said, looking at the crowd.

"Today, I'm going to talk about the immune system, how it works, what it does, and how skills can influence it – for better or worse."

I started my lecture, talking about the basics, white blood cells, their role in fighting off disease. How most weren't even noticed.

How Light could bolster and strengthen the system.

How Dark could purge disease.

How the immune system didn't learn anything when a direct purge was done, making the person vulnerable to re-infection.

Well, more vulnerable. There was nuance, especially since the immune system would've gotten a look, and had at least some immunity, and could potentially build off of that, and...

"Remember. Medicine is *complicated*. It's an art." I said, as a bell in the back of the room lightly chimed.

[**ding!** [Oath of Elaine to Lyra] leveled up! 234 -> 235]

One of the apprentices had gone up and hit it, indicating he'd leveled up. A particularly brilliant suggestion from Artemis, it went off two, three times a lecture. People rarely got more than three levels from listening to me lifetime, even if the material was wildly varied, but as word spread that one could literally level up just by listening to me talk, well.

I had a nice revolving door of low and mid level healers coming by to listen.

I was making a *difference*.

Maybe I should travel more?

The lecture wrapped up, and Artemis, Julius, Artemis's helper, Julius's bodyguard – Commanders were *expected* to have bodyguards, unlike Sentinels, who had to look invincible – all settled in for a lovely nightcap.

"I'm pretty sure I'm going to get at least five applicants for Ranger Academy." Julius said, sipping at his mug.

"Oh? That many talked with you?" Artemis asked.

"A heck of a lot more than that talked with me." Julius responded. "But I only think a small number will actually join."

I smiled, and we clinked mugs.

"No poaching my students!" Artemis fiercely told Julius. "They're mine!"

"I'd never poach them." Julius said with a straight face.

And he wouldn't. He'd just dangle the potential of being like *Artemis* in front of their face, and they'd sign up in droves. Most students of hers seemed to think "going to Ranger Academy" the natural, logical next step once they'd learned a ton of magic from her. Passing the entrance exam was being seen as the "graduation test" from the school, no matter how hard Artemis tried to disabuse them of the notion.

Ah well.

Her problem.

Life, for me?

It was *good.*

[Name: Elaine]

[Race: Human]

[Age: 19]

[Mana: 58840/58840]

[Mana Regen: 49245 (+23244.375)]

Stats

[Free Stats: 407]

[Strength: 271]

[Dexterity: 199]

[Vitality: 770]

[Speed: 770]

[Mana: 5884]

[Mana Regeneration: 5635 (+2324.4375)]

[Magic Power: 5121 (+60171.75)]

[Magic Control: 5121 (+60171.75)]

[Class 1: [Constellation of the Healer - Celestial: Lv 256]]

[Celestial Affinity: 256]

[Warmth of the Sun: 215]

[Medicine: 240]

[Center of the Galaxy: 256]

[Phases of the Moon: 256]

[Moonlight: 256]

[Veil of the Aurora: 245]

[Vastness of the Stars: 147]

[Class 2: [Ranger-Mage - Radiance: Lv 215]]

[Radiance Affinity: 215]

[Radiance Resistance: 215]

[Radiance Conjuration: 215]

[Shine: 104]

[Sun-Kissed: 165]

[Blaze: 215]

[Talaria: 215]

[Nova: 215]

[Class 3: Locked]

General Skills

[Identify: 151]

[Pristine Memories: 200]

[Pretty: 152]

[Bullet Time: 230]

[Oath of Elaine to Lyra: 235]

[Sentinel's Superiority: 240]

[Persistent Casting: 111]

[Learning: 256]

Chapter 3

Massage

The lecture wrapped up fairly late at night. Fortunately for everyone involved, it wasn't short like the Ranger Academy one, where I needed to dump as much info as I could in as short a period as possible. I had *time* to properly explain everything, and explain how everything intersected, how magic applied to it – mostly.

I was still mostly clueless on what Wood stuff could do, besides "make potions". As to what they could make? My best guess was walking into a store and seeing what was for sale.

I wasn't nearly good enough to present lectures on the stuff, although I'd been chatting with one particularly high-level dude, trying to convince him to start his own lecture series in tandem with mine.

All I could offer him was advertising, and "why would I give away all my secrets for maybe a few sales from people who don't need my stuff" was his current logic.

I think I might be getting to him though!

"Hey! We're leaving!" Julius announced to the healers, who'd taken the time post-lecture to mingle somewhat while Artemis, Julius, and I spent time chatting.

That quickly killed the socializing, and Julius and I had a crowd following us as we made our way back to the gates.

By sheer virtue of our positions, the guards would open the gates for Sentinel Dawn and Commander Julius – and basically *nobody* else. They'd begged, pleaded, and tried to bribe me to host my teaching sessions inside the city walls, but I was unmovable. Helping Artemis, boosting her school, was more important to me than inconveniencing some guards – as much as I liked guards.

"Sentinel Dawn. Commander Julius." The captain said, saluting us as we entered, and as all the other healers started to stream down the streets, to where they lived.

"Heya Cicero! How's it going?" I asked him, waving happily.

I got a pained look.

"It'd be much better if you didn't teach so late at night. Please. The bribe's at 7000 coins now." He pleaded.

I laughed.

"Wellll… I could say yes… but then you'd still need to bribe Commander Julius. He'd keep going out to flirt with Artemis." I said, shamelessly deflecting the blame onto him, letting him take some of the heat.

"Wait – Artemis told you? That was supposed to be a secret!" Julius complained.

"Sh- YOU WHAT!?" I said, turning to Julius and looking at him open-mouthed. "you- Artemis – What!? *When!?*"

I wasn't exactly coherent.

Julius had color in his cheeks.

"Oh, she hadn't told you. Um. Can we pretend you heard nothing?"

I shook my head at him as the guards wisely vanished. When powerhouses argued in the street, the guards were there to arrest them.

When powerhouses who outranked them a hundred times over argued in the streets, the guards *vanished.*

"Oh no, you gotta tell me *everything.*" I said, walking towards him.

Julius was, fundamentally, a speedster. In spite of us being similarly leveled, his class was a higher tier quality-wise than mine, and, well, speedster vs mage was tilted towards the speedster.

Especially when they decided to run away.

Humph. I was going to *ask Artemis really nicely* about this tomorrow. Artemis had no trouble zapping me if I was sassy – I'm pretty sure she went extra-hard, knowing how unkillable I was.

Kinda made sense, thinking about it. Julius had been hanging around Artemis's school *constantly* for... oh shit. Quite a long time now.

He'd been spending way more time than what could be explained by just wanting to pop in to see an old friend or see how the school was going. *No wonder* he was always there when I popped by.

I felt a grin crack my face as I wandered through the streets, back home. I did a little hop, skip, and a jump, clapping my hands together. Ooooh, I was going to have *so much fun* with this!

The city had a fairly active nightlife. A different set of vendors took over, selling more late-night snacks. Jugglers, bards, and other entertainers took to the streets, strutting their stuff as crowds of colorfully dressed people walked around, occasionally stopping to watch amazing displays of athletics and skills.

It was *amazing* what people could do with skills.

I turned [Shine] off while I walked through town. The tiny chance that someone was sneaking up on me invisible, vs ruining a third of the acts I came across – well. One was a lot more dangerous than the other, and angry jugglers could really pack a wallop.

There were a number of prostitutes out and about, and I got a few good eyefuls until I saw one that brought me up short.

She was wearing a very short leather skirt, a sort of silvery shirt, with a great big sun on it. Kinda, almost, if you squinted really hard, looked a bit like armor that the army used.

That Rangers used.

That Sentinels used.

"Come have a lovely night with Sunrise!" She called out. "Stay until the sun rises!"

Yeah, what? Tonight was great for short-circuiting my brain.

Was that supposed to be me!?

Holy.

Shit.

I hadn't quite realized I was so famous that prostitutes were dressing up as me. On one hand, it was kinda gross. On the other, much larger hand – I was weirdly flattered.

I *had* to know more.

"Hi!" I said, waving to her, walking over.

"Hello." She said, with a sultry voice. "Want to have some fun until *dawn?*"

Yup. That was not an accident.

I took out my badge.

"Hi. I'm Sentinel Dawn. I've got a few questions…" I said.

She went from pale to white, and sat down fast, burying her head in her hands, mumbling something.

"Sorry, what?" I asked her.

"I'm so dead." She said a little louder.

Oh shit. I made her cry. I didn't mean to.

I sat down next to her, slightly awkwardly patting her back.

"No, no, it's ok. I just want to talk. Is there somewhere a little better…?" I asked her, looking around at the street we were on. Kinda awkward place to have a chat.

Sniffing into her shirt, with a defeated look on her face, she nodded and got up. I got up as well, feeling awful.

We entered what was probably a brothel, and after I got inside –

Yup. Definitely a brothel.

We got stopped halfway across the first main room, which was large, full of people, and roughly one tunic for every three people.

"Hey Sunrise, is everything ok? She's not bothering you is she?" A large man asked, putting a hand between me and her. I let him.

Sunrise nodded, and yeah. I mean, she was clearly crying, I would see what was wrong. I figured I'd step in.

"Heya! I'm Dawn. I saw Sunrise here, had a few questions for her, made her really upset, and now I want to make sure she's ok."

The bouncer crossed his arms.

"She's ok. Now scram."

Sunrise tugged on his arm.

"No, no, it's ok. She's Dawn." She said.

"Yes, and you're Sunrise. Who cares?" The bouncer said.

"No. She's *Dawn*." Sunrise said.

The penny dropped for the bouncer. It *never got old*. The situation was serious, but I couldn't help but have a huge grin crack my face.

"*Sentinel* Dawn, nice to meet you." I said, extending my hand.

The bouncer gave me a terrible salute instead, like someone who'd watched a dozen guards in plays, but was never a soldier himself.

"I apologize. But… I have to know. Is she going to be ok?" He asked.

I *liked* this brothel! They looked after their own. Half the stories I'd heard would have them throwing Sunrise out before the night was over.

"Well, that's the hope! That's why I want to chat. She broke down crying when I introduced myself, and, well, I feel kinda responsible."

The bouncer nodded, and we found ourselves in a back room.

"You're not mad?" She said through some sniffles.

"Well, only if someone's making you do it." I said.

She mutely shook her head.

"What's your story anyways?" I asked, figuring to change the topic somewhat. People liked talking about themselves, right?

Slowly, hesitantly, she started telling me her backstory. It was pretty straightforward. Orphaned at an early age, was a **[Thief]**, grew up, got older, and turned to the oldest profession to make ends meet.

There was an awkward gap in the middle that I interpreted as "became a slave, ran away, and am still technically a runaway slave", but I didn't ask more.

"And then I heard more and more about a *Sentinel Dawn* who was a *woman,* and I got this idea. It worked *so well!*"

"Well, then go for it, but be a little more discreet." I said. "I know how hard it is for you. Scratch that, I don't. I know how hard it was for me, and I know you've gotta have it harder than me. I'm not going to begrudge you making a living however you can, as long as nobody's forcing you to do this. It's more than a little creepy that people are paying that well to pretend to have sex with me, I'm not going to lie. But they're the creepy ones, not you. You're cool." I said, patting her.

"For real?" She asked me.

"Yeah. For real." I said, almost getting strangled by her hug.

"Thank you thank you THANK YOU!" She said, and I realized she had to be around my age.

I had a sudden vision of our roles being reversed, if dad's eye injury had been worse when I was a kid. How close had I been to this?

"What can I do for you? Anything? I can probably talk Marcellus into giving you a session if you'd like – he's stupid high level. Or, um, " She said, thinking fast, then listing off a bunch of options.

I laughed.

"No, no, I'm good. Although, I do have a free clinic if anyone needs help. I know some diseases can cause serious problems."

Sunrise nodded at me. I'd gotten her real name, but Sunrise just *fit*.

"Please? Are you sure? I can't even give you a massage or anything?" She asked.

She really, *really* wanted to say thanks somehow, and it had been a long day.

"Yeah, sure, a quick massage, why not." I said.

"EEee! Yes! Ok, lie down real quick, on your stomach." She said, and I complied.

Her hands tentatively, gently, reached my shoulder, and oh *goddesses*. There *had* to be skills involved, and fairly high level ones to boot.

I let out a pleased noise, and Sunrise leaned in, finding her confidence, which made it even *better*.

I was wobbly-legged on my way back home. That was *amazing*. Fabulous. I could see why some people spent all their money at a brothel, and Sunrise hadn't even been super high level!

I was *totally* going back. Would probably get the VIP treatment, especially after I'd given everyone free healing.

Well, everyone who'd been available. Hopefully word of my healing stall in the marketplace would spread to boot! Some of the girls had been *really sick.*

They were better now, and it warmed my heart.

I got home in no time at all.

"Heya dad! Good day?" I asked him.

"Ugh. Same old, same old. I was with Senator Kosmimatus today. Some farmers want there to be a tax on bamboo." He rolled his eyes at that.

"An entire day. Bamboo taxation. The *worst.*"

Master spy stuff was generally *extremely boring.*

"Why did they want a tax on bamboo?" I asked him.

"Honestly? Because they sell wool, and they'd sell more with a bamboo tax. That's it. That's the entire story."

Sometimes government got it right. Other times, they wildly missed the mark.

"Welp, sounds like you had fun." I told him.

"Fun? *Fun!?* I had to stand there all day! My biggest challenge was *not yawning.*"

I laughed at his, as I waved, heading to bed.

"Goodnight dad. You know what I'm going to say."

"Yeah, yeah. Don't go near your rooms when you're sleeping. I got it." Dad said.

I took a quick dip in my bath – the villa was big enough to have more than one, and I'd claimed one as my own, personal bath – before going to sleep.

Daytime was great. Friends. Family. A great job, freedom to do what I saw fit, a calling. People liking me. Preferential treatment. The ability to pursue my hobbies.

Nighttime – less so. That's when the dreams came.

I'd almost ended up addicted to sleeping potions at one point. I'd cut them out entirely, and sworn to never touch one again.

I got into a fresh, simple tunic, and laid down in bed. A whole bed, all to myself.

Come on.

Gotta sleep.

Maybe tonight will be fine.

I let my eyelids get heavy and close.

I opened them to a sea of blood, all caused by me.

"Murderer." Iola, the bandit leader whispered to me. "You killed me. Just too cowardly to do it yourself."

I tried to shoot her, burn her alive. I had no magic, no skills. I just waded against the tides of blood, trying to escape from her.

Tides of blood, that I'd spilt personally.

"Murderer." The pirate captain spat at me. "You weighed your freedom against twenty lives, and decided they had to die. Probably killed the merchant and his family as well, after ruining their livelihood. How is that a fair trade? How is that an ethical trade?"

I tried to run from him, only to encounter members from the rebellion.

Survivors of Destruction's skills, who I'd healed.

"Bitch. You healed them, just to divide us. You're responsible for the in-fighting. You killed all the survivors, as surely as if you'd wielded the knife yourself."

Lyra.

Oh goddesses *no,* not Lyra, not tonight. Please.

Anything but Lyra.

"You." She said, forever eight in my dreams, forever staring at me with pained eyes. "You –"

It was blessed relief when the door to my room exploded inwards, a huge man bursting in. I was awoken, adrenaline flooding my system, fight-or-flight kicking in.

41

I blasted the man with a thin beam of Radiance, designed to kill – or at least burn his eyes, so he couldn't see, while unleashing a **[Nova]** right at him.

"Da- **WHOA CHILL**" He yelled, taking the **[Nova]** head-on.

"wha- *Brawling!?"* I yelled, confused, still waking up.

"Holy shit, are you ok!?" I asked, crashing as I realized I wasn't in fight or flight.

Oh fuck **[Oath]** don't punish me for this, I genuinely thought I was under attack.

No punishment. Bless the reasonable aspect of it. That was *close.*

Sadly, a good chunk of my room hadn't survived my **[Nova]**. I winced. I'd need a new wardrobe.

I snapped back to Brawling. He waved his hand.

"Just a little warm, I'm fine. Anyways. Emergency. Gear up."

Oh fuck this must be one hell of an emergency. Nothing – *nothing* – couldn't wait until the morning meeting.

Until this, clearly.

I looked at him. He looked back.

"Come on! Move!" He tapped his foot, looking at me.

I finished waking up, and one and one clicked.

Holy *shit* we were in a bad emergency, if Brawling was waiting in my room for me to gear up.

Modesty forgotten, I jumped out of bed, stripped out of my tunic, and started to gear up.

New tunic – designed to be worn with my armor.

Laminar vest. Sunstone and Moonstone woven throughout, internally, along with a ton of Arcanite. Inscriptions woven throughout, for toughness. Strength. Speed. Dexterity.

A minor one to keep my badge on, no matter what happened.

Sandals. **[Talaria]** required them.

Shin guards. More inscriptions. More stones.

Vambraces. They held my special, one-off gemstones. All the Sentinels traded skills with each other, giving us part of each other's kit.

42

Helmet.

No cape.

Our "serious" gear.

I went around the room, making sure I had the last pieces of my kit. Short sword. Inscribed again, but nothing special, nothing out of the ordinary.

I glanced at Brawling.

"Threat level?" I asked him.

"Bring it all." He said.

I took down my tower shield off the wall. Grabbed the spear behind it.

I hadn't used this shield since I became a Sentinel. Same with the spear.

Small round shield got added.

"Got everything?" Brawling asked, having helpfully stamped out the small fire.

"Check me over." I said.

"No time. We'll do it on the way."

Before I could object, he'd picked me up and we were *moving.* Brawling was not only higher level than me, but had a higher tier class, and was all physical stats and buffs.

I didn't like being carried like this, but it was the fastest transportation possible. I kept my mouth shut for expediency.

In a flash, we were in front of Ranger HQ, where a number of guards were clearing the street in front of the building. Some people were curious and looking on, but being pushed back.

"Here we are – whoa!" Brawling said, putting me down, then immediately picking me up and moving me.

I hated being an almost literal stick that could be thrown around, but I could see the reasoning as the *Pegasus,* our rapid deployment sky ship, landed *hard* in the street.

Mostly in pairs, the rest of the Sentinels showed up, usually one of the more physically minded transporting one of the slower, more magically based ones.

Quartermaster was awake, and organized a few of the guards to start throwing bags into the *Pegasus.* A shattering noise accompanied one of the bags, and with a curse he just threw the bag off to the side.

Holy.

Our penny-pinching Quartermaster just throwing stuff around? Breaking tons of valuable stuff and not caring?

We were in deep shit.

I got onboard the *Pegasus,* finding a seat near the front, and staying out of the way. I started giving my gear a double check. I'd put it on in a rush, and I wasn't going to die due to a loose strap.

We finished getting ready, when Night showed up at last, with one of the people I least expected.

Priest Demos.

"Excellent. We are all here." Night said. "Ocean. Acquisition. You two stay behind. The rest of you – board. We leave now."

Ocean and Acquisition saluted.

I didn't question him. We had seven large, glowing Arcanite crystals in the middle of the boat – extra fuel for wherever we were going.

We all boarded in short order. No double checking. Quartermaster desperately throwing as much stuff as he could in the boat.

"Ocean. You're in charge if we don't come back." Night said.

"Sky. Max speed. Frontlines." Night said, and in just a few moments, I felt myself becoming lighter as Sky reduced gravity's influence on all of us, then a large breeze came, filling the sails, lifting us up, up, and away, speeding us westward, one last pack from the Quartermaster falling short.

"I apologize for the short notice." Night said, seeing that rushing wouldn't get us there any faster.

"The Formorians have breached the walls."

[Name: Elaine]

[Race: Human]

44

[Age: 19]

[Mana: 58840/58840]

[Mana Regen: 49245 (+23244.375)]

Stats

[Free Stats: 407]

[Strength: 271]

[Dexterity: 199]

[Vitality: 770]

[Speed: 770]

[Mana: 5884]

[Mana Regeneration: 5635 (+2324.4375)]

[Magic Power: 5121 (+60171.75)]

[Magic Control: 5121 (+60171.75)]

[Class 1: [Constellation of the Healer - Celestial: Lv 256]+]

[Celestial Affinity: 256]

[Warmth of the Sun: 215]

[Medicine: 240]

[Center of the Galaxy: 256]

[Phases of the Moon: 256]

[Moonlight: 256]

[Veil of the Aurora: 245]

[Vastness of the Stars: 147]

[Class 2: [Ranger-Mage - Radiance: Lv 215]]

[Radiance Affinity: 215]

[Radiance Resistance: 215]

[Radiance Conjuration: 215]

[Shine: 104]

[Sun-Kissed: 165]

[Blaze: 215]

[Talaria: 215]

[Nova: 215]

[Class 3: Locked]

General Skills

[Identify: 151]

[Pristine Memories: 200]

[Pretty: 152]

[Bullet Time: 230]

[Oath of Elaine to Lyra: 235]

[Sentinel's Superiority: 240]

[Persistent Casting: 111]

[Learning: 256]

Chapter 4

Formorians I

There was dead silence at Night's pronouncement. He would say more, in time.

I looked around. Magic. Destruction. Sealing. Sky. Night. Nature. Brawling. Demos. Myself.

The peak of humanity, speeding along in a little boat, high in the sky, off to contain the breach.

"From the courier's report, both official and what he saw, this is it." Night said. "The Formorians have brought everything to this battle, which is how they breached the walls in the first place."

Destruction swore.

"Wait – they got through *all* the walls?"

"*Yes.*" Night nearly hissed at him.

"How the fuck did they do that?" Brawling asked.

I was wondering that myself. Humanity was able to hold the line with soldiers on the ground, the wooden palisades behind them the first line of defense. A maze of smaller, wooden walls was behind that, where we were occasionally pushed back, but had extra defenses.

Then there were three gigantic walls, layered, high and thick, made out of stone. The only times they ever went down is when humans did something monumentally stupid, and broke them. Or when the army decided to "leap frog" a set of walls forward, claiming more ground against the Formorians.

"For the most part, we mostly just see what I shall call 'Formorian Soldiers' or simply 'Soldiers'" Night said, getting into teacher mode. I was used to his lectures, having been on the receiving end for almost two years.

"There are a number of other types. I believe we do not see these types normally, because they are much more expensive for the Formorians to produce, and they are used for defensive purposes." Night said. "Only when we push deep, when we begin to threaten their nests, do they appear."

"Nature, please let me know if you've encountered a type I have not." Night said. "It has been quite a few years since I last attempted a dive, and new Formorians may have been created since then, or some rare breed may now exist."

Nature nodded.

"There are Shooters, Spitters, and what I shall call Royal Guards. Shooters are beetle-like, with a large number of sharpened, poisoned spikes on their back. They specialize in shooting down fliers, and are the primary reason we do not simply drop poison on top of the Formorian nests. Spitters, as the name suggest, spit streams of acid out of their mouth. They resemble large worms. They are used inside their nest, to ambush and attack invaders from all directions."

Night's muscles rippled as he suppressed a shudder.

"The last type I have directly seen and engaged in combat are the Royal Guards. They are ten meters tall, a bulbous body with massive mandibles and thick armor. None of my attacks could penetrate their armor and cause harm to them. By the same token, they do not handle small, nimble targets well. That was inside their lair, however, with dozens of other Formorians assisting, and outside, without additional distractions, well. They may be more manageable."

He paused a heartbeat. Wait, did he even have one...?

"I do not know why the Formorians saw fit to have such large guards. What they are supposed to defend against, I do not know. Nature. Are you aware of any other types?"

Nature grimaced.

"Maybe. I had bursts of acid come out of the ground now and then. It sounds like the Spitters. Maybe. Doesn't sound like their method of operation."

Night nodded.

"Should we expect attacks from below?" Sealing asked.

Night hesitated a moment.

"Possibly. Generally, the Earth mages present on the frontlines collapse any tunneling attempt. However, I believe they will be otherwise occupied."

That was one way of putting it.

"Hang on, hang on, how did they breach the walls!?" Sky asked.

"Reports say it was a number of Royal Guards. The exact details are unknown to me at this time, however, with their size and bulk, I can believe this to be the truth."

"That matter is irrelevant. It has happened. The Formorians bringing their defensive units forward suggest that the Formorian Queens themselves have emerged, and are coming. This may be our single best chance to slay them." Night said.

"Assuming there are no other Queens in reserve." I pointed out. Night tilted his head in agreement.

"Assuming there are no other Queens that have stayed behind, correct." Night said. "However, even if there are some in reserve – slaying this many, when they are out of their domain, when they have left their lair, should be enough to tilt the odds in our favor to the point where we may take the offensive."

I looked around at us.

"So, what's the plan?" I asked.

"I am hoping to discuss this with all of you at this time. I believe the objective is to slay the Queens. The breach, and the containment of Formorians who have made it through the wall, is of secondary concern. Any objections?" Night asked.

There were heads shaking around the open air sailboat, except for Priest Demos, who was frowning.

"I object." He said.

"Noted. Reason?" Night asked.

I blinked. Night was treating Demos as, well, not an equal, but the same as the rest of the Sentinels.

"Isn't your job to protect humanity? Shouldn't we be mending the wall, stopping the spread, and then handling the Queens?" He asked.

"I regret to inform you that Bulwark is away on a mission." Night said. "The location isn't conducive towards picking him up. We shall have to make do without for the time being, and what I propose to slay the Queens will likely destroy the walls anyways." Night said.

Ooooh shit. The walls. The massive, thick stone walls were going to be *collateral damage!?*

"With no further objections. The plan is simple. Destruction, begin channeling what you believe to be your best spell for the situation. Demos, pray for a miracle. The rest of us are to defend them while they prepare their skills. Once they have done that, we attempt to clean up."

Well, when Night put it like *that,* who was I to object? Just, you know, casually wait for Destruction to channel one of his stupid long channeled skills, pray for a literal miracle to bail us out.

"Why don't we just kill the Queens directly?" Brawling asked, some frustration in his voice.

"I do not believe we are strong enough." Night said. "I could not slay a Royal Guard, and while the Queens are *unlikely* to be combat-focused, I do believe they should be a higher level than the Royal Guards. Tougher. If we find, for whatever reason, that we are capable of slaying Royal Guards, we shall re-evaluate."

Brawling nodded.

"Sky. Once you have dropped us off, I expect you to retrieve Bulwark. He is currently in Buthrotum."

Sky saluted.

"Do we know how long Hunting's going to be?" Magic asked.

"I believe he shall be a day or two behind us. However, the larger issue at hand is him getting to us."

"Wait, we're not going to be behind the army lines?" Magic asked.

We all sorta gave him a Look. Seriously dude? Us, *behind* the army?

"No." Night gave him a curt response. "We will not. Destruction's magic rapidly loses potency the further from him it needs to be, and by having Destruction cast on top of himself, we reduce the amount of time needed to hold."

A memory of a small tornado ripping through a rebel camp flashed before my eyes.

"On TOP of us!?" I practically shrieked.

Night gave me a flat look.

"Yes."

Welp, suicide missions. The price I pay for the good life.

Then again, half our missions were suicide missions. I generally tended to show up after, but, well – I'd be lying if I said stuff tended to be safe.

Destruction closed his eyes, and I recognized the meditative pose. He was gathering mana, gathering power together. He had a skill – [Channel] or something – that let him cast a skill over time, instead of instantly. Took longer, but he could pour a lot more power into the skill in the end, unleashing *destruction* on an apocalyptic scale.

"Initially landing will be the most dangerous portion of this." Night said. "Gods willing, we shall arrive at nighttime. Now. Does anyone else have long preparations to make? Dawn?"

Ooof. I knew exactly what he was asking.

"I could class up now." I said, thinking about it. "Or… I could change my [Persistent Casting] on [Phases of the Moon] to turn myself into a 'healing touch stone' so to speak. Touch me, get instantly healed."

"That would work even when you're sleeping." Magic said approvingly.

I continued to think out loud.

"I just barely got to 256, it's not like I'm sitting on a bunch of levels. It's my last class up. It should improve my skills. It's not like I need to mass heal, just heal a few people. Any levels I get while doing this provide stats which I can then use. This isn't the optimal class up. There's no use being optimal if I'm dead. At the same time, my skill set will be entirely new, I won't have any time to practice with them. I don't know how long it'll take. Thoughts?"

I didn't mention that I probably had access to a Blue class. Although, they probably wouldn't insist I take it, with it probably being a non-healing class.

"Don't class up."

"Don't."

"Do."

"Don't."

"Don't."

Right then. That seemed to make it clear. I wasn't going to class up.

"Hey all, I know we're about to start planning and all, and Dawn's going to be working on her thing while Destruction channels and Demos prays and all, but – I need half the boat." Nature said.

Most of us shuffled over, giving him plenty of room. It was getting real cozy over here, but I wasn't going to ask why. We were all a strange bunch in the first place.

"Whyyyy?" Magic asked, petulantly.

Night slowly turned his head and affixed Magic with a Look.

"Ok, ok, fine…" he said, shuffling over.

"Nah, it's a good question." Nature said. "I'm going to prep a bunch of seeds to start growing, and I can get them started now. They'll explode with growth once we land. Much easier on me."

Magic also muttered about some prep work he wanted to do, and Night and Sealing started going through the packs, seeing what we had.

My eyes went wide as I watched Sky walk forward, grab one of the large, now spent, Arcanite crystals in the middle of the boat, and just *heave* it overboard.

"Um." I couldn't help myself, leaning over the edge to try and watch it fall into the darkness.

Sky shrugged.

"This is do or die. What was I going to do, keep it the whole time? For what? We can always buy more one day."

I swallowed a nervous lump. He had a point. Time for me to do my part.

I wrapped myself in [Veil], tying it off. With great reluctance, I undid my previous [Persistent Casting] of [Phases of the Moon], the great safety net which had kept me alive dozens of times falling away.

I immediately started working on it again, this time making it so anyone touching me would be healed. Kinda dangerous in some ways – I might try to heal a Formorian touching me.

I might not. My current healing kit was pretty human-focused.

My full review of healing, injuries, and medicine went quite a bit faster this time than last. Constantly teaching helped, and this not being the first time I did it made it easier. Before long, I was dropping [Veil], looking back around.

The *Pegasus* was even more cramped. We were all still crammed in one half, with Nature taking up the other half. A thin layer of dirt covered the floor, with a bunch of tiny seedlings popping up, sun shining brightly on them.

Sealing handed me some wrapped food – field rations, blah – and a water skin, which I greedily downed.

"How long?" I asked him.

"Two days." He replied.

Welp. That was better than the three days the last time I did this.

"Do not forget to allocate any free stats any of you may have." Night casually said from deep inside a thick covering, and I felt like the comment was directed at me. Given the scale of where we were going, given that this was going to be a marathon fight against not particularly bright enemies, given my role was to be a healer – Mana Regeneration it was, all 407 free points I'd been sitting on.

I was also handed a heavy pack.

"Arcanite and field rations." Sealing told me. "We split everything up equally. If we're separated, you should have everything you need."

"Thanks!" I said, meaning it.

He patted my arm. I noticed my mana dropping a hair, then recovering.

"Thank *you*. Without a healer…" He trailed off, not finishing the sentence.

Yeah. Without a healer, we wouldn't last three days against the Formorians, let alone three weeks. Or however long Destruction needed.

"Any timeline on that miracle?" I asked him, seeing Demos awkwardly kinda-kneeling in prayer. We were all real cozy with each other, and there wasn't the room for full proper kneeling-in-prayer-ness.

"These things take time, and are fickle." Night grumped from underneath his layers. "The gods – or god, in this case – may choose to answer now. He may never choose to answer, and bringing Priest Demos turns into an exercise in futility. Still. I do not believe this god will choose not to respond to our prayer, not in our dire hour of need. Enough on that. We have determined our initial plans, which while we shall need to heavily modify as the course of battle demands, is a starting point."

Also known as "no plan survives contact with the enemy". Usually, we were trained to be the one interrupting the plan though. Unpleasant for the shoe to be on the other foot.

Night, Sealing, and Nature all detailed the plan to me, and I was able to provide some additional input, a few minor modifications, which were discussed, and added or rejected as needed. In the end, we had a round dozen plans, covering a number of likely contingencies.

I didn't like plans E or F. Those plans assumed I was dead.

All too soon, the sun was setting, as we approached the walls from up high.

I looked down. How could I not?

I couldn't see details, just masses of bodies, and the walls. The three gleaming walls had a single, huge gap punched right through them, in a single line. The black tide was pouring through, with the occasional brown spot slowly moving through and around – what I had to assume were the Royal Guards, visible from such a distance.

Not all was lost in the space between the exterior and middle wall though. While there was a massive breach going through all three of them, between the middle wall and the wall against the Formorian side had been the soldier's encampment. It was clear they had rallied, and on either side of the breach, were holding the line, stopping them from flooding inside.

It was a terrible position, but it was better than the "camp follower" side, which had no such soldiers to hold the position.

There were no Formorians flooding in that portion of the wall.

There was no point.

Just a few straggling Formorians, dragging bodies away to be recycled.

Well. Not really *recycled* when they started off human.

And then the breach itself! A puncture wound, direct into the heart of human territory. A black stain, a plague, a blight spreading throughout.

Or it would be, if it wasn't being contained by a thin red line, soldiers desperately rallying to *hold the line* here and now, one last thin veneer preventing utter devastation.

Even as I watched, I saw a Royal Guard all the way on the Formorian side of the wall start to run, the brown blob starting to pick up incredible amounts of speed and momentum, run through the breaches in the wall, and simply run straight through the last defensive line, crushing hundreds of Formorians and dozens of soldiers.

A squad was dispatched, and a number of still brown bodies suggested the army had figured out some method to deal with the Royal Guards, but the damage was done. Formorians flooded through the gap, and the thin red line became impossibly thinner as soldiers were shuffled around to accommodate the new, larger battlefield they now had to contend with.

There were a few little spots of humanity on the walls, but only on the wall closest to humanity's side.

And then, there were the Queens.

It was obvious what they were.

One hundred meters tall, vaguely crab-shaped, wider than they were tall, the Queens were wreathed in Mist, only the outline visible, distant on the horizon. We could only just barely see them, and that's because we were flying so high up. Tentacles that could only be called "small" in relation to the main body were visible, wriggling through the Mist, constantly dipping down to the ground, then going back up.

Eating bodies?

Laying eggs?

Who knew?

What did it matter?

We   were   totally   fucked.

Chapter 5

Formorians II

Sky kept us flying right over the battle lines, over the walls, and with slowly dawning horror I realized what "the deeper in we get the better" meant.

We were going to land right inside the horde. All the plans we had on hiding and shielding and holding ground suddenly made a lot more sense.

Like.

It was one thing to plan to be in the middle of the fighting. It was another to see us flying high over the endless horde, and realize the closest human would be thousands of Formorians away.

Destruction opened his eyes, and slowly – slower than a normal human, forget his massive System enhancements – got up. Without saying a word, he slowly put his arms out, and Night put on his backpack.

Destruction could move, and fight somewhat, while channeling his huge spell. Nothing impressive, but it wasn't like a level 160 combat Classer could get the drop on him in single combat while he was channeling. He wasn't going to pull an Artemis and rip through hordes, but he wasn't defenseless.

However, defending himself had a price, namely, mana. Mana that could be used to fuel his spell instead. The more Destruction needed to defend himself, the longer this would take. He also went slower and slower the more he channeled, and at a point, moving would destroy the spell entirely. That's how it was explained to me.

"Higher. Sky, HIGHER." Night yelled.

Sky's eyes went as wide as mine, as we sharply tilted upwards. Night *never* yelled.

Then we were over the endless army, flying fast. The moons were up, half-full, waxing larger, staring at our adventure, crimson light flooding the plains, watching the army.

Watching us struggling against the ceaseless black tide.

I jumped up and down experimentally, making sure my pack was fastened well to me, mentally checking that I could "tap" into the spare Arcanite. Triple checking that my **[Feather Fall]** gem was well-charged.

I was not looking forward to this next part. I knew why it was better for it to be during the evening – Night – but I'd *kill* for some sunlight right now for **[Talaria]**. At least it was dusk, so I wasn't totally blind.

I *really* regret giving up **[Eyes of the Milky Way]** right now. If only I had known, I'd have given up **[Vastness of the Stars]** instead.

I disabled all System notifications. I didn't need the distraction, no matter what it was. I might miss a skill, but it was better than a bad distraction at the wrong moment.

"Go!" Night yelled, and that was it.

We were off.

Brawling was the first to run off the back, giving a side-five to Sky as he jumped off.

Nature's plants suddenly started growing, some of them forming a thorny armor over his gear, the rest "nestling" inside the thick vines that were now covering him. He also ran off the back of the skyship.

Then it was my turn, and with a yell, I ran off the back, hitting Sky's hand right before I jumped off.

Sky was a powerful Gravity mage, among other things. Usually, I'd seen him use his skills to make us lighter. Now, he was using another skill. Not make us heavier – apparently, that did nothing – but to make us fall faster.

We were jumping off in order of tankiness, and that had me Concerned with a capital C that I was third in line. Magic was arguably tankier, but he needed to blow a gem every time he had to defend himself. Sealing was jumping with Destruction, to protect him, while Night was personally escorting Priest Demos.

And then I was off the end with a scream, jumping from way too high up without a parachute, dropping fast, wind whipping around me. I briefly considered doing a skydiving pose, where I was spread-eagle, before remembering that defeated the point of trying to go *faster*.

I twisted in mid-air, and made the snap call to go down head-first. I wanted to be able to see what was happening.

What was happening, was that the horde had noticed us. Rather – the shooters had, and I twisted my head as **[Bullet Time]** activated, dodging a nasty-looking spike that whizzed past my cheek, drawing a thin line of blood that was instantly healed.

That seemed to almost be a ranging shot of sorts, and as I dove down, faster and faster, more and more shots headed my way.

Dozens of spikes, fired up from the ground at me.

I twisted and turned, dodging some of them, but the speeds I was working with didn't lend themselves to dodging a ton. **[Bullet Time]** was a literal life saver. Whenever a shot came too close, whenever a spike threatened to pierce my head, it would activate, spiking my perception of time. I then had a multitude of choices. Try to incinerate it with a beam of Radiance, twist out of the way, shield it with **[Veil]**, deflect it with my physical shield, or take the hit.

A high-stakes, high-speed version of the "tank it or shield it" training I'd gotten with the Rangers so many years ago.

I tended to combine "twist out of the way" and "tank the shot", letting poorly-angled shots deflect off my armor. Anything that looked like it'd land solidly on my body I used **[Veil]** for. I didn't want to foul up my vision. Lastly, anything heading for my face got aggressively destroyed with Radiance. Last thing I needed was a spike through the head. I didn't think I could recover from that.

I also had my physical shield, which I held tight against the front of my body, shielding half of me from attacks. I could "fall" on it, but with the angle it was at while I was falling, it helped deflect shots. I had no doubt that the spikes fired by the

Formorians could go through the Inscription-enhanced shield, at which point the time I had to see and react to the attack would be dramatically lowered.

Plus, I wouldn't really have a working shield at the end of it.

I wasn't perfect. I was dropping faster than any human could fall naturally, and Shooters were firing incredibly powerful shots, strong enough to shoot down fliers much higher up than I was. Speed turning into height and all that. I couldn't get them all. a grunt, I wrenched a spike that had sunk into my shoulder out, shooting out five more beams, incinerating five more shots, as **[Veil]** flickered around me, catching another six shots.

It got easier once **[Bullet Time]** stopped turning on and off, and just permanently stayed on.

I cursed as what I could only call a "puff ball" exploded around me, and started coughing violently as dust, spores, particles, whatever, entered my lungs instead of air.

Which of course led to a *lot* more spikes making it through my "pin-point" defenses, slamming into my gut, piercing my calf- and staying there.

Then another puff ball exploded on me, and as I cleared my way through a chain of clouds, eating a dozen more spike shots, suddenly the ground was close – real close.

Way too close.

I didn't have enough swears and curses in my vocabulary for what was going on as I tried to activate **[Feather Fall]** in time, while flipping myself mid-air to not land head-first.

Well.

At least I was close enough to the ground that the anti-air Formorians had stopped shooting at me.

I summoned a **[Veil]** under my feet, almost immediately breaking through it, but bleeding a good amount of speed as I did.

I was still going far too fast as I landed, fortunately not on the ground, instead going *through* some poor Formorian Soldier. Chitin cracked as I exploded through the soldier, rapidly turning it into some puddle of goo and gore.

Most of it on me.

In me.

And oh so awkwardly, having gone feet-first when wearing a leather skirt. I needed a bath. Stat.

I landed hard on one knee, surrounded by Formorians, spitting Formorian guts from my mouth. I'd managed to slow myself enough between [Feather Fall], [Veil], and using a Formorian as a landing pad, that I didn't turn myself into paste when I hit.

Did turn a Formorian into paste though.

The Formorians immediately noticed my landing – honestly, it'd be kinda hard to not notice – and I was beset on all sides, unable to fly up and away.

I threw a [Nova] behind me, killing another Formorian with a thrust of my spear, killing another two with beams of Radiance. Had to go kinda wide on them, burning a hole through their "head" didn't drop them the same way it dropped a human.

I had a lot of experience killing Formorians.

And yet.

There were way too many of them, crowding around me, pushing in at me.

I would've died in a minute or two, if another Formorian hadn't exploded next to me in a shower of gore.

"Ha! Dawn! You're crazier than I am!" Brawling roared, as he started to kill Formorians in a circle around him with rapid thrusts of his spear – and giving me a bit of breathing room.

He took a brief moment of respite to grab the spikes that had gone into him, and just yank them out. I eyed him jealously. While they'd gone fairly deep into me, they'd barely scratched him, his high vitality letting him almost literally shrug them off.

His hand blurred as he moved it forward, touching my nose – one of the only exposed parts of me. His slowly bleeding wounds snapped closed in front of my eyes, a nasty bruise on his face just vanished.

My new [Persistent Casting] of [Phases of the Moon] working well.

Barely speaking, we went back-to-back, and I drew my short sword. Brawling covered most of the circle we were in, while I covered his back, securing his blind spot.

I have no idea how long we were fighting, back-to-back against the endless horde, when Nature *dropped in* on us. Given how short the time between each of us jumping off was, it had to be under a minute. Time did weird things in combat like this.

He simply shrugged, and the spikes caught in his thorny vines wrapping around him simply fell off. He made a motion like a farmer throwing seeds, the tiny seedlings he'd been growing flying into the ground around us.

Verdant trees, more thorny vines, entangling bushes, tripping roots and more – all manner of deadly plants, centered by a huge plant with a bulbous red center, and sharp "teeth" with a maw large enough to eat me in a single bite.

Obviously carnivorous, it lashed forward, grabbing a Formorian in its jaws, and with two sharp bites, ate it whole.

I gave it a wide berth. I wasn't going to risk the barely-controlled plant deciding to try a little Elaine snack.

The plants started to crowd the area, making it harder for the Formorians to reach us.

I looked up, only to see Night and Sealing dropping fast, angled to land near us. Destruction was near Sealing, and they had a shimmering barrier of light, of Brilliance, around them, a pair of wings made out of hard light helping Sealing fly towards us. Shots just bounced right off, although the extra glowing light had attracted more attacks towards him.

Night just had what I now recognized as blood violently flowing around him, intercepting all spikes and just... vanishing... them. Priest Demos was held in his arms, as he dropped towards us, feet-first.

Sealing and Night landed with basically no problems, which had me more than a bit jealous.

Night dropped Demos into the circle of what I was calling the Grove, and Destruction made his way over as well. Night, Brawling, and Nature without a word, executed the next part of the plan, which was basically – they ran around the perimeter of the grove, killing as many Formorians as possible as quickly as possible. Night and Brawling had the majority of the perimeter, while Nature handled only a small slice of the circle, along with maintaining the entirety of the defenses.

Sealing was working on his magic, glowing lines of white radiating from his position, as Priest Demos was encased in blinding light. Demos was encased in Brilliance, having his backpack of supplies inside with him. I had no idea what his combat capabilities were, but from what I'd gathered, "non-existent" summarized them. Destruction had more of low walls made of Brilliance, that completely covered him when he was sitting, but low enough that he could easily pop over and lob a few shots over if he felt like it.

With that, Demos and Destruction were relatively safe and secure.

Push came to shove, the barriers wouldn't stop the Formorians breaking them down and killing Demos and Destruction. They'd last as long as Sealing's mana did, which wouldn't be super long under a sustained assault. No, they were good for preventing stray shots from accidentally killing one of them when nobody was paying attention.

I had no idea where Magic was or what he was doing. He was supposed to be here! He was supposed to be the emergency backup! If something was going wrong on Brawling, Night, or Nature's side, he was supposed to jump in and cover them.

Like. It was entirely possible that he was lurking here, hidden, invisible, and would only jump out of his invisibility when he was needed. It was totally what Magic would do. It was still winding me up, not being able to see or hear him.

My job was, in theory, straight-up healing. I was supposed to be obvious, and keep my head on a swivel, checking if anyone was taking too many hits and needed a dose of healing, and to stay obvious if, say, Brawling wanted to duck inside the grove and get healed.

A lack of Magic made that problematic.

"I'm now backup!" I yelled, firing a [Nova] in the space Night just left. Screw it. I was going to operate like Magic wasn't here, and oh boy was I going to give him an earful once I found him again.

By the time it landed, Night would be gone, and a new Formorian would be there – hopefully blasted to pieces by [**Nova**]. It wasn't much, but I didn't have a ton of mana right now. Sure, I had a bunch of Arcanite lying around that I could grab, but that was for emergencies.

This was going to be a marathon, not a sprint.

Chapter 6

Formorians III

The grove was the centerpiece of our strategy here. Short, stout trees formed a medium circle around us. Right now the space was luxurious – well, as far as luxurious is when what you're talking about is described as "miniature" – but as more Sentinels showed up – namely Hunting, namely Katastrofi – it'd get real cramped, real fast. At the same time, the smaller the perimeter, the less we needed to defend.

We had five trees and one massive carnivorous plant anchoring the grove, solid wood and greedy greenery forming the pillars. Grasping bushes and thorny vines would make it a struggle for any Formorian to reach us, while we could easily just stab them with a spear while they tried to get in.

The Formorian Soldiers were blessedly dumb. They had exactly one tactic – wave assaults – and their threat was in their sheer number and mass. There was a reason humanity had been able to hold the line for untold centuries, with the greatest threat being ourselves.

Dumb, and no real obvious skills to boot. There were no caster Soldiers, they only had a single class, unlike, say, goblins. There was a reason Night had been able to straight-up walk to their hives in the past, and attempt to kill the Queens. Staying in one place was almost easier than walking through the horde.

Nature had spent a good amount of time practicing this particular trick to boot. When Night had taken me and Toxic to the front lines, Nature had hitched a ride. I realized now that he'd been practicing just this among other things, how to make little sheltered groves inside the Formorian horde. It probably wasn't for this exact scenario, but we were all adaptable.

It helped that Night could single-handedly keep the entire horde off of us during the night.

Sealing stood up, and the inscriptions that he'd been working into the ground flared up with pure light, then dimmed down, into a simple glow, casting the interior of the grove in a soft light.

"I'm no Bulwark, and my Inscriptions are mediocre." Sealing said. "This should be enough to stop Spitters from ambushing us from below though."

"Wow, that's amazing!" I said, trying to put more happiness and amazement in my voice than what I actually felt. It could be amazing, but I was so ignorant on Inscriptions, I couldn't be properly amazed.

I looked around, Night, Brawling, and Nature outside the bushes, Sealing, Demos, Destruction, and myself inside the vines.

"Where the hell is Magic!?" I cried out in frustration, seeing more bodies go flying as Brawling simply moved through them, outside the grove's protections. "He's supposed to hide us!"

Sealing gave me a look.

"If he's not here by now, I'm assuming he's dead."

That sobered me up real fast.

This was going to get much harder.

The first night was the hardest. I spent most of the time fidgeting, throwing out ill-advised [Nova]s just to keep my mana from being full, while Night, Brawling, and Nature did their bloody work. Having full mana at this point was practically a sin.

We were assuming Magic was dead, and we were falling back on our plan D. Sealing was erecting complex barriers to funnel the Formorians into a single choke point, where any one of us could, in theory, hold them back.

The tricky part about the barriers wasn't raising them. The tricky part was the "Formorian-be-gone" aspect, where they wouldn't try to just bash the walls in directly. Sealing mentioned something about "reflecting the Formorians back on themselves", or some other complex mirror nonsense.

I was pacing in circles, around and around the barrier protecting Destruction and Demos. I'd claim I was doing it so I could constantly see the battle, get a 360-degree view of what was going on. No. It was because staying here, being the support, was driving me *insane.* I felt like I should be there. I felt like I should be fighting directly.

I popped out a few times to tap everyone, making sure they were fully healed. A few scratches fixed, a nasty cut healed. Nothing major. At the same time, if we allowed injuries to pile up on themselves, we'd slowly get bled to death. That's what I was for!

"Speed up, Sealing!" Night yelled. "Daybreak arrives!"

I started, seeing the now-ominous glow on the horizon. Surviving without Night, without the barriers, would be tricky, to say the least.

"I can't do one hole! Three holes!" Sealing yelled.

As alike as all of us Sentinels were, we all had different curses at his pronouncement.

His barriers rose, leaving three equally spaced gaps around the circle. Two of the gaps were wide enough for two Formorians to get through at once – or three people shoulder-to-shoulder to block. The last was narrower, enough so that only one Formorian could squeeze through at a time.

"Dawn. Nature. Brawling." Night ordered, pointing to each one of the entrances in turn.

Sealing sat down with an exhausted look on his face, safe inside the grove. Recovering his mana. I dunno what else all the stuff he was doing took, but he looked *exhausted.* I didn't tend to get nearly so tired casting my stuff, but for all I knew he had to do some terribly complex thing to get his stuff working. Was probably some sort of power stunt or skills working in tandem, like my **[Phases of the Moon]** with my **[Persistent Casting]**.

Naturally, I got the small hole, where I'd only need to contend with one Formorian at a time.

"Yell if you need healing!" I reminded everyone as I ran to my position, the bushes and vines parting unnaturally as I passed the barrier, spear out in front of me, ready.

With a blur of motion, Night moved into the grove. He took out two brightly glowing gems. As the light dimmed from one, a small earthen part-umbrella, part-mushroom structure rose up. Then the second gem dimmed, and what I recognized was Sealing's barrier snapped up around it, leaving a small opening. Night slipped in through that, and used a sheet to cover the entrance to his miniature "hut".

Well. That explained how he kept himself safe during the day. He probably had enough room in there to do a little bit of fighting, in case of emergencies. Then again, if Night was fighting inside his hut, we were all doomed.

I didn't have too much time to think about it though, I was now in the thick of it.

The first Formorian soldier charged at me, an ant-like being taller than I was. Large clicking mandibles were on the front of its face, its main weapon. It charged at me, and I downed it almost instantly with my favorite trick – Radiance through the head.

I needed to burn through quite a bit more of its body before it actually stopped, but that just took more mana. It fell with a thud in front of me, entirely blocking the entrance.

I had maybe half a second of gloating that the entry was now fully blocked and safe before the body was picked up and flung back by another Formorian Soldier, while a third one proceeded to charge at me.

So I killed that one.

Rinse.

Repeat.

Rinse.

Repeat.

I kept an eye on my mana – it wasn't dropping super fast, but it was being eaten up quite a bit faster than my regeneration could keep up with. As the sun finished rising and hit me, my **[Sun-Kissed]** kicked in. My mana dropped significantly less quickly once the first rays of light hit me, but the damage to my mana bar had been done.

An hour and a half passed, my mana slowly but steadily draining down. At about 30% left, I felt the need to change my technique. At this rate, I wasn't going to make it to lunch, let alone nightfall. It was fortunate that the Formorians were morons, and I just needed to stick with the same formula. Again. And. Again.

I figured it was time to mix it up a bit, and try to kill a Formorian with my weapons.

I killed one, then I killed two more behind it for good measure once the body got cleared, just to give myself a little bit of extra time to set myself up. I braced myself the way I'd been taught by Artemis, so very long ago. Kneeling on one knee. Shield planted in the ground in front of me. Spear up and out, braced against the ground behind me. Eyes peeking over the top of the shield – barely.

The next Formorian charged at me, like they usually do, mandibles opening and closing, promising a swift end if I found myself inside of them.

Well.

Probably significantly less swift for me than someone else.

It charged, I braced, and it hit me like a truck, knocking me flat on my back, tumbling through the dirt and getting unceremoniously stopped by the tree trunk. I groaned, looked up, and realized more Formorians were starting to come in through the passageway, removing the body of their fellow.

Shit!

"Brawling!" I called out, starting to blast away – a **[Nova]** directly at the entrance blowing up all the Formorians.

"You're fine!" He yelled, glancing at me, seeing a bunch of charred bodies and nothing else.

"Don't do that!" Sealing yelled at me. "Do you have any idea how badly that destabilizes the barrier!?"

I flipped him the bird as I got back into position.

"I need some damn help! I don't have infinite Arcanite anymore!" I yelled back, drilling and taking down another Formorian.

"Fine. Kill two I'll kill one." Sealing snapped at me.

I killed one.

"One!" I yelled

Killed a second one.

"Two!" I yelled back.

"Drop." Sealing ordered, and I took a knee, to better spring back up once Sealing was done.

Another Formorian charged me, and I stared at it as it approached, feeling nervousness bubble up in my chest. Sentinels were like a family – a distant family. Sure, we hung out every day, chatted, and worked together. We almost never *worked* together though, never fighting as a unit. Two Sentinels sent on a mission was the top, the absolute cap that we'd ever seen, and half those missions involved me.

As a result, while we had some ideas of each other's capabilities, while we rarely sparred with each other to keep ourselves in tip top fighting shape – or in my case, keep trying to bring me up to an acceptable level of close combat competency, "acceptable" here being "beat people with twice my stats and experience" – we didn't practice working together, the same way Ranger squads practiced working together.

The first practice being in the heat of battle where humanity's fate was in question, was, putting it politely, a *strategic mistake.*

I only hoped that I wouldn't end up in the **[Historian]**'s scroll as "Dawn died due to a strategic mistake. Motion for Sentinels to practice fighting together rejected, 3-5."

And yet. We were not at the peak of humanity for no reason. It wasn't like this was Sealing's first rodeo. Given how old the dude looked, he must have decades of combat experience under his belt. We had all started out as Rangers, working together in teams of eight. We all knew how to work as a team. And a single Formorian? With basically no pressure on him?

A spear of Brilliance impaled the Formorian, going just as deep as I recognized as "lethal". Obviously not Sealing's first time against Formorians himself.

We kept going in this pattern, and only needing to kill two out of three was enough. My mana was back on the upswing.

Time passed in the most boring way, my mana fell, and then, blessedly, it was nighttime.

Or rather – it was *Night time.*

Basically, the moment the shadows hit us, Night emerged from his little hut.

"Mine." He called out, a single word, and we all retreated back into the grove. Sweat was pouring off of Brawling and Nature, and my stomach was growling. I hadn't eaten since before we jumped off the ship – a mistake on my part, not eating last night, but I'd been so worried.

I took a look around. Night was easily, single-handedly, holding all three entrances alone.

"You good Night?" I asked him.

"Rest, Dawn." Was all he said.

I stayed standing, struggling with my own emotions. I should be there. I should be helping. I should-

Brawling gently, with a force I couldn't resist anymore than I could resist a mountain being pressed on me, pulled me down to the ground, in a sitting position.

"Eat." Nature said, shoving a ration bar in my hands. "Maging is hungry work."

My stomach growled in rebellion, but he was right. First things first though. I leaned over, making sure to touch everyone, blasting them with some healing. I gave Brawling a Look.

"You obviously can cover your entrance and do more. See. Me. When. You. Get. Injured." I said, smacking my fist into my hand on every word.

"But-" Brawling started to say. I felt comfortable cutting him off. I was the healer.

"No buts! I *will* walk over to make sure you get healed next time." I threatened him. "Remember Pompius?"

He looked suitably chastised, and figuring that my work here was done, it was time to look after myself.

I chowed down voraciously.

Brawling brought a sad looking water skin up to his mouth, tilted it all the way back, and cursed. He turned it around in his hands, and showed up a nasty gash in it.

"Blasted spikes got it on the way down." He complained, throwing it across the grove.

71

"Shame." Sealing said. "What went wrong, what can we do better?" He asked.

"I'm the weak point." I promptly pointed out. "I'm not a physical Classer, I can't hold my entrance the entire day."

"You came damn close though!" Brawling said, happily patting me on the back with spine-shattering strength.

"Yes, but 'close' will leave us all dead." I pointed out unhappily, wordlessly handing my own waterskin to Brawling, who proceeded to drain the whole thing. Fuck! I should've topped myself up first.

"Ideally, Brawling doesn't need to cover two entrances." I said. "Although, maybe it would work?" I said, tilting my head at Brawling.

"It does… and I can do it…" Brawling said, thinking about it. "But it has us skirting on the edge of disaster."

"I'm already the backup." Sealing said.

"I think I can help with this." Nature said after a few moments of silent eating, the only noise being Night dismembering a Formorian limb from limb. It sounded like someone breaking crab legs.

"Oh?" I asked, eager to hear more.

"Yeah. Let me grow some particularly resilient thorns. It won't stop them, but it will slow them down, and it sounds like that's all you need. Heck, it might even let you fight them without going heels over ass like earlier."

I flushed and looked down, focusing on my ration bar. I hadn't realized everyone had seen it.

Ooor, the crumbs of my ration bar. I grabbed my backpack, and started to dig through it to get out more.

"Pace yourself." Destruction said, carefully saying each word, eyes still closed in concentration.

Aww fuck he was right. I was ravenous, I could eat a whole cow, but we only had so many rations. I was going to go to bed hungry, to better pace myself.

"Break out a **[Water Conjuration]** gem?" Sealing asked.

Nature's fingers twitched as he performed some calculations.

"Yes. Plants are all new, they could use the water."

My disappointment must've been clear on my face, as Brawling laughed and gave me another overly-enthusiastic "pat" on the back, air exploding out of my lungs.

My mana dropped. He'd somehow hurt me enough to trigger my healing.

"Easy!" I complained at him.

Brawling just laughed at me.

"We all ready for a **[Water Conjuration]**?" Nature asked.

I leaned over and grabbed Destruction's waterskin. Priest Demos was still sealed away, deep in prayer. I nodded at him.

"What about him?" I asked.

Sealing made a sound like an aborted snort.

"He's barely going to move, or do anything. His stats will keep him going, and he's got three waterskins in there. He'll be fine until this is over."

The "one way or another" was left unsaid.

"Ready? Set? Go!" Nature said, water appearing from his hands like a hose.

I knew it had to be a Sapphire he had in his armor – probably his vambraces, if he had the same arrangement I had – but it was still cool to see. In order, we quickly put our waterskins up to the faucet, then stepped back to let someone else fill their skin up. After I'd filled my waterskin up, I drank deeply from it, until it was entirely empty, then stepped up again to refill the skin. I also made sure Destruction's skin got a full refill, and handed it back to him.

It didn't take too long for all of us to be sloshing, and Nature then turned and started to water his garden. The incongruous sight of a gardener tending to his garden in the middle of a warzone, in the middle of what might well be humanity's last hurrah was, well…

Difficult to process.

We got our sleeping rolls out, nothing more than a thin blanket to put between us and the ground. My stomach was all butterflies.

I was really supposed to sleep? Here? Now? Hungry? While a war was raging on not five feet away from me?

73

"Pssst." Brawling "whispered" at a volume that could deafen a child. "How long until you think we start eating Formorians?"

I made a gagging noise, and got a serious answer from Sealing.

"You'll start eating them tomorrow, Nature two days from now, and Dawn and I will partake on the third day."

Oh gross.

I looked around, and decided that a calculated risk was in order. I stripped out of my armor and gear, and maintained it, digging all of the Formorian goo out from the cracks, checking that my shield hadn't been too badly compromised, and more.

I still couldn't get the idea of eating Formorian out of my head though.

With that lovely image in mind, I hoped my nightmares would be more flavored towards unsavory cuisine, as opposed to my   usual   fare.

Chapter 7

Formorians IV

I snapped upright as I heard someone moving, instinctively preparing an attack. I relaxed as I saw Brawling acting like a sneaky bull in a china shop, trying to get a bit of a fire going as the sky started to get lighter.

I eyed one of the trees, now somewhat de-branched. I shook my head. Those were part of our protection, and Brawling was cheerfully burning it for some morning heat and light?

I got up – I'd slept lightly in the first place, and it was bloody cold in the morning. I shook off a thin layer of dew, and huddled around the fire Brawling got started. All judgement aside, I was pretty thankful for the fire. I was unhappy about the damage, but hey. I wasn't going to let that sour the results for me.

My stomach protested, and I grabbed my bag, hauling it around, and even less sneakily than Brawling, rifled through it until I found more rations.

I eyed them. I thought about how hungry I was. I thought about Sealing's prediction.

Fuck it. I was going to eat Formorian *today,* just to show him up. The Hell Months hadn't been too long ago, just what? Three years ago? They probably made us eat worse then. Compared to Sealing, who'd probably been on a steady diet of good food for decades.

Ok, that probably wasn't fair to Sealing, who'd been a Ranger for far too long before being a Sentinel for far too long.

Still! I was *hungry,* and feeling somewhat adventurous! Bring on the Formorian legs! I'd like to place an order for one Formorian steak, done extra-extra-extra well!

Sealing and Nature eventually woke up, and we huddled around the fire, eating breakfast and getting some water inside of us. I was lucky – I could drink and fight at the same time. I didn't need to physically *do* anything to cast, just will Radiance into being. Brawling and Nature? They needed to physically thrust a spear for most of their kills.

Nature *could* use his plant-magic to kill stuff, but that was tricky. Much easier to just use a spear.

The only sounds was the fire crackling, food being chewed, Formorian bodies breaking under Night's tender ministrations, and the sound of Formorian Soldiers being thrown back by their fellows. It was eerie how quiet they were.

"Same 2-1 as yesterday?" I asked Sealing. He frowned a hair. "Could we do 3-1?"

"Sure!" I said. My mana had held up well enough with him taking so many off my plate, I figured I'd return the favor. I was pretty sure I could manage 3-1, or even 4-1.

Brawling finished his business – thank all the gods and goddesses above that we had Nature making bushes and trees – grabbed his equipment, and walked to "his" entrance, cursing about the early dawn.

Right. Because the sun would be rising directly in his eyes.

"I'm in!" Brawling yelled at Night, getting into position.

The blur of motion that was Night stopped making rounds between all three entrances, and just blurred back and forth between two of them, now pausing for a moment here and there, letting us see him as he lazily waited for the next Formorian to attack.

"You probably want to beat Nature to your post." Sealing whispered to me. I gave him a quizzical look, but he only smiled mysteriously at me.

Deciding that Sealing knew something I didn't, I decided to take my position. I grabbed my spear, double-checked that my sword hadn't, like, gotten grimed stuck inside the scabbard, picked up my dented shield, and walked to my spot.

I mean, I maintained my gear every evening, but double and triple-checking never hurt.

"Dawn. Excellent initiative." Night complimented me, before zipping off to the last entrance.

76

One shot. Two shot. Three shot. Kneel, Brilliance-spear from Sealing, and one-two-three-four, the musical dance of death resumed.

"Dawn. Hold your own entrance. Sealing. Maintain the last." Night said.

I heard an inventive curse from Nature – vines going there sounded deeply unpleasant. I was too busy looking and fighting, killing the endless horde, while I overheard the conversation behind me.

"Does it have to be me?" Nature – *whined!?* Dude barely spoke at all, and whining wasn't what I expected from him.

"Yes." Night said, and the pieces clicked.

We were Night's dinner – or in this case, breakfast. Obviously it wasn't going to be that bad, but from the sound of it, none too pleasant.

As I heard all manner of interesting noises behind me, I resolved to always, *always* be first back into the fray. I ate other creatures. Other creatures didn't eat me.

The law of the jungle had never been so clearly on display here. Eat, or be eaten. Kill and eat the Formorians, or be killed and eaten by them.

Also, there was always a bigger fish – or in this case, vampire.

After the noises stopped, and Night seemingly – I couldn't see behind me – went back to his hut, I called out.

"Nature! Tap my shoulder before you get back in the fight!" I called out. "You'll feel better and fight better."

Bless **[Phases of the Moon]** evolving at 250 to include blood loss.

Nature tapped my shoulder, getting healed up, then sprinkled some seeds in the entrance.

"Keep the passage clear for a minute." He said, and I started blasting quite a bit further out. Thick, thorny, low to the ground vines erupted, crawling and growing along the ground.

"They won't stop a Formorian, but they will slow them down. They're also fairly resilient. They'll survive being stepped on more than others."

"Thanks!" I said, appreciating his help.

"Sealing! Let me try this solo, see if I can do it alone!" I called back.

"Understood. Let me know if you need help." He responded.

And I could! Nature's twisty vines slowed the Formorians down enough that my regeneration could just barely keep on top of it.

Day 2 had nothing special. Simply a repeat of day one, without needing to land first. Nature's vines helped, and I was able to finally hold my entrance alone.

"Hey Dawn! Try to drag some of your Formorians in! Yours are the least mashed!" Brawling yelled as night was falling.

I'd shoot him a dirty glare if I could. I was *not* a physical Classer! I wasn't fast enough, strong enough, to dart in, grab a body, and throw it back. Heck, I wasn't entirely sure if I even could drag one of the bodies back in. Sure, I had solid strength, but Formorians were big, heavy suckers.

Nature, blessedly, knew the score, and threw back a few bodies.

"Idiot." Was all he yelled at Brawling.

Night took over shortly after, and we retreated back into the grove. Nature took to butchering the carcasses with practiced efficiency.

"Dawn! Would you do the honors?" Sealing asked me, handing me a gooey slab of Formorian.

I eyed it doubtfully. "Green goo" described it well. I was seriously reconsidering my resolve to eat Formorians today.

Ah well. I'll cook it first, see what happens after.

Using some careful Radiance control, I slowly cooked the meat, watching my mana drain away. Ironically, it took a lot more mana to cook meat than to kill a Formorian – killing just required a thin, narrow beam while cooking took a lot of energy over a large area.

Still. Formorian steaks were cooked in short order, and the smell was indescribably *foul*. I cut myself off a hunk, and suddenly I was the center of attention. Even Destruction took a moment to crack an eye open and look at me.

I eyed the somewhat more solid green goo. Welp. Nothing ventured, nothing gained. I took a bite, and retched.

Wet socks. That was the best way of describing it. Wet. Socks.

No wonder this wasn't a staple food. No wonder we didn't try to capture and eat as many bodies as possible to supplement army rations. There'd be a rebellion in three days, never mind that the frontlines rebelling would spell doom for all of humanity. I was seriously considering going hungry, but no.

I had a point to prove.

I gamely chewed on, not bothering to try hiding the revulsion on my face. I swallowed.

"That was terrible." I spat out – quite literally, I was spitting out tiny pieces still stuck in my mouth.

Brawling threw up his hands and cheered, while Sealing and Nature looked sour. Bags of money traded hands.

"Seriously!?" I asked. "When did you get the time to gamble on this!?" It made no sense! We were all in close quarters! When had they managed to pull this off!?

Brawling laughed, and took a bite himself.

"Oh dear gods this is worse than I remember." He said, twisting his face in a grimace.

The evening continued. A moment of peace and quiet, before the slaughter tomorrow.

Day 3 rolled around, and the sun was up high. I was blasting Formorians, bored out of my skull. There was only so much "the fate of humanity hangs in the balance" that could keep me interested, along with "These Soldiers will murder you dead if they get the chance" that kept me focused. My thoughts were wandering, and my mind wasn't on-task *at all,* when I got a surprise that had me jump seven feet in the air.

Quite literally – I started climbing with [**Talaria**].

"Heya Elaine." Arthur said, popping up next to me.

"ARTHUR!?" I yelled, before **[Bullet Time]** activated, warning me of incoming spine attacks. The Formorians didn't tolerate fliers, or anything too high up, at all – that's why nobody was on the walls. The Shooters couldn't shoot stuff on the ground though – they were pure anti-air.

"What's going on? How've you been? How did you get here?!" I asked him, landing again, continuing to shoot Formorians.

I took a moment to look at him, the fire-wait-wait-wait-fire pattern well-ingrained at this point. He looked like hell. Huge racoon eyes, a scraggy, untrimmed beard poorly hiding sunken cheeks, and other signs that he'd completely let himself go.

The smell was *probably* related to that, but after having bathed in Formorian guts then getting cooked in the sun for three days, I probably didn't smell like peaches either. I wasn't going to judge him on that.

The giant of a man licked his lips nervously.

"I-" He started to say, before Night interrupted him.

"Toxic. Report." The voice echoed from Night's hut. I half-started. I didn't think he was awake! Then again, his sleep needs were probably minimal. It kinda made sense that he stayed awake as emergency overwatch. Maybe?

Arthur gave me a look, then vanished, to report to Night. He spent the entire day inside the hut, and no matter how I strained my ears, I couldn't hear anything that was going on.

He was fast asleep by the time the rest of us finished up for the day.

Day 4 came all too fast, and Arthur took over handling my section. He was fairly physically focused, poison not requiring huge amounts of stat investment. While using his bow and arrow might've been better, Arthur was still Arthur, a giant of a man with a wagonload of physical stats. He hadn't come with his spear and shield, so I lent him mine, and he went to perform his bloody work.

That put me back in the grove with Sealing, and I ended up on "break" duty. Basically – I rotated through the different openings, single-handedly keeping them safe while Brawling,

80

Nature, or Toxic took a fifteen minute or so break – basically as long as I could keep two Formorians constantly coming at me down before my mana started to get low, with enough padding in case something went wrong.

The jump in time I could last between one and two Formorians at a time was massive. Against one I could last much longer, because my regeneration was helping. Indeed, I could even keep it up all day, with Nature's vines giving me a hand.

With two though, that math went out the window – all my regeneration was accounted for and then some, and my mana went down at a solid clip. It did regenerate nicely once I was back on overwatch duty. It also meant that I could regularly walk around, tapping everyone to make sure they were fully healed, that a little cut they were brushing off wouldn't turn into something worse. Making sure that nobody died from a thousand cuts, that injuries didn't slow anyone down.

Still, everyone appreciated the breaks.

I swear Arthur was still avoiding me, as he almost instantly "fell asleep" the moment we were done. I wasn't going to force the issue.

Day 5 everything went to shit mid-afternoon.

The Formorian powers that be had *noticed* us. A Royal Guard came charging at us, basically an entire city block of chitin, flesh, and mandibles, trampling over dozens of smaller Soldiers in its effort to get to us. We'd be flattened in a heartbeat.

Sealing sprang into action with a curse.

I figured the walls he made before, with "Formorian-be-gone" basically on them, had to be some sort of power stunt, combining skills together in new and different ways, similar to how it took me time to make myself a "healing beacon". I got to see his skills in action, in their element, as he stared down a charging Royal Guard, the monstrous creature towering over us, and seal it in shimmering light. He grunted as the Royal Guard hit the side of the barrier and broke it, but the Royal Guard had lost significant momentum breaking the cage. Sealing immediately reformed a new cage, a second barrier. The Royal

Guard hit that one, and I could almost see the cage bending – but holding.

The monster started to thrash inside, as glowing runes lit up the inside. The Royal Guard's attacks started to slow down.

"Dawn! I can't hold it! Go!" Sealing yelled at me.

Time for a fun move!

Using [Talaria], I flew up, dodging some shots that Shooters fired at me, [Veil]ing others, and shooting down the rest with Radiance. I went above the seal, where the Shooters couldn't see me anymore, and hovered right above the Royal Guard.

I could land on the barrier, but that'd just tax it more, and the normally unflappable Sealing was yelling at me to hurry it up.

Keeping in mind that Night mentioned struggling with these, I went a little nuts. My standard drill of Radiance through what I thought was the head, fully powered up unlike the weak beams I'd been using on the Soldiers – and I unleashed not only my own [Nova]s, but all of my stored ones.

The beauty of Radiance was I could straight-up bypass Brilliance barriers. Sure, by the same token, Mirror wrecked me hard, but right now, Sealing and I made a great one-two punch.

Sealing also coated the inside of his barrier with his other element – Mirror – which had the effect of amplifying and redirecting a good amount of the damage. Any stray Radiance just went right back to roasting the Royal Guard.

I had quite the collection – it was basically the only skill I kept inside my Sunstones.

The cube containing the Royal Guard lit up like a sun – but even brighter. I squinted, then conceded, turning my head away from the incandescent explosion below me, all while keeping up the beam roughly where I thought the Royal Guard's head was.

I turned on System notifications just for Royal Guards, to see when I got it.

[*ding!* Your party has slain a [Formorian] (Erosion, lv 750)]

I had no time to admire myself as I was nearly entirely out of mana. I'd gotten to the point where I could fly forever, in the sunlight, without any gear on.

I was fully geared, and wasn't *quite* able to keep myself up forever. Still, it only took me four mana per second, and I wasn't that far from the grove. I made my way back in, landing with a lot more grace and elegance than I was feeling.

"Good work Dawn." Sealing said.

"Nah, it was all you." I modestly said. "Without you dramatically weakening it, I would've had no chance. Plus, those were *all* my [Nova]s." I said, grimacing.

"Less than wise." He pointed out, grabbing a ration bar and digging in. I felt I deserved one as well, and joined him.

"Yeah, sure, but what else was I going to do?" I asked, mostly rhetorically.

Sealing chewed in contemplative silence.

"I don't know." He finally admitted.

"I'm not a blasted combat Classer, fundamentally." I pointed out. "Get Brawling to do it next time. Or Nature. I dunno."

"Getting someone in with the Royal Guard is extraordinarily high-risk." Sealing pointed out. "Not only do they need to be engaged before my barriers and weakening kick in, but then they need to engage them in hand-to-hand combat."

He had a bunch of good points.

"I guess I'm going to start recharging my gems." I said. "And pray no more Royal Guards attack."

"Dawn. Sealing. Come closer. I dislike needing to yell." Night called out to us.

We approached Night's hut, then we went to either side of it, and stood, backs to the hut, keeping an eye out on Toxic, Brawling, and Nature, making sure they were ok, that they didn't need help. Or rather, being in a position to help them if something happened.

"Sealing. Are you capable of only crippling a Royal Guard inside your barrier?" Night inquired.

He spent a few moments thinking about it.

"Kinda. See, the way it works…"

A long technical explanation followed, which apparently Night understood and it went way over my head. I'd love to know more, but this wasn't exactly the time and place to get a comprehensive education on the matter.

Short version: Yes, he mostly could, but he lost a few tricks.

"Right. Dawn. Work on recharging your Sunstones. I shall wake you up during the night to better assist. When you are fully charged, you are on Royal Guard slaying duty. However, that shall not always be possible. When you are not ready, the three of us will work in concert if it is day time to slay one. Dawn, you will escort me under [Veil] to the Royal Guard. Sealing will seal myself and the beast together, using the methods he described. You shall keep the sun off of me withyour [Veil of the Aurora] while I kill the monster." Night decreed.

I felt the urge to salute overcome me, and I did. No reason not to. For all I knew Night could tell.

"Possible problem." I said, thinking about it. "I'm not sure how to make the transition."

"Explain yourself." Night said.

"So. [Veil] is generally a single solid sheet that I can conjure up. It's – ah I've got the answer. Night, my [Veil] is moveable by someone who's not me. I can make it, and move with you while you move [Veil], and keep the sunlight off of yourself. You can then reposition it right before you get there, and I can fly on top of Sealing's barrier to keep myself safe!" I proudly worked out.

"It is dangerous to take to the air with the Shooters around." Night pointed out. "Additionally, a number of their attacks will land on Sealing's barrier, stressing it even further."

"It held up to my attacks." I pointed out.

"Barely. Only due to how Radiance and Brilliance interact." Night pointed out acridly. "Sealing's barrier will also need to contain *me*."

That was an excellent point. I shrugged, before remembering they couldn't see me.

"Sure, but I'm at high-risk *inside the middle of the damn horde*. I'll also be missing one of my key combat tricks – namely, my [Veil]. Sorry. Flying on top is my best – hence our best – chance. If it's not possible for whatever reason, we'll do something else and figure it out on the fly."

"Fine. Do what you must." Night coldly dismissed me.

I knew a dismissal when I heard it, but I was curious.

"Hey Night." I asked.

"What?" He grouched back.

"I mean, I'm no slouch, but I was just able to kill a Royal Guard. I'm not exactly a combat-focused Classer like you are, but you mentioned struggling with them. How? Why weren't you able to kill them like I did?" I asked, dead curious.

I got a long-suffering sigh back.

"It was outside its lair. It did not have a Queen in direct support. It did not have Spitters or Soldiers working with it. A small fortune of gemstones was used. You had Sealing's full might – a specialist in handling large creatures exactly like said Royal Guard – giving his full support, in his area of expertise. I last tried some forty levels ago. Lastly, I did not use my final killing stroke when I last fought a Royal Guard. I did not want to let the Formorians know I had it, not when I hoped to use it on the Queens themselves."

Ah. Right then. Time to stop annoying the ancient vampire, not when one of his life-long goals was in front of him – and when failing at his self-imposed lifetime mission was a possibility.

Plus – Night always seemed grouchy when the sun was out. A hidden aspect to his curse? I remember him being much more pleasant when we had our long evening discussions together in Ranger Academy.

It could also be stress, I suppose.

I slumped to the ground, keeping one eye on Brawling, and the other eye on Nature, kinda splitting my view. Sealing had Toxic's back, and I started to recharge gemstones once I was over half my mana.

Depending on the size of the gemstone, I could recharge roughly five gemstones per hour. It would take me, what, a little less than two days of constantly recharging gemstones to get myself fully back up?

That assumed I did nothing else. Like heal Brawling. Or give Nature a break. Or…

Yeah. I had way too much to do, and not nearly enough mana.

I got to work.

Chapter 8

Formorians V

Day 6 started off like the rest, although the night was a pain in the rear. Night kept waking me up every 30 minutes or so to keep working on recharging my gems. Waste not, want not was the motto on mana. The morning was boring. The afternoon was interesting.

I was bored, holding my entrance, looking around, when I saw a familiar tie-dye splash of color come barreling towards us, surrounded by what looked like a cloud of dust or something.

I blinked and rubbed my eyes, making sure I wasn't hallucinating from a lack of sleep, some new poison the Formorians were using, or anything else.

Nope. That was Hunting and Katastrofi, plowing their way through the horde to reach us.

"Hunting incoming!" I yelled. "He's moving fast! Royal Guards are starting to go after him!"

The last part I yelled as I saw not one, but *two* Royal Guards take notice of Hunting, and start charging towards him as Katastrofi scythed through the Formorians.

"Night!" I yelled back, throwing up a **[Veil]** like we'd planned. "Going to need some help here!"

Night was next to me in a flash, the only indication of his passing being a strong breeze making my leather skirt flutter. He started barking out orders.

"Nature. Hold all three entrances. Sealing, Dawn – on me, like we planned. Brawling, Toxic – work with Hunting to stall the second one."

Nature cursed, and got to work. I didn't see what was going on, but I figured I'd see what was happening when we got back.

Night held up his hand in a fist, while the other one held up a part of the **[Veil]** I'd brought down. **[Veil]** was like a giant, absurd umbrella right now, but huge – large enough to give Night a solid amount of darkness to work in.

Katastrofi was charging towards us, full-speed. The Soldiers were practically a speedbump, but I suspected I'd need to tend to Katastrofi's legs when this was done. There were only so many razor blades one could run through before they started to have an impact.

We stood at the entrance. I was nervously bouncing on my feet, Toxic was thumbing arrows, Sealing and Night were both standing unnaturally still, and Brawling was keeping the gap clear with *great enthusiasm.*

We watched the three of them converge, and when it became obvious Hunting wasn't going to make it, Night simply dropped his hand.

We *moved.*

Brawling was the vanguard, the spear through the horde, merrily beating the shit out of the Soldiers, and carefully blasting them out of our way.

I was frankly a little impressed at his controlled violence. It was far too easy to swing a spear hard enough to go through a Formorian, simply bisecting them. The problem with that was, there was a Soldier body left over that we'd need to climb over. Sure, we were all superhuman enough to pull it off, but it would still slow us down. Instead, Brawling was carefully applying and exerting force in a way that just "flipped" Formorians like a pancake back into the horde, keeping a path clear for us.

He was flipping enough that even as the horde tried to close back in on us, we had enough room to keep going.

Brawling. The best physical combat Sentinel. Given that, what, half of all Rangers if not more were physical combat fighters, it meant something. Unlike myself, who one could argue I was promoted on the basis of "nobody else is a healer", Brawling had more than enough competition for the position. He showed us why, how, he'd earned it.

"We're not going to make it!" Brawling yelled at us, and a moment later there was a collective wince as the first Royal

Guard plowed into Katastrofi's side, the two locked in mortal combat.

Hunting jumped off her back as the Royal Guard hit her, and started stabbing with his spear. The name of the game was "avoid the jaws." I had no doubt that even Katastrofi would be sheared in half if she ended up in the deadly mandibles.

"Toxic! Brawling!" Night yelled, pointing at the Royal Guard locked in combat with Hunting.

Night then peeled off, Sealing and I following him, as we headed directly for the second Royal Guard, the [Veil] still acting as an absurd umbrella. It was starting to take some fire, some Shooters objecting to the object in the sky, but it wasn't anything that [Veil] couldn't handle. Nothing was so strong that it threatened to break [Veil], although my mana took a hit on every shot. It was why I didn't use it to stop sustained attacks – it was a great way for me to lose all my mana.

There was no such thing as normally in the situation, but *originally* I had planned on dropping back, then flying up and over, and staying safe above my own [Veil] and Sealing's own barrier. The Formorians had Shooters, but Sealing's barrier, plus me kinda hiding, would solve that.

Of course, no plan survives contact with the enemy, and this one was no exception. The plan had assumed that Sealing would be safely inside our defenses, and not in the middle of the horde.

Which naturally led to me, by myself, surrounded by Formorian Soldiers on all sides, needing to hold them off of Sealing single-handedly while he channeled his barrier, sealing Night and the Royal Guard alone together.

This wasn't the time for finesse or subtlety. This wasn't the time to carefully conserve my mana, not when I needed to cover more than just myself in the middle of a gods-dammed horde.

I blasted and blasted and [Nova]'d and blasted away. [Nova] was good for clearing a chunk of Formorians, but it was horribly, horribly inefficient. I could kill a lot more Formorians with the same amount of mana that [Nova] took. It just took a lot more focus to do so – hence the occasional use of [Nova].

"Sealing! Get your back to your damn barrier!" I yelled at him, continuing to run around him in a circle like some kid on a merry-go-round.

Blessedly, he didn't argue with me, instead taking slow steps to get his – well, he didn't bother turning around – his front to the barrier, just staring in at the cage fight between Night and the Royal Guard.

I wasn't paying too much attention to the other fight, but a high-pitched scream caught my attention. I watched in horror as the Royal Guard's jaws closed on Brawling, slicing him cleanly in half at the waist, guts and blood spilling out.

"Night! Finish it *now* and *get me to Brawling!*" I yelled. "I don't give a shit about saving some long cooldown move! *Save Brawling.*" I said, starting to run towards him.

Sealing must've popped several gems, because he was suddenly surrounded in a secondary barrier, glued to the first one. A number of Formorians moved in to attack him, but I wasn't paying too much attention.

Had to reach Brawling.

I fought my way through the horde, indiscriminately firing away, not being too careful about preserving my mana, drawing on my reserves.

"Dawn! **[Veil]**!" Night yelled from behind me, and I reflexively toggled my **[Veil]** off, then back on, creating a new, larger 'umbrella' for Night. There was a brief, inhumane scream from behind me as Night encountered daylight – kinda surprised it hurt so much, although maybe it was due to injuries suddenly kicking in or something – then he was next to me, carrying the umbrella, moving us through the horde at an unbelievable speed.

Even with **[Bullet Time]** I couldn't process how fast we were going, until **[Veil]** above was replaced by a solid, never-ending ceiling of flesh and chitin, the weight of a hill psychically pressing down on me. I saw bodies flash and Formorians die by the dozen, as Night used his blood blades to carve a path through them, depositing me next to Brawling.

Well. Next to half of Brawling, the half that was "him". I had no time to try and find his other half, no time to ask Night to hunt it down. Emergency stabilizing medicine time.

I landed next to Brawling, the light fading from his eyes, hands slowly clawing futilely at his guts, trying to put them back inside his body.

"Daw….." He started to say, head slumping back.

My hand was already moving, already reaching for his face. I touched it, and thanks to **[Persistent Casting]**, I didn't even need to focus, or make an image, or anything.

Pelvis and waist, legs and feet were recreated in a second, as my entire mana pool emptied out into him. I drew more mana out of the Arcanite, and watched more vanish, until it stabilized. Brawling groaned and rolled over, clutching his head.

"What a headache." He moaned. "I'm never drinking again. Worst. Dream. Ever."

"Brawling!" I couldn't help it; it came out as a shriek. "Not a dream! GET US OUT!" I yelled, slapping at his back with both my hands like beating a drum.

Sure, I could walk out, but Brawling was orders of magnitude faster than I was.

Or Night could just carry us out I suppose.

To his credit, Brawling rolled over and jumped up. I mock-shielded my eyes.

"And get some damn pants!"

I needed a clothing-regeneration skill.

Night carried me while Brawling just ran out, cursing his lack of sandals as he squished through Formorian guts. We made it out, and Night yelled. "They are clear! Sealing!"

A barrier sprang up around the Royal Guard, Night, Brawling, Katastrofi and Hunting inside. Sealing, Toxic, and myself outside. Toxic and I got to work keeping Sealing safe.

It was a lot easier with help, especially of the physical classer type.

I had no idea how long it took, but I was tapping my Arcanite reserves again just to keep up, Toxic and I having our backs to Sealing, who had a hand on his barrier.

I got lucky. I glanced in at the right time, to see Hunting on top of the Royal Guard, thrusting down with his spear to perform the lethal takedown.

The barrier went down, and the Sentinels came out, bloody and bruised. I drew in more mana from my Arcanite, and healed up Night and Brawling. Hunting waved me off, pointing to Katastrofi. The injuries were a bit more serious this time – Hunting had an arm dangling uselessly, while Brawling was limping. Well, more serious than the usual bumps and scrapes. Less serious than getting sliced in half. Katastrofi had a series of nasty-looking gashes on one flank, great bloody footprints trailing behind her.

"Dawn. Katastrofi. Everyone else, escort back. Move!" Hunting barked out orders, which even Night complied to.

I nimbly climbed up and onto Katastrofi, watching my mana drop to nothing and stay there. Dangerous move that, but any mana I pulled at this stage would drain right into her, healing her numerous injuries, while not protecting me any further. I was completely reliant on the other Sentinels to defend me, while my mana drained into healing Katastrofi.

I glanced down, getting a better idea of her injuries. She had some nasty, *nasty* injuries on her flank, to the point where I was wondering how she was still moving. Super-dino, I guess. Companions, and creatures in general, also got a number of skills. They were just usually less than visible, although something had to be keeping her going.

I stayed basically flat to Katastrofi while we headed back to the grove, where Nature was busy holding all three entrances. The massive carnivorous plant was holding one entrance, while Nature was bouncing between two more entrances, one coated in vines, the other having a bush in the way, killing Formorians.

"Hunting. How are you?" Night asked.

Hunting gave Night a look.

"Katastrofi's injured." He flatly said.

"And Dawn is managing her. Can you hold an entrance?"

Hunting hesitated, then nodded.

"The small one." He said, pointing at it with his still-good arm.

Sealing made a strangled noise as Katastrofi nearly stepped on the barrier. I didn't know much about Sealing's magic, but it couldn't be good for it. He conjured up a quick ramp, which she used to step up and over.

Nature had no such luck with the grove, and I winced as Katastrofi trampled most of the perimeter, before settling down, wrapped about Destruction and Priest Demos's barriers.

Ugh. We were going to have to get *real* cozy with each other. It was going to be cramped before we added a large dinosaur to the mix. Maybe I could sleep on Katastrofi? Then again, did I want to be that high up?

Toxic, Hunting, and Nature each took an entrance, with Nature stoically taking the responsibility, not even muttering about needing a break or anything. Night retreated to his hut, and I mentally checked him off the list of "needed healing". He'd gotten a solid touch after his battle with the Royal Guard.

However – we were back now, and while Katastrofi was busy draining all my mana, she was clearly stable enough. She had crashed, physically and metaphorically, and was busy sleeping. My regeneration was respectable, but she was massive, and I was eating a gargantuan penalty for her being so far away from being human.

I figured it was better to touch everyone up, then get back to healing her. Hunting, after all, needed healing. He'd brushed me off before, wanting Katastrofi to get medical attention before him. I could respect the sentiment, but given how long it would take me to finish healing Katastrofi, versus how long it'd take me to fix Hunting, it was a no-brainer whose turn it was.

I got up, and did a round, making sure everyone else was also patched up. Nature was practically untouched, and Arthur needed some nasty slices healed up. I paused when I got to Hunting.

"Your feet!" I said, pointing to the huge bloody footprints his half-feet were leaving. "Holy! Why didn't you say anything!?" I yelled at him.

He fixed a steely look at me, mechanically thrusting and killing Soldiers.

"Katastrofi gets attention before I do." He said, in a tone that said "Duh, and you'll never get a Companion if you ask dumb questions like that."

I folded my arms.

"She's resting, and she takes way more mana than any of you do. You're defending her right now while she's hurt. What good is your defense if you fuck up because you're hurt?"

Hunting wavered a moment, before nodding at me. I touched him.

"Lift one foot up, then the other." I instructed him, and he did, the bottoms of his feet magically recreated. I couldn't do it when the ground was in the way. He winced as he put them back down.

"No callouses." He said, answering my unasked question.

"How'd you kill the Royal Guard anyways?" I asked him.

He shrugged with his non-spear shoulder.

"I'm a Void mage. I'm Hunting. I'm *really good* at killing stuff."

I mean, sure. That was as much of an explanation as anything.

"What happened to your feet?" I asked.

"The Royal Guards are Erosion. Started eating into me the moment I touched them. We need to be careful for more than just their jaws. Their entire body can erode us away simply by touching us."

I nodded, and with not much else to say, wished him luck and carried on. The part about the bodies potentially eroding away anyone or anything that touched them was interesting from a healing perspective, but I was going to do my damnest to never be close enough to touch. I'd be so dead if that happened.

Sealing was fine, although he looked drained, and had some Arcanite out in front of him. Made me think he had to go through some of his reserves as well.

With everyone else topped up, I went to see Brawling, who'd blessedly found something resembling pants.

Sure, he was going to have an even worse time sleeping now that he'd cannibalized his blanket, but at least he wasn't streaking anymore.

"Heya Brawling." I said, sitting down next to him. "How are you holding up?"

I wasn't prepared for the bone-crushing hug from him.

"Dawn! You literally saved my life! Seriously thought I was a goner there. *Thank you.* Best healer ever. You ever need anything let me know. For real."

Brawling was fairly effusive in his thanks, and I got the life-size doll treatment. I couldn't even get a word in sideways!

After a few minutes of my view rapidly changing, I'd had enough.

"Brawling! Let me go!" I yelled at him, and with a look of minor chagrin, he did.

"One minor complaint though. Not everything's the same size." He said, with a completely straight face.

I thought fast.

"I'm sorry. There was only so much enlargement I could do, given the initial small size I was working with." I said with my best poker face. "On the bright side, you're twice the man you were earlier."

Brawling groaned and mimed an arrow through the heart, mock-falling over. I cracked a grin.

My healing couldn't change anything. It simply restored back to the bodies natural state. How it knew how much muscle mass Brawling had before? Only thing I had for that was magic.

I looked around. Everything seemed ok for now. I went back to Katastrofi, and the mana I'd managed to recharge vanished in an instant as I touched her, one of the injuries on her side getting noticeably smaller as I did.

I refrained from sighing. At least I'd get a good night's sleep tonight. All I had to do was stay touching Katastrofi, and all the mana I regenerated would go right back to healing her. Making good use of every drop of mana I had!

Chapter 9

Formorians VI

Day 7. It turned out that my blowing up the Royal Guard with all my **[Nova]**s on day 5 had basically lit a massive beacon, and what remained of the army had seen it. When Hunting had shown up, they were able to point him in roughly the right direction. Brave man, charging into the horde, having complete faith that we were still there, and would help him make it the rest of the way.

Also, there was no more defensive line. The Formorians had breached it, and were busy pouring into the countryside. The army was hunkering down wherever they were, keeping themselves safe in little pockets, like we were, hoping the flood would slow down enough that they could regroup, reseal the walls, and purge all the Formorians that had leaked in.

Given the situation, I had my doubts that the "usual" methods would work, especially now that the Formorians had demonstrated an ability to breach the walls themselves.

Not terribly much happened today. I finished healing Katastrofi, and Hunting declared that she needed the day to finish healing, and there was no sense in switching up the working method. Brawling also had the day off, which he used to perform stretches and exercises, "making sure everything still worked".

I didn't point out the obvious. I didn't want him making sure EVERYTHING still worked.

Had to be quite something, getting sliced in half and surviving.

Day 8. Brawling was back in action, although he mentioned if there was another Royal Guard, he wanted to be the one

holding down the fort. Losing everything below his belly button seemed to have shaken some core belief of his, cut his personal illusion of invincibility in half.

I kept an eye on him. Being a healer wasn't just giving him a new pair of legs. Right now, I was willing to be an ear as well, listening to his concerns and fears.

Katastrofi took one of the large entrances, happily chomping down on Formorians. Snack, snack, throw, snack.

Hunting was hanging out, carefully watching her throughout the day, making sure she was back in peak physical condition. On one hand, it hurt a bit to think that he thought I'd do a subpar job. On the other – I'd seen their bond; I'd seen how they worked together. In my shoes, I'd also be carefully checking my companion over to see if there was anything wrong.

Arthur pulled me aside once the day was over, and Night had taken over. He still looked terrible.

"Elaine, can – can we talk?" He asked, hesitantly. Not at all the strong, confident Arthur I remembered.

I wrapped us up in **[Veil]**, since there was absolutely no room in the grove in the first place, not with Katastrofi settling in happily. She'd eaten probably a third of her weight in Formorians, and the glutton was now settling in for a long snooze.

"What's going on?" I gently asked. Arthur had been avoiding me every time I visited the frontlines, had been avoiding me ever since we got here, and now, finally, seemed ready to talk.

"I – promise you won't tell the others?" He started off asking.

I weighed the request in my mind.

"If it's not causing immediate risk to us, I won't say anything." I promised after a moment. "Although if it's medically related, I'm **[Oath]**-bound to keep your secrets."

I really *really* hoped that it wasn't a medical secret that threatened everyone's health. No idea what one could be, but hey. Weirder things had happened.

"Ok. Um. It's not. Um. How do I put this…" Arthur trailed off. I kept my silence, not wanting to spook him here.

He closed his eyes and visibly steeled himself, confessing his sins.

"Elaine. I'm killing people."

The words tumbled out of his mouth explosively. I caught myself from saying anything, from immediately blurting out accusations or recriminations. Arthur was clearly being tortured by this, he obviously wasn't gleefully murdering people in their sleep and bragging about it, like some of the Classers we'd handled when we were on a Ranger team together.

I forced a smile on my face, and nodded at him, encouraging him to keep going.

"It's the poison. We designed a slow poison, one that would persist and stick, one that would poison water, that would poison the ground. Working off your food chain idea. Working off how heavy metals work, how they poison people. I studied people, studied cases, and with a few other poison experts, we made something new. Poison has a habit of back blowing onto us, and we guessed this might do the same. It's why we brought you to the frontlines initially. We wanted, we needed, to know if this was going to cause the same problem."

I nodded, not letting the horror I was feeling show on my face. I saw exactly where this was going.

"Well, usually poison acts fast, and we see it back blowing into us within a week. We decided to be extra-conservative, and basically have you stick around as long as possible until your graduation came up. Six months. Six months without a single problem, without a single notification that the poison was hitting us. Figured that was good enough, and with how sensitive the System can be on kill notifications, we were cautiously optimistic about it." Arthur continued.

He closed his eyes, and his voice became strained.

"The gods have a sick sense of humor. I got the notification that I'd killed a soldier the same day I got a notification that I'd killed a level 180 Formorian. Obviously, the poison was now in their hives, and it was working. At the same time, it was now hitting us."

Arthur paused, and the haunted look came back to his eyes.

"Night and I met and discussed it. Eventually, he decided that it was 'acceptable collateral damage', and that I was to continue on."

I couldn't keep my face entirely straight and smiling at that. Heck, my supportive smile had been fading the whole time.

"Come on Elaine. Please don't give me that look." Arthur begged. "Night's logic was that we lose soldiers all the time. Now we were trading them for potential, real gains. And. He. Was. Right." Arthur said that last part in a depressed triumphant tone. "Spitters started to die, then Shooters. Some other variant we haven't seen. But the kill notifications on people started to speed up."

Chemotherapy. Arthur had been effectively performing chemotherapy on a grand scale. "I've got poison, and I think the poison will kill you before it kills us."

I think.

Of course, it could go horribly wrong – like it was now – but as a grand scheme, I had to admit it was exactly like treating cancer.

I disapproved. Strongly. Vigorously. The chemotherapy analogy broke down almost immediately. First, people with cancer had almost no other options, besides "just die". Second, people with cancer *chose* to have chemotherapy. Nobody had chosen this, besides Night and Toxic. For all I knew, Night hadn't even told Ranger Command about it. It was also being kept under wraps, kept secret.

And speaking of. Nobody had told the people here, on the frontlines, that it was happening. A slow poison like Arthur was talking about? It probably looked like natural causes half the time, or just slowed a soldier down enough that they were eaten by a Formorian, the kill credit and experience split between Arthur and the Formorians. Heck, it might not even register as an army kill in that situation.

Or if it did, it might just be put down to another brawl or something. I didn't know enough about self-kills like that. "Your army has slain one of its own" probably wasn't a System concept.

Argh! Where was Maximus when I needed him?

Actually.

Focus.

Arthur was here, and he needed my help. Needed my absolution at least, which I could give him.

"Hey, listen, listen, you did the best you could." I said. "What's done is done. What matters is how we tackle this going forward. We're either going to win or lose. If we lose, what does it matter, we're all dead. If we win, I'll declare the area a disaster zone or something, and we'll just pack up and leave. Shouldn't be too hard to handle from there, especially since it's a slow poison."

I stood up to pat him reassuringly on the shoulder. Damn he was big.

"Worst part is, I feel this is all my fault." He said, gesturing round to the walls. I know what he meant though.

"It's not your fault!" I protested.

"It is." He said, looking at me with a steely gaze. "I managed to kill a Queen."

Well then. That explained a bunch. Like why they were now all-out attacking.

My repertoire of comforting maneuvers was weak. I patted him on the shoulder again.

I quickly checked Arthur's level. [Ranger]. Wow. I didn't have Artemis around to compare, but he was giving her stiff competition, if not outright higher than she was. That must've been, what, 80 levels in three years or so? And he'd only get stronger the longer this fight went on.

Rapid leveling in dire straits. It was a well-known phenomena, although one only the most desperate voluntarily went through.

"Good job! And hey! Now we'll get the rest of them! By the way, what level were they?" I asked.

"The one I got was level 1021. Three classes though, not one. They're clearly smarter than straight up monsters, even though they're tagged as monsters." Arthur explained to me. "Mist, Forest, and Decay. I got the impression that Mist was their combat class, Forest was their production class, and Decay was a recycling class for them."

"Makes sense. Do you think we should tell everyone else that?" I asked. It was skirting the line if he said no – the information seemed relevant.

Arthur hesitated a moment.

"Let's get Night to tell everyone. Nobody will question him how he knows. I just. I don't think everyone else would understand, you know?"

Privately, I disagreed. All of us had been tasked with defending humanity. We had all been Rangers, gone through trials that proved we were in it for the mission, not for glory or money. I couldn't even see Sky being so callous as to make jokes and poke fun at Arthur for accidentally killing people – then being told to keep going.

"Yeah, sure, that sounds good."

"Also, I'm sorry for avoiding you." Arthur looked down, shame-faced. Didn't mean much when I was still at belly-button height on him. "Night ordered me not to tell you, because you'd go ballistic, and probably end up causing problems. It's why I was avoiding you." He said, and a huge weight seemed to lift off of him at the confession.

I patting him reassuringly. "I'll do what I can to make it right. I promise." I said, mind already whirring with what would need to be done to fix it.

We made some more small talk, then rejoined the rest of the group.

Day 9 rolled around, and we had a good rotation going, to the point where Brawling was helping Night during the night.

Also had a good rotation of warm bodies to feed Night. I hadn't been on the menu yet, and I was making myself far too useful and busy in the mornings when Night went looking for dinner.

We were also comfortable taking on a single Royal Guard at a time, although knowing the Queens were coming was filling me with an existential dread.

Early morning, and we were all in position, doing our thing. I was focusing on refilling my gemstones with [Nova], just keeping an eye out on things. The gemstones still weren't full, because I kept needing to do minor healing things. Honestly, now that so many of us were here, it was getting easier as the pressure was reduced on us.

Brawling called out. "Look! The *Pegasus!*"

Most of us snapped our heads to look, and yes, high in the sky, barely a dot, was a little brown smudge.

Cripes. Just how much perception did the dude have? Did he have additional vision skills, something like [Eagle's Eye]? Or was it raw vitality that was letting him see it?

And with perception linked to vitality, and vitality linked to toughness, and Brawling undoubtedly having skills to make himself tougher – I wasn't going anywhere near a Royal Guard's jaws.

"Dawn! Toxic! Sealing! On me!" Hunting yelled, getting on Katastrofi. The rest of us climbed on, as Hunting shielded his eyes, keeping an eye on what was going on.

"Bulwark's unlikely to land directly here, so we're going to go out and grab him." Hunting explained to us. "I want us ready."

"I'm going to use [Shine] to let them know we're here." I said, giving Hunting a chance to strike down my proposed move.

"Good call. Do it." He said, and I gave everyone a moment to look away before turning the light show on [Shine] to the max, along with flickering bright Radiance. I was almost impossible to miss.

Instead of seeing a tiny figure though, the *Pegasus* started to get larger and larger, drawing a massive amount of anti-air fire from the Formorians.

Absurd amounts. I thought we'd gotten it bad when we dropped in on them, but obviously, the larger the object, the more Formorians noticed and started shooting at it. At the same time, the hull of the boat formed an armor of sorts. Either way, the *Pegasus* was dropping like a rock, straight down.

Hunting cursed.

"The idiot's going to land on us at full speed! Sealing! Dawn! Barriers! Brawling! Prepare to catch!" He called out.

I hopped down off of Katastrofi, and made my way to the edge of our defenses, putting my back to the wall. My barrier and Sealing's didn't play terribly nicely together.

Sealing put up his barriers, wonderous multi-layered things that you could still see through. I added mine on top, a single layer of Aurora Borealis, looking like a way too thin coating of chocolate icing on a massive vanilla cake.

I missed icing. And vanilla. And chocolate. And raw sugar. And so many more foods. **[Pristine Memories]** let me know *exactly* how good it all tasted.

Honestly, I missed food that wasn't live and murderous 20 minutes ago. My standards were in the mud right now.

Focus.

Sky came in like a meteor, Bulwark clearly having worked his magic to reinforce the hull. It was covered in layers and scales of overlapping stone, spikes mostly bouncing off, shattered. A few embedded themselves into the rocky exterior, but none penetrated. They weren't slowing down in the slightest, and I refrained from wincing as my barrier was instantly shattered.

Sealing was a certifiable monster, but then again, so was I. I'd just healed a person who was bisected. Sealing only lost two of his barriers to Sky's stunt, leaving them an awkward height, with the boat broken in half.

I looked up, and refrained from groaning.

"Brawling, careful when you catch them." I said, starting to head over.

It turned out, even superhuman bodies didn't do well going from 200 to 0 in about half a second. Extra-not-well when your name was Sky, and you were a magical Classer.

Sealing released the barriers, and Hunting and Brawling caught Bulwark and Sky respectively, extra supplies raining down around us along with all manner of wood and broken stone.

I used **[Veil]** on myself to shelter from the raining debris, then walked over to Sky and Bulwark and touched them, healing them back up. I kept a poker face as I heard their bones crack back into place.

"How does freaking Dawn land better than you Sky?" Brawling demanded. "You're *Sky*. Doing dumb shit like that....?" He trailed off, shaking his head as Sky wormed out of his arms, floating in his aggravating way.

"I was fine! Honest! I just didn't expect some idiot to put a blasted barrier between me and the ground! I'm Sky! I totally could've stuck the landing!" He protested.

"Yeah, but you'd have killed half of us if you goofed. Including Priest Demos. We couldn't take that risk." Hunting pointed out, looking somewhat grumpy. "As-is, you only showered us in crap."

"Yes, but I brought food. Good food!" Sky protested.

All of Sky's sins were forgiven in an instant. At least by me. He could've broken half the walls if he'd brought *good food.* I tuned out the argument, and started rummaging through the bags he'd brought. There had been enough time, and Sky had clearly made a pit stop at the capital. The Quartermaster, given more than 15 minutes notice, had properly managed to get everything settled and ready, and we had a heck of a lot more stuff now.

I grimaced as I opened a bag, and a bunch of freshly-broken Arcanite was revealed to me. Like. They'd still work, and still hold mana, but two small stones didn't quite hold as much as one stone twice as large. Sure, it was possible to fuse them together, but it was a time-intensive activity.

Like the bag, that was irrelevant. I kept digging, as some of the others went back to defending the choke points. Bulwark had already started to work. He first went up to Priest Demos, and layered additional protections around him, both in stone and in glowing inscriptions. I figured that Demos was the most vulnerable of us all, and Bulwark was making extra sure that he would be fine. Bulwark was relentless. As soon as he finished that task up, he was already circling our defenses, stroking his chin and muttering under his breath.

There was a bag that literally had my name on it, obviously meant for me. I opened it and started digging through it, to see what was meant for me.

At last! I found it! The Grail, mana almost literally from the heavens! Salvation! Redemption! I was blind, but now I can see! I was lost in the barren desert, but now I am found! The sun had risen, chasing away the dark time of Formorian for food! Through many toils and dangers we preserved, only to arrive at the holy land that was in front of me! My wretched self was saved!

It had been smushed flat, wrecked by the massive forces placed on it by Sky's abrupt stop, followed by a second insult from the fall to the ground. Its skin was rendered, flesh spilling from the insides to form a sticky, gooey mess inside the bag, smearing itself over all the other vittles in the bag, and yet, the most beautiful thing I'd ever seen. The one object that would make me forgive Sky all his slacking off, which would have me singing the Quartermaster's praises – and making sure I donated extra to his coffers.

I grabbed it quick, holding it to me like it was the most precious thing in the world.

A   lone,   solitary,   slightly   mashed   *mango*.

Chapter 10

Formorians VII

Day 10. Sky had not only brought us a bunch of supplies from the Quartermaster, but the Quartermaster, bless his shriveled little heart, had gotten all of our families to gather up and send us each a small pack. Hence the mango. I only found the letters in the morning, when taking an early-morning inventory of everything I'd been brought. Autumn had gotten the mango for me, along with a letter, written in neat, Very Careful words.

Elaine!
*Be careful out there! They said you're doing something dangerous, and you might be gone awhile. **<u>MAKE SURE THEY PAY YOU EXTRA</u>**. I'll be really disappointed in you if you don't get them to pay you more. Stay alive. I miss you. We get a lot less business when you're not around, and frankly I want the extra cash.*
Cheers!
Autumn.

I laughed at the little merchant's sheer transparency. I had no doubt that she wanted me back for me. I also had no doubt that she was bemoaning the lost coin while I wasn't around.

Mom and dad also sent me a letter, along with a few changes of clothes. I appreciated the gesture, but I was going to be quite literally living in my armor for the foreseeable future. Then again, the moment this was over I could change. So it was worth it in the end, I guess.

Elaine,
We've gotten told some of what's going on. Be safe, oh beloved daughter of ours. We sent you a few things we think you'd need! We've also fixed your room back up. Can't wait to see you back safe and sound!

Love,
Elainus and Julia.

They had taken up most of my bag with a pillow. Not exactly standard wilderness fare, but…

"Bugger off Sky." I said, clutching my pillow to me. "You had every chance to get yourself a pillow on your supply run."

"But Daaaaawn" Sky whined at me.

"But nothing. My pillow. Git. Shoo. Leave me alone." I said, making a shooing motion.

"It's already so cramped though! Come on, just half." Sky pleaded with me.

I decided to take the risk, and sleep under the bushes that night. Sure, it was about as comfortable as "sleeping in a bush" could be, but Sky and Bulwark being added to the mix made the place even more cramped.

I mentally cursed to myself as I saw Sealing and Bulwark decide to sleep in Night's hut. Damnit! That could've been me!

Almost literally though – I snoozed, I lost.

Bulwark had helped out a ton. He performed some large-scale Arcanite inscriptions, along with having classes based on warding and protection. Sealing's power stunt was Bulwark's walk in the park. He laid down a number of Inscriptions to boost our stats while we were on our 'home turf', increased stamina regeneration, made sleep better, made us appear even more hidden to the Formorian senses, and a dozen other minor quality of life improvements.

Day 11. Thick clouds covered the sky, starting a miserable downpour on us. The winter rains were arriving a bit early, and this far south, they were *cold.*

Thunder and lightning started to rumble in the clouds, as the deluge got everything soaked. We stuffed Night's cabin full of all of our supplies – much to his grumping as we started chucking stuff at him while he slept – but he'd live. We weren't going to start eating moldy food, or sleeping on wet blankets.

"Elaine! Quick, come here!" Hunting called to me urgently, and I ran over to him as fast as I could.

I put my hands on him, expecting some grievous injury to get close. Hunting just patting my hand with his left hand, his free hand a blur as he kept stabbing Formorians.

"Whoops! Nothing's wrong. No. Look up! In the sky!" Hunting said, pointing up with his left hand.

I shielded my eyes and looked up into the pouring rain, flashes of lightning across the sky lightning it up.

"What am I looking for?" I asked, not seeing anything.

"There! Two thunderbirds!" Hunting said, pointing again with emphasis. "They're traveling westward. Maybe when this is over, we should go take a look!"

I squinted, trying to see.

Maybe. A flash of too many wings, a crack of thunder, and I could vaguely see the outlines of two massive birds, each with far too many wings, dancing around each other, lightning playing around them.

Lightning making it really damn hard to see them.

"Yes. We should take a look." I agreed with Hunting. "If we survive this." I added dryly.

My humor in contrast with the pouring rain wasn't lost on me.

After much muttering and consulting and discussion, Bulwark slowly erected a pavilion of sorts to keep the rain mostly off of half the grove. Katastrofi was too large to make a shelter over her as well as the rest of us. That seemed somewhat suspect to me – wasn't it just the support pillars that needed to be enlarged? – but what did I know, I wasn't an engineer. For all I knew, "Just make the supports bigger" was like someone saying "Why don't you just make their bones bigger to make them taller?" It didn't work that way.

Long story short, I darted around, making sure everyone was fully healed up, before settling back under the pavilion, enjoying the lack of rain. I cranked up **[Warmth of the Sun]** to the max, which promptly backfired on me as I got zero personal space as everyone not on "holding the gap" duty crowded around.

Such was the price of being a heater.

Day 12 saw the Formorian Queens show up on the horizon right as the sun was starting to set. We had a full rotation at this point, where Night no longer needed to single-handedly hold all three entrances at night.

Day 13 everything went to shit again. The Royal Guards were called that for a *reason*, and the few we'd seen here and there were clearly just advance scouts or something. We killed two in the early morning, then three more came for us.

We had about a minute to plan our defenses.

"Brawling! Take over the defenses! Everyone else! Here!" Hunting yelled out, and we dashed over in seconds. Hunting was already drawing little figures in the mud. Night even showed up, the heavy cloud cover hiding the sun. He normally didn't even show up when there were clouds, but hey. The *stakes* were high.

"Three Royal Guards coming in fast. I don't think we can kill them all easily, not before they overrun us. Sealing, Dawn. The two of you have one Royal Guard. Katastrofi and I have a second. Toxic, Nature, Bulwark, Sky – you're on the third. Night, can you assist?"

Night spent less than half a second thinking.

"I will watch, and jump in if assistance is required. Otherwise-"

"Ok, great." Hunting interrupted him. I appreciated it. Night tended to pontificate, and without Hunting interrupting him would take seven minutes to say "I'll be on backup."

"Shame we don't have Ocean here, not with the rain. Dawn, blow your gems on this one. Everyone else. Try not to blow any gems. Once we're done with ours, we'll swing by to help. Questions?" Hunting asked.

"Sky, can you give us a float over?" I asked. I didn't want to plow through the horde if I didn't need to.

"Yeah, but there's a narrow band between the Formorian Soldiers being unable to reach you, and the Shooters attacking you. You won't have the same control I have to stay in the band, not with your flying skills."

"Don't risk it then." Hunting said. "Move out."

Toxic and Nature blazed a trail for Bulwark to follow, while Sky stayed in the narrow band he had deemed as 'safe', dipping down to pick up rocks and throwing them at Formorians. He was really out of his element here.

Hunting jumped on Katastrofi, who roared a challenge at one of the Royal Guards before charging out.

Sealing and I stayed within the defenses, waiting for the last one.

I will say, in all the fights I'd been in, in all the challenges I'd faced, with all the adversity I'd overcome – a monster the size of a three-story building charging at me never failed to strike fear deep into me. Like before, like always, I let the fear in, acknowledged it, and let it pass through.

[Center of the Galaxy] helped.

Sealing layered barriers up, bleeding momentum as the Royal Guard crushed through them all, finally judging that either enough speed had been lost – or more practically, that the Royal Guard was practically on top of us. His barrier thankfully held; the beast trapped within.

It was with a lot less stress that I stepped closer to the barrier, and unleashed all of my stored **[Nova]**s.

A brilliant eruption of heat and light exploded out from me, passing directly through Sealing's barrier, exploding directly onto the Royal Guard. The heat and the light of the Radiance lit the place up like the sun was directly ahead, never mind the clouds.

I blinked as the fiery inferno calmed down. My eyes widened in realization.

"Sealing! No notification! It's not dead!"

He cursed as the Royal Guard became visible again. I guess it was a tactical mistake on my part. The front where it chewed things up was a lot tougher than the rest of it, by sheer virtue of that's where it usually got hit. Last time I'd hit it from above. However, it was moving slowly, unsteadily. Sealing made a snap judgement call.

"I can hold it until Hunting or someone else gets back. Might even be able to kill it. Keep a mana reserve for healing. See if anyone else needs help. Go!" He ordered.

I mean, he can tell me to go, but it's not like I needed to actually go and do anything. I took a look at Hunting, and how he was doing.

I didn't see Hunting, but I did see Katastrofi, his enormous – well, against the Royal Guards, small – Abelisaurus no longer charging at the Royal Guard, but locked in a deadly dance, as she dodged attacks and continued to roar challenges at the Royal Guard. It wasn't going great for her – the Soldiers were working her over, as she was unable to defend herself on all sides, in spite of her tail sweeping away dozens of Formorians at a time – but I had full faith that Hunting was hard at work *somewhere* in the mess.

Even as I watched, Hunting leapt up, nimbly climbing the Royal Guard, expertly avoiding its mandibles. I mentally winced – with how corrosive the skin was, with their "anti-small stuff" defenses, Hunting had to be losing layers off his skin at a bare minimum. My bet was he'd have something close to bloody stumps when he got back.

And yet.

He reached the top of the monster's head, and seemed to just drop straight down. Through the beast.

Just – a nice, wide hole under him where there no longer was Royal Guard, just a void, rapidly sucking in air.

The Royal Guard collapsed, dead, but I didn't see Hunting emerge.

Doing some quick math… yeah. He was probably stuck in there until he could either dig himself out, or climb back out. Neither option sounded pleasant.

"Sealing. Night. Might need to rescue Katastrofi." I said. "Hunting took down the Royal Guard, but looks stuck as a result."

Night was next to me – not quite in a flash. Moving at more normal speeds.

"Accursed clouds. Half the time I have my System-access. Half the time I do not. Dawn, if you would do the honors?" Night asked.

I wordlessly made a large umbrella out of [Veil]. Night grabbed me in one hand, grabbed the umbrella in the other, and was off like the world's deadliest lady.

Making it to Katastrofi was hardly a challenge, although I wanted to keep an eye out on the third fight. Persuading Katastrofi to leave Hunting's side?

"Here dino dino dino dino!" I said, much in the same tone that people called cats. "Bluebeard's safe inside! You're not safe. Let's get you back to safety, then come back out when Bluebeard comes back out, ok?" I said, as Night kept the area around us safe.

Katastrofi leaned into me.

Oh my. What big teeth you have.

She sniffed. Once. Twice.

I was getting to her!

"Yeah, that's right. Let's keep you safe so Bluebeard doesn't worry, ok?" I told her in my best soothing voice. I had no idea if she could understand me or not, and I briefly considered what the heck my life was coming to that I was trying to negotiate with a dinosaur in the middle of a monster ant horde while a vampire progenitor was keeping me safe, but hey! I gotta just roll with it. If I didn't roll with it, I'd go nuts.

I was forced onto my knee and clamped my hands over my ears as Katastrofi objected to my proposal, roaring her defiance.

"Ok! OK! I get it!" I said, thinking fast.

"Night! What do we do!?" I asked.

"I will attempt to dig him out. Please secure the rear with Katastrofi."

I wanted to groan. More defending myself in the middle of the horde. I wasn't equipped for this.

The worst part was, Katastrofi had picked a position by the Royal Guard's head to wait for Hunting. Reasonable, when you consider that's where he went in. But instead of a half-circle to defend, we needed to defend almost an entire circle's worth. Just me and Katastrofi.

Katastrofi was at least smart enough to see what we were doing, and helped us out by being the terror she was built to be.

Quite frankly, I was almost more of a hindrance on the ground than a help.

"Good dinosaur you know me please don't eat me." I said in a calm, soothing voice as I grabbed one of Katastrofi's harnesses, and hauled myself up, onto her back. "I'm here to help, good dino." I said, patting her neck.

"Right! Kill them all!" I proudly announced, having no illusions about how well my orders would be followed.

There was a world of difference between seeing Katastrofi in action, riding her, and then actually being on her when she was in action. My perception couldn't keep up, and since I wasn't in 'going to be dismembered in the next second' danger, **[Bullet Time]** didn't activate.

[Center of the Galaxy] was the only thing keeping my lunch in, as she whirled and struck, slaughtering Formorians by the dozen. I stayed looking to one side, then the other, occasionally firing out a strong beam of Radiance when I saw a target of opportunity nearby. I was in no position to do fine beams, to make sure I exactly killed a Formorian and nothing else.

I didn't dare use a **[Nova]**. For all I knew, Katastrofi was mid-swing, and I'd just friendly-fire her.

In a brief moment of pause, I saw the team that had gone after the 3rd Royal Guard limping back to the grove, injuries clear on a number of them. I hit my thigh in frustration. I wanted to be there! I needed to get to them, to heal them! Instead, I was stuck here, because freaking Hunting didn't have a blasted escape plan properly worked out!

I have no idea how long Night and I stayed here, but the sun was setting, and the clouds were starting to part. Which meant Night might be in trouble when he got out of the blasted body. How long did it take to dig someone out of a body anyways?!

The Queens had been getting larger and larger, and as they got closer, dread was mounting within me. The crab-like beings

113

were *massive,* on a scale I couldn't properly comprehend. Through the thick mists surrounding them, I could see one massive crab-like leg rise, slowly move forward, then plant itself down again. Tentacles writhed from every surface, some dipping down to the ground and back up in a never-ending dance, feeding and laying more eggs.

I couldn't see any way to even slow it down, let alone anything as crazy as *kill* it. If it stood still, and I had twenty years, I might be able to do some damage. Depending on how tough naturally it was. Probably tougher than I was thinking. I could maybe beat a tentacle. One of the smaller ones.

How, by all the gods and goddesses, were we supposed to kill one, let alone three!? The task seemed impossible to me. Generations of combat before my time attested to the fact that, yes, it seemed impossible.

And this was with them out of their lair to boot! How much more dangerous were they when they had the home field advantage, when they were on the defensive?

No wonder Night had never gotten anywhere. No wonder Toxic's move was such a breakthrough.

He'd killed one of *those!?* How had he only gotten 80 levels?!

Still. Hunting and Night eventually exploded out of the Royal Guard, coated in goo, signature blue beard *gone.*

"Night. Dawn. Thank you." He said, glancing around, immediately assessing the situation. "Katastrofi. Follow." He said, and took off through the Formorian Soldiers. I had to grab on as Katastrofi loyally bounded after her companion, and Night followed at what could only be described as a "leisurely" pace, never mind the speed we were going at.

We arrived back at the grove, and I promptly hopped off to heal everyone. A variety of moderately bad injuries all around, with Hunting having gotten the worst of it. Not only was the outside of the Royal Guard corrosive, but everything on the inside was as well. It was like he'd gotten steadily rained on by deadly acid, eating away at him.

Night also needed a solid amount of healing, managing to once again drain all my mana out. I had saved him for last for that reason, his inhuman nature straining my skill.

I could totally see him touching me in my sleep in the middle of the night. In a non-creepy way, of course.

Healing didn't bring back his magnificent blue beard, and he ran his hand over the shiny dome of his bald head.

"Well. Guess I've got a new look now." He said with good humor.

"Ooooh, I can see myself in this!" Sky said, hovering over Hunting.

Hunting swatted at him. Sky dodged.

"Dawn. Toxic. Bulwark." Hunting said. "Defensive duty for now. Brawling's been on it long enough."

I refrained from grumbling. It had been long enough since I last took a full shift, and not just relieving someone, that it was fair for me to do it.

Ah well.

Day 14?

I was woken up in the middle of the night by Night yelling.

"It is time! Everyone, to arms! Bags on! Destruction! It is *now or never!* We can not wait for Priest Demos any longer! Do it!"

Adrenaline was one hell of a wake-up drug. Seeing the Queen only a few miles away, seeing what looked to be a wall of Royal Guards charging towards us, and I was awake, alert, and in full fight-or-flight mode within seconds.

Everyone else was jumping to attention, with Sky shooting off into the air as fast as he could. I had no time to wonder where he was going, as everyone was desperately throwing their bags onto their back. I hurried to follow suit.

The moons were out again, full. Staring. Watching. Unnatural. Crimson light flooded the plain, basking everything in red.

Then Destruction spoke.

It was only a single word.

It spoke of Mother Earth, turning over in her sleep. The planet, taking a breath. The rock and mantle below, scratching an itch. Tectonic plates shifting and sliding, of great tension relieving itself with a sudden, quick snap. The forces that skills could bring, of the might any living being on this planet could wield. As he spoke, it sounded like rocks and stones tumbling over one another, gravelly voice exerting his will upon the world, reshaping it. Destruction Spoke, and the world responded.

"[Earthquake]."

I didn't feel it at first. I didn't see the impact, didn't see the effect. I had a brief moment of wondering if it had been a dud, before a sudden large jolt occurred, the ground underneath me deciding that it was going to be somewhere else, and damn all the people and things above it. I went tumbling to the ground, head smashing on a tree.

"Careful Dawn!" Night reprimanded me.

I bit back a curse. No shit I was trying to be careful.

The ground buckled and heaved, Nature's carefully-grown trees falling. Bulwark's earthen barriers reinforced by Sealing's skills also couldn't survive the disruption, and they collapsed.

The Formorians weren't having a great time of it either, and as I watched, a great rift split the ground, swallowing hundreds – thousands – of Formorians, as they tumbled into the abyss. Soldier, Shooter, Royal Guard – none of that mattered, the earth ate them all.

The rift continued to expand, snaking its way in the wild, unknowable method of an earthquake towards the Queens. Even as I watched, the crack opened up near enough to the Queen's feet, and her great weight was too much for what remained of the cliff wall. Half the Queen fell into the chasm, only her great bulk reaching from side to side stopping her from falling all the way through.

But the earthquake wasn't done yet.

With a snap that no force on the planet could survive, the chasm closed, crushing a good third of the Queen with it. The tentacles on that Queen went crazy, flailing all over, crushing

116

and killing dozens of Royal Guards who were moving towards her, to better aid and assist the fallen behemoth.

The earthquake continued, bucking and heaving, us Sentinels thrown around like a leaf on the wind. Through it all Priest Demos remained knelt in prayer.

Until he wasn't.

He got up, and spoke with a soft voice.

The world stood still for a moment.

"Ah. That did it. We have our miracle."

Warm waves of divine power started to radiate out from Demos.

The sky was cloudless, and yet, the heavens split open, and a radiant glow brighter than the sun burst forth, lighting up the plains with golden light. The air shuddered as the God made his judgement and intervention known, all living beings within sight of the miracle cowering before the raw divine power on display.

Sentinels and Formorians included.

A pillar of divine flames reached down from the heavens, seeming to almost gently and tenderly wrap around one of the remaining Queens, then purging and scouring the Queen from existence. The blast of heat and power hit us with a roar, returning sound to the world. The force blasted around anything that had been in the camp and not nailed down.

I was a lightweight, and got included in the "not nailed down" portion, tumbling and cursing as I was blown back. Not terribly far, but enough for it to be a pain.

The heavenly flames were merely the announcement, the initial strike opening the skies. The inferno faded, leaving behind a charred husk of the Formorian Queen, and a notification that our party had slain it. I wasn't going to argue with getting credit. Behind it, a legion of angels poured through the burning rift. Humanoid, with great white feathered wings and enormous burning swords, they descended down from the heavens above, down to our mortal plane, and fell upon the last monstrous Queen.

Scorching swords sliced through vicious tentacles, cauterizing purple flesh. Heavenly weapons sought out chinks and nooks and crannies, plunging deep into the Queen's shell, and emerging with an explosion of steaming flesh and golden, holy flames.

The angels were clearly corporeal, less than fully divine. A tentacle wrapped around an angel, crushing him, throwing the body with broken wings plummeting to the ground. Another had her wings torn off, turning herself into a final strike with her sword as she plunged down.

She landed on the Queen, and kept furiously hacking away at tentacles until another one turned her into paste.

The Shooters noticed the new aerial threat, and turned their attention to the angels, hundreds, thousands of spikes firing up towards them. Most were deflected, or did nothing to the heavenly beings, but now and then one would fall, pierced by too many attacks to keep going.

The earthquake was keeping them in check though, side rifts opening up and consuming hundreds of Formorians, Shooters included.

Then the earth got back to heaving and bucking under my feet, and I was back to keeping myself alive.

Chapter 11

Formorians VIII

Suicide missions were called that for a *reason*. In this case, namely, we were channeling and launching an earthquake on top of us, as powerful as could be. We were at the epicenter, where the ground was constantly deciding to be somewhere else at high speed.

Sky promptly took flight, flying high, going up, up, and away, speeding towards the angels.

"Sky! Don't do it! The Shooters-"

Night bit off what he was going to say, as Sky was clearly ignoring him.

From what I could briefly see though, the Shooters weren't ignoring him, never mind the earthquake, never mind the legion of holy angels.

I really, really wanted to try and heal some angels. See them up close and personal. Maybe talk with them? Get a few feathers?

"Bulwark. Toxic. Dawn. Escort Priest Demos to the walls, and attempt to secure them. Sealing. Hunting. Brawling. Nature. On me. We will strike at the Queen while she is weakened. We shall ensure our victory."

I opened my mouth to argue, to advocate for me getting to see the angels, then closed it. It was right for me to head back. I would be a massive force multiplier among the soldiers defending themselves, while I'd barely be a help here. Sure, I might pull someone from the brink of death, but I might also end up being a liability where they were going.

All Sentinels were equal, but some – namely Night – were more equal than others. I wasn't going to start arguing here and now. Not when it was such a coin flip.

"Hang on." Destruction said, holding his hand up. We paused.

119

"I keep notifications on." He said, unable to hide a smug grin passing over his face. "And with that little stunt just now, I hit level 520."

Holy – I whistled and clapped like everyone else did. He'd just gotten what, a eighty levels in one go or something absurd like that?

"Turns out, you get your 3rd class at 512 like we were thinking. I'd love to grab a class now, but since the experience stays and I need to do some thinking on what to grab, I'm going to delay." Destruction said.

There was some grumbling at the announcement – we all wanted to see him grab a third class, to see if there was anything special about it.

Destruction yawned.

"Do wish I could sleep though, or grab a nap. My [Sleep Storage] skill only goes so far." He grumbled.

The four of us on the "return and defend" team grouped up, while the strike team grabbed what they could, getting the lion's share of the remaining supplies, then started running. They needed to do a long loop – the earth was split, forcing them to detour. Katastrofi couldn't make the gap.

Watching Destruction work on his own, when he wasn't channeling a skill, was quite something. It was like Artemis on steroids. Artemis, if she had unlimited mana. Pebbles kept levitating themselves around Destruction, then firing away in every direction like grapeshot, leaving dozens of Formorians dead and twitching behind him. An uncountable flurry of stones were whizzing around him, creating a deadly shield that would shred anything near him.

Almost all regeneration. He could keep this up for hours, and that was after he'd unleashed a massive earthquake.

I mentally shook my head. Sentinels. Crazy powerful, the lot of them. Which had me eyeing Priest Demos, who'd pulled off a stunt nearly as crazy and as strong.

"Miracles, eh?" I asked Priest Demos, keeping my footing through the shaking earth. Like, mid-earthquake wasn't really the time for a casual chat, but like, what else was I doing? Well, besides rapidly finding religion. All praise… who again?

He closed his eyes.

"A lifetime of service, of devotion, all for this one moment." He said. "It wasn't for this moment. It wasn't with ulterior motives that I worshipped the God of Conquest. It just felt *right.* He rewarded me with the ability to see lies so many decades ago, touched me in a manner similar to Papilion's touch on you, although different in so many ways. Then it came to now, came to this moment. I begged intervention. The temple back in the capital also had worshippers beg for intervention. Finally, the god decided to intervene. It comes at a significant price to his divine power. Angels come from faithful mortals that are selected and asked to join. Those that died are forever gone. The god will need centuries, if not longer, to recover from this intervention."

Priest Demos smiled, with his eyes closed.

"Lastly. I'm not going to make it." He said, and at that, I leaned forward, touching him, making sure he was fully healed. Only a few points of mana left, which I surmised was from how banged-up he'd gotten – we'd all gotten – in the earthquake.

"No Dawn – eh, Elaine. This is my time. See. My old friend White Dove has come to take me away."

I'd be dammed if there wasn't a white dove now sitting in one of the branches of a downed tree. I eyed it somewhat unhappily.

I'd initially taken to White Dove/Black Crow being a superstition until I'd been visited by the specter of Black Crow on the pirate ship. I *still* kept falling for the "but it's just a folk story". One day I'd stop making that mistake.

Probably just in time for the story to actually be a folk story. That'd be the day, when Sentinel Dawn's scared of the chicken-legged house. Hang on, chicken-legged housed sounded totally plausible on Pallos.

Mimics? Yeah, I could see some chests holding voracious all-consuming monsters.

A living cookie?

Ok, no, that was going too far. Cookies couldn't live. Maybe they could be puppetted by someone else – that was all too easy to believe – but being alive? No way.

Anyways.

Black Crow I'd fought hundreds of times, with each patient I'd pulled back from the brink, with each life I'd saved. White Dove? She was a whole different kettle of fish. She came to those who were at peace with death, who were ready to go.

What did I do?

I was sworn to help, to heal, to fight off death, to do grim battle with Black Crow over lives. To shoo him away, to give people more time under the sun, to let them see another *dawn.* If Priest Demos was suicidal – a fairly common case for White Dove to show up, as the stories went – it'd be easy. Sit on top of him, talk him out of it.

But he wasn't. He simply knew his life was at an end, and was happy to take the grim reaper's hand, and walk onto the next step of his journey, the next chapter in his...

... *life* felt like the wrong word here.

"Elaine. Do not worry about me." Priest Demos said, locking eyes with me, giving me a kindly, grandfatherly smile. "I assume your healing beacon is still on. Listen. Take my hand, so you know you did all you could, so you don't need to worry about what happens next." He said, offering me his hand. I took it.

"Tiberius." Priest Demos said, turning to Bulwark.

"Priest." He respectfully said.

"You've grown up to be a fine man. I couldn't be prouder. I would never imagine the kid I sheltered from the streets to become the man you are today. Be at peace. Marry that woman. Name a kid or three after me." He said, cracking a grin. Bulwark cracked one right back.

"Alright, just for you, I will!" Bulwark said, wrapping Demos in a hug.

I let go of his hand, to better let Demos and Bulwark say goodbye.

They eventually let go.

"Toxic – Arthur, if I remember correctly?" Demos said. Arthur nodded stiffly.

"I don't know what haunts you so. If it is atonement and absolution you seek, I can give it to you. If it is penance, I can also give it to you. Go forth, and do good in this world. Do good, until you believe you have done more good than harm. Go out, and improve the lives of your fellow man, however you best see fit. One day, the scales will be balanced, then tip back towards you, and you shall know peace."

That short little speech seemed to lift thousands of pounds off of Arthur, as he wrapped the Priest in a large, fierce hug.

"I will. I will." Arthur sobbed. Bulwark and I exchanged a glance, a silent vow to never mention his crying.

"Right. I do believe my time is up. Elaine, if you would do the honors?" Demos said, holding out his hand again. I took it again, my heart racing, my palms suddenly sweaty.

I just realized that this could go *terribly wrong* for me. If I somehow kept Demos alive through the attentions of White Dove, I'd have the literal grim reaper mad at me – possibly going after me.

I steeled myself. Every day was a battle against Black Crow. I wasn't going to get scared now. I wasn't going to back down now, not when this was just another fight, another time and place to push back a death-date.

It didn't stop a nervous lump from forming in my throat as Demos faced the white dove – White Dove – and spoke to it.

"I do believe my time has come, and I am ready." He said.

There was no fanfare, no trumpets, nothing.

Priest Demos simply dropped dead from perfect health while holding my hand, while my healing was pulsing through him, without me spending a single point of mana.

So ended the tale of Priest Demos, a boy who loved the gods, and was loved in return by them. A teenager, who'd been visited by one god in particular, touched and blessed by him. A young man, who'd taken up a blue class in the name of his god. The high priest, who'd guided and mentored dozens of other god's touched in the decades, nearly two centuries that he'd lived. The man who'd taken kids off the street, sheltered them, given them life and meaning and purpose. And lastly. Humanity's great savior, who'd called down a miracle in our hour of need.

Such was the tale of Priest Demos.

Chapter 12

Formorians IX

I gently lowered Priest Demos's body to the ground, stepping back. Bulwark moved in, and I tugged on Arthur's arm, to better give him some privacy.

It was weird. I'd never gotten the hang of sea legs, but my earthquake legs seemed to be fine.

Arthur was also deep in thought, and I wasn't going to disturb him. The Formorians had stopped attacking for now, but I suspected it wouldn't be too long before they were back at it.

I shut up, and said nothing, letting the two of them have their moment of peace. Heck, I had some thinking to do myself.

Demos letting me hold his hand did just as much as he'd guessed it would. I wasn't struggling or self-doubting my actions or choices, which immediately gave me a measure of peace.

However, there was now the certain knowledge that there was no fighting White Dove. If she wanted someone, there wasn't a damn thing I could do about it, at least as my skills were now. It was likely my skills would never be good enough.

At the same time, as the stories went, White Dove only took those who were willing, and Priest Demos had gotten more than a little bit of divine attention just now. I had brushed up against the gods once again, and the sheer scale, the sheer difference in power, made me want to run screaming the other way.

I was *so glad* I had never taken one of Papilion's classes.

A loud noise came from where Bulwark was, and Arthur and I turned and looked. A large stone statue of Priest Demos emerged from the ground, larger than life, standing protectively over a tomb made of stone. We let Bulwark take his time, carefully having the stone imprinted with fancy patterns, putting up a plaque describing Demos and his life's work. Putting down basic defenses and complex inscriptions, so the Formorians wouldn't bother the tomb.

As impatient as I was, as much as I wanted to get moving, I left Bulwark alone. Instead, I idly punched Arthur's leg. Left. Right. Left. Right. Dude was unfairly tall. He just glanced down and basically shrugged.

Thinking about it, he probably had more stats at this point than anyone else on the old team. His massive evolution at 256, combined with all the levels here? Yikes. Heck, he might be rivaling some of the other Sentinels in stats, given that he seemed to see a nice big level spike as well.

I was getting kinda excited to class up myself, and I was going to do so the moment I could. I'd been checking on my stats and level ups now and then as we fought, but now I took a high level summary look at everything I'd gotten up until now.

[*ding!* Congratulations! [Ranger-Mage] has leveled up to level 215->256! +10 Free Stats, +5 Speed, +5 Vitality, +20 Mana, +20 Mana Regen, +20 Magic power, +20 Magic Control from your Class! +1 Free Stat for being Human! +1 Strength, +1 Mana Regen from your Element!]

[*ding!* [Warmth of the Sun] leveled up! 215 -> 217]
Oh wow. If **[Warmth of the Sun]** was leveling up, I was in for it. In a good way.
[*ding!* [Medicine] leveled up! 240 -> 251]
[*ding!* [Veil of the Aurora] leveled up! 245 -> 256]
All my Ranger-Mage skills, except for **[Shine]**, maxed out as well.
[*ding!* [Shine] leveled up! 104 -> 111]

I mentally cursed. I should've kept **[Shine]** going semi-permanently at night. I probably would've maxed it as well.

At the same time – I was spending most nights recharging my **[Nova]** gems. I didn't exactly have mana to luxuriously waste.

[*ding!* **Congratulations! You've unlocked the Class skill [Sun Spike]! Would you like to replace a skill with [Sun Spike]? Y/N]**

Sun Spike: You are the inviolate sun, high above all other beings. With this skill, you strike down all small things that dare approach you. Increased number of projectiles that can be shot down, increased power of attacks, increased range per level.

I thought about the skill. Basically, it seemed to be a point-defense system. A reward for diving through the Shooter's spikes from high up, a skill that would let me do it again.

At the same time, it seemed like a skill that just mimicked stuff I could already do with a combination of other skills. Plus, and this was super petty, I didn't like the phrasing of the skill.

I denied the skill.

[*ding!* **[Bullet Time] leveled up! 230 -> 256]**
[*ding!* **[Oath of Elaine to Lyra] leveled up! 235 -> 252]**
[*ding!* **[Sentinel's Superiority] leveled up! 240 -> 256]**
[*ding!* **[Persistent Casting] leveled up! 111 -> 182]**

[Sun-Kissed] maxing out was sweet though! I'd been struggling to raise that skill's level for some time now, and getting it capped here and now was great!

I glanced at my stats. On one hand, I didn't want to punt and screw up my stat allocation. On the other, *this was it.* My last evolution for my Celestial class that I'd ever get. I'd hate myself if I missed a good evolution because I was short a few stat points. At the same time, we were still in the middle of a war zone, and I didn't exactly have time to chat with Night, Julius, Artemis, and the rest of the Sentinels to optimize my build.

Then again, I kinda knew the score at this point. I knew what to expect, I knew my build.

Stats

[Free Stats: 451]

[Strength: 312]

[Dexterity: 194]

[Vitality: 975]

[Speed: 975]

[Mana: 6704]

[Mana Regeneration: 6903 (+4417.92)]

[Magic Power: 5839 (+68608.25)]

[Magic Control: 5839 (+68608.25)]

Right. My Dexterity-Speed ratio was starting to get a hair worrying, but I was still within tolerance. I was also pretty close to 1000, and that seemed to be a nice, round number. 50 points there!

I did some quick math. I had 401 points left. I'd need, baseline, 161 points in both Power and Control to get them up to 6000, and that was before the Power-Control trade-off hit. That wouldn't leave me enough points to boost my mana regeneration over 7000.

Now, I could do both Power and Control, a nod towards the evolution that was coming. However, my stats were frankly absurd with [Oath] boosting them. What did Power and Control do to help? I mean, apart from the all-too-obvious 'it helped with my [Ranger-Mage] class.'

However, looking at my stats more – Mana to 7000 and Mana Regen to 7000 was just a hair under 400 points total. Given the current situation, that seemed to be the best use of my stats.

And with that, I had a measly 8 Free Stats left. I tossed a bone to my Dexterity, getting it to 200. I kept the remaining 2 Free Stats.

Alright! I was ready to class up, as soon as I wasn't in the middle of a hostile army.

Bulwark seemed to have wrapped things up as well, and said his final goodbyes.

"Let's get moving." He said, and Arthur and I pretended to not notice him wiping his face.

"That way." Arthur pointed, and we were off.

Arthur wasn't nearly as good as Brawling was at hacking through the Formorians, but them being disorganized and somewhat confused was working well in our favor. I was quite liberal with my blasting, although we were getting bogged down. Sucked that he was still using my spear and shield, although it wasn't like I was going to get much mileage out of using them myself.

"Toxic! Just pick me up and run or something!" I called out in frustration as the Formorian body Toxic effortlessly hopped over was nearly as tall as I was, requiring a lot more time and effort for me to get over it, slowing us all down.

Bulwark was quite a bit taller, but no giant, nor was he a physical classer either. He was able to throw bodies out of the way though, and effortlessly jump over others.

Toxic kneeled down, and I climbed up onto him, piggyback style.

I suppressed the urge to make horse noises, say something like "Onwards my noble steed!", or hit his sides, like a horse.

My traitorous tongue made a few clip-clop noises though, as Toxic charged ahead, much faster now that I wasn't slowing us down. I helped by shooting Formorians from over his shoulder.

I mixed in a few Radiance shots from my eyes, just for variety's sake. Mobile Radiance eye-turret! Pew! Pew pew!

This was a lot more fun when it was just "getting from A to B" and not "Defend this narrow gap, the fate of all humanity rests on it." I mean, sure, if we died here it would be Bad, and I'd feel pretty sorry for myself. But hey. A spoonful of sugar made blasting Formorians that much more fun.

Gods, I'd love a spoonful of sugar right now.

It helped that the Formorians were acting weird. Almost like they were confused or something. They didn't have their usual mechanical precision, the relentless unending waves of flesh and mandibles. They were still deadly, still attacking, but not working in tandem as flawlessly as before.

We ran, jumped, blasted, and generally made our way to the once perfect, gleaming walls, now with a hole blasted through them.

The earthquake had done quite a number on the walls to boot, large swaths of the walls broken and crumbled, a rift breaking another segment. Honestly, it looked like there had been centuries of wear and decay on the walls. If you told me that a month ago they were whole and complete, I wouldn't have believed you.

I twisted and looked at Bulwark, who had a sour, "I totally have my work cut out for me" look on his face.

"Good luck!" I cheerfully gloated to him.

"Your work is even harder, and more time-sensitive." He shot back. "The more goofing off you do now, the more people die. Go on now, chop chop."

The smile vanished off my face faster than a snowflake in hell. I bit my lip and turned away, stopping myself from retorting, from getting deeper into the pissing match, and thought about it.

Bulwark was, technically, correct in what he said. The longer we took, the more people would die.

He'd also just seen someone pretty close to him die, and this wasn't exactly a low-stress situation. I'd been a bit carefree, and it might've grated on him a bit.

Ugh. *Social Niceties.* At the same time, spending a moment and thinking about it probably avoided us getting into a stupid spat over nothing.

Arthur wisely shut up and said absolutely nothing.

Good oversized horsey.

We moved towards one of the holes in the wall, and I started conserving my mana, trying to get full up before I needed to start healing.

"Skip the entryway. I'll make us an entrance." Bulwark said. "All the Formorians are funneling into one spot, and if there are members of the army still around and alive, we don't want to make it any harder on them, not after we already dropped two walls on them."

I winced. I hadn't quite put one and one together, but yeah. There had been a bunch of soldiers holding the line between the walls when we traveled in, and said walls had just gotten an earthquake delivered, in geographical terms, directly on top of them.

We continued to fight our way to the walls, and made it, somewhat relieved that we weren't fighting off Formorians from every direction.

"Move away from the breach!" Bulwark yelled. "It's more likely that we'll encounter soldiers, and not Formorians, on the other side if we're further away!"

Made sense. We peeled *away* from the entry hole, and found a nice stretch of unbroken wall.

"Over, or through?" Bulwark mused. Nodding to himself, he seemed to come to a decision. "Over it is. Toxic! Look alive!" He said, putting his hand on the wall. Little bits on the wall twisted out, giving a small series of expert-level handholds too far apart for me to try them. Toxic grabbed on to the lowest handholds, I made sure I had a tight grip on my steed, and we went up the wall like a shot, Bulwark following closely behind.

Toxic and I got to the top of the wall, and laid flat on it, to better avoid the Shooter's line of fire.

I tried to twist my neck around to better see behind us, to better cover Toxic's back from Shooters, but honestly, he moved so darn fast there was no point. Bulwark followed; a hair slower. He dropped down next to us; a few spikes stopped by tiny stone plates. I raised an eyebrow.

Anyone else I'd say it was a skill, [**Pinpoint Stone Defenses**] or something like that. On a Sentinel? Raw reflexes and ability was my bet.

"Ahoy! Are there Legionnaires of Remus below?" Bulwark called out. No idea why he wasn't just poking his head over the side.

There were noises from below – human noises.

"Yes! Who are you? How did you get here?" A tired-sounding voice came from below.

"Sentinel Bulwark, Toxic, and Dawn. Dropping in." Bulwark said, rolling off the edge of the wall.

I got off of Arthur's back, and mentally cursed Bulwark seven different ways. Yes, I could probably make the drop. It would cost me mana, and we wanted to – needed to – look good, especially here. Especially if we were going to project the image of the invincible Sentinels, here to save the day.

This is what it all led up to. This is where keeping our image good came into play, where it mattered. There was a massive tonal shift between "Sentinel Dawn slowly and awkwardly scrambled down the wall – the rookie." And "Sentinel Dawn dropped in like an avenging goddess – all hail."

At the same time, if Bulwark had used some damn mana to make some damn stairs or footholds, I could've gone down elegantly, mana-less. Sure, he'd be spending it, not me, but as he pointed out – my mana and use was critical here.

I wrapped myself in **[Shine]**, just going all-in on the imagery, and I jumped off the wall. Toxic landed right before I did, next to Bulwark who already had his badge up in the air, proving his authority.

Bulwark was barking orders already, and I remembered our time in Massalix somewhat fondly. He also needed to organize stuff, but his method and reasonings were different. He didn't need everyone to cooperate, just the people he found, and he was good enough at that. His method was to get a bunch of strong dudes together, have them pick up rocks, put them roughly where the wall should be, and he did the rest.

I took a moment to acquaint myself with my surroundings, to see how the soldiers had set themselves up and arranged the fight.

We were in the midst of a half-trampled camp, basically. Most of the neatly arranged tents were mushed off to one side or the other, making the center lane through the camp much wider than usual. Broken spears and torn canvas were thrown off to the side, obvious indications of 'this is broken but we're so hard up on supplies and can't physically throw anything away so we're keeping it just in case we need it.' Little contained fires flickered here and there, while some bright beacons of light came from a few tents, obviously the rare soldier with [Light] or some variety of the skill.

Off to one side there were clear sounds of battle, of the soldiers fighting with Formorians and holding the line in the middle of the camp. Losing some ground here meant lost tents and sleeping space, although I was willing to bet large amounts of money that significant amounts of room had been cleared behind them. Which was probably part of the "thrown wherever" debris that was littering the normally clean and well-organized camp.

Toxic whispered to me out of the corner of his mouth.

"Dammit. I'm going to have to be the great big amazing Sentinel holding the line in the middle forever aren't I."

I patted him on the arm, talking out of the side of my mouth again.

"Probs. Going to find a soldier and the infirmary." I said. "I'll try to swing by now and then to give you a break."

I looked around for a likely candidate. Too shell-shocked, too leadership-like, too high level to get pulled away to show me things. Ahha! Perfect. A nervous, young-looking soldier. Back when I was regularly on the front lines, I would've mentally pegged him as the type to always manage to avoid being in the fight. And hey! Now I could give him a legit excuse to be away from the fighting, and everyone won.

"Soldier!" I said, pointing to him and striding forward, as Toxic hustled over to the fighting and Bulwark vanished with a team instantly assembled. "Show me to the infirmary!"

To my surprise, he balked, and hesitated.

"Um, I dunno about that, I'm supposed to-"

I didn't care.

"I am Sentinel Dawn. Your orders are to show me to the infirmary. Now."

"But-"

133

"I outrank everyone here except *Sentinel* Toxic and *Sentinel* Bulwark, who are my equals. Now move!" I yelled. "Unless there's no infirmary?" I asked with what I hoped was my best 'dangerous' voice.

The soldier, bless his cowardly little heart, snapped into a salute at my berating. Clearly something got through to him.

"Sir! No sir! I mean yes, sir! Er, ma'am? Ah, yes, there's an infirmary, it's right this way." He said, pointing.

"Lead the way." I said, then corrected him as he started to climb over a pile blocking a side lane. "Through the main path."

I'd picked an idiot to escort me.

With the multiple false starts out of the way, we started to move through the center lane, my badge held up high backed by my **[Shine]** being great for parting the sea of soldiers. A Sentinel, in the camp, clearly in a hurry? Clear the path!

This is what all of the politeness and careful navigation and generally not being a jerk came to. When one of us needed to *move,* when one of us needed things to happen *right now,* we could – and did – start barking orders, overriding anyone and everyone, and commandeer whatever we needed. The understanding was that we wouldn't abuse it – and Night came down *hard* on anyone who did – which gave us a pristine, immaculate reputation.

So, when I came in, and started barking orders, I didn't get grief. I didn't get people thinking "oh, it's just another Sentinel throwing their weight around." I didn't get too much sass, or backtalk, or double-guessing. I got what I wanted, when I wanted, which was *right now.*

It helped that it was the army, who we outranked. It helped that they were used to taking orders. *In theory,* it would be just this easy to command civilians, and order them to help us.

Interestingly, it was just as hard to order civilians around as it was to order soldiers around. You'd think civilians would be harder to order around, not just as hard. Civilians weren't always used to being ordered around, so they had a moment of surprise before agreeing to whatever we were asking.

The "I have the combat capabilities to murder you and take what I want and people will be mad at *you* for slowing a Sentinel in an emergency down" aspect helped grease cooperation quite a bit.

Soldiers had a moment of blinking like before, usually because they were trained on a normal chain of command, and orders coming from someone outside their chain of command was unusual, to say the least.

Either way – I got what I wanted. I was tempted, oh so tempted, to blast out **[Moonlight]** as we ran through the camp, but I refrained. The problem with doing that was the first blast was great. Then anyone I was healing I healed at the absolute maximum range of **[Moonlight]**, which meant taking the maximum penalty. It made small injuries murder my mana, and I'd just lose all my mana for almost no tangible benefit once I got in range of the infirmary. Better to leave **[Moonlight]** off until I made it to the infirmary, assess the situation, and go from there.

"We're   here."

Chapter 13

Formorians X

I took a look around the infirmary, a frown on my face. *Usually,* there were booths of healers, and a line of injured soldiers waiting their turn, sorted by severity. That's normally how this worked.

Instead, what I saw were rows upon rows of injured soldiers, with a number of slightly-less injured soldiers running around with buckets of filthy water and bandages. It was still night time, and the long, long tent was poorly lit. All I saw were unending rows of men, going into the darkness. The stench of rot and decay, blood and vomit, bile and gore filled the air.

Nothing new there.

Screams and cries filled the air, men in agony begging for relief. Crying out for their families, for their loved ones.

"Find me the healer, or whoever's in charge." I ordered my gofer.

I missed Kallisto already. He would've preemptively read my mind, and already had the whole story for me. Instead, I was back to doing this the hard way.

I grabbed one of the soldiers who was running around, and not wanting to go through another song and dance routine, started by flashing my Sentinel badge.

"Hi. Area with the most critically injured?" I asked him. I didn't get a salute in return, on account of him missing the needed hand.

He hesitated a moment, just from the sheer surreal nature of a Sentinel showing up in his tent, but pointed me in the right direction.

"Thank you." I said, tapping him, letting a grin go from ear to ear. The *look on his face,* as his arm regrew, and a dozen minor cuts and bruises got fixed.

Gratitude and relief, thankfulness and joy. A new lease on life, a body made whole again.

There was an argument to be made to wait until I had a full sense of the situation. Until I had an eagle-eye view of everything going on, to put my mana to the best, optimal use. That we'd need my power somewhere else.

I couldn't do it. Not here, not now, not this time. I went from soldier to soldier, lying side by side, packed like sardines in the infirmary, touching each one, healing them. Getting them ready enough to get back in the fight.

Which naturally had the soldiers further down in the line start to clamor and shout for me, for me to skip the line and heal them *now*.

"I'm the grandson of Senator Lucius! Heal me next!" One voice cried out.

"I have a wife! And kids! Do me next!" Someone else added in.

In the most pompous and arrogant tone I'd ever heard, so over the top as to be ridiculous.

"Well, bugger to all of you. **I** am the son of a baker. I *obviously* take priority."

I cracked up laughing at that, hitting another person, and if I didn't think it'd cause Serious Problems, I would've gotten to him next just for the joke. If I started down that path though, it could end up problematic. Better to have the appearance of fair and neutral in my healing.

However, I'd been a bit arrogant coming into the infirmary, and starting to heal.

Magic worked on a bunch of different things. Skills. Stats. Difficulty. Size. Image. All were factors in how much mana I used in a skill. One of the biggest, most important aspects was the size of the injury. A small cut took hardly anything, while regrowing an entire arm cost thousands of mana. Disease was easy and hard in that respect. The better I knew what I was dealing with, the more efficient I was, the less mana I used. However, fundamentally, disease didn't have a huge amount of mass to it, which seemed to be one of the most critical aspects of not using lots of mana to cure it.

A poor image of the disease Hesoid was using, the fact that it was a magical plague and not natural, the fact that it was backed by skills as well, was why it had cost me so much more to cure his diseases, versus the natural outbreak of cholera that had been going on in tandem. I also needed to heal the damage done by the disease.

However, it was generally on a small scale, as these things went. It was why I could attempt to cure an entire tiny town of a weak plague. Diseases just didn't cost that much mana. Part of why Dark and Water healers were more popular than Light healers. You could see a lot more patients for the same amount of mana, on top of a higher effectiveness at lower levels.

Only at 100, when I'd first gotten [**Detailed Restoration**] did I start becoming an effective Light healer. Even then, I'd needed the boost from [**Oath**] just to start getting anywhere.

Restoring limbs was an entirely different ballgame. There was a reason it had taken me three castings of a skill just to restore a kid's arm back when I first got the skill, and that was a *kid.* A single, scrawny kid, with a small arm. The larger the person, the larger the arm, the more mana it took.

The question wasn't my power, or my control. I'd demonstrated that with Brawling, curing him being bisected.

It was easier to reattach a limb than to recreate it. All the flesh was still there, it just needed to be reconnected, and what little rot and problems had set in needed to be fixed. Growing a limb wholesale was a different problem, by an order of magnitude.

The question was the sheer scale of the problem.

The first dozen patients were easy, and I hardly noticed the problem.

The second dozen the half-eye I permanently kept on my mana was sending a little warning bell that my mana was dropping *fast.*

By the third dozen, I knew I was in trouble.

I started to slow down. Chat with each soldier for a minute, stalling for time to think, and stalling for time for my mana to regenerate. The beauty of the "booth" method of healing is it took some time between patients, time that I could regenerate my mana, as opposed to the "blitz through everyone as fast as possible" method that I was currently employing.

I looked around, and spotted exactly the person I needed.

Well. Thought I needed.

They looked well into their middle-ages, and identified at level 240. His insignia suggested that he was a Centurion, one of the lower-leveled commanders. A young Centurion likely had bought the spot, or had gotten in on connections and the like. A battle like this, being on the frontlines, might have knocked some sense into them. It might not have. However, someone who'd broken past 180, and gotten themselves all the way to 240? Someone who, in spite of an age that suggested decades in the military was a Centurion? I couldn't guarantee it, but it hinted at a lifetime of service, of being promoted from the lowest ranks all the way to Centurion on sheer merit and skill. Exactly the sort of person who could discreetly lend me a hand.

"Centurion! It's been so long!" I gleefully said, arriving by his side. A quick look at his injuries suggested that falling rocks was the cause of his injuries, not Formorians. Made sense. Didn't get to be this old on the front lines, without knowing how to best battle Formorians. Night and General Augustus talking about "not using large-impact skills" way back when I first arrived at the front lines had a much more sobering reminder.

"Here, let's spend a few minutes catching up!" I said, wrapping us with **[Veil of the Aurora]**, the initial privacy aspect of the skill coming back. The skill was *so useful!*

He looked at me as I touched him and healed him.

"Begging your pardon, Sentinel, but I've never seen you before." He said.

"I know. I apologize." I replied. I could see the gears turning, and before I could say anything else, he started speaking.

"Which means you need something from me. Something private, that you don't want getting out." He paused, continuing to think. I figured I'd spare us the game of "figuring it out", and just talk with him.

"I'm going too fast, and running out of mana." I said. "It'll look more than a bit bad when I heal a bunch of people, and suddenly stop. Mind giving me a hand?"

The Centurion was sitting up and stretching, checking that, yes, he did indeed have his stomach back. He looked at me, spent a moment thinking, then nodded.

"Mostly. I can move down and partition the area. Once you reach the end, you'll have 'healed' everyone present. Can't stop people talking though."

I shrugged.

"Can't stop them talking, or making it back indeed. I just need things to not turn ugly when I go 'heal, heal, heal, sorry you drew the short straw', without burning through all the Arcanite I have in reserve. My regeneration is high, and I will be able to get to everyone in time. I just need the time!"

He frowned.

"We don't have time. Not with the way the assault is going."

"I'm not the only Sentinel here, and I can only do so much." I pointed out. "But I can do something. Come on. Work with me here."

The Centurion seemed to think that, yes, indeed, he was back in one whole piece, and saluted me, fist over chest.

"As you command, Sentinel." He said, and I dropped the **[Veil]**, moving onto the next patient.

The Centurion moved down the line, deeper into the dark confines of the infirmary. I continued my work, spending a moment chatting with each soldier, carefully checking what had happened.

I could've probably gotten away with it anyways, but I had to acknowledge that being a **[Pretty]** healer in the middle of a warzone was probably helping. Nobody was minding me spending a few moments chatting them up.

If I could somehow stretch each conversation to a minute or so, I'd be able to do this forever. A secondary plan.

"This looks bad, how'd it happen?" I said, chatting with a soldier sans a leg.

A minor look of disbelief crossed his face – obviously a Formorian had taken it off – but it was quickly replaced with a misplaced confidence. Surely, *he* could tell an epic tale of heroism and valor, enough to woo a maiden's fair heart.

"It was a Formorian! Twice as large as the norm, it ripped its way through our line! Soldiers fell left and right as it barreled through us. It was just me between it and the vulnerable camp! 'This is it.' I told myself. 'This is what I've been training for, this is my moment of glory.' Ah, alas, as I struck it with a mortal blow, it hit me right back with its dying breath, taking my leg with it! Such a monstrous Formorian wouldn't die without extracting a price!"

I kept a smile on my face, mentally rolling my eyes in the biggest circle possible. Translation: He goofed killing a perfectly normal Formorian, who took his leg off in a moment of inattention. Someone must've screwed up the shield wall to boot, to allow it to happen.

I had no doubt by the time he got back home that he would be slaying a Royal Guard in single combat, the only soldier between it and the rest of Remus.

Still, his long-winded nature gave me *time,* time for my mana to regenerate. I patted him on the shoulder and plastered a smile on my face. Good bedside manner, that.

"How heroic! A new leg, for your service. Can't help you with getting new armor though. Good luck!" I said, slowly standing up and moving to the next patient.

Zig-zagging across the aisle every time also burnt more time, so I did. The Centurion came back, and noticed me.

"Sentinel!" He said, in the fake-friendly voice. "I'm impressed! You've almost entirely cleared this tent, as usual!"

I mentally cursed.

How I translated what he said: "No way to break the tent in half or anything. Gotta go until the end. Not a ton more patients left."

Curse the shit lighting in here. I had no idea how much more tent there was.

Although, the light was starting to get better. I made a poker face.

Dawn had arrived. In multiple senses.

I carried on regardless.

I was starting to tap my Arcanite, dropping the dangerously low reserves even further, when I reached the end of the tent. I looked back behind me, and smiled.

From what little I could see, the tent was nearly empty. Most of the soldiers, having gotten fixed up, decided that getting out of here was the right move. Occasionally I'd seen a squad leader move through, grabbing the members of their squad that had healed up but were loitering around, not terribly eager to get back in the action.

It couldn't be good for their mental health. Imagine. Losing an arm, not being healed, spending who knows how long staring at the dark tent ceiling, thinking he'll be a cripple for life – or at least until a good healer can get to him, if he could ever afford one. Most likely reliving the moment they were injured.

Then boom! I come through like the sun rising over the horizon, breaking their night, bringing the day. They're healed! Whole!

I loved the title Dawn.

And with military efficiency – which is to say, incredible at some times, horribly inefficient at others – they're yoinked right back to the front lines where they were injured, to be fed back into the all-consuming grinder that was the Formorians.

As much as I wished I could do some sort of mental health counseling – now was not the time or the place. Nor did I have any sort of training or skills for it.

I wish I did. I could probably handle my nightmares better if I did.

The gofer was waiting near the end of the tent. I eyed him. I was regretting picking him, of all people, to help show me around. Should've just grabbed the most competent-looking person around.

Then again. The fact that he was showing me around meant he wasn't in the line right now, and from what I'd seen so far, I wasn't impressed. For all I knew he'd get his shield-mate killed – or sent to this tent.

"Um, head healer said, um, he wasn't going anywhere for anyone, and if you want to speak to him, you'll need to go to him yourself." He stammered out.

I suppressed a flash of anger and irritation. I'd pulled similar stunts myself, and I couldn't complain when someone did it to me. Didn't stop me from getting annoyed.

The gofer led the way, and I found myself in a large, well-lit tent. There were a large number of injured soldiers, clustered in groups. A full line of well-armed soldiers were around, nervous, on edge. Clearly in some sort of "riot control" mode.

I blinked, processing.

Ah.

They didn't want soldiers resorting to physical violence. Fairly standard guards for a healer. Took me way longer than it should've for me to realize that. I was obviously tired, and it was starting to show.

I kept looking around. There was one healer, and a few helpers that were performing basic triage.

Except – the triage was different from what I was used to.

I was used to a three-tiered system. Green was for walking wounded, people with injuries, but eh, not only would they live, but they could still move under their own power. Orange was for the badly injured, those who needed medical attention, who couldn't really move under their own power. The tent I'd just cleared, I was realizing, was entirely full of Orange-tier injuries.

Last was Red. "Immediate attention or death" was the Red criteria, and whenever triage was being performed, no matter where in the world, Red was seen first. They got to skip the line.

Which was still happening here.

However, I saw a soldier get bustled in at full speed, screaming in agony, crying for his mother, and trying to hold his guts inside with one arm. He'd been sliced down his left side, everything from his left shoulder to left hip was gone, ribs exposed to the world, and he was trying to keep what was left of him inside his body. Even as I watched, something – a kidney – fell out, as everyone shifted slightly to get the man to the healer first.

The healer touched him, and instead of a body shimmering back, the wound was simply closed.

I narrowed my eyes. Dude was straight up dead with what he was missing. Like. Not immediately, but I could think of a dozen different ways he'd end up dead anyways.

Yet, everyone seemed to accept this as normal, and I begrudgingly had to admit that he was no longer a Red case, just a severe Orange.

Still – not terribly unusual.

Where it got weird was a Green was next. A relatively minor injury – a nasty gash to the shoulder – was entirely healed up. The soldier saluted, grabbed his gear, and hustled back out the door.

There was still a never-ending bombardment of people coming to the healer, and the dude looked exhausted. Like he hadn't gotten a good night's sleep in a month.

Right. Time for me to step in, and if nothing else, help this poor healer get some damn sleep.

I started to march over, only for the guards to move to block me.

I'd so had it with this shit.

I just gave them my best death-glare, and pointed to my badge. Gave it a bit of a [Shine] to boot.

The guards decided that being on the wrong end of a Sentinel's ire – even if she was short and female – wasn't the best career move, and gave me no problems. I made my way over to the healer.

"Healer." I said, arriving next to him.

"What." He said monosyllabically, exhaustion coating his every word. I made a snap call.

"Take a break. I'll take over. Sentinel's orders." I said, nodding to his guards.

"Need-" He said, and knowing he'd do exactly this, I cut him off.

"I'm a healer. I'm taking over. Take. A. Break." I said, as his guards – friends – grabbed him under the arms and started to move him to a little cot in a corner.

I recognized the cot. Same type I'd used in Perinthus. The "crash where I've arranged my healing station because it's just me against the unending tide" cot.

Poor dude. I sympathized.

I turned to see the crowd, half-grumbling that the Sentinel had basically just axed their healer. I checked my mana, still low after having stretched it thin clearing out the tent. I threw my backpack into a corner, out of the way.

Right. The only reward for good work – more work.

Chapter 14

Formorians XI

The first order of business was reassurance, to calm and placate the crowd. Yeah, I was a Sentinel, yeah I could say jump and everyone in the tent would ask me how high. Didn't mean that angering a bunch of already on the edge people was a smart move. I actually had no idea what I **[Identify]**'d as right now. My highest class was displayed – and I was tied, 256 to 256. I had no idea what the tiebreaker rules were. First class in the list? Prior highest class? Or did it "look" and see how much experience I had stocked up, and display that?

My heart skipped as I realized something *terrible,* an awful possibility occurring to me. If my **[Ranger-Mage]** class was displayed first, that might mean my eyes were showing Radiance, not Celestial. I liked my star-speckled eyes too much to lose them, even briefly!

Either way, I had the crowd of injured men looking at me, and pain caused people to do stupid things. It was easier to lash out at people, especially when it looked like I'd taken away their lifeline.

I thought as fast as I could while I started speaking to the crowd.

"I am Sentinel Dawn." I announced, cursing that my short stature meant that most people couldn't see me. Not everyone knew what all the Sentinels did, especially when my name wasn't something like 'healing'. "I am Sentinel based on my healing powers and abilities, and I'm here to provide assistance."

My mind was racing as I went over some basics. One healer. Huge crowd. Lots of injured people. A healer ran ragged. Shit triage.

"I already cleared out a full tent of wounded, and they are now back in action." I called out, which got a number of appreciative murmurs. It wouldn't surprise me if most people knew at least someone badly injured, a squad mate if not a friend, and hearing that I'd single-handedly cleared out a tent of wounded?

Immediate street cred. There was now another healer around, one with some serious juice if my Sentinel title was anything to go off of.

Thank goodness for the careful reputation and image management we all did. It was paying off in spades right now, as we needed to land and have people listen to us *now*.

"Who's next?" I asked, and the people who were keeping things straight and sane shuffled the next person forward.

I looked at him. A Green, by any metric. I wasn't going to start throwing stones here and now, and my mana hadn't recovered yet from clearing out the entire triage tent. I healed him, noticing only a small dip in my mana, and I refrained from slapping my forehead as the puzzle finally clicked.

I must be tired and exhausted. That was the only reason it took me this long to figure it out. Wish I had **[Greater Invigorate]** right now.

They were desperate, and their healer – I'm not even sure they had more than one – couldn't keep up with the casualties. Someone had made the call, either the healer or whoever was in command, to throw a quick-fix bandaid on whoever was about to die, and to fix up people who had minor injuries, so they could get back in the fight. Prioritizing getting as many people fighting-fit *right now* with as little mana as possible.

It made cold, sickening sense. Fortunately, my mana was regenerating a hair faster than the minor injuries coming in could drain it – and I had the healer busy sleeping and regenerating himself.

In addition – the call hadn't been made yet to abandon Reds, and only work on Greens. If the situation got worse, I could see that call being made.

I spent a little more time thinking about it. Why were there so many wounded soldiers in the tent, when Green and Red were getting priority?

Glanced at the snoring healer.

Ah. He probably had a skill similar to my **[Warmth of the Sun]**, and by cramming a bunch of people together, he was maximizing the impact of the skill.

How similar healing skills overlapped with each other wasn't an area I had much experience with. That would require time and research, and while I was all for the pursuit of knowledge, what would be required to pursue that knowledge I was firmly against.

If nothing else, it would mean that I'd need to be in close contact with a large number of injured people, and not heal them. That wasn't kosher, nor was that in line with my **[Oath]**.

I mean, yeah, I was in close contact with a bunch of people right now that I wasn't healing, but at the same time, I was trying to heal as many of them as Elainely possible.

The only time to even get some information was in situations like this one, and it wasn't like we could easily compare person to person. Healing was an art.

Either way, I was feeling somewhat pleased that my mana was regenerating at an acceptable rate, when another Red casualty came screaming in on a stretcher.

Literally screaming.

I took a quick diagnostic look as he was rushed to me, and touched him as soon as he arrived, entirely fixing his injuries. I didn't just downgrade him from Red to Orange, I downgraded him to "battle ready". Well. Except for all the broken and missing gear, but that wasn't my problem.

"Thank you so much, I thought I was a goner!" The soldier said.

I plastered a smile on my face.

"You're welcome. Next!" I called, channeling Autumn. I had no desire for small talk right now. Not when the little reserves of mana I'd gotten back had just been wiped out entirely.

Arguably I should make small talk. I should delay, get my mana up. I was just so *tired* though. On the small decisions, I was making the easy choice, not the right one, and being a brusque grump was what I wanted to do.

I was mentally thanking myself for deciding to see how the current system worked before making changes. No wonder it was "stabilize Red, fix Green." Dealing with the masses of Orange would drain more mana per soldier, resulting in fewer soldiers back on the front lines.

I glanced back at the healer, still dead to the world. I pitied him. He must've been stuck in this cycle for ages, with no relief. A quick nap here and there, interrupted by soldiers barging in with another Red that needed stabilization *right now,* only to get back in the healing groove until he passed out again, exhausted. Day after day, week after week, of non-stop back-to-back healing.

No wonder he was at level 256. The stress and environment were perfect for power leveling, but he obviously never had a time to grab a class up. Heck, with how his cheekbones were showing, it looked like he barely had time for a meal.

This sucked, but I needed the other healer alive. My demonstration earlier had me believing that one healer couldn't keep on top of things, with Orange casualties steadily piling up. However, I'd gone through like a whirlwind, and knocked out an entire tent full of Orange casualties. I think it was enough to tip the balance.

Even as I was looking through, new Orange soldiers were entering the tent, while some who'd been in here some time were being encouraged to leave, to make room for newcomers. Made sense. A deep cut needed basic clotting, but once a soldier was no longer at risk of bleeding out, for example, it was prudent of them to move onwards to one of the tents, and give a spot for someone else.

It had been a long night, followed by a long day, fighting for our lives. I'd seen earthquakes, divine fire, angels descending from the heavens. The end of Priest Demos, fighting through the endless Formorians, climbing a wall, orienting ourselves into a new place, a new camp, healing an entire tent of grievously wounded soldiers, and now this. Frontline triage.

Of course, none of the soldiers here knew what I'd just been through. They didn't know the bone-deep weariness that was setting in. They just saw a Sentinel, an invincible presence in their mind, show up, relieve their healer, and start healing. I couldn't flag now, couldn't call it quits after an hour or so and trade off with the still-resting healer.

By all accounts, I should wake the dude up so he could use his mana, then go back to sleep. At the same time, the healer was clearly in need of a long, long rest.

I weighed it in my mind as I continued healing. The needs of the many, versus the needs of one. Obviously, the healer had been picking the needs of the many every single time. How much was enough? How much sacrifice could a single person be asked to make? Where was the line?

I made the snap, arbitrary decision that the line was here and now. Also, I was ravenous. Starving, even.

"Heya." I said to one of the guard-soldiers, who had seamlessly transitioned from guarding the still-nameless healer, to guarding me as I did my work. "How do meals around here work?" I asked him.

He looked at me with an "oh shit" look, and saluted.

"Apologies, Sentinel." He said. "It didn't occur to me."

He gestured with his head to one of the other guards behind me, who I heard leaving the tent.

"Get a bunch! I've had a crazy night!" I turned and called to him.

Room service. Perfect.

Then again, the current healer probably already had a similar set up.

It was like having Kallisto around! Except I could almost literally walk in and hijack the entire arrangement.

I didn't entirely want to be chatty, but I did need info. Blargh. Sleep is what I needed.

"So." I said conversationally to the chatty guard, as I continued to deal with the steady trickle of soldiers coming in. In, touch, leave. In, touch, leave. "Why's there only one healer?" I asked him.

He saluted me, which I thought was a bit over the top, but then again. Chain of command. Better to be safe than sorry when one's a grunt, dealing with the highest levels.

"Begging your pardon Sentinel, but most of the healers were quartered in another portion of the wall to begin with. The Formorians breached the walls in multiple locations, and it was only a lucky fluke that Healer Myron was in our section to begin with. Something about hanging out with friends. We're able to communicate with some of the other sections, but we're not exactly able to properly meet up with them to exchange supplies – or healers." He said. "The huge suckers keep randomly charging through."

Welp. Ok then. That explained a bunch.

"Can one of you get me a runner, courier, messenger, whatever?" I asked. Gofer was still hanging around, but his stunning lack of competency had me wishing for an actual runner of some variety. For all I knew, I'd ask him to find Bulwark, and he'd end up inside the Formorian lair.

Another one of the guards vanished, off to do my bidding.

The next wounded to show up was Green. Green. Green. Red!

It was like a demented game of red light, green light, and I was thanking my lucky stars that I wasn't the one needing to have the conversation with injured legionnaires that, no, sadly, they didn't fit into the right healing category, and would have to wait.

The endless treadmill of casualties continued. Breakfast arrived, and I happily ate with one hand, while continuing to heal with the other blood-soaked hand. I winked at one soldier who looked particularly repulsed that I was cheerfully chowing on chicken while healing. Much better than Formorian!

The soldier who'd gone out came back, finding his way back into position. I eyed him as I continued healing, but said nothing. He'd report soon enough.

"Sentinel. The Legate says he has no messengers to spare." He said. "He also ordered you to come see him."

I twisted in my seat to look at him, arching an eyebrow. The soldier was staring ahead, ramrod straight, with a face that said to never play poker with him.

"He is familiar with the chain of command?" I asked him after a moment, turning back, continuing my heal-a-thon.

"With all due respect, Sentinel...." The soldier trailed off.

Ah. Quite possibly one of *those*. The polar opposite of the grizzled veteran I'd asked for help earlier.

Oh well. Wasn't much I could do about it. Barring him trying something *incredibly stupid* like trying to arrest me mid-healing, and I could ignore him.

And it wasn't like I was alone. Bulwark and Toxic were also running around. Plus, said idiot would need to convince a number of other soldiers to go along with his plans, and when it came to being between a rock and a hard place?

It wasn't like I was the one ordering soldiers into battle. I was the one saving their lives, saving their comrade's lives.

Being a healer was *awesome* at times. I felt nearly untouchable.

I stopped a manic grin from crossing my face as I kept up the healing line. Wouldn't be good for people to think I was grinning at their misfortune.

"Well, if he needs me, he knows where to find me." I said, with a nonchalant shrug. "It's not like I'd be anywhere else, or doing anything else."

My stomach rumbled in protest. Heaping breakfast had barely put a dent in it.

I decided to straight-up own it. It'd only be embarrassing and awkward if I made it embarrassing and awkward.

"Any chance anyone could rustle up some breakfast?" I asked with an entirely straight face. "I just showed up, and I have no idea where the mess is."

I got three strange looks and one strangled chuckle at that. I somehow managed to keep a poker face the entire time.

I acquired a second breakfast, midday snack, early lunch, regular lunch, an "oh look at the time, we should get lunch", a nice afternoon snack, early dinner, regular dinner, late dinner, and I was chowing down on a midnight snack when healer Myron woke up.

I nodded over to him, blinking sleep out of my eyes. I was talking with my mouth full, but who cared about etiquette in a warzone?

"I think both of us could use a large meal." I said loudly, to nobody in particular. Screw it. I was still ravenous from the marathon healing session.

The designated meal-fetcher rolled his eyes, and left the tent. I had no idea what the poor **[Quartermaster]** or **[Chef]** thought – "No, no, for real, I'm getting all these extra meals for a Sentinel. No seriously, we have one in our healing tent now, and she's hungry. Yes, she. Dawn. Healing. Yes, there's a healing Sentinel."

Communication in Remus was spotty at best. Good songs were the best chance of word getting around about us, and it wasn't like people had been singing about me for decades, long enough for me to be a household name. I had some notoriety in the capital, but outside of there? No idea.

Myron bolted upright, having gotten a solid 14-16ish hours of sleep. He hit his forehead with his hand, and scrambled up.

"Dolts! Imbeciles! Fools! Why did you let me sleep so much!?" He roared at the guards, shaking his finger at them. "People are dying! They need me! It is- "

That was my cue!

"It's time for you to chill." I said. "I got this. Or rather, now you got this while I take a nap. Wake me up in…" I trailed off, doing some quick mental calculations. "64 patients. Cheers!"

I waved off the spluttering indignant noises the dude made, and skipped over to the corner.

My gear included my blanket and pillow that I'd been using while in the grove, and I'd settled an internal debate ages ago.

Where should I sleep?

I wasn't a dumbass. I wasn't about to put myself in a position of vulnerability around a bunch of strange men. That was just inviting trouble, Sentinel or not.

No, the easiest, safest place to get a good hour sleep was… right here.

I set my cot up next to where Myron had his cot, closed my
eyes,   and   was   out   like   a   light.

Chapter 15

Formorians XII

Fortunately – or unfortunately, depending on how you looked at it – I was woken up a short time later, feeling somehow worse for the power nap.

I had the presence of mind, and I was in that weird place between too tired and not getting enough sleep, that I didn't wake up blasting.

The eternal curse, the quandary surrounding naps. Be tired, take a nap. When you wake up, you somehow feel worse than when you went to sleep.

Still, I'd gotten a solid chunk of sleep, no matter how short. I got up, saw the second midnight dinner I'd ordered but never managed to eat next to me, and inhaled it.

Almost literally.

I got up, stretching liberally to work out the kinks in my neck and my arm. Somehow, I'd pinched myself slightly on my armor as I slept, and it was obnoxious. I didn't get myself fully awake though, there'd be no point.

There was still the permanent multitude of Orange tier wounded waiting for healing, and with basically no warning, I started walking through them.

"You're healed. You're healed. Healed. Healed, now shoo. Healed, get out of here. Healed, go away. Healed, clear out. Healed. Healed, goodbye. Healed."

I blitzed my way through the tent, clearing nearly every soldier who was waiting for healing, except for those at the back of the line. I managed to empty out my entire mana bar, and with a yawn, stumbled my way back to my cot.

People were trying to talk at me, but I was still exhausted. I'd pulled off a solid 24-hour insane marathon, and I wanted my beauty sleep. I basically ignored everyone, except the food-retriever.

"You." I sleepily said, singling him out. "Is there some dire emergency I need to know about?"

"Well, no, but-"

"Right. Food please. Wake me up in fifty patients." I said, collapsing back down.

I had the option of telling people that I was a healing beacon, that touching me while I slept was enough to get them fully healed.

The natural consequence of that would be a bunch of strange men pawing at me while I slept. I'd run completely out of mana, then I'd have strange men persistently touching me while I slept, trying to slowly heal themselves up.

No.

I don't remember my head hitting the pillow, but the soldier was insistently shaking my shoulder.

I brushed it off with my hand, head in my pillow.

"I said 50 patients." I grumped, mostly into my pillow. No idea what it sounded like on the other end.

"Begging your pardon Sentinel – it has been 50 patients." A nervous voice came from the side.

I got up with a groan. It felt like a blink, and my head felt even *worse*. The tent was full again. Naturally. No rest for the wicked.

No rest for the good either.

Heal. Chow. Drink. Sleep.

Repeat.

After another six rounds, I got up, bleary-eyed, but realized I wouldn't be able to fall back asleep. I mentally cursed. I hate that. The stage of 'I got enough sleep to not go back to sleep', at the same time as 'sleep deprived enough to be suffering'.

Nothing I could do about that. Might as well get back to healing.

"Healer Myron." I said as politely as I could, shuffling up next to him after clearing the room again.

"Sentinel Dawn." He said with stiff formality. "Sorry for my outburst last time we spoke."

I shrugged.

"I've been there, more than once. I get it. No hard feelings."

I gave him a critical look. Still looked like he'd been through the wringer, but hell, everyone here did. I had to give him credit. Whatever ego he had, whatever quirks and demands he had, he'd single-handedly kept this unit alive.

Breakfast was acquired, and the marathon was on.

A guilty, fleeting thought was sent towards Toxic. I'd promised I'd see and relieve him on the frontlines, but I'd gotten no chance to.

But oh, the difference a single healer made. One of us could just barely keep on top of the critically injured patient, and patch up the lightest, easiest to cure of the wounded. Two of us?

I was ripping through patients like a tornado.

Thinking about it, that analogy might not be my best phrasing.

Either way, three intense days of trading off, with only one bad aftershock of Destruction's earthquake in the middle, and we were down to a magic number.

Zero. Patients were healed as they entered the tent, by Myron or myself.

I didn't have a way to calculate it directly, but it seemed like the rate of new patients over time was diminishing. I could totally believe it was Toxic doing enough work to slow things down, Bulwark making improvised defenses, or enough fresh soldiers on the line that generally upped the safety.

Or that massive walls weren't being dropped on their head anymore. Earthquakes and poor building codes were a deadly mix. The frontlines had been here long enough that a number of semi-permanent structures existed. Had existed.

Anyways. No matter how it was sliced, we were on top of things.

I wanted to stretch, but didn't. I was coated in filth and grime. I'd never truly gotten clean ever since I landed feet-first on a Formorian, and it'd only gotten worse from there. Dust got blown up, coated the freshly-sprayed on gore, then it dried into an unholy mess. Being elbow-deep in dried blood and desiccated gore would be an improvement, because that would imply it stopped at my elbows.

My efforts hadn't gone unrewarded though.

[*ding!* [Medicine] leveled up! 251 -> 256]
[*ding!* [Warmth of the Sun] leveled up! 217 -> 231]
[*ding!* [Oath of Elaine to Lyra] leveled up! 252 -> 256]
[*ding!* [Persistent Casting] leveled up! 182 -> 189]

I suspected I'd managed to get a solid amount of stockpiled experience to boot.

"Cheers Myron." I said, heading towards the door. I was leaving my backpack behind. Seemed like a safe enough spot. "I'll be back later to patch up anyone who slips through the cracks."

I heard some dark muttering behind me, and I cracked a self-satisfied grin. Perks of being a Sentinel, even in a warzone. I got to do what I wanted.

At the same time, only people with the right mentality ended up as a Sentinel. I somehow doubted I'd be in this position if my inclination towards seeing a large number of injured and wounded soldiers wasn't "stick around and help".

I headed towards the frontlines, and since there was a fairly direct route between the emergency triage and healing area, and the frontlines, well. It was pretty easy to intercept and heal everyone who needed it. Not like I could ignore them, not with my **[Oath]**.

Still, the attitude, and the feel, of the camp was significantly different from when we'd dropped in earlier. Little structures were popping up again, tents were whole, and the rows between tents were military neat again. People were cheerful, almost upbeat. Wildly different from the healing section, but then again, people missing limbs tended not to look on the bright side of life.

I frowned as I kept moving. The deadly meatgrinder was far. Much further than I expected.

Heck, for that matter, why was the healing section so far from the battle in the first place? We should've been on top of it, to more easily get people to us.

I did eventually find my way to the battle, Toxic's massive form unmistakable. I didn't bother calling out. I wasn't loud enough, and I was small enough that I'd never be seen. Didn't help that Sentinel armor was like Ranger armor, which closely mirrored Legion armor. I was just another short form in the press of soldiers.

I did have skills though, and there were some rickety, unstable platforms for mages to use.

"Hey!" I called up to an Earth mage on the platform closest to me. "I want that platform!" I yelled to him.

He barely glanced down at me, before shooing me with his hand.

"Bugger off! First come, first serve! You know the rules!"

You know what? I was actually fine with this style of rudeness. No sexism, no elitism, no whatever-ism – just plain, simple, "I was here first." I could totally respect that. I'd do the same thing.

Didn't mean I was going to let it slide.

I held up my Sentinel badge, and let it **[Shine]**. I coughed.

No reaction.

"Ahem."

Nothing.

"**Ahem.**" I said, quite a bit louder.

"Now listen here you – *holy shit Sentinel please take it!*"

I couldn't help but chuckle at the abrupt tone shift, and the sheer speed the mage moved at to vacate the spot. Didn't bother walking down, just jumped off and vanished, presumably to dodge my non-existent ire. Couldn't have moved faster if I'd lit him on fire.

Not that I'd extensively considered lighting people on fire and what their reactions would be when I had a Fire element. Noooooo.

Ok, fine, I had, it was a practical combat aspect to it. I blamed Maximus.

159

I climbed up on the mini-outpost, and took a good look at what was going on.

Let's see...

Four rows of footsoldiers, shoulder-to-shoulder, shield-to-shield, from one wall to the next. Spears flashing with deadly grace and precision, careful rotations preventing the Formorians from getting any deeper. Toxic, centering the line against the endless black tide.

I blinked.

Hang on – not an endless black tide. The Soldiers weren't nearly as densely packed as they usually were, nor were they as organized and mechanically dangerous as usual. Were the Formorians running out of soldiers? Were we *winning?*

Right, things seemed fine here, with Toxic mostly as moral support. Time to get his attention!

I fired a few [Nova]'s into the Formorians, having them skim close to Toxic, but not too close as to possibly hit him. Close enough that they'd be impossible to miss though.

I also toned down the power significantly. I wanted something bright and distracting, something to get Arthur's attention. Didn't care about doing damage, and I wanted to preserve my mana for healing.

WeeeeeeeeeeeeeeeeeeeeeeeeeeeBOOM!

It was a heck of a lot more relaxing when the pressure was off.

A half-dozen [Nova]'s later, and Toxic glanced back. [Shine] full blast, and I jumped up and down, waving my hands.

I literally couldn't be more obvious if I had a neon sign.

Actually, for that matter, I could kinda make a neon sign.

I used [Veil] to make a large arrow pointing downwards at me, continuing to jump up and down like a maniac.

Arthur waved back, and turned back to face the Formorians. He stepped forward, out of formation, and continued to fight as his spot in the shield-wall was filled by another soldier.

He then did what I could only describe as the "Sentinel Special", where he single-handedly went back and forth along the line, killing dozens upon dozens of the Soldiers single-handedly, in front of all the soldiers.

Which got them all sorts of riled up.

"Tox-ic! Tox-ic! Tox-ic!" The chant came up from the crowd, as Arthur did some grandstanding, killing Formorians in particularly large and showy motions.

I stifled a laugh. Sneaky snipey Arthur, expert in bows and poisons, fighting Formorians with a spear and grandstanding? He must be hating every minute of it, but probably saw the need to show off, to boost morale.

'There's nothing wrong here! Look at me! We're invincible!'

Or some message like that. I left that type of stuff to other Sentinels whenever possible.

Eventually Toxic finished his grandstanding, and made his way through the lines, the shield wall unsafely parting like the Red Sea to let him pass. I hopped down as he got near.

"Arthur! Good to see you! Sorry I didn't swing by earlier; the casualty rate was atrocious."

I got a grin from him, probably the first one he'd had in months.

"Elaine! Glad you made it. What's up?" He asked.

I shrugged, suddenly realizing I didn't have much to say, no real plan or anything.

"Not much. I promised I'd swing by, and I am. Is there a place where we can quickly catch up?" I asked him.

"Yeah, we got our place set up. Tried to find you to let you know, but had no luck."

I gave him a flat look.

"Did you try, oh, I dunno, *the infirmary!?*"

Arthur looked at me.

"Yeah, first place we sent a runner to. Said you weren't there, which confused us."

We walked in silence a moment, while I processed what he said. A light went off, and I snapped my fingers.

"The idiot Legate. He's been trying to get me to see him. Kept sending people to 'order' me around. The guards working the infirmary are fairly protective, and probably just brushed your dude off." I said, putting a likely solution to the puzzle together.

Arthur shrugged.

"Totally possible. That, or the dude was straight up incompetent."

I nodded in agreement. I'd gotten some recent, hands-on experience with incompetent gofers.

"Well! Here we are!" Arthur said, throwing open the tent flap of an extra-large tent. The interior was "as luxurious as possible considering the situation", which basically meant extra layers of blankets on the three cots in the space, little dividers splitting the room up, and a table with food on it, surrounded by four stools. Sorry Nature. The grove was nice and all, but the tent was just flat-out better in every aspect. Like privacy!

It was weird. Of all the things, the fact that they'd gotten a spot ready for me touched me the most. I gave Arthur a grimy hug.

"Lunch?" He asked, gesturing to the table. I needed no encouragement, as I sat down at the table, grabbing a plate and digging in.

"Lunch!" I agreed happily.

"What have you been up to?" Arthur asked, digging in himself.

"Oh, nothing surprising. Found the first aid tents. Healed until I was out of mana. Rinse, repeat for days. They had another healer, we basically traded off. Nothing super special." I said, downplaying it a bit. "How about you?"

Arthur groaned.

"Oh, it's been terrible. It's all morale management. First had to come in like one of Artemis's lightning strikes, shock and awe, the great big bad Sentinel come to save everyone. Nearly had to beat the entire line back on my own for the desired effect. Then I needed to play at being a [Bard], and work up the great big battle we had against the Queens. If anyone asks, they're all dead, and I killed one in single combat."

I laughed at that.

162

"They're all probably dead at this point. We only saw one alive before we left." I said, swallowing a bite. "Otherwise, we would've seen it by now. We weren't that far away from the walls that we wouldn't see it days later."

"Sure, but then where are the rest of the Sentinels?" Arthur asked, my train of thought clearly derailing his.

I shrugged.

"No idea. They might be holed up deep down for whatever reason. They might have returned to another section, and are working as a stabilizing force over there. They might be doing one of a dozen other things."

"Reasonable. Anyways. I've been working with Bulwark when I'm not projecting confidence. We move forward, he has his crew move in and put enough stone in the broken wall, then works his magic. Fixed wall! We've more than tripled the size we have secured, and joined up with a number of other groups."

I frowned at that.

"How did I not notice more healers, new healers, or a change in patients?" I demanded.

Arthur shrugged.

"I think it's because it's happened more on the other side. The gap here is too large to easily bridge, so Bulwark's been working more on the other end. I imagine the injured from this side stay the same, and healers take over more on the other side. You mentioned having a bunch of extra people that needed healing, and it took you, Dawn, *the* Sentinel for healing, three whole days to work through the backlog. Imagine other healers, but they only get relieved once we've expanded far enough that new patients aren't making it to them."

I groaned, and put my hands in my head.

"What's up?" Arthur asked me.

"I was planning on classing up now, and I was going to ask you to guard me while I did it." I said. "Now I feel like I need to go out and help the other healers instead."

"Were you planning on classing up both classes?"

"Just the healing one for now."

"Hmmm. Well. We've got a momentary lull right now, and your **[Oath]** doesn't demand you run out right this second to help, right?" Arthur asked me.

I reluctantly nodded.

"For just a few hours to a day of classing up, at the bare minimum, you get more mana regeneration. The pressure's low here, and you can figure out your new skills without getting everyone killed. Who knows when you'll next have a chance to class up? Plus, Bulwark swings by every night. He can help as well. Who knows when we'll end up too busy to help out."

I spent some time thinking about it. The dire emergency was over. I'd stabilized the situation. There wasn't an immediate demand for me. Heck, I was running around right now on a semi-social call. I was probably sitting on a mountain of experience points, which would help me out with my regeneration, which was my current bottleneck. I was in a position to get some solid practice in with my new skills. Also, Arthur was right. I had no idea when the next time I'd be in a somewhat safe position, with someone I trusted to look over me.

Still. I felt bad about it.

I closed my eyes, coming to a decision.

"Right. I'm going to class up. Just the healer class though. Let me grab my stuff from the healer's tent, fix up anyone I can to give them some breathing room, then I'll be right back to class up."

I jogged slowly down to the infirmary, intercepting and healing up soldiers whenever I could. Benefit of moving slowly. Made it, wished the healer luck, mentioned it might be awhile before I showed up again, grabbed my stuff, and I was off like a shot. Before the idiot Legate's messengers or whoever could try to waylay me.

I hurried back, making sure to heal anyone I encountered. I still felt bad about this, but I was back in the tent in no time. I chucked my stuff into the little divided out portion of the tent that was 'mine'.

"Ready?" I asked Arthur. He shot me a thumbs up.

"Ready!" He said.

I settled onto my cot, full gear still on, helmet and all. I closed my eyes, and let myself fall into the world of my soul.

[Name: Elaine]

[Race: Human]

[Age: 19]

[Mana: 70000/70000]

[Mana Regen: 62338 (+44800)]

Stats

[Free Stats: 2]

[Strength: 311]

[Dexterity: 200]

[Vitality: 1000]

[Speed: 1000]

[Mana: 7000]

[Mana Regeneration: 7000 (+4480)]

[Magic Power: 5839 (+74739.2)]

[Magic Control: 5839 (+74739.2)]

[Class 1: [Constellation of the Healer - Celestial: Lv 256]+]

[Celestial Affinity: 256]

[Warmth of the Sun: 231]

[Medicine: 256]

[Center of the Galaxy: 256]

[Phases of the Moon: 256]

[Moonlight: 256]

[Veil of the Aurora: 256]

[Vastness of the Stars: 147]

[Class 2: [Ranger-Mage - Radiance: Lv 256]+]

[Radiance Affinity: 256]

[Radiance Resistance: 256]

[Radiance Conjuration: 256]

[Shine: 111]

[Sun-Kissed: 256]

[Blaze: 256]

[Talaria: 256]

[Nova: 256]

[Class 3: Locked]

General Skills

[Identify: 151]

[Pristine Memories: 200]

[Pretty: 152]

[Bullet Time: 256]

[Oath of Elaine to Lyra: 256]

[Sentinel's Superiority: 256]

[Persistent Casting: 189]

[Learning: 256]

Chapter 16

Celestial Class up! I

I opened my eyes, seeing Librarian again.

"I'm back! With a second class in the tank, ready to upgrade whenever!" I said, pumping my fist.

"Yeah! You go!" Librarian said, holding her hand up for a high-five, which I happily hit.

She was in comfortable, simple clothes this time round, a lovely cyan tunic which was my favorite. Current favorite.

"No time to read right now." I said, pulling an exaggerated sad face. "But! Next class up I'll make sure I have all the time needed to read!"

Librarian tapped her nose.

"You know, if it was all about reading, you could just reset your class, and keep resetting it every time you hit level 32."

"Ooooh! That'd be so fun! I'd probably end up dead. No defenses, and if nothing else, I'd annoy people to the point where they'd want to murder me with too many week-long binge reading sessions." I said.

It suddenly hit me, and I felt a tear or two well up. I moved to hug Librarian, who hugged me back.

"This is the second to last time I'll ever see you." I said, stifling some tears. "Once I class up **[Ranger-Mage]**, that's it. I'm done forever. I'll miss you."

Librarian patted me on the back.

"Cheer up! Destruction hit 512, so did Night! We're part of a generation that's hitting 512, and you were with them as they took down the Queens! We've got a strong shot at hitting 512, and we'll see each other again!"

I smiled at her, gave her another hug.

I was her, and she was me. She'd miss me as well. Hopefully she was right, and we'd meet again.

Would she even still exist? Doomed to wander the library forever, alone? What did Librarian do when I wasn't here anyways?

Or were we the same person, one whole entity, when not here? Did she simply split off when I came?

I shook my head.

Enough metaphysical questioning. While I wasn't on a time crunch, I didn't have a ton of time to waste.

"Let's see them!" I said. "Although, I should probably skip all the non-healing sidegrades. No way am I taking them, and I'm not exactly in a position to take my sweet time on this."

"Reasonable!" Librarian responded.

I had a sudden brain wave, as Librarian led me up the stairs.

"Unless there's something, like, *really epic* I should know about?" I asked her inquisitively.

"Hmmmm." She said, pausing, one hand on her hip, the other finger tapping her lips. "There is a class related to killing Formorians. Green-tier. Also the usual 'you met Papilion and survived' class."

I waved her off.

"No interest. Also, 'survived'? By whose definition?!" I asked her.

She shrugged.

"The System's."

I honestly didn't know if I expected anything else.

We resumed our trek up the stairs, higher and higher until we got to the 4th floor. A number of books, all glistening like the night sky, sat on pedestals, surrounding a multi-colored door that led nowhere.

That would naturally lead somewhere. This wasn't the real world; it didn't have to make sense. More trippy magical world stuff.

I'd make a bet that whatever class I took would be through that door, but I was going to be thorough. Maybe that was some super special class or another, but it'd have some heinous drawback. I wanted to know what my other options were first.

Given the colors, everything was Celestial. I felt a bit locked in, but hey. That was the price of an advanced element.

Plus, I loved my Celestial healing. Wouldn't want anything else.

My first choice was [Oathbound Healer]. I idly flipped through it fast. The class somehow managed to strengthen my **[Oath]**, giving it a +7% per level instead of the current +5%, and also impacted mana regeneration, giving it a +2% to regeneration per level of **[Oath]**. It also made **[Oath]** a class skill, and while the class book didn't directly say it, I knew that **[Sentinel's Superiority]** would then kick in and apply, boosting it even further. My Magic Power and Control would end up at quite frankly ridiculous levels when I was healing.

The stat distribution was amazing to boot. +5 Free Stats, +50 Magic Power, +50 Magic Control, +80 Mana Regeneration, +80 Mana per level. That was nothing to sneeze at, offering almost four times as many stats per level than **[Constellation of the Healer]** had given me.

At the same time, it added to my **[Oath]**, making it more restrictive. I'd need to actively seek out people I knew were in trouble, and I'd need to always put them before myself. I'd also no longer have the option of making a choice – it would be made for me.

Nooooooo thank you. It would probably get me killed, with the type of situations I found myself in.

Still. It was kinda nice to see that my adherence to my **[Oath]** was recognized by the System. I thought back to Idiot Mage, the mud mage who'd been one of the adventurers trying to kidnap me, who I'd healed even after all he'd done to me. My actions being reflected back, granting me a class option? Probably.

Would the class be even stronger if I hadn't screwed up in Perinthus?

The next book had me stop short, and was tempting just from the title, and some minor infamy.

[Ranger-Healer]. I'd literally be the first person ever to have this class, and it shot to the top of the shortlist. It wasn't the flashiest class. It didn't have anything super special in it, but it was strong. Slightly improved healing, a solid stat distribution, and a focus on keeping me alive, so I could keep a squad alive.

It came with an interesting skill – **[Lifeline]**. I could designate up to seven other people to "connect" with, and while they were in a generous range – that expanded with the skill level! – I'd automatically heal them from my mana pool, at a significantly reduced distance penalty. It would almost be like they were on top of me.

This was one heck of a skill! I wouldn't need to do suicidally brave stuff like run towards a monsters eight times my level to save someone.

Then again, at this point, fighting something eight times my level was completely hopeless. Which made having a skill that meant I didn't need to be so close to the action more appealing. Naturally, anything eight times my level would be over level 1500, which, like, I dunno if all of the Sentinels combined could fight against.

Not exactly my current forte. Sure, I'd just done small squad tactics with the rest of the Sentinels, but that was more of a once in a lifetime occurrence, rather than my daily job.

I found some wood and quickly knocked it, after having mentally jinxed it. I didn't want a repeat of the Formorians.

Mass casualty events were more what I was dealing with these days, and my ability to run those wasn't improved at all.

Still. There was nothing *wrong* with the class.

[Magical Plague Doctor] was next up, a mimic of Caecilius's class, a reward for my work in Perinthus. Not only was the class amazing at handling mundane plagues, but it could also handle plagues of a magical nature. What was pants-shittingly terrifying though, was the implication that there were natural magical plagues. Ones that obeyed their rules, and their rules alone, and all my medical knowledge would be mostly irrelevant in the face of them.

A side-grade, mostly downgrade honestly, was presented to me in the form of [Constellation of the Midwife], which was interesting in some respects. It would hyper-focus me on babies and childbirth, but I'd be the single best person in the world on it. From conception, to gestation, to childbirth and infancy, a mother and child under my care wouldn't fear anything, from defects to death. Heck, I could even help a mother produce milk, and a baby latch and feed.

At the same time, it was a side grade *at best*. I'd lose a bunch of my current healing prowess. The stats per level were pretty bad. Less than half of what I currently got per level, about a tenth of what [Oathbound Healer] offered. I wouldn't be able to cure a plague – unless it was in a mother or baby. I wouldn't be able to restore limbs – unless it was in a baby.

It did let me fix things I normally wouldn't be able to fix though, which was interesting. Normally, if a child was born without an arm, my healing wouldn't be able to change that.

Remus was a shit place though, and children born without an arm were left to die. Still had me furious that the practice existed, although I understood the *why*. Wound me up to no end though. This class would give me the chance at stopping that. Locally, at least.

I felt indecision take me. That was a part of society I deeply hated. The System was offering me a way, a chance, to change that, single-handedly. Was turning my back on this class the same as turning my back on the innocent babies?

I kept the class in my shortlist. I'd need to do some serious philosophical thinking on the matter.

[Kekkaishi] was up next, and it was mostly a side-grade again. It took **[Veil of the Aurora]** and made it the primary focus of the class, instead of **[Phases of the Moon]**. I could make more barriers, move my barriers, strengthen them. I could make sharp barrier edges for cutting, animated barriers, and more!

I suspected that Sealing had an advanced Brilliance version of this class, never mind that it was the same tier as his class.

It was interesting to read about, but my healing would become self-only. I wasn't terribly interested in that. Fundamentally, I believed myself to be a healer first and

171

foremost. Losing the ability to heal others was a no-go in my book.

Sure, there was an argument to be made that if I prevented anyone from getting hurt, that was better than healing them. Except I couldn't be everywhere. Wasn't possible.

[Eternal Blazing Sun] was the next book on offer. My stunt with the pirates had unlocked it, and the short version was I lost the ability to heal others, in favor of healing myself. I'd be, for all intents and purposes, practically unkillable. I eyed the name of the class, and I eyed the contents.

[Undying Cockroach] would be a better class name for this. Decapitation, thrown into acid, cooked by flames, frozen solid, digested, and so many more ways to not die. The only things I'd fear were imprisonment, suffocation, or stakes through the heart. Or stakes through the brain. Really, staking was...

Actually, reading more – I'd get a skill at level 400 that would make it damn hard to stake me.

I could do crazy things, like take acid baths, enjoy super-poisoned cakes, and more!

Imprisonment was still a possibility, and I shuddered as I read about it. The class was *entirely* self-preservation, and it'd be all too easy for an Earth or Metal mage to encase my feet in stone, and throw me into the sea. I'd sink down to the bottom, drowning, suffocating constantly until I either starved or died of old age.

Horrifyingly, I could probably catch enough stuff at the bottom of the sea to make death by old age the only real possibility. That was a fairly messed-up chapter, where I'd let fish eat me as bait, only to catch them back and eat them alive.

There would be no [Center of the Galaxy] to stabilize my mind, to make me not suffer. It sounded like a terrible way to go, and worse – I couldn't heal others with the class.

Same issue as the [Constellation of the Midwife]. The Sentinels might be Unhappy that I wasn't a strong healer anymore, and there was a non-zero chance I'd get the boot. It'd be like if Sky no longer had his flying Gravity class. He didn't really belong in the Sentinels without it.

I didn't quite know how Sentinels were terminated, but I suspect I'd be taking an early retirement. "Sentinel Dawn has decided to spend more time with her family" or some other nonsense like that. Would probably ruin it for women for centuries to boot. "Oh, last time we tried it was a disaster. No can do."

I was well aware of the unfairness of being a trailblazer. I had to be more than perfect in some ways, and it was aggravating to be held to standards that others weren't.

[Professor from the Stars] offered me a chance to move more into the teaching role, a reward and amplification for all the hard work I'd done teaching the Rangers, mentoring Autumn, lecturing at Artemis's school, writing and spreading my *Medical Manuscript,* helping out other apprentices, and so many other things I'd done! It preserved most of my current healing abilities, but I would give up most of my utility for teaching skills.

Interesting. Not quite the direction I saw myself moving in, but I saw the appeal of the class, and how I'd earned it. The ability to use skills to make teaching easier was appealing, and I wouldn't be burning out quite so hard on the teaching.

The last class book was [Radiant Nebula of the Healer], and it opened my eyes to a possibility I just hadn't considered yet, and I honestly felt stupid for not having thought it through before.

[Constellation of the Healer], for all that I loved it, was focused on healing one person at a time. I'd gotten lucky with not one, but two area heals, but both of them were, quite frankly, weak. [Warmth of the Sun] simply boosted an individual's natural regeneration, while [Moonlight] was a bit stronger, the stacking distance penalty was painful.

[Radiant Nebula of the Healer] fixed both of those issues. Technically, I'd be losing out on some individual healing power, but my [Oath] was boosting my stats to a ridiculous degree. So much so that the small loss of individual healing power wouldn't be noticed.

In exchange, my healing aura got a significant boost, and I lost a portion of the penalty on **[Moonlight]**, while increasing the range.

The class looked and felt custom-tailored to the current situation. Bulk, mass healing. Interestingly, it looked like the area of effect healing was "natural" healing. In other words – better make sure bones aren't misaligned or anything.

At the same time, if someone did heal improperly, I could always swing back after and fix the individual problems. Another nice benefit was that since it boosted a person's natural regeneration, fighting off diseases and plagues would be guaranteed (ok, fine, *likely*) to result in natural immunity down the line.

I chewed my lip in thought.

Three classes that all gave me pause. Three different directions. Being a squad healer, being a midwife, or being a massive area of effect healer.

While I didn't quite know all the ins and outs of how this place worked, the multi-colored rainbow door in the middle of the room was basically screaming "the class you're going to take is here!". The other books were good for thinking, good for reflecting on. Heck, I hadn't thought that **[Warmth of the Sun]** could be that powerful, when focused on. I hadn't realized that a skill like **[Lifeline]** could exist, nor that it was possible to fix some physical birth defects. Checking the other classes, reading about them, was educational.

Chapter 17

Celestial Class up! II

I put the books back down, mentally marking their location.

"Hey, I can come back here if I don't like what's through the door, right?"

"Yup! It's just, ah, complicated through there." Librarian said.

Good to know I wasn't locking myself into anything.

Complicated, eh? I opened the door, and saw...

... the other side of the room. Anti-climatic in a way.

I stepped through it and ended up in a starfield, floating in space. Dozens, hundreds of stars surrounded me, connected to each other in clusters with thin little lines, forming a field of constellations around me. Some of the stars were brightly lit, most of them were dim. The constellations were of all different sizes, some big, some little. The stars themselves had as many sizes as there were stars, from tiny pinpricks that I could barely see, all the way to some "stars" that looked more like small moons.

I had a large glass cylindrical container, taller than I was, wider than I was, hovering in front of me. It was filled with a glowing, shimmering substance that looked like bottled starlight. The top was open, and tiny little motes of starlight, little twinkling points that looked like fireflies occasionally came off the top.

I looked down. I was floating in space, more stars and constellations below me. I tried to move around a bit, finding that I was able to reposition myself at will. The door was gone, but I had no doubt that it'd be easy to find my way back to the library if I needed to.

A book was on display in front of me, on a stand hooked up to the glass container. It was a strange, shifting multi-colored thing, like the doorway I'd come through.

[The Dawn Sentinel] Requirements: Sentinel. Title "Dawn". Healed over 100,000 people (non-unique). Killed a creature over level 750. Participated in killing a monster that threatened humanity that was over level 1000. Cured plagues. Handled volcanic fallouts. Dealt with tsunamis flooding cities. Trailblazer. Contributed to human's medical knowledge. You are Sentinel Dawn, and you bring light and hope to those who see you. A peerless healer, you have worked your way to the top, selflessly sacrificing yourself whenever needed for the betterment of others.

Although – there were no stats listed.

I looked down, and on the stand, there were nine marked indents. I experimentally pressed the first one once.

The book changed slightly, and the summary at the end now had a "+1 Strength per level" on it. It seemed like the starlight level in the container went down just a hair.

Pressing on each of the icons did exactly what I'd guessed – put one point into each of the stats for the class. The level of starlight dropped a tiny fraction of an amount.

Alright, time to check the most important thing – could I put the points back?

The answer was yes! I could put them back in! Success!

I played around with it a bit more, and did some experimenting. Turns out, I had a whopping 631 stat points *per level* that I could allocate. I was stunned. That was more than eight times the number of stat points per level that I had access to before. There had to be some catch.

I checked what would happen if I made all the starlight Free Stats. Turns out, I could only get 504 stat points out of it. Message received. There was a penalty for the flexibility that Free Stats offered. It was worth properly planning out what I needed and where, and minimizing the number of Free Stats that I used.

I looked around at the stars and constellations around me. There were dozens, if not hundreds, of constellations around me, but only a dozen or so constellations had stars that were brightly lit. Eight of those were lit up with a faint yellow glow, while the rest were a blazing white.

I looked at one constellation that was glowing yellow, and it was simply composed of four stars connected in a line, each one larger than the prior one. The last one was "small moon"-sized. It was almost the center of everything, tiny threads in the sky linking it to every single other constellation up there, like the heart.

Like the center of the starry sky.

It seemed fairly simple, and I focused on it, trying to study it.

The sky helpfully expanded around it, most other constellations vanishing to give me a better look at this one.

One star at the bottom was lit up, glowing yellow, and the rest were dark. All four stars were big though. Not the largest, but hefty. There was a faint image around the entire constellation, making it clear that the constellation was a scepter, the sovereign ruler.

Or I was just reading too much into it.

Looking at the one star that was lit up in the constellation, I could faintly see what skill it represented.

[Celestial Affinity].

It was the lowest star in the constellation. I focused on the second star, large in the sky, and with a force of will, made it light up!

[Celestial Authority] it said. It took me a moment for the penny to drop.

It was a skill tree! I could customize what skills I got!

I was pretty sure.

I glanced at my vat of starlight.

My now heavily drained vat of starlight. A solid chunk had gone into lighting the star up. I went back to the stats, and put all the starlight into mana regeneration. 375 stat points. So, lighting up the **[Celestial Authority]** star cost me 256 stat points.

Hang on, where was Librarian when I needed her? This seemed to be exactly the sort of question I had her for.

"I thought it'd be more fun if you figured it out yourself." She said, popping up. "Spirit of adventure and exploration and all that."

I grumbled to myself, a huge grin on my face. She knew me too well. I totally enjoyed figuring it out.

"What am I missing?" I asked her. "I think I've got it all set."

"Yeah. Except you can also strip points from the constellations you already have skills in." She said. "This is it. Last chance we're going to get to upgrade this class. We've gotta make it good. We should take a look around, and look at all the skills. Then pick eight skills we want, and put all our points into them. Buy all the perks we want. Put whatever starlight remains into our stat allocation."

"There's gotta be more to it than that." I said.

Librarian nodded.

"Yup! Depending on how much we put into a skill, passive skills might take up more mana – or more starlight. Also, if we put fewer points into a skill, we might get it later on. It might require that we get a higher level before it'll unlock, and it might be weaker as a result. Still, it's a trade-off worth thinking about and analyzing."

"Any idea why I'm basically getting to build my own class, instead of taking something the System's offered me?" I asked.

Librarian shrugged. "No idea. Got lucky, maybe the System thinks you're worthy, maybe you hit some accomplishment. Heck, maybe this is how monsters class up or something! Honestly, I have no idea."

The monster thing sounded dubious at best. I was going to make the most of this though. Once in a lifetime opportunity and all that.

I looked around and cursed.

"There are hundreds of constellations here. Literally. Hundreds." I said. I picked a random unlit constellation. A raven in flight, twinkling stars making everything from the beak to the wings, shining eyes and sharp claws.

Allergies. This set of constellations was everything to do with allergies. Detecting what someone was allergic to. That ranged from getting weak responses, to getting exact details, depending on how many points I put into it. Stopping a response. Helping the immune system at the start. Straight-up rewiring the immune system at the end, to remove the allergic reaction.

I looked around some more.

There was a constellation full of what I could only call "dead" stars. It wasn't that they were unlit, just – straight up dead. It was in the shape of a stuffed children's toy. With some imagination, it could be a teddy bear, a bunny rabbit, a fox, or if you squinted hard, a bird of some sort.

Seemed kinda interesting. I focused on it to see more, and groaned when I realized what skills the constellation was for.

Bedside manner. A social skill.

Apparently, my allergy to social skills went deeper than I thought, and even the representation of the skill in celestial form was indicated by dead stars. I couldn't think of a better way to indicate that it was a hard no on the skill.

I tried to light up the stars, for the sake of thoroughness and completeness. Nothing happened. They were dead, and the skills were clearly closed off to me.

"Any chance I can get this all in book form, to better organize what's going on?" I asked Librarian. I loved books, and we were in a library. Why was I stargazing? I could see someone stargazing to pick classes, but that would be for a completely different person. I was a book gal. Give me paper and ink to manage!

With a wave, Librarian gave me a cozy little book cubby, with the hundreds of books surrounding me. Eight of them glowed yellow – my current skills. More glowed white, but they were dwarfed by the hundreds that were mundane. A few blackened, charred books were my dead skills.

Way to rub it in System.

I grabbed the eight books representing my current skills.

[Celestial Affinity] was an automatic keep. The fact that every single class came with an affinity skill, and that it looked like it was the center of absolutely everything, with everything seemingly relying on it? I wasn't taking my chances on not

179

having it. Also, being the middle of everything had it as a contender to upgrade – although the prohibitive cost was making me hesitate.

[Warmth of the Sun] was a keep, and I was looking to upgrade it heavily. **[Radiant Nebula of the Healer]** had shown me just how powerful area of effect healing could be, and I wanted to open myself up to the possibility. I wanted to have a healing aura strong enough that simply being in the triage tent would get most injuries that could heal naturally, to heal naturally. It was represented as a grand tree, a trunk leading to many different branches. I had a few core stars lit up along the trunk, surrounded by a few smaller stars. Just one branch had a few stars lit up. I took a close look at them – it was the warmth aspect of the skill.

[Medicine] likewise was a keep. I was a hair leery on how much knowledge I could possibly lose without it. It combined with **[Pristine Memories]** was the entire basis of how efficient I was. Of all constellations it could be, it was represented by a lantern. Most of the frame was lit, and a dozen little stars were shining inside of it. A fairly complete skill, although a number of dim stars inside it suggested there were untapped depths to the skill.

With that being said, it was low on the list. If push came to shove, I might – maybe – under dire conditions – axe the skill. Sure, my ability to lecture at Artemis's school might also be axed, and I'd probably end up a much worse mentor to Autumn, but I might be able to remember enough off of my scrolls, and it would be possible to re-learn it all the hard way. Especially with **[Oath]** and **[Pristine Memories]** boosting me.

For now, my knee-jerk reaction was that I was going to keep it. I would do some thinking and meditating on the issue though.

[Center of the Galaxy] had saved my life a hundred times over, if not more, and I was eager to make it more powerful. No question there. The constellation was an elegant tiara, a band of smaller stars with larger stars forming the points.

[Phases of the Moon] I was confident was a top-tier, almost perfect healing skill. I planned on taking a look, and seeing how complete it was. Maybe I'd finish the skill off by being able to handle lead poisoning. Would be kinda cool.

I took a look at the constellation, and promptly ate crow.

[Phases] was represented by a massive constellation of an angel, with only one of her wings ignited, shining brightly. The angel held a harp, and completely disconnected from the wings representing [Phases], a portion of the harp was lit up, looking like a crescent moon. I took a look at that portion, and saw it was its own skill.

[Moonlight]. My best guess was the disconnect between the two portions of the constellation is why it was in two skills, and if I could somehow connect the two, the skills would merge.

Speaking of [Moonlight].

[Moonlight] was a skill I was looking to upgrade. Or maybe sidegrade? [Lifeline] from [Ranger-Healer] had looked sweet, and if [Warmth of the Sun] was upgraded into an aura as strong as I wanted it to be, my ranged healing would only come into effect when I was directly in a fight, probably with another person or two.

Putting it another way – I didn't think I'd need to hit dozens and dozens of people at once. I was looking to change this skill up. Depended how everything else shook out.

[Veil of the Aurora] was also on the table for serious upgrades, although I suspected I was starting to get greedy. I wanted to be a super single target healer + area of effect healer + utility + amazing barriers. I had a ton of starlight, but I probably didn't have *that* much. The constellation was almost predictably a shield, with a single large star ignited, and like three other smaller stars burning with light.

Dozens, if not hundreds, of other stars were in the constellation, and I took a quick look over them. My bet was if I'd taken the [Kekkaishi] class that most of this constellation would ignite.

Also, if I blew all my starlight on super cool skills, I might not have the stats to back them. It was a careful balance I had to walk. If I turned all my starlight into stat points, my skills would suffer. If I turned them all into powerful skills, I wouldn't have the stats to back them.

And the last skill was why I had so much trouble. If only I liked **[Vastness of the Stars]**, I'd just keep all my current skills, and to heck with the other stuff. Sadly, I disliked it, and it had to go. Which meant I needed to browse all these other skills for a good one to replace it.

Time to blatantly cheat!

"Hey Librarian! Can you get rid of a bunch of these that I won't like or won't use?" I cheerfully asked her.

Librarian had grabbed her own cozy chair in the reading cubby, and was engrossed in a book of her own. Typical me behavior. I was slightly jealous that I wasn't the one doing that, but as it was, I was going to be spending a huge amount of time here, browsing through books.

She held up her hand, one finger up.

Tick. Tock.

I looked around at the night sky, deciding to take a peek at a few more skills that I'd never have access to, whose stars were dead.

A rainbow, therapeutic skills to help me talk people through trauma. Apparently, that was too social for me, but I noticed with interest that magically healing the trauma wasn't part of the skill. Perhaps it was in another skill, and I would have access to that?

A gavel, which somehow translated to public health management. No thank you. A minion with skills like that would be nice though.

She got to the end of her chapter, carefully put in a bookmark, then looked up as she snapped the book closed.

"Right. Let me get on that." She said, and a whirlwind of activity occurred. A small pile of books ended up next to me, while the vast majority stayed on the shelves. Two of the books next to me were even glowing white!

I paused, inspiration suddenly striking.

"Heya Librarian. Is there a skill to bring someone back from the dead? Revival, or something?" I asked her, crossing my fingers.

"Sorry. That's impossible for the System." Librarian said. "Namely, the part where it all goes wrong is it'd require manipulating the soul, and there's no class or skill that can do that. Gods and Goddesses can do some soul manipulation – like with us, and with Priest Demos – but even they can't fish a soul back from Samsara."

"So, short version, no revival skill?" I asked.

"No revival skills." Librarian confirmed.

I was disappointed, but what could I do? I couldn't force a skill to appear that wasn't there. It was satisfying to know that it wasn't because I couldn't get the skill, that it wasn't part of the class, but instead that it was flat-out impossible for anyone. Even goddesses.

It was always a bit strange when Librarian busted out knowledge like that though. I clearly didn't know it, but Librarian suddenly knew it, in spite of being me. The System making things a bit easier.

Right! Enough with the impossible, back to the possible!

I decided to tackle the two glowing skills next to me first. What skills did Librarian think I would like, that I'd already been offered and declined?

The first one was the constellation that [Eyes of the Milky Way] had come from. Seeing under the stars. Although there were only a few little points in the skill. It could get much more powerful. There were hidden depths to the skill, potential for evolution, that I hadn't considered.

Of course they were all eye skills, and *of course* the constellation was a beautifully detailed pair of eyes.

I wished I had a mirror, and extensive time to compare. I wondered if the pattern of stars I was seeing in the eye was the same as my eyes.

Shortlist.

The next one was a diagnostic skill, an elegant cloak speckled with stars. I had to get me a cloak like that. I looked at it briefly, and remembered getting offered the Astrology-like skill. Well, how the stars were lit up in the constellation explained it. Great on the diagnostic part. Terrible on the communicating the information to me part. I'd suspect it was more of the allergy to social skills if the stars weren't alive. Unlit, but alive.

Shortlist. Didn't hate the idea, but I still felt I could just throw mana at the problem, especially with [Medicine]. Like, it would replace [Medicine] in all likelihood, but that would mean rejuggling things, and it might not even be as strong.

Well. Probably different. I don't think I was giving the skill enough credit, especially when some of the stars hinted at offering the ability to detect magical problems.

I'd need to cross-reference [Medicine], and see if there was a way to evolve it to check for magical problems. I never got a good read on Hesoid's disease, and maybe I could strengthen [Medicine] to get a read on problems like that in the future.

Ugh. This was going to give me a headache from how complex it was. Still. It was literally the rest of my life. I wasn't going to rush it. Although, I was slightly regretting classing up *now,* when I was a hair crunched for time. It was going to add a bit of extra stress to the whole process.

A book that was holding the [Lifeline] skill was next up. I took a close look at the [Lifeline] skill. Stars for more people. Stars for longer range. Stars to more efficiently heal over a distance. Stars to reduce the cooldown of "hooking up" someone to the skill. Stars for communication, from me to them. Stars for talking back.

The skill was an entire section of the angel constellation that held [Phases of the Moon] along with [Moonlight], and I shortlisted it as well.

Everything being on the shortlist was kinda meh, but what else was I to do? The skills were all solid, and making cuts was difficult.

Seven books relating to children, childbirth, babies, mothers, and defects. Specialty skills. Skills to remove foreign bodies. Like swallowed pebbles, peas shoved up noses, or harpoons in chests.

Constellations. So many constellations everywhere.

A quill and inkpot, for teaching skills that I would've gotten if I'd taken the [Professor] class.

A lion, for buff skills to make people stronger, faster, tougher. I earmarked that one. If nothing else, being able to turn off someone's mana regeneration would make me significantly more comfortable trying to take them prisoner, which would allow me to be less lethal in fights.

I still had some of that shiny naïvety, some deeply seated belief to not kill people *when possible*. Sadly, most of the time it straight up wasn't possible, and it hurt on the inside when I had to kill to defend myself. I wasn't going to stop, but it wasn't like I enjoyed it.

A tidy stone well, a skill that increased my mana pool. I hesitated, before deciding that this wouldn't make the shortlist.

A bonfire, a skill that removed curses and debuffs. I'd been hit by a few curses here and there, but I'd always had the right gemstone on me to purge it and deal with whoever was trying that nonsense. I decided against shortlisting the skill, because I had other ways of handling the problem.

The halo of the angel, making me realize just how absurdly large the [Phases of the Moon] skill was. The halo portion was good for a healing buff that I could put on people. I checked it carefully, getting more and more interested the more I read.

For the price of a chunk of mana, I could strongly improve someone's natural healing. It would take up most of their mana regeneration, but while they were near me, they'd heal like my [Phases of the Moon] was on them. When they got further away, the magical healing would wane, and their own body's natural healing would be kicked into overdrive, naturally fixing and healing them.

It was a single-target, buff version of what I wanted my [Warmth of the Sun] to turn into at a distance, and a single-target, moderate distance ranged heal for [Phases]. Bonus – it let me disable someone's mana regeneration!

The more I looked, the more stars I saw, the more hidden depth to the skill I was starting to realize. I forced myself to close the book with a snap, marking it and putting it on the top of the shortlist. The full in-depth analysis would occur after I finished getting my entire shortlist together.

A banner, a skill that would let me use my healing skills offensively. I recoiled at it, and shot a nasty look at Librarian as I pitched it.

Healing was my *art,* my calling, my reason for being. I wasn't going to twist and pervert it into something that killed. That was all manner of *wrong.*

A shining gemstone, and I saw my old friend **[Invigorate]** in the constellation, along with **[Greater Invigorate]**. Ooooh, I wanted my coffee-in-a-skill back, the ability to be instantly up and refreshed and energized returned to me.

Bonus – some of the stars were even partially lit! Onto the shortlist – now a longlist – it went!

Chapter 18

Celestial Class up! III

Of course, once I saw that perk in a skill, I wanted to go back and cross-reference my **[Phases of the Moon]**. I'd try to find the corresponding stars inside the constellation. Not every skill I was offered, not every new thing, was a subset of the constellation. Some were their own, but I took the chance to look around and see what I was missing in the constellation, check if it was reasonably close enough to ignite and make mine, without needing to make a long string of stars to the skill. After all, igniting random stars in the middle of the constellation, that weren't connected to anything else, was a good way to get it offered as a new skill, not as an expansion of a skill.

At least, that was my understanding of it.

Magical herbs. Petrification. 'Strange metal sickness', whatever that was. Something about being close to some types of metals could make you sick? It was considered a *mundane* ailment? How did I not know anything about this? It was *weird*. I thought I had knowledge of everything mundane. Yet, looking at this skill, it was clear that, yes, I did have some hole in my knowledge, something so large that I didn't even know I had a hole. Nor did it neatly connect to anything else, no obvious trails that lead to a gap.

I knelt and groaned, holding my head. It *hurt*. Pain. Nothing external, just pure internal agonizing and headaches.

I put a few points, grabbing the skill, and moved on, determined to ignore it.

Lead poisoning was a different ailment, and a bit more obvious, and I was going to be happy grabbing that skill. At last! Mercury poisoning. Gold and silver poisoning – each one got a tiny little star. Stars to boost efficiency. Stars to connect to the **[Moonlight]** portion of the constellation, which would merge and fuse the two skills. That was a long, long, long chain of stars. I could barely make it if I spent way too much starlight on it. Stars to make my healing automatic, which gave me a moment's pause.

"Hang on." I said, pointing to the 'automatic' star. "This isn't factoring in my other skills at all, is it?" I asked Librarian.

"Nope!" She cheerfully informed me. "Except yes. Some skills will be based off of other skills you have. Makes them easier to get. Other skills don't. It's not quite arbitrary, but the rules around it are complex enough that they might as well be. It'll cost a heck of a lot more to remove it from your other skill entirely, and move it over here. Pay a premium to cram it all into one. Or rather, gotta pay either way – with using more skill slots, or using more starlight."

Which interestingly implied that stars cost more starlight the more that were lit up. I decided to quickly check on it, picking two random stars inside **[Phases]**.

Actually – hang on. Let's be smarter about this. I took the starlight out of the callous star, and allocated all of my points into mana regeneration. I then carefully took starlight out of mana regeneration until I had enough starlight to ignite the star, giving me a careful measurement of exactly how much it took to make it happen. Giving me units to work with.

Ignited the first one. It took me 10 stat points to make it happen. Removed the starlight. Ignited the second one. 12 stat points. Ignited the first one again.

This time, it cost me 11 stat points to ignite it, instead of 10. Message received. The bigger and better the skill, the more it would take to continue to expand it. Made sense. Meant I couldn't just make one uber skill and call it a day.

Well, ok then. Most of what I couldn't handle was in what seemed to be the "magical ailments" section of the constellation, and I quickly wrapped up grabbing the few tiny stars in the "mundane" section.

I was delighted that parasites, viruses, bacteria, prions, fungi, cancer, blood loss and all other manner of mundane problems were lit up, along with restoring flesh and carving out dead material. The 'Restore muscles properly' perk was also lit, which explained why Brawling didn't need to start working out again once I'd restored his legs. It was satisfying to know that my skill was pretty damn good.

It just could be *better.*

Just not everything. Fixing autoimmune diseases was still beyond my reach, although I'd somehow never encountered one so far. Lucky me!

Unlucky them. I probably hadn't encountered one, because nobody had survived long enough for me to get to them.

I made an impulsive move, and lit up a "restore callous" star. It was tiny, and would barely cost me anything.

There was a skill book for magical ailments to compliment the **[Phases of the Moon]**. Skills for everything under the stars, skills for everything the moon had seen. It was exhausting, seeing every book, every skill, then cross-checking it against what I had. Weirdly, this constellation wasn't part of the **[Phases]** constellation, but there was near-perfect overlap. Anything in this book had a corresponding star in **[Phases]**, while being a completely different skill.

Weird. If I was going the route of wanting to heal magical ailments, if I wanted these perks in the skill, I'd just upgrade **[Phases]** instead, grab a cluster inside the skill as its own stand-alone skill, and hope it merged with the main healing down the line. Still. It made it a bit easier to see how it all worked together, seeing what the System considered the "magical ailment healing" skills all bundled together.

To call this complicated would be an understatement. I would love to take a thousand notes on everything in the library and bring it back and supplement my *Medical Manuscripts* with the information. Sadly, **[Pristine Memories]** didn't work here, and all my mental energy was being devoted to not screwing up this once in a lifetime chance. I was pretty happy that decision paralysis hadn't struck, and that I was chugging along, putting in the needed legwork to make this all work out properly.

Although, I didn't have **[Pristine Memories]** back when I was on earth, yet it was clarifying those memories. I'd need to check, but I wasn't hopeful. The System didn't seem to be the type to helpfully give me free information from classing up.

Librarian was a lifesaver, and she'd gotten me a blank book for me to take notes in. There were somehow sticky notes as well, and I was getting deeply buried in piles and piles of paperwork, as I carefully checked and cross-checked every potential skill, and how it could possibly slot in against the rest of the skills. If what I wanted from skill A was doable from skill B, or perhaps expanding skill C could make it work?

It was a dizzying labyrinth of skills and combinations, and I had barely even touched on more stand-alone skills like [Warmth of the Sun], to see what and how I wanted to upgrade that skill!

Thinking about that – I should go through the skill and check what I wanted from it. Increased size, increased healing speed. Oooh! There was a perk to make some of the resources come from my mana instead of the patient! Basically, not starving people as I healed them.

A restaurant might pay me good money to not take that perk though. Ah well, their loss. I didn't see myself getting into the restaurant business anytime soon.

Also, the warmth aspect was a few stars in and of itself. I didn't think I needed that, not when I had Radiance, and I was probably going to yoink that part of the skill. Technically a downgrade, but it'd give me more starlight to allocate elsewhere. Would also make the rest of the tree a hair cheaper to upgrade.

I didn't put starlight into them yet – I was still in the note-taking part. Back to the books!

The next constellation – a mask – caught my eye, a few of the stars not quite lit up – but neither were they dim.

"What's going on here?" I asked Librarian. She took a peek over my shoulder.

"Cosmetic surgery." She said. "Reshaping faces, bodies, etc. The half-on stars are where you're getting some support from [Pretty]. My guess? It's how and why general skills influence class skills. Bet that [Ranger-Mage] also has some impacts here and there, meaning it's a heck of a lot cheaper to turn those stars on."

I thought about it for a moment. Not out of any consideration for taking the skill, but for the implications and what they meant.

"If I take a bunch of stars based off of that, would **[Pretty]** merge into it?" I asked.

Librarian thought about it for a minute or two.

"Probably." She said cautiously. "No promises."

It was good to know, and I put the book off to the side. I liked being **[Pretty]**, but I had no desire to get into the cosmetic flesh reshaping business.

Books upon books, stars upon stars. There wasn't an obvious "save" or "undo" method, just lots of notes, so I was a hair reluctant to pull all the starlight out of all the other skills, and get cracking. I wanted a full picture of everything before I started working on stuff.

Of course, all that got thrown out the window when I stumbled upon a particular book, deep in the stack of "potential skills".

It started off innocently enough, an ouroboros for the constellation. Fancy, but there wasn't any real rhyme or reason relating the constellation to the skill. I started to read the skill, feeling some strain from the mountain of books and notes I'd already taken. Mental fatigue was still a thing here.

I read the skill once, not quite properly processing what it said, and what the perks did. I must've misread it.

I stood up and stretched, chatting with Librarian.

"I've been at this too long. Misreading stuff now." I said. "Gotta focus more."

She arched an eyebrow at me.

"Be careful. This is it." She gently rebuked me. I held my hands up.

"I know, I know. That's why I'm taking this short break. Right! Back to it!" I said, sitting back down. Ready to read the skill properly, see what it did.

I read the skill again. It did… wait.

I hadn't misread it.

It did *what!?*

And the other perks also did... holy shit.

When they were combined together, that would mean...

My heart started to speed up, my throat tightened up in nervous anticipation as the pieces of the puzzle clicked together

"This is it." I forced the words out of my throat. "This is the skill."

I didn't bother with the math, with carefully checking how much each star cost. I just moved all my starlight from stats, back to the container.

I tried to light all the stars up, and only got through seven of them before running out of starlight. I needed all of them lit up. I *needed* this skill.

I made a strangled noise, and grabbed the unused skills, ripping the starlight out of them and dumping them back into the skill. Nine out of twelve.

"Whoa, whoa, chill!" Librarian said, as I started to reach for my current skills, intent on draining those. "First off, breathe. Think. It's not going anywhere. It's not going away. Second, you don't need the entire skill lit up. Third, what about everything else? What about the rest of our plans, what about stats? We need those."

What I should do is put the book down and go for a short walk to clear my mind. Instead, I just sat there, not even blinking, not wanting to risk the skill somehow vanishing or being misplaced if I looked away for even a moment.

Librarian sat next to me on the fuzzy chair. She put her hands over mine.

"Ok, look, I get it. Yeah, super exciting. The best skill ever. Calm down. Think."

My mind was whirring, unable to calm down. Unable to think. Stuck in an endless loop.

I had to have this I had to have this I had to have this I had to-

Librarian cuffed me over the head, as hard as she could. I almost saw stars from the blow.

"Ow! Fuck! What was that for!?" I yelled at her.

"Resetting you." She said, one hand on her hip, other hand pointing an accusing finger at me. "It's. Not. Going. Anywhere. Now focus. What do we need?" She asked.

I just gave her a Look and pointed to the skill. She rolled her eyes at me.

"What *else* do we need? What do we want upgraded from our other skills?"

Fortunately, I'd been taking copious notes. Everything I'd been thinking of had been knocked right out of my head. I pored over the notes, pointing to a few dozen different stars I'd been wanting to ignite.

"Ok, good. What are we willing to sacrifice?"

Well, that had been all the other skills, but I already yoinked their starlight. I looked through stuff some more.

"The privacy aspects from [Veil]. While shielding Night was nice, I doubt we need to keep it just for that.Also the colors and light from it." I reluctantly admitted. "Heat from [Warmth of the Sun]. A bunch of the anti-emotion stuff from [Center of the Galaxy]. I'm on the fence with [Medicine] as well, we've got a bunch of great options, and I think we can manage with [Pristine Memories] and [Oath]'s knowledge boost."

"Alright, good. Now, we don't need this skill to be at full power right now. We can lower the amount of starlight in it, which means it'll unlock when we're higher level. This will give us enough starlight to get most of what we want, although they might also be dim, and unlock when we're higher level. Plus." Librarian waggled her finger at me. "We can't use everything on skills! We need to have stats at the end of this!"

Oh shoot, she was right. I'd almost forgotten that.

Librarian looked over the book containing the skill, and pointed to four stars.

"We really only need those four – oh, and grab that fifth one as well. Let's put as little starlight in it as possible, and it'll unlock later on."

I frowned at that.

"But I want it now." I half-whined at her.

"Yeah, but you don't need it now, do you?" She said. "You need it later on. It's basically useless today, right?"

"Right..." I reluctantly admitted. Librarian was right about that. I didn't need it now; I didn't need it today. Heck, I had no use for it this year!

"Ok, good. Now, we've got a choice. We can power up our skills now, but get fewer stats per level. However, we'll probably level a bit faster. Or, we can put less starlight into the skills, and get more points per level, but it means we delay some of our skills upgrading."

"We're sitting on a pile of experience, right?" I asked, trying to confirm. I'd been at 256 for a few months, but I hadn't done anything that would've been worth a bunch of levels. Just standard city healing. However, participating with the attack on the Formorian Queens, being part of the party that killed two of them, along with hundreds of Royal Guards – mostly killed in the earthquake – followed by the marathon healing here had to be worth quite a lot of experience. Heck, Destruction had gotten almost a hundred levels, jumping him from the 400s to the 500s, which was pure insanity.

"Should be!" Librarian cheerfully agreed, and I cursed the only partially-knowing aspect.

"Should probably rearrange it back to the starfield." I said. The books had been fantastic to see and cross-reference stuff, but it's not like my notes would vanish. There was something about seeing the sky in the full visual that just appealed to me for this last step. "Let's only have the eight skills I'll be using. We've yoinked the starlight from all the other skills, right?" I asked Librarian.

She gestured, like grabbing a moonbeam out of the air.

"Yup! Now we do!"

I eyed up the now very full container of starlight. It was moderately tempting to keep it as pure stats.

Then again, better skills? Even more tempting. A delicate balancing act that I'd need to walk. I'd gotten a treat with being able to essentially build my own class, but the power came at the price of complexity. The eternal trade-off.

194

I decided to call each stat point worth of starlight a single unit.

I decided to keep [**Moonlight**], even though something like [**Lifeline**] might be better. Turns out that [**Moonlight**] was pretty cheap – hence it not being that strong – and I invested some starlight to make it a hair less restrictive. Not a ton, it was still going to be a conditional skill, but for only 12 starlight across four stars I was upgrading the skill by leaps and bounds.

There were a half-dozen stars in [**Moonlight**] which would help with "multi-tasking" so to speak, where I'd be able to focus on and improve everyone's healing. Like, right now when I did massive area of effect heals, I just focused on "heal", which worked but was a *terrible* image, and hence terrible efficiency. With the little cluster of stars, I'd be able to picture everyone's injuries at the same time, and think about and focus and heal each one in a custom manner, dramatically improving my efficiency.

It sounded neat, and I took the stars. Those were a bit more expensive, costing me 40 starlight.

[**Celestial Affinity**] I left it as-is. It was expensive to upgrade, and while it probably got stronger, I wasn't chomping at the bit to change it. It would help if I knew what the upgraded version did, and I might regret it, but at the current cost? I was going to pass.

[**Warmth of the Sun**] got a lot of love. Stars to boost the range. Perks to boost the speed, by a significant factor. The ability to go through mundane walls. Being able to go through magical walls and barriers was crazy expensive, and I didn't really see the need for it. An entire branch towards using my regeneration to improve the power and quality. It cost me a total of 82 points of starlight, and I was looking forward to seeing what it could do after these upgrades.

[**Medicine**] I decided to axe after way too much time spent thinking about it. I got back over a hundred points of starlight from it, and I invested them into the healing buff skill, the halo portion of the gigantic angelic constellation. There were just so many hidden depths and complexities to the skill, I was eager and excited to try them out.

I wasn't looking forward to leveling the skill up from level 1 though. That was going to be painful. Maybe sticking it on some of the Sentinels before they sparred with each other would be a good way to help it level. Plus, I could be a bit lazier when they were sparring.

[Center of the Galaxy] had a bunch of things stripped from it, but I increased the pain resistance and the calm and collected aspect when in a fight. That was the part that had saved me a hundred times over. All in all, it was starlight neutral, as I reallocated starlight around the perks.

I had enough introspection to realize that I'd grown up and matured while leaning on the crutch that was [Center of the Galaxy]. I hadn't needed to handle the fallout from intense negative emotions for years, and I'd need to work on my self-control. It was going to suck, but I *couldn't* be seen as a whiny brat who threw tantrums and complained about small stuff.

The mere fact that I was aware of it would probably help.

The angel constellation that [Phases] was in now had three separate portions lit up, that would all work with each other. I'd tackled the [Moonlight] portion, I'd handled the halo that dealt with the buff. Now it was time to work on and upgrade the healing portion directly. The stars I was eyeing up to full light up *right now* mainly dealt with things being stabbed in me. A few to deal with suffocation.

[Phases] was my keystone skill in my primary class. The skill, more than anything, defined who and what I was, and a total of 98 points of starlight illuminated the skill. Improvements. Improvements all around. Magical ailments, the stabbing thing, and a dozen more items that looked like they might be useful one day in the future. Like heavy metal poisoning. A dozen points towards handling what I thought Arthur's poison was, based on our brief conversations. Most of them would be coming down the line in the future, but I felt I could wait.

Heck, I was sitting on a massive pile of experience. "Waiting" could easily just be "until I woke up and everything leveled up like crazy." With that being said, I focused on getting more stars partially lit, rather than making sure a few stars were lit *right now.*

"Removing objects that were stabbing you" was an expensive set of stars though, and I didn't have that much spare starlight. I decided not to light *all* of the 'stabbing stars' up. I focused my starlight on items in my upper torso and my head. In theory, I could still get staked through the gut or something, and I'd just have to deal with it. Honestly, I was fine with that.

My logic was that being staked through the gut wasn't a swift death, so I'd have time to handle it. Being staked through the heart, vampire-style, would kill me in seconds. I wanted my skill to be able to handle it. Mundane stabbing wasn't a concern, so I didn't see the need to even partially buy the skill off. Why waste my precious starlight on something like that, when they could be stats instead?

It was with great sadness that I barely upgraded anything in **[Veil of the Aurora]**, instead mostly hitting it with nerfs. Minor, technical nerfs, but nerfs nonetheless. Less privacy. No more light, or pretty colors. Actually, that second part was arguably a buff, and a pretty strong buff to boot. I could now try to hide with the **[Veil]**, instead of lighting a beacon that screamed "Dawn is RIGHT HERE!". Being a solo operative now, stealth was more important than signaling to teammates. Also, I could see what was going on the other side of my shield. Previously, I had no idea what was happening on the other side of my shield. Had the attack landed? Missed? Or was Artemis preparing another nasty trap?

I wouldn't have that concern anymore, so it was a win in my book.

The System considered it a nerf, but when I looked at it that way, I felt like Prometheus stealing fire. Not only had I improved the skill for my purposes, but I also got starlight out of the deal. A total steal.

I used the bonus starlight I'd gotten to grab a few little stars. For myself only, I could attach it, I could move it around a little, and it was now flexible when I wanted it to be. I might be able to do cool stuff with that, especially now that it was a more close-in to myself skill, focusing properly on the aspects of keeping myself alive and well.

I still think that being able to full-on do all the cool barrier stuff would be awesome, but I hardened my heart and made the choice.

Stars for sharp barriers. Multiple barriers. Moving barriers. Conditional barriers. Those, and dozens, hundreds, of additional options remained dark. Only a small part of the constellation was lit, and the rest would remain forever outside my reach. Possibly.

What I found super interesting was it seemed like I didn't have the full constellation. It seemed like some stars had lines that led nowhere – or led to stars that I couldn't see.

I suppose I did start from **[Constellation of the Healer]** and not **[Constellation of the Barrier-Mage]**. It wouldn't really make sense to have access to all the powerful barrier skills and aspects in what was fundamentally a healing class.

And that was it. I was done with the initial pass-through.

I eyed the starlight. It had a good amount, but I was greedy for more. Every point mattered, because every point would turn into stats. Every stat I had would always be applying to everything I did. I'd unlocked everything I thought was cool; that I felt I needed.

Iteration time!

Time to see how useful things were, evaluate skills and perks not only on their own merit, but how they synergized with and interacted with everything else I had.

I cut the suffocation aspect from **[Phases of the Moon]**, seeing a significant amount of starlight return. That had been a crazy expensive perk, and I avoided water like –

Well. I didn't avoid it like the plague, given that I dived into plagues head-first. Still. The starlight didn't justify the investment. Like, if I was suffocating, the skill would just keep me alive while I had mana, then I'd die anyways. Expensive skill, niche use, that was a formula for elimination.

Healing animals and dinosaurs from **[Warmth of the Sun]** bit the dust as well, returning a whopping 35 starlight. I'd had the awkward realization that it'd also heal animals and monsters hostile to me, unless I specifically bought the perk to exclude things from my aura, which was expensive. Also, healing animals and dinosaurs with **[Warmth]** was a pretty niche use anyways. Spend more starlight on a niche ability, or get it back? It was pretty obvious what the correct choice was.

All but one perk from healing non-humanoids from **[Phases of the Moon]** also got axed. Rough translation – I could heal Night and other vampires, following his old request, but I was going to continue to have a steep penalty healing other creatures. The further away from a human the System considered someone or something to be, the worse my healing efficiency would get, eventually turning into a "are you sure you want to lose all your mana for no reason?"

I frowned, and hesitated over that. I wanted a companion, and if I didn't have the stars at least partially lit, I'd always have a gigantic penalty when healing said companion. Hunting had mentioned possibly going after the thunderbirds, and, well...

I lit up one more star in the "non-humanoid animal healing" section.

I looked at my starlight. I looked at my skills. Improvements!

I cut the "super efficient mass visualization" aspect from **[Moonlight]**. I hated it, but I didn't do mass heals under **[Moonlight]** often enough to justify needing the extra efficiency. Plus – I'd just upgraded **[Warmth of the Sun]** a bunch. It was cannibalizing where I needed the skills, and a solid amount of starlight returned for it. Heck, if I threw that starlight into mana or mana regeneration, I basically got back everything I just lost from having the skill! After getting a few dozen levels, of course. Super-duper long run, it was going to work out even *better*.

I looked at my starlight, and I was now much happier with how much I had left. I had enough to think about what my skills would look like.

I was going to have only seven skills for quite some time, given how dimly I'd lit the ouroboros skill. I had room for a cheap pick up to temporarily hold onto and fill the slot, and with great glee, I grabbed a few points from the **[Invigorate]** skill.

I reviewed it, eight times, to see if there was anything else I wanted. I kept going back and forth on stuff, turning a star on one round, turning it off the next. Skill, or stat. Stat, or skill.

I looked back, finally content with my skills and my remaining starlight. It wasn't the best. When push came to shove, I leaned towards powerful skills, going a bit lighter on the stats. Stats came from everything, while skills were unique and one-time.

Now it was time to figure out what stats I wanted, and in what ratio.

To begin, Free Stats were significantly more expensive than assigned stats. As much as possible, I wanted to carefully and properly plan out my stats, and minimize how many Free Stats I'd get. Like. Why bother getting four Free Stats per level when I'd just put them all into Speed? Might as well use that starlight to get five points of Speed.

I had a delightful amount of starlight left. 487 stats to distribute, which was simply crazy. I rubbed my hands in glee, eager to start distributing.

First off, my Magic Power and Magic Control as it pertained to healing was flat-out batty. The boost that **[Oath]** was providing was significant, to say the least. I'd probably put a few points in Power and Control just so they wouldn't stagnate, so I'd be able to slowly improve over time. It was also useful when I needed to perform bulk, mass-healing all at once. I could only heal as many injuries as I had power. The quality of the healing would also be impacted by my control. Plus, it helped out my **[Ranger-Mage]** class. Still. Not the primary focus.

Physical stat-wise, Speed and Vitality were the name of the game, and I could use some of each. A bit of Dexterity to keep up with it would be nice as well. Strength was useless, as far as I used it.

No, the stats I needed the most were Mana, and Mana Regeneration. There was a tension between the two.

Mana was good for fights. Mages died when they ran out of mana, and my healing was strong enough to drain my entire bar in an instant. At the same time, as Sentinel, I had constant access to huge reserves of Arcanite, able to pull and extend my staying power.

Mana Regeneration was good for enduring, and long-lasting problems. Most of the problems I ran into these days required massive regeneration, from holding the Formorians, to healing tents upon tents of injured soldiers.

I was frankly exhausted. Not physically, but mentally. I was in the world of my soul, in soul form. It was impossible to be physically exhausted. Mentally though? I'd been slicing and dicing skills and points for what was probably days on end, and having had "mana versus regeneration" debates in the past, I decided to say screw it.

Even split on the two. Most of my points were going into it anyways.

I started pressing icons.

Strength was almost pointless. If nothing else, I'd consistently get a few points of it here and there from leveling up **[Ranger-Mage]** once I finished classing it up.

Three points to Dexterity.

24 points to Speed and Vitality.

48 points to Magic Power and Magic Control.

170 points to both Mana and Mana Regeneration.

Zero free stats per level.

I looked at the book, exhausted.

[The Dawn Sentinel] it proudly displayed, having turned a dark green. On top of being dark green, powerful on stats, I knew that most of the power of the class was in the skills, not in the stats. Being able to entirely customize the class was an unbelievable power, and it was probably even stronger than the raw numbers suggested. It was better than tailored for me – I'd tailored it myself.

Most of my skills would probably change their name, to reflect the new abilities I had. I was going to flat out lose **[Vastness of the Stars]**, and after getting my replacement and temporary skills, I wouldn't be getting another skill for a long, long time.

It was all going to be worth it. I'd gotten to see what the skill was going to be called once I'd get it. I knew what it would do, and the mere thought of it sent my heart racing as I bit my lower lip in nervous anticipation.

[The Stars Never Fade].

I would be able to see Librarian again in the future.

I would be able to turn back the clock of time on myself, effectively rendering me ageless.

Or, to put it another way -

Immortal.

Chapter 19

Skills Skills Skills

I opened my eyes, eager to see what I got, what the name of the skills would be, what level everything would hit. Before I could see anything, a powerful wave of nausea overcame me, the loss of the high-level skills hitting me hard. I turned over, tried to hold it in, failed, grabbed a random *thing* and vomited hard into it, retching and heaving as my empty stomach demanded that *everything* left, resulting in me spitting bile.

Wiping my mouth, I ignored the rest of my surroundings, the disgusted noises I heard, and immediately focused on my notifications.

I'd left the name of all of the skills to be something of a surprise. Well, except for the *bloody Immortality* skill, but I just *had* to know.

[*ding!* Congratulations! [Constellation of the Healer] has upgraded into [The Dawn Sentinel]!]

[*ding!* Congratulations! [The Dawn Sentinel] has leveled up to level 256->305! +3 Dexterity, +24 Speed, +24 Vitality, +170 Mana, +170 Mana Regen, +48 Magic power, +48 Magic Control from your Class per level! +1 Free Stat for being Human per level! +1 Mana, +1 Mana Regen from your Element per level!]

Cha-CHING. Holy stats. I'd what, doubled my mana and mana regeneration in one go? Yikes. That was good stuff. No wonder Artemis had seemed so much stronger than everyone else. No wonder Sentinels were so powerful.

Then again, **[The Dawn Sentinel]** was by all accounts an absurdly powerful class. The only other person I knew of with a dark green class was Arthur, but on the other hand, I didn't know the quality of the other Sentinel's classes.

Magic claimed his were pink, but that was probably a lie designed to throw me off. I really hoped we'd screwed up, and the ever-paranoid, always-cautious dude would show up again.

Back to my new skills!

[*ding!* Congratulations! [Warmth of the Sun] has upgraded to [Cosmic Presence!]]

Cosmic Presence: The cosmos is omni-present, always roiling and moving, always reshaping itself over eons. Your presence is like the cosmos, omni-present around you, and you renew and fix those around you. Increase the natural healing of everyone around you. Increased speed and range per level. Passive skill, costs 7777 Mana Regeneration.

First new skill! **[Cosmic Presence]** sounded totally cool, and I was excited to see it in action, to see what it could do.

[*Error* You have lost the skill [Medicine]]

I had this sudden moment of horror. What if I was completely wrong, and I wasn't getting a replacement skill for quite some time? What if I'd just screwed myself hard?

[*ding!* Congratulations! [Center of the Galaxy] has upgraded into [Center of the Universe]!]

Center of the Universe: Your ego has only grown over time. From the center of the galaxy, you now see yourself as the center of the universe, as all of existence revolves around you. Improved pain resistance and mental stability per level.

[*ding!* Congratulations! [Phases of the Moon] has upgraded into [Dance with the Heavens]!]

Dance with the Heavens: The heavens cycle above you, each object participating in the grand dance of life. The sun heals and restores, the moons remove that which does not belong, while the stars adjust everything to their proper place. Panacea skill. Improved efficiency per level, improved power per level.

I was thrilled with the new name, but I wasn't completely sure what the leveling up would do. I already had a terrifying amount of power, and I was pretty darn efficient with my images.

Then again, with losing **[Medicine]** my efficiency was going to dip a hair.

[*ding!* Congratulations! [Moonlight] has upgraded into [Wheel of Sun and Moon]!]
Wheel of Sun and Moon: Your power to restore life comes from the sun, as your power to remove harmful substances comes from the moon. Now, heal those that are touched by either the sun or the moon! Ranged healing. Range increases per level. Penalty reduced per level.

[*Error* [Veil of the Aurora] has downgraded into [Mantle of the Stars]]
Mantle of the Stars: You weave a cloak of starlight to wear for yourself. Improved manipulation and defense per level.

[*Error* You have lost the skill [Vastness of the Stars]]

[*ding!* Congratulations! For hitting level 300, you've unlocked the Class skill [Solar Infusion]!]
Solar Infusion: The sun burns brightly, forever fueled, immune and immutable. With this skill, you'll be able to impart your healing on someone else, letting the power persist in them, keeping them hale and whole. When they are further away from you, the skill will also increase and improve their natural healing. Increased radius where **[Dance with the Heavens]** applies per level. Increased amount of mana that can be placed in the skill per level. Increased efficiency at transforming their mana regeneration into natural healing.

The skill had almost double the range of **[Wheel of sun and Moon]**, and it came without the distance penalties, along with letting me donate more and more generously into the "mana pocket" that came with the skill. Situations like Brawling being cut in half wouldn't be nearly so dire. Still bad, I'd probably still need to help, at least until the skill leveled up a ton, but it was better than what I had before.

I could also disable someone's mana regeneration. I was fairly certain that since it was a healing skill, **[Oath]** would apply when I tapped someone with it, which meant a corresponding increase in the maximum amount of mana regeneration I could "eat" from them. Or, putting it another way, I felt more comfortable disabling someone, without worrying about a skill coming out of the blue and killing me.

[*ding!* Congratulations! For hitting level 300, you've unlocked the Class skill [Sunrise]!]

Sunrise: Good morning, rise and shine! Have a nice big cup of sunshine, and be awake, alert, and energetic, ready to meet the day! Warning: Not a sleep substitute.

[Sunrise] and [Solar Infusion] starting off at level 1 each was going to be painful. Then again, I felt like I had unlimited mana and regeneration, and I could just spam the skills non-stop to help level them up. Onto the level up notifications!

[*ding!* [Celestial Affinity] leveled up! 256 -> 305]
[*ding!* [Center of the Universe] leveled up! 256 -> 285]
[*ding!* [Dance with the Heavens] leveled up! 256 -> 305]
[*ding!* [Wheel of Sun and Moon] leveled up! 256 -> 271]
[*ding!* [Oath of Elaine to Lyra] leveled up! 256 -> 270]
[*ding!* [Sentinel's Superiority] leveled up! 256 -> 305]
[*ding!* [Learning] leveled up! 256 -> 280]
[*ding!* [Bullet Time] leveled up! 256 -> 268]

Sweet, sweet levels. Yessssss. I looked over my new and improved stat sheet.

[Name: Elaine]

[Race: Human]

[Age: 19]

[Mana: 153790/153790]

[Mana Regen: 133517 (+98425.6)]

Stats

[Free Stats: 51]

[Strength: 293]

[Dexterity: 347]

[Vitality: 2176]

[Speed: 2176]

[Mana: 15379]

[Mana Regeneration: 15379 (+9842.56)]

[Magic Power: 7897 (+106609.5)]

[Magic Control: 7897 (+106609.5)]

[Class 1: [The Dawn Sentinel - Celestial: Lv 305]]

[Celestial Affinity: 305]

[Cosmic Presence: 231]

[Solar Infusion: 1]

[Center of the Universe: 285]

[Dance with the Heavens: 305]

[Wheel of Sun and Moon: 271]

[Mantle of the Stars: 256]

[Sunrise: 1]

[Class 2: [Ranger-Mage - Radiance: Lv 256]]
[Radiance Affinity: 256]
[Radiance Resistance: 256]
[Radiance Conjuration: 256]
[Shine: 111]
[Sun-Kissed: 256]
[Blaze: 256]
[Talaria: 256]
[Nova: 256]

[Class 3: Locked]

General Skills
[Identify: 151]
[Pristine Memories: 200]
[Pretty: 152]
[Bullet Time: 268]
[Oath of Elaine to Lyra: 270]
[Sentinel's Superiority: 305]
[Persistent Casting: 189]
[Learning: 280]

Oh. My. Goddesses.
That was *insane.*
Over 200,000 mana per hour when in sunlight?

Over 110,000 magic power and control when healing?

A mana pool over 150,000?

Heck, with that Power and Control, anything that didn't instantly obliterate my entire head I could recover from at least once. I was unwilling to put that hypothesis to the test, but given that I could immediately restore half of Brawling in a single go, and I'd just gotten a massive jump to both my power, control, and mana, it seemed likely.

Also, I'd fixed my little problem. Previously, I had so much effective Magic Power when healing that I could instantly drain my entire mana pool in a single sitting. I had Magic Power in excess, which was a waste. Now I didn't, and while I didn't think it'd matter on a direct basis, it was a nice little bit of efficiency gained.

Having finished basic processing of my new abilities, I decided to focus on the world around me. My mouth still tasted foul. I groaned, as muscles protested and joints creaked from being still way too long, never mind the emergency 'find a place to vomit' from earlier. I hit myself with **[Sunrise]**, and smiled as energy flooded through me, and my muscles became loose and limber.

[*ding!* [Sunrise] leveled up! 1 -> 2]

Heck yes. Even better.

"Welcome back Dawn." A distinctly unamused Night said, wrinkling his nose at the mess I'd made.

Plate of food, rumbling stomach, mug of water and parched throat. A standard "I've been under *how long!?*" combo. **[Sunrise]** was obviously useless for food and drink, and I started to chow down without a word.

"You said you were going to be fast!" Arthur glared at me accusingly, and I looked around the tent.

Toxic was seated at the table with Night, Nature, and Brawling, dice, drinks, and tokens scattered all over the table. Hunting was in another cubby, the curtains half-heartedly closed. He was sitting on a cot, looking away from us. A few kegs had found their way into our tent, and from the look – and the smell – there were more empty kegs than people. Destruction was in a third cubby, small motes of light around him indicating that he was also classing up.

Upgrading his mythical third class.

I idly wondered if he was getting the level 8 or the level 32 class up, before physical needs reminded me that they needed tending to.

I held one finger up in a "wait one moment" gesture as I grabbed the water and drained the entire thing in one go, taking huge gulps as I tried to get water back into me. I put it down, smacking my lips.

"Right. Sorry about that. I was spending the entire time working on my class-up. I promise!" I said, looking at Arthur's raised eyebrow. "Somehow, I was given the chance to customize and *make* my own class. I was given the chance to grab whatever skills I wanted, and have them do whatever I wanted. It took me some time to properly build the best possible final healer class I'd ever take."

Poker face. Gotta keep a poker face. I should really keep this a secret –

"Or it might not be my final healer class." I said with what I hoped was a mysterious grin. I wasn't going to say more than that but – *I was just too excited!*

Night slowly turned and looked at me.

"Tell me about it." He said, and I explained about the door, the constellations and the starlight, and how extra starlight turned into stats.

"Fascinating." He said, tone of voice back to the normal aloof and superior tone. "That sounds remarkably similar to my last class-up, however, I had tables and chalices to fill with blood whereas you had constellations and stars to ignite with starlight. I have only rarely heard of similar occurrences, but then again, the number of individuals who wish to share the going-ons of their class-ups is exceedingly rare. Nevertheless, it is a golden opportunity for those who properly seize it, and from your description and the time taken, I do believe you have." Night said, once again using fifty words instead of fifteen.

"So... did everything go ok?" I asked. I mean, Night and company were back, which implied things went well, but hey. I'd been out of it.

I got the first look of real joy on Night's face. Sure, I'd seen him smile. I'd seen him laugh; I'd seen him happy. It was always careful though. Always thought out. Not that he was wearing a mask or being manipulative or anything, but this was pure, unfiltered joy on his face.

"Victory." Night said, raw jubilation in his voice. Thousands of years of combat, and this was it. He finally declared victory. "The Formorian Queens have been slain, and most of the Formorians are likewise dead."

"Not all of them." Hunting yelled with a pained voice; grief raw. The jubilation I'd been feeling got instantly erased at the sound of his voice.

I briefly wondered what could've happened, before settling on the most obvious solution.

Katastrofi.

I looked around the room.

"Who?" I asked, trying to keep an even tone. I was mentally cursing myself for ditching parts of [Center of the Galaxy]. I wasn't enjoying this emotional rollercoaster one bit.

Toxic, Nature, and Brawling all looked at Night. The responsibilities of leadership.

Didn't help that they all looked sloshed.

Night's face grew sober as well.

"Sealing is dead. Sky is presumed dead. Magic is, as of now, officially missing in action, presumed dead." Night slowly pronounced.

I closed my eyes, each name like a punch in the gut. I curled up, and buried my face in my knees. I didn't want to let the others see me cry.

"Katastrofi." A tortured sound came out of Hunting's throat. "Katastrofi's also dead."

"Their sacrifice was not in vain." Night said. He didn't need to say more.

More dead friends. More names to carve on the Indomitable Wall. More people to grieve.

Some soft sobbing let me know that Hunting was being significantly more open about his grieving.

Night could clearly read the room.

"We shall properly celebrate their lives, and mourn, this evening once Bulwark has returned."

That   was   good   enough   for   me.

Chapter 20

Party

I was still curled up and feeling miserable when I felt a mass that could only be Brawling's plonk down next to me.

"Heya." He said. "Yeah, this sucks. We won, at what price? Tell you what. Best thing for it? Go out and do something. Take your mind off of things. I'm sure there's a dozen soldiers that need some help. From getting too drunk, if nothing else. Or heck, have a drink or five, wander around, get in trouble. Find a handsome soldier and get laid. Dance on the walls. Join us playing dice. Nature's cheating, but Toxic isn't. Just find something to do, something to keep your mind off of things as you process."

I sniffled.

"Are you cheating or not?" I mumbled into my knees.

Brawling guffawed at that.

"Not telling!" He said, with what I could now kinda tell was forced, fake cheer. He was hurting like all of us, but had better coping. Somewhat.

"That's a yes." I said, lifting my head and giving him an accusing look. "I suck at cheating. No way am I going to play."

"Awww, come on! Just a bit?" Brawling said, cajoling me.

A plan came to me. In spite of the heavy weight on me, I cracked a grin.

"Ok, fine, just a bit." I said.

Brawling bolted up, and offered me his hand. I took it, accepting his help to get up. We wandered over to the table.

I was being eyed up like a seal in front of a bunch of sharks. I gave them wide, innocent eyes. Like a lamb to the slaughter.

"I'm out." Nature said. "She's got something up her sleeve. Nobody looks like that." Nature said, pointing at me. "Nobody with Dawn's experience looks that innocent and naïve going to a game where she knows people are cheating."

"Oh come on!" I protested. "How is that fair? Both you and Brawling are cheating horribly – heck, for that matter, Toxic's also cheating, you just haven't caught him yet – and when I come to the table, suddenly you're out?"

Nature smirked, and I suddenly realized I'd been had.

"See. Told ya she's got something up her sleeve. Come on, let's go." He said.

I sat down at the table, mentally cursing. He might've ruined everything.

Still. I ponied up a few coins, and threw them into the pot.

"Night?" Brawling prompted, after everyone else – Nature included, I guess curiosity won out – had thrown a few coins or chips in.

With a long-suffering sigh, Night threw a few coins in as well, and dice started to shake.

I wasn't cheating. Well, I kinda was, but I wasn't. I was banking on everyone else cheating *for* me. See, how else were you going to get the reluctant, but loaded, sucker who was terrible to the table?

The dice finished rolling, and it took me a moment to process what they'd landed on.

"I won!" I cried out, playing up the excitement, scooping the pot over to me.

"Yeah! Fun, right?" Brawling said, a huge smile on his face.

"Yup. Anyways, thanks all. I'm out." I said, a predatory grin splitting my face as I scooped up my winnings.

The look on Brawling's face – *priceless.* Stunned disbelief. Nature just started laughing.

"Told you she had something up her sleeve! She played you all like a lute! Oh man, losing that round was totally worth it just to see the look on your faces! Ha!"

The answer for how you get the reluctant sucker to play – have her win a few times. Get her hooked on the feeling, wanting to play more.

It wasn't like we hadn't played similar games when I was a Ranger.

Toxic winked at me. I flipped him his coins back – and a few extra.

"Wait! Why does he get his coins back!?" Brawling sputtered with indignation.

Night snorted at our antics, and deigned to chip in.

"Because Toxic and Dawn were on the same Ranger team together. He clearly has a strong grasp of her talents and abilities, and assisted with her victory just now. Most likely he even knew what would happen after. Instead of ruining her fun, he participated as a willing accomplice. Dawn is simply repaying the favor. Also, how you lot have not caught onto Toxic's method of cheating is simply disgraceful. Honestly." He said, shaking his head.

I glanced at Night.

"How are you cheating?" I asked him.

"I do not need to cheat. I am too wealthy for that." Night said, practically sniffing with his nose in the air.

"He flips the dice when he feels like it." Toxic stage-whispered to me.

Night gave Toxic an affronted look.

"I have not informed the others of how you are manipulating the game of chance to favor yourself." He pointed out dangerously.

I grabbed a double handful of rations, and left before another one of the Sentinel's famous brawls erupted.

I wandered around camp, munching on the rations. There wasn't a shred of good food left – everyone had eaten it in the earlier celebration, which I had missed, and the logistics were still interrupted. That'd need to get fixed quick, before it became a larger issue. Didn't seem to concern most of the soldiers, however. The mood, from how I could gauge it, was mixed. Some soldiers were celebrating, loud parties around non-regulation fires. The Centurions obviously didn't care, as I saw a number of them celebrating and joining in themselves.

Others were sad, mopey, tucked away in corners with a mug.

I wandered around, not quite sure what I wanted to do.

"Hey girly! Wanna have some fuuuuuuuuuuuuun?" A drunken soldier asked, leering at me as his friends laughed.

I shot him a disgusted look and a finger, and got struck by inspiration. The sun was out, my range had increased, and I had a new skill to test out.

[Wheel of Sun and Moon] was my new ranged skill for **[Dance with the Heavens]**, and I focused, applying it to just the one dude. I wanted him cured of his 'alcohol poisoning', and with a slight mental frown, I realized a few things.

First off – my image on **[Persistent Casting]** was entirely *gone*. I'd need to rebuild the whole thing from scratch.

Second off – an image, the knowledge of how getting drunk worked on a fundamental level in the human body, and what I'd need to do to cure intoxication wasn't springing into my mind like I was used to. I had to spend a moment straining and thinking.

Right. Alcohol. The active ingredient – and the thing that was causing most of the issues – was the namesake alcohol. As it was digested, the liver produced a substance that counteracted the alcohol, breaking it down. Getting drunk, however, was a product of drinking more alcohol than the body could break down at a time, resulting in alcohol in the cardiovascular system, interfering with parts of the brain. The coordination part of the brain was particularly susceptible to the effects of alcohol – hence a loss of balance.

It also had a release of dopamine, which made people feel good. I couldn't – wouldn't – interfere with dopamine and other natural side effects, but the alcohol itself? Yeah, I could handle that. Technically a poison, although handling and managing alcohol had been its own unique star, given the unique status of alcohol in society.

Once the alcohol was gone, everything else would clear itself up. With a thought and a glare, I instantly sobered the soldier up, and kept on going, ignoring the confused cries from behind me.

Ethically, I was walking a bit of a thin line here. I was pushing a boundary, and I could almost feel **[Oath]** grumbling at me. My justification for why I was on the right side of the "informed consent" portion of medical ethics was the dude was clearly so sloshed that he'd completely missed that he was harassing a Sentinel, which suggested that he had more in him than was healthy.

I felt the loss of **[Medicine]**. It was going to take me a bit more mental effort to heal someone efficiently.

Then again, I'd gotten *so much mana* that I wasn't going to notice the slight decrease in efficiency. I'd also gotten an entire new skill!

Well worth the trade-off.

Brawling had suggested getting laid but I had *standards.* Probably wasn't happening.

What else had he suggested? Helping people out.

I figured I should see if there were any people at the infirmary, and practice my new skills while I was at it. I wanted to get a good handle on them.

I wanted to squeal with joy. My new skills were *so damn cool!* Like, I'd already cast a ranged heal *in daylight!* The moons were one heck of a restriction, but the sun? It had cost me hardly any starlight to buy that particular perk, and was more than halfway to removing the restriction entirely!

And, that was just one tiny perk on one tiny skill!

We'd left for the frontlines in a rush, and we'd naturally grabbed our combat gear. Our "looking good" gear – namely, our red cloaks – had been left behind. Good way to get tangled then killed in a fight. Now we were out of the fight, in camp, and I had the perfect idea.

With a careful thought, I used **[Mantle of the Stars]** to create a shimmering cape of stars down my back, clasped around my neck. I took an experimental step forward, and not only was I able to move my cape of starlight, it also fluttered mysteriously as I moved, no gust of wind needed.

I bit my knuckle to stop myself from squealing in girlish delight in the middle of camp. *This was so blasted cool!!!*

I puffed my chest out as I strode through camp, feeling like a total badass with my shimmering cape of stars trailing behind me. Right. **[Mantle of the Stars]** tested, **[Wheel of Sun and Moon]** tested, **[Sunrise]** used earlier. **[Center of the Universe]** wasn't super easy to test, but it was so similar to **[Center of the Galaxy]** that I didn't bother. Plus, similar to **[Bullet Time]**, it usually only activated in bad situations.

[Solar Infusion] was up, and ideally I'd like to get some time to properly examine what **[Cosmic Presence]** was doing. I'd poured a ton of starlight into the skill, and I wanted to know how it worked.

Problem was, **[Solar Infusion]** was almost a "pre-healing" skill. I should find Brawling or someone who was going to spar, and hit them ahead of time.

[Cosmic Presence], on the other hand, I could try to test now. Would've been better if the fighting was still going on, but eh. I couldn't complain too much that people weren't dying anymore.

I continued to wander through the nigh-endless camp, crossing the occasional awkward stretch of extra-muddy ground, with no tents, and suspiciously smooth walls with an obviously different texture. Clearly where the Formorians had broken through, and where Bulwark had worked his magic to reform and reseal the walls.

The celebration was one long never-ending party, from squads grouped together, celebrating their time and survival, to soldiers who just so happened to have their tents nearby – it looked like almost everyone was partying. Everyone had broken out whatever little comforts they had with them, and was liberally sharing them around.

It was a tragedy that the camp followers section of the walls had also gotten broken into. I'd like to imagine that as soon as the first Formorian had gotten through the walls, that they'd all run away. I studiously avoided thinking about the narrow gates between the walls, how when people panic they stampede, and the likelihood that a crush of bodies would've trapped the camp followers in-between the walls, their safety turning into a death trap as Formorians scythed through them, grabbing and dragging their bodies back to the Queens to be eaten and turned into nutrients for more Formorians.

Nope. Nuh uh. Wasn't going to think about it. There was nothing I could do for them, although it was clear that the lack of camp followers was being sorely felt. I don't think I'd passed a party yet where I hadn't been invited, and the sheer number of invitations that got walked back when someone saw the Sentinel badge let me know it wasn't my status that was earning me invites.

To be fair – everyone was in a real friendly mood, and most of the other soldiers wandering around were getting invited to little parties here and there. Still. I resolved to find my way back to the Sentinel's tent soon enough.

Entertainment of all flavors was on display. Dice, dancing, and drinking were popular, but games of all sorts were also on display. Heck, one Centurion looked like he'd organized all the squads under his command into a miniature sort of Olympics, which had a roaring crowd of their own.

It was inevitable that small fights and brawls would break out, and anyone I saw nursing an injury I hit with **[Dance with the Heavens]** at range with **[Wheel of Sun and Moon]**. I missed **[Medicine]** again, and felt the loss of the skill with the inefficient healing. At the same time, I had *so much mana,* I only noticed that it was less efficient because I was looking for it. Didn't want to get bogged down in social niceties, but it was entertaining to hear the cries of realization that a broken arm was suddenly fixed, or a twisted ankle rightened. Stealth healing! Still didn't get me what I wanted, which was testing my remaining skills.

Soldiers were a violent bunch, and more than a few liked blood sports. It was with no surprise in the slightest that I heard the distinct sound of weapon against armor, and I had enough experience to identify these as "sparring blows", and not blows that were aimed to injure and maim.

I took a quick right turn, and followed my ears, discreetly putting my Sentinel badge away. If I showed up with my badge, the soldiers would assume I was there to shut them down entirely, and it could get ugly. I had no intention of doing that. Where there was fighting, there were injured people. This was a chance for me to see just how powerful [Cosmic Presence] was, while making sure the fights stayed non-lethal.

Heck, if I was lucky I could try [Solar Infusion], although I was pushing my [Oath] a bit here. I was enabling people to hurt each other, with the fact that they were going to hurt each other anyways acting as a balancing or mitigating factor. The fact that they might hurt each other more pushed back on that, and I was walking a thin line here.

Like. I really *shouldn't*. But I was too excited! I wanted to try out my new skills! It was the perfect chance!

I ignored the little voice in my head saying that I should turn back.

I did stop and pay attention when the little voice in my head reminded me that I'd dumped the emotion-dampening aspects of [Center of the Galaxy], and that I'd resolved to check my emotions.

I wasn't being a whiny brat though, or throwing a temper tantrum. I was simply taking a risk, eager and excited. Were those such bad emotions?

Resolved, I pressed on, squeezing myself into an extra-large tent. The stitch marks along the side spoke to a clever soldier, a half-dozen tents joined to form an extra-large fight club.

There was a packed crowd. Of course there was a packed crowd, shouting and jeering and waving coins around.

My biggest challenge was seeing what was going on, as I cursed my short height. I could *hear* what was happening no problem. Seeing though? I could see backs, and that was it.

An adventure that consisted of slipping, sliding, pushing, swearing, climbing, and a whole lot of cursing got me a better view of what was going on.

Two men wrestled in the central arena. One was big and burly, the other smaller and nimbler. Some half-naked men jumping up and down excitedly off to one side, and another banged-up soldier being half-carried away by his buddies, who were patting him in a reassuring way. I heard the standard roar of the crowd, baying and hooting, cheers of joy when their dude got a solid punch in, which was immediately mirrored by cries of dismay by people rooting for the punchee.

I pushed and shoved my way over to the section with the waiting fighters.

"Hey. Hey! Hey!" I called out, barely able to hear myself over the crowd. No way the people warming up would be able to hear me either. Ugh.

Also, the thought crossed my mind that by using skills on the people about to fight, that there'd be a lot of deeply unhappy people as a result. Blargh. Combine that with using **[Solar Infusion]** on people about to fight, which would let them fight harder and hurt each other more – never mind that they'd heal it right back up – and I gave up on testing **[Solar Infusion]** for now. I'd just need to wait for a more reasonable spar, instead of dealing with a fight pit.

No, this was a great chance to test out **[Cosmic Presence]** though. I groaned with half the crowd as the small nimble dude got a grip on the bigger dude's arm, and threw him across the arena. The *crack* of breaking bones announced the end of the fight, and the winner raised his arms up in victory, to the cheering of the other half of the crowd.

Body size and obvious strength weren't everything, not when skills and stats came in to put their weight on the scale.

I lasered in on the poor fellow being carted away by his buddies, and started to follow them, overhearing the first soldier bemoaning their loss, and their lack of drinking funds.

I made a detour towards some of the other fighters who had lost, and were nursing injuries. I mentally cursed not getting ranged healing indoors, but then again, that had been an expensive, expensive star to light, and it was rare that I needed to heal at a range inside.

Naturally, since I'd jinxed it, fate conspired to immediately put me in a situation where I wish I had it.

[Oath] satisfied, I made it out of the tent, and spotted the injured dude being carried by his fellow soldiers. I noticed with a critical eye that a number of nasty bruises were starting to blossom on the dude who'd lost the fight.

They made it to the tent, and I was in a bit of a pickle. Just standing out here was all sorts of awkward, and I was getting some funny looks.

I felt a bit awkward, like I was kinda stalking him – well, I guess I was stalking him – so I figured I might as well introduce myself.

"Hiya!" I said, walking up to them.

One of them opened his mouth, only for the second one to elbow him.

"Welcome, healer." The second one said, throwing a significant glare at the first one. "What business do you have here?" He asked, throwing another pointed look at his friend.

I mentally rolled my eyes. Yeah, yeah, hint taken.

"Here to help out. Have a new skill I'm looking to test." I said, deciding to have some fun and threw my most sinister smile on. With the most cartoonishly evil voice I could muster, I pointed to the fighter who'd lost. "And I've found my test subject!"

Ok, maybe not the best introduction, but hey. Gal's gotta have fun somehow.

They looked at each other, while the injured dude just groaned.

"What are you going to do to him?" The first one asked.

"Absolutely nothing!" I proudly declared, which got some confused looks. I rolled my eyes this time.

"Trying out my new passive skill." I said, clearing up the confusion a hair.

"Maybe you should just move along…" The first soldier said doubtfully.

Eh. I suppose I deserved that.

Having run out of social tolerance, I decided to press the magic "I get my way" button.

I pulled out my Sentinel badge.

"How about now?" I asked them conversationally, and got salutes in return.

I loved the Sentinel badge. I don't know what I'd ever do without it, or the authority and listen-to-me-ness it granted me.

"Honestly – just upgraded a skill, and I'd like to see it in action." I explained, moving closer and sitting down. "Supposed to be a passive heal, and I want to know how well it works. Your buddy here's perfect, because he's got a dozen bruises all over the place. Nothing life-threatening, and bruises are easy to watch heal. Long enough timeframe that I can get an idea, guaranteed to heal, not life-threatening in any way, shape, or form. Figure I can hang out here while he's healing up, see exactly how well it works."

Alcohol was the great social lubricant, and I'd make the two soldiers all sorts of nervous. I didn't have alcohol but I had the next best thing – money.

Even better, it wasn't my money! And they'd been complaining about a lack of drinking funds. Time to make some new friends!

I grabbed my smaller coin purse, and tossed it to one of the soldiers, who caught it with a satisfying noise.

"Why don't you rustle us up some beer?" I 'suggested', and with my badge on my chest and my coins in his hand, the soldier moved like it was an order from a god above.

Which made me all sorts of sad again, remembering Priest Demos, which led to me remembering everyone else who'd died.

The dude who'd been left behind sensed the mood, and we sat in morose silence until the beer showed up. We all cheered up considerably after it appeared.

I had some fun chatting and trading stories with my three new temporary best friends. They had all sorts of crazy stories, and the fish kept getting larger with each one. I kept an eye on the pit fighter, and I was surprised and pleased with how he was healing.

It took about thirty minutes for his bruises to go through the entire rainbow, and at two weeks for bruises to fully vanish, that was one hell of a pace. That was what, 168 hours in a week times two, into thirty minutes? I had no way of keeping good time, so I was what, improving someone's natural healing speed by 600 times or so?

However, vitality was throwing a massive wrench into the equation here. People with higher vitality naturally healed faster than people without it, and soldiers tended to have a good grasp on that concept, along with other physical classers.

I eyed him up, cursed that I'd dumped **[Medicine]** instead of expanding it to help me know how stats interacted properly with magic skills. I checked his level, mentally cross-referenced it with numerous Ranger Academy trainees I'd dealt with and their injuries, and guessed that his own natural healing was roughly twice what it would normally be, just from his stats.

A much better guess was probably speeding up naturally healing by a factor of 300, which would multiply against whatever vitality he had naturally.

[Cosmic Presence] wouldn't restore limbs, and I needed to re-set one bone which healed wrong, but at the rate I was healing, I was more than pleased. Heck, a number of injuries that would normally be slowly fatal would now just straight-up heal on their own simply by my presence.

Blood loss and related problems also shouldn't be a problem anymore, not unless the blow was so massive as to likely be fatal anyways.

For example, if someone had their femoral artery sliced open, a knife slicing their inner thigh open. A traditional example of a blow that, while not immediately lethal, would quickly turn lethal from a loss of blood.

Now? With me around?

Not only would the injury clot incredibly quickly, in spite of the size, but the cut itself would almost immediately scab over and repair itself. On top of that, any blood lost would be rapidly – in terms of blood restoration timeframes – restore itself.

It wasn't *just* a 300x or so rate of improvement with healing. The body helped itself, and the effects on one system improving helped other parts of the system improve as well. Everything was connected in the body, everything worked with each other.

And this was just for a single person! My aura could fill maybe half a stadium.

I suspected, but had no real way of finding out, that the only thing I needed to be concerned about were immediately lethal blows, and injuries that removed significant portions of the body. Apart from that? My mere presence was enough.

Well, that and some aspects of diseases.

Take the Black Plague for example. People got sick with all manner of symptoms. Then, like a miracle, like a Goddess had descended from the skies and touched them, people would feel miraculously better. They were cured! They'd avoided the grim reaper!

Then they'd drop dead two days later.

Most symptoms of a disease weren't the disease itself. Most symptoms was the body's own immune response kicking in to fight the disease. Fever? A raised temperature made the body a more hostile environment for disease, killing it off faster than a human would die. Headaches? Lethargy? The body's way of saying "Whoa, slow down, we're sick here. Don't do something dumb like try to hunt. Go rest."

The feeling better was a complete and total collapse of the immune system as the Black Plague overwhelmed the body's defenders, killing them all. People felt right as a fiddle! Then the Plague finished killing everything else in the body, and people dropped dead.

[Dance with the Heavens] solved that issue entirely, and it combined with [Wheel of Sun and Moon] gave me strong anti-plague skills, along with the ability to troll drunken soldiers.

I mentally cursed not getting [Cosmic Presence] while the war with the Formorians was still going on. I'd have saved uncountable numbers of people just by standing there.

At the same time, without the war coming to a close I would've never gotten the skill. No use crying over it, I had a cool new skill! It was as awesome as I could've hoped for.

Even better – my estimates were just estimates. For all I knew, it would range from three hundred times as fast, to six hundred times as fast. Good timekeeping. I *really* wanted good timekeeping.

Whistling, a bit tipsy, I made my way back to the Sentinel's tent,   eager   to   share   my   discoveries.

Chapter 21

Mourning

I skipped along, singing drunkenly and off-key. Didn't care, was too happy. Cool new stuff everywhere!

Awesome healing skills away! I could heal a person fully that I was touching, I could heal them at a distance, I could preemptively heal with **[Solar Infusion]** – in theory, still needed to test it – and I passively healed people around me!

All that, in one class! Most healers that I'd chatted with needed two classes dedicated to healing to properly work their stuff, and here I was, having compressed it in one class! I was pleased with my class and my skills, and I felt like it was justified.

Randomly **[Identify]**ing people indicated that I wasn't the only one who'd gotten a ton of levels. People tended to cap out at 180 on the frontlines if they were "only" fighting Formorians – **[Scribes]**, **[Camp-Followers]**, **[Generals]**, and more not included – and yet, most of the soldiers I saw were well above 200. The added stress and peril of the walls falling, of humanity getting pushed to the brink of extinction, fighting Royal Guards – well, that was enough to push the survivors up significantly.

I pitied any soldier who'd taken a **[Formorian Slayer]** class or something similar. If the Formorians were gone – truly, actually, totally dead – then they'd have a hard time leveling the class, and their specialized skills were likely useless. Additionally, the hard time leveling meant they'd be unlikely to hit 256 to be able to change their class.

Then again, while I appreciated the sacrifice any soldier who'd taken a dedicated killing class had made, I was slightly skeptical as to what, if any, long-term plan they had. Soldiers did retire eventually – doubly so if they had a strong combat class to help them survive, like, say, **[Formorian Slayer]** – and if they went into it without a plan of what to do after, well, that was kinda on them.

The stats they'd gotten from leveling up would stay with them forever though, and one of the beauties of physical Classers was they weren't tied to their skills. Having 4000 strength was 4000 strength, regardless of what else your skills said and did. Didn't need a skill to pick up and throw blocks of bricks around, nor to till a field. Sure, they helped, but physical Classers were crazy flexible.

Unlike magical Classers, who lived and died by their skills.

Flexibility versus specialization. When it came to fights, it was more a question of burst versus sustained.

I shook off my mental mutters as I made it back to the Sentinel's tent. A roaring fire was outside of it, and all the Sentinels were around it, staring into the flames, chatting and drinking.

The weight of our presence kept nearly everyone else away. There was one person I vaguely recognized, and I did a double-take as I finally placed him.

A Ranger. He was the head of team.... 9? Maybe? It'd been quite some time since the last Convocation, but it would make sense that any nearby teams got ordered over here, or just came of their own volition when they heard the news. Only dude comfortable enough, unawed by our presence, to come up and chat.

At the same time, "Head of a Ranger Squad" didn't exactly remove our aura of mystique, and I joined the rest of the Sentinels.

"Welcome, Dawn!" Night cheerfully greeted me, clearly in a much better mood now that the sun was gone.

"Night! I'mmmmm back!" I cheerfully, not-at-all-drunkenly, called back to him. Must not say the vampire thing must not say the vampire thing must not –

"Didja get your third class?" I blurted out, managing to not say the – you know what, I was going to stop thinking about it.

Night smiled.

"I have gotten the opportunity to do so, yes."

228

I made some more polite conversation with Night, reminded strongly of the many nights we spent together, slowly walking around the Ranger Academy island. After some time, I spotted Bulwark and headed over, eager to share a few words with him. Hadn't seen him since we'd gotten here, after all.

"Bulwark! Good work on the walls! They looked good!" I said, cheerfully toasting my mug at him.

"Dawn. Excellent work with the soldiers. Caught a whole stream of them exiting one of the infirmaries you were in. Don't mind the walls though, they're a rough job. I need to go back over them and fix them properly later."

Note to self: Chat with all the Sentinels about this area being a disaster.

I kept moving around, chatting with the rest of the Sentinels. Toxic, all moody in his mug, permanently tilted back as he tried to get hammered. Hard work, with all that extra mass and vitality. Then again, alcohol brewed by people with the right classes was good for counteracting high vitality. Which is why I had to be somewhat careful about what I grabbed. Then again, I could always partially cure myself down to the right level of drunk. Destruction, making water sculptures, having them move around in a jerky, uncoordinated fashion. Practicing and showing off his fancy new class. First person any of us had ever heard of reaching 512, and getting a third class.

Poor Night. Relegated to a footnote, since Destruction classed-up first, and would get all the fame for the act. I could practically hear the tune that the Ranger's bard would use, both for the epic battle, Demos's sacrifice, and Destruction's power and growth.

That was assuming the bard was honest. Or that the Sentinels gave him the honest, real story, for that matter. We were the victors, we were writing the history. It'd be whatever we said it was.

I was strongly on the "tell the damn truth" side of things, but it occurred to me that if we all agreed that something happened, it'd be in the history books as having happened that way.

Scary.

For that matter – Night might've had Destruction go first, just so he could stay in the shadows.

Too much thinking for how many drinks I had in me.

Brawling and Nature were arms-over-shoulders with each other, loudly belting out songs. Nobody was bold enough to tell them just how horribly off-key they were, but there it was.

I didn't see Hunting around the fire, and I decided to poke in and check up on him. I entered the tent, and saw him curled up and lying down. I hit myself with **[Dance with the Heavens]**. I wasn't going to fuck this up horribly by being too drunk.

I sat down next to him. I didn't say anything, I didn't do anything but sip my mug.

I didn't think anything else needed to be done. Just some companionship, letting him know he was not alone in the world.

I don't know how much time passed before Brawling popped in.

"Dawn. Hunting. The memorial's going to begin." He said.

I got up and left, and after a moment I heard Hunting get up and join me.

Night stood in front of us all, fire flickering large behind him.

"Sentinel Hunting. Sentinel Dawn. Sentinel Destruction. Sentinel Bulwark. Sentinel Nature. Sentinel Brawling. Sentinel Toxic." Night said. "Thank you all for coming here tonight."

"Tonight we are gathered to remember our brothers-in-arms who have died, fallen against the Formorians in their last, desperate strike. Each one a master of their craft, protectors and defenders of humanity."

Couldn't help it. The waterworks started, and the only dry eyes were Night's inhuman ones. Even then, there was a glimmer to them that wasn't entirely explained by the lighting.

"Sentinel Sealing fell fighting against the Formorian Queen, stopping nearly a dozen Royal Guards simultaneously. His efforts opened a pathway, allowing for myself and Sentinel

Hunting to strike at the Queen. His work was not in vain, as all of humanity can now rest more easily as a result. He made the highest sacrifice possible, the last sacrifice, and his name shall forever be remembered on the Indomitable Wall."

Night closed his eyes, and with a start I realized this wasn't any easier on him than it was on us. Losing another Sentinel was like losing a friend to him, regardless of how many centuries had passed. He still *felt*. He still grew attached and lost, let the pain and the grief rip through him time, after time, after time.

I should have a chat with him. I should start working on some long, long, *long* term plans, along with acquiring coping methods. Why stumble through it in the dark, when I've got someone to give me a hand?

I mentally slapped myself. Funeral. *Fucking focus.*

"Sentinel Sky fell fighting against the same Formorian Queen, as he moved in to assist the angels that Priest Demos called down upon them." Night said, keeping it short and sweet.

Or rather – this was the kindest possible description of Sky's end, who'd been a *fucking idiot* to think that he was invincible in the sky, that "lowly ground-grubbing bugs" weren't able to take him out. I hadn't seen his end, but from what I'd gathered up in bits and pieces and snatches – he wanted to see the angels, be close to them, fight with them. Ignoring the fact that they were probably significantly more powerful than he was, and they were dying anyways. Sheer hubris had brought Sky low, disregarding entities on the ground.

I bet that if the Formorian anti-air had been fliers, that Sky would've treated them with the proper respect they deserved, and he wouldn't have ended up dead.

Or hell! If he'd just bloody *stayed with the rest of the team!*

It made me so mad. Sky was essentially dead because he'd been an idiot, and did something dumb.

I was stewing in such a self-inflicted rage that I'd missed the rest of the short portion of Sky's speech. Which just got me madder at myself, and more than a bit sad. This was Sky's end. This was his funeral, and I got fucking distracted. This. Sucked.

"I would like to bring our attention to our last casualty." Night began, and the outraged look on Hunting's face just poured oil over my anger. Night's callous dismissal of Katastrofi was earning him no brownie points here.

"Katastrofi, while not a Sentinel, was companion to one. Brave. Fearless. A terror to all who beheld her magnificence."

Hunting let out a choked chuckle at that, his face rapidly turning from rage to relief, from anger to gratefulness.

"Bound Companion to Sentinel Hunting, Katastrofi was more than just a beast of burden. More than the deadliest killing machine in a century. She was *aware*. She made friends, held grudges, was a part of our family like any other Sentinel was. Indeed, I believe that her name belongs on the Indomitable Wall. Now. I wish for a moment of silence, of remembrance."

I closed my eyes and bowed my head, repeating their names in my mind. Sealing. Sky. Katastrofi.

Katastrofi. First one I'd met, my introduction to real, live Sentinels, in the flesh and blood. Sentinels had been creatures out of myth and legend until I'd met her, and she had been my first chance ever to ride a dinosaur. Her tie-dye color scheme was etched into my memory, the riot of color unforgettable.

Sky. One of my teachers, who, in spite of his poor reputation and even poorer teaching methods, had successfully helped me to get a flying skill. As much as he gave off an aloof air, as much as he just winged his lessons, he was around when I first started. He caught my fellow trainees as they fell. He was careful to warn me about the skies, and the perils they could hold.

Sealing. I hadn't had as much time interacting with him, but he'd given off a kind vibe. Made sure that I was shielded when one of the Sentinel's brawls broke out. Selflessly helped me out, without teasing or rebuke, as I'd had trouble holding my portion of the grove.

Lastly, there was Magic. I spent a brief moment wondering why we weren't mourning him, before remembering that he'd been declared missing in action. The ultimate magic trick – he'd made himself disappear! He was presumed dead, but barring additional evidence, the passage of enough time, or, we hoped, him popping up one day declaring himself alive, he was going to stay as missing in action.

The more time that passed, the less likely it seemed. Magic's paranoia, illusions, and invisibility was great for dodging the arrow with his name on it.

The barrage of spikes labeled "To Whom It May Concern", however, was an entirely different story.

Magic was no coward. He was no shirk. He wouldn't have bailed on us, he wouldn't have gone invisible and stayed on the *Pegasus*. He had been a soldier, then a Ranger, then selected from the Rangers as one of the best of the best, an elite, a Sentinel. For all his quirks, for all his paranoia, he wasn't one to run from a fight.

I was hoping that he'd broken his leg in the fall, and being unable to reach us, had holed up somewhere, quiet, invisible. Part of that theory was dampened by the knowledge that he had a half-dozen Moonstones with my old **[Phases of the Moon]** in them, a cure-all that would fix any injury he had.

My heart refused to write him off. I'd have faith that he was still alive out there, until Night declared otherwise. We were Sentinels. Stranger things had happened than vanishing on a mission and showing up a decade later, with wild and fantastic tales.

"I first met Sealing when I was a fresh recruit at Ranger Academy." Brawling spoke up, breaking the silence, words punctuated by the fire crackling. "He told me that I was a muscle-bound idiot, and that I needed to start thinking one day."

Brawling shrugged.

"Still wondering when that day will be."

A few cracked smiles, a half-hearted chuckle.

"I first met Sky at Ranger Academy." I said, surprising myself. "His lesson on flying was basically 'don't hit the ground', which was about as useless of a lesson as you can imagine. Somehow, that was good enough to get me a flying skill."

A couple more chuckles. A few more smiles.

On and on we went through the night, each of us trading stories of the Sentinels, of Katastrofi. Sharing memories, making a new one. Trading, just a little bit of each other.

My resolve strengthened. My desire grew stronger.

Sky. Sealing. Katastrofi. Their names would end up on the Indomitable Wall, carved in stone to remember for all eternity.

Screw that. I was going to carve them into my memory, into my recollections. I'd have a **[Pristine Memory]** of them. I was going to become immortal, and remember them forever, a never-ending living legacy for all of them. All I needed to do was level up like crazy, and unlock **[The Stars Never Fade]**.

It wouldn't be the same, but they, too, would be timeless, forever immortalized in my memory.

My list was growing longer.

Lyra. Origen. Sealing. Sky. Katastrofi.

I closed my eyes again; more tears squeezed out.

More names would join the list. It was inevitable.

Chapter 22

Aftermath

Our celebration of everyone's lives had gone on for hours, and the sky was already starting to lighten as we all went to sleep. I hit my pillow and was out like a light.

A soft hand on my shoulder, and I bolted upright, ready to fight, to blast, to protect myself and – oh, it was just Night.

"Huh? Night? Whazzup?" I asked him, adrenaline fleeing and the siren song of sleep soothing me back down. My eyelids were so heavy, I was ready to go right back to sleep.

A pounding headache was letting me know that I'd gotten maybe 15 minutes of sleep *tops*, and the tent getting slightly lighter as the sun threatened to break over the horizon let me know that, yes, almost no time had passed. I was totally ready for more sleep.

"Dawn. I apologize for disturbing your rest. However, I wish to speak with you, alone." Night said.

Welp, up and at 'em. **[Sunrise]** was a miracle skill, and I was happy to see a notification for it leveling up.

[*ding!* [Sunrise] leveled up! 2 -> 3]

My eyes flew open as energy bounded through me, although my headache was a persistent reminder that I was running on practically no sleep.

Note to self: Spam the heck out of the skill to try and get it leveled up faster. With my power and regeneration shooting up, I should be able to level it quickly.

Assuming the amount of power I shot through the skill impacted the leveling speed, and there weren't more arcane aspects to leveling up that I was unaware of. Danger I knew about, stress I knew about, properly using skills was a yup.

Right, well, I'd try to remember to use **[Sunrise]**, although it was a risky move. If I spent all my time thinking about using my skill, I wouldn't be paying attention to other things.

Like the private conversation my technically-not boss and 5,000 plus year old vampire and I was going to have.

I shook my head as I got up, and followed Night out of the tent.

Focus.

I fell in naturally by his side as we walked through the cold and dark camp, passing by the occasional party that refused to die, in spite of most of the participants being stone-cold out.

I was reminded of our many walks together, our discussions. If I had my way, if I managed to do everything right, we'd have a bunch of centuries like this. Kinda intimidating to think about. At the same time, Night clearly knew how to stay alive. It was probably safe to get somewhat emotionally attached, since he wasn't going anywhere anytime soon.

"Dawn." Night said, and paused.

Step.

Step.

"Yes?" I asked, thanking my lucky stars (ha! I probably had a few of those, given that my element was Celestial) that **[Sunrise]** had woken me up, stopping me from slurring my words in spite of the massive sleep deficit I was running.

Classing up wasn't really sleep, and I'd been running myself ragged for awhile, before the party and the mourning.

"First off, I would like to say, excellent work. You are a credit to all of us, to all Sentinels, and to humanity as a whole."

My heart swelled three sizes at his praise. Praise I didn't know I wanted, but nonetheless struck deep inside, resonated with me. Put a great big silly grin on my face. No matter how hard I worked, no matter how hard I tried to school my expression, it was stuck on.

"Thank you." I managed to say, with only a bit of warbling.

Step.

Step.

I loved the processing time built into Night's discussions. Let me organize my thoughts.

"Before I forget, I wanted to let you know I got offered **[Ranger-Healer]** when I was classing up. Given the history of the Rangers, I think it's a first. Wanted to let you know about it."

Night gave me a long look, a smile tugging at the corner of his mouth.

"Excellent work Dawn. From our prior conversation, I recall you did not take said class?" He half-asked, half-stated. I had told him about the special class after all.

I shook my head. I figured I'd eventually tell him, given the long history I expected us to have together. Why not tell him now?

"I got **[The Dawn Sentinel]**." I told him. I wanted to explode and tell him all about **[The Stars Never Fade]**, but I didn't even have the skill yet. It'd feel a bit like bragging.

I also kinda wanted to feel out Night's reaction to it ahead of time. He'd been a paragon of reason and virtue the entire time I'd known him, if a bit long-winded. However, as a human I'd level up significantly faster than he would, and would eventually overtake him, in relatively short order. Well, as far as the timeline he worked on was concerned. And that I would soon be working with. Either way, I'm pretty sure his reaction would be favorable, but eh. I was in no rush to tell people about a skill I'd get many years in the future.

"An excellent choice. There have been a few Sentinels over the years who have had the choice to perform their level 256 class-up, and out of those, the ones who have taken the class corresponding to their titles have all done well. I believe a part of that is since Sentinel encompasses a great many things, you acquire strong experience for a wide variety of activities, which should help you level at a rapid rate."

We paused for a moment, to keep walking as I digested that.

I wasn't too surprised that I wasn't the first Sentinel to perform their 256 class-up. Heck, thinking about it, my level had never been called out when I was being promoted. I assumed it was because they didn't want to bring attention to my low level, but perhaps it was just that it wasn't anything special. "The 11th lowest-level Ranger to be promoted" didn't quite have the same ring to it. For all I know, in the earliest days of the Rangers and Sentinels, they just took who they could until a solid system was sorted out.

Which in some ways made me being the first woman Sentinel all the worse, but I wasn't about to explore that tangent.

"I would like to speak about the main subject at this time. While this may be a touch premature, I believe once everything has been arranged and analyzed, most of us will be heading home." Night said.

'Most of us', and 'private conversation' translated into 'you're not coming with us.' At least, that's how I saw it.

"What do you plan for me to do?" I asked bluntly, still on the high of Night's compliment.

Step.

Step.

Night *hummed* to himself, a single held note.

"It is complicated. Let me attempt to give you the compressed version of what I believe will be happening next, along with skipping over a thousand tiny details. Like the inevitable coup that at least three generals are planning. Oh, sure, it will occur after the cleansing of the Formorians inside of human lands, but as the Generals finish mopping up the remnants, their armies will only grow more loyal, their fame spread, and themselves closer to the capital."

"Wait, but –" I started to say, only for Night to whirl and slash his hand in front of me in a violent motion, cutting me off.

"Permit me to finish." Night said, a note of displeasure in his voice. "We have much to cover, and your namesake arrives. No, we will not be participating. We are Sentinels. We are *neutral.* This is no mere rebellion, no slave uprising. The government is scratching and turning itself over. It happens. Remus will survive. No, a side issue, a minor note in all of this, is you would be all-too-tempted to join the fray, not to fight, but to heal. Inevitably it would be noted that a Sentinel was participating, assisting some general or another, then ugly politics would rear its head and drag us in, kicking and screaming. Either we are seen to be fermenting and participating in the rebellion, assisting one general over the rest, or it is civil war among the Sentinels, which detracts from our primary purpose and mission. Either way, we lose."

Night fiercely breathed in and out, and I realized this was no picnic for him either.

"We are taking the long view, staying neutral, and our mission of protecting humanity will continue uninterrupted. Now. As I said. This is a minor side-note. The Formorian Queens are all dead – so we believe. The endless waves of Formorians have ceased."

A pause, a note of victory and triumph.

Step.

Step.

"Now, Hunting has just lost his sworn companion, the other half of his soul, the reason for his being. I have seen it before. It is devastating him, tearing him apart. I do not wish to lose another Sentinel, not when we have three seats to fill already. Especially not when two of those seats are critical seats, and Hunting's seat is also critical."

I half-opened my mouth to object to Night writing Magic off like that, but closed it. Magic was likely dead. It was no treachery to assume that was the case and operate like he was gone. It was just cold pragmatism. Made me wish we had properly mourned Magic like everyone else though.

The "critical seats" thing I hadn't even heard of, but with Night's habit of letting us think and process, I was able to examine the idea. Kinda made sense, from his point of view. We always needed a Sentinel that could get us moved around quickly, that could let us deploy to any place in the Republic within two days. Without that, we'd lose a huge amount of our effectiveness.

I couldn't tell if Night considered Sealing's or Magic's seat to be critical – I could see arguments either way – but I could see Hunting being critical.

I had no illusions that I was critical. Maybe if I demonstrated my usefulness over the decades and centuries, my seat would morph into a critical one, but that'd be kinda moot, since any plan that involved "Replacing Elaine" usually also involve "Because she died."

I *could* eventually retire though. A thought for another day.

This immortal stuff was ridiculously trippy. It was almost as bad as when I got promoted to Sentinel, and all my plans got thrown out the window. Was it too much to ask for that a 5-year-plan get properly executed for once!?

… I said, being 19.

"It is my experience that the best thing possible is for Hunting to be given a mission, a quest, a job to take his mind off his grief, and keep him focused on other things. It is no guarantee, and I could be incorrect, however, simply allowing him to wallow is a poor move. Especially as he is prone to retreating to his estate, which has marks of Katastrofi all over it. I believe it will simply fuel his despair."

I could see where this was going. I gave a customary pause, as short as possible, before replying.

"Let me guess. You want to send him into Formorian lands to check that everything's properly dead, but mostly to keep him busy."

Night nodded at me once it was clear that was all I had to say.

"Correct. Now, for the tricky part, the part that I do not wish to state in front of the rest of the Sentinels, and the reason for our private discussion."

I was all ears. I didn't even need **[Sunrise]** to get me all perked up and listening.

Actually, for that matter, I should probably use a **[Sunrise]** just to keep myself going. Grinding experience and all that.

[*ding!* **[Sunrise] leveled up! 3 -> 4]**

Hurray! More levels! I should do it some –
I should listen to bloody Night and not get distracted!
Focus.

Sleep deprivation was one way to make sure my mind was on permanent wander mode.

"I wish for you to accompany Hunting on his mission. Nominally, it is to provide him support and back up, along with allowing you to flex and practice your new abilities somewhat away from prying eyes. Prevent Toxic's poisons from getting to him. I truly have this concern, as the concentration should be significantly higher the deeper into the Formorian lands the two of you travel. Additionally, it is to give Hunting some relief, and allow him to take breaks and have support."

He was right – the excuse was fairly weak, and I'd normally object to it. I wasn't just a support minion. I was the one with support minions.

Step.

Step.

"In reality, I wish for you to watch over him. Provide him support, yes. Support of the type he'd get from Katastrofi, in a sense. Prevent him from mentally reaching out for her, only to find a gap, an emptiness. It should help distract him. Lastly, I do not wish for him to commit suicide, and I believe your presence nearby will help. You are calming. Soothing. You blunt rough edges. You are often happiness and light, and I believe you will prevent Hunting's mind from straying towards darker territory. However. If I state this in public, in front of the others – especially Hunting – most of the purpose of sending you is lost. Thus, our conversation now."

We reached some mysterious point as the sun's rays were starting to creep down the wall, walking at a brisk clip back to our tent.

I thought over what Night was saying.

Basically, he was killing thirty birds with one stone. We needed to check that the Formorians were fully uprooted. Hunting needed something to do – and his role happened to coincide with 'go find Formorians and make sure they're dead'. There was a potential civil war brewing, or so Night believed. I hadn't seen hide, hair, nor whisper of anything like that, but I trusted Night's analysis on that. I wasn't the most politically astute, and it wasn't like I hung out with generals, nor would the generals send a polite letter to the Senate telling them about it.

Heck, it was almost Julius Caesar-like. Or Sulla. I didn't know my Roman history all that well. Massive victory, huge, loyal army, no external enemies left – only thing to do was to march home and declare oneself emperor.

Sounded like more than one general had that plan. There was probably some vast web of politics and intrigue, and the more I thought about it the sicker I felt. Night was totally right. I would try to get involved, if only to heal people, and simply hanging out would cause problems. Heck, knowing me, I'd end up getting roped into some scheme or another, think I was being nice and helpful, and OOPS! Turns out I'd accidentally dragged everyone into some massive mess, just by trying to be helpful.

I knew I could be a bit of an idiot with politics and the like, which is why I tried to run screaming from it. *Usually* that wasn't a problem, because "kill the monster, save people" wasn't terribly complicated, but when people were fighting each other, it got real tricky real fast.

Getting me out of the way, out of the mess before it could properly begin was an okay move. I'd honestly rather stick myself in a wagon, close the door, and get carted back to the capital while sleeping and eating good food, but hey. There were more problems to fix. For all I knew, the cart would get hijacked without me being aware of it, and I'd be carted around as a healing beacon, all while thinking I was out of the mess.

Sending me with Hunting seemed to be the second or third best solution to the "Dawn's going to cause problems" problem, but it did solve a number of other problems.

It wasn't like most of those other problems that I was solving could be easily aired out in public, in front of the rest of the Sentinels.

Right then. I was feeling the steam coming out of my ears. This wasn't the type of problem I was equipped to handle, and I was going to happily pass it off to someone who I believed had my best interests – all of our best interests – at heart, and listen to what he wanted to do.

After all the time processing, we were nearing the tent, Night looking distinctly nervous.

"Right. I'll do it." I told him, as the tent came into view.

Night smiled, a huge, predatory slash across his face.

"Most excellent."

I paused outside the tent, and a grumpy look crossed my face.

"Night. Can we have some privacy – some real privacy – for a second chat?" I asked him.

He looked at my face, and slowly nodded.

"Follow." He said, opening the tent-flap, allowing me to enter first. I did, thanking him, and we made our way to Night's portion of the tent, where with a thought red liquid snapped around us, surrounding us, cutting us off from the rest of the world.

"Night." I said, organizing my thoughts.

"Dawn. I am listening. Speak." He said, with a serious look on his face. I'm glad that he treated me seriously, that he listened to me.

"I recognize that your position is difficult." I said, trying to be somewhat diplomatic. It was *hard,* interacting with people and yelling at your boss, especially when stupid sleep deprived. I felt a cold trickle of sweat going down my back that had nothing to do with the temperature.

"However, that's no excuse for not letting me know what was going on here! I could've been here! I could've been saving people! Heck, I was here, if I'd known there was a problem, I could've been working on it! People are dead as a result, that didn't need to be! Why didn't you tell me!?"

I'd started off calm, but got more and more upset as I went through my rant. Fuck. No more emotional stability from **[Center of the Galaxy]**. It's what I wanted, but…

What was done was done.

"Dawn. If you were here, you could not have been deployed to Aquiliea. If you were here, you would not have saved the souls in Pompeius. There are dozens of calls for Sentinels every month. You know that we must choose when and where to deploy, to optimally save the largest number of people. You know this. The balance of the scales would not be appropriately

243

tipped by your knowledge and presence. It was a decision I made. Now, do you have any further objections or comments?"

I turned and angrily stamped off, Night dismissing the barrier before I hit it.

I hated how right he was.

I got a few more hours of sleep. All of us needed the rest, and it was late afternoon by the time I was woken up again.

My internal clock was totally screwed. Getting back on a normal sleep cycle was going to be all sorts of fun.

All of us, except for Destruction, got up, fixed some food – rations were starting to run low, with the supply lines having been cut off when the Formorians broke through, then the huge party following our victory was pushing our supplies dangerously thin – then we sat around the central table, Destruction's snoring punctuating our conversation.

He'd stayed awake for almost three weeks straight. We were all willing to cut him some slack.

Night laid out the situation once again, going much more in-depth into the upcoming movements and potential changes in governing structure that was being planned. I was half snoozing through it, half doing my own thinking.

Just because a rebellion was headed by a general, with a significant portion of the army behind him, didn't make it any less of a rebellion. Night having spent thousands of years in the military might be skewing his view a hair on the matter. It wasn't like this was the first time someone had taken a chunk of the army on their way to 'correct' things in Remus.

At the same time, by the sounds of it, something like 70%+ of the army was getting involved in some way, shape, or form. I was no political genius – heck, I was a political moron – but when that much of the army, the people with the sharp swords and deadly skills were saying 'this person's the new boss', well. It was kinda hard to argue with them.

The only people that would be arguing with them were the other parts of the army that wanted someone else to be the boss, and yeah. It was shaping up to be real ugly, real fast, if there wasn't some nice place for the army to be. In a way, the Formorians had been good. They were a source of external pressure keeping everyone united. Almost the literal minute the external pressure was gone, we fell into infighting and bickering.

Blah. Working together for the common good was just too much for some people.

I kept listening in on the conversation, not having much to add. It was all 'implied support' this and 'appearance of neutrality' that. I got a bit more interested once we moved on from the topic.

"Do you want me to stay here to turn the fortifications into a town?" Bulwark asked. "It's out of the way, and it's part of what I do. It helps that the only people it'll look like I'm helping are the soldiers staying out of the fight, which should help with our appearance of neutrality. We already have walls, the expensive part's done. If it wasn't for the breach, the place would already *be* a town." Bulwark said, to almost everyone nodding along to what he was saying.

Toxic and I exchanged horrified looks. A quizzical tilt of my head, a sharp jerk by his. Silent, non-Ranger-standard communication.

Afterall, everyone here could read Ranger communication.

"No." Toxic and I both said together.

Night looked at us and frowned.

"Are you certain?" He asked.

"Absolutely." I said, giving him a *look*. One that tried to say that he better go along with my plan if he wanted me to go along with his.

Ok, fine. I was going to help Hunting out either way. I didn't want him diving deep into despair anymore than Night did. I liked Hunting too much for that.

Toxic took in a deep breath.

"It's the poison I was using." He said, chin up, staring unblinkingly at each one of us until he moved onto the next person to lock eyes with.

"It's poisoned the land, the soil, the water. It's poisoned everything, and it's cycling back through. Anyone that lives here, anything that's grown here, will have small traces of the poison."

Brawling sprayed the water he was drinking out of his mouth, onto all of us. A shield flickered in front of Bulwark and Night as they expertly deflected the surprise attack.

Toxic stoically accepted the spray as his due punishment. Nature seemed delighted to get some water for his plants – well, water that didn't come from his mug, and Hunting seemed to just not care.

Destruction was snoring through it all.

Which left me, spluttering with indignation as I got sprayed. I didn't have the reflexes to handle surprise water attacks from close-range, not without **[Bullet Time]** giving me a hand. For all that **[Bullet Time]** occasionally stretched to help me with not quite lethal situations, there was *no way* it was going to help me with surprise water.

I shot my deadliest, most withering look at Brawling, who was still staring at the mug with a look of horror.

"Dawn! Quick! You gotta save me!" Brawling said, reaching across the table to touch me.

I kept up my mad face as I touched him, letting **[Dance with the Heavens]** pulse through him.

No mana drained.

"Thanks! Thought I was a goner. Cute angry face by the way."

Right.

"You idiot! If the poison was bad enough to kill *the* physical Sentinel after being diluted a million times, we wouldn't be sitting here discussing it, now would we!" I shouted at Brawling. "We'd all be dead a dozen times over!"

Brawling looked kinda sheepish at that, and was getting unimpressed looks from the rest of the Sentinels.

"If Toxic were that lethal, there wouldn't be a single living soul in the camp." Night softly said. "Nor would we have had this issue with the Formorians. We digress. Back to the subject at hand. Dawn. Toxic. New towns and cities are troublesome to arrange and build, to say the least. Properly founding a new location is a massive undertaking, requiring scouts, an army legion, a nearby quarry, and mining large quantities of stone to build walls in the first place. We have an opportunity here, a town, ready-made and able to accept settlers, with pre-established trade routes. On the other hand, the area is slightly poisonous."

Night closed his eyes, thinking about it, then opened them up.

"Right. While this situation is larger than just us, we move as a unit. We move as one. Our words have weight, meaning, gravitas. What will our recommendation for the future of this encampment be? Discuss."

Chapter 23

Sentinel Meeting

The conversation about what to do with the frontlines, now maybe being turned into a town, went on for hours. I was surprised that we got so sidetracked on the issue, but then again, I suppose we weren't all going to be in the same place for some time, and Toxic and I were *the* experts on the subject.

With the current plan Night and I had hatched, my expertise was going away for some time. If we were going to resolve the issue, we were going to resolve it now.

On the "turn the place into a town" side, we had Nature and Bulwark, with Night leaning in that direction.

On the "call the place a disaster" side, Toxic and I were the staunchest supporters, with Brawling providing eager, if haphazard support.

"The economic realities, and difficulties of forming a new town, strongly support that we divert the current resources in an optimal fashion." Bulwark pointed out, circling back to the fundamental argument that he was working off of. Large-scale construction like this was insanely expensive. It was hard to overstate how expensive.

"Getting a number of healers to immigrate to the new town shouldn't be terribly difficult. Indeed, it should be simple to lure them to this place, with the allure of a constant stream of patients." Night pointed out, trying to be somewhat neutral but once again showing that he was leaning towards the "Town" faction.

"Yeah, but then how are you getting people to join?" Brawling 'innocently' pointed out. Dude was shrewder than he let on. Asked 'dumb' questions, which were striking at the heart of the problem.

Half the time he acted like an oaf, and the other half he acted like a cunning strategist. I kept yo-yoing if the first one was entirely an act that he put on, to make people fall for the 'dumb brute' stereotype, then he could whammy them when they weren't looking.

"Telling people 'Move here! Pay frequently for healers because it's poisoned!' isn't going to encourage a lot of movement." Brawling continued to point out.

"Speaking of the economics of the situation." I jumped in. "What's this place even going to produce? All the money that had come in here was from soldier's pay. Without that money coming in, what would this theoretical town even make?" I asked. "With no trade goods, nobody will come. Like Laconia."

I swear I almost saw Origen's smiling face, as I half-parroted his arguments, his reason for becoming an Inscriptionist and his detailing of the problems that Laconia faced. Arguably the last thing he'd ever managed to teach me.

"People will come." Nature argued. "Cheap, plentiful land is attractive to any number of retired soldiers, and others who are being crowded out of some of the more compact cities. Where would you rather live? In a small apartment in the capital, or being able to purchase a large tract of land, inside city walls, for the same price? Not everyone will take the offer, but enough will. What people do from there is up to them, but there's more than enough land to grow enough crops to support the city on its own merits. Heck, the Formorian land might be some of the richest land we'll ever have the chance to expand onto. They would've cleared out anything and everything that could be a threat. Almost monster-free land? People will be lining up for it."

I decided to switch track, to a potentially more profitable line of argument.

"Sure, people might grow stuff. Wheat, even. Poisoned wheat. Who's going to want to buy it? Putting that aside for the moment, what woman's going to want to come here, and poison all her kids? Knowing that kids are more vulnerable, that it takes less poison to kill one."

I glanced over, and saw Arthur's blanched face.

"Sorry Toxic." I said, patting his arm in what I hoped was a reassuring way.

"How many?" Hunting asked, contributing for only the third time in three hours.

Toxic instantly knew what Hunting was asking, and had a response.

"371 people in the last 430 days." He said, without a moment's hesitation, a small shudder going through his body. Numbers that must be carved into his mind, a litany recited.

"The camps are – were – huge." Hunting pointed out. "The number of dead versus the number present are highly suggestive that, while it will be a problem, it'll be a minor problem at worst. Also, conjured material decays over time. Worst-case, eight years from now there'll be no poison."

"It's accelerating. Also, we thought this might take years. I didn't directly conjure the poison. I enhanced an existing poison. It acted a bit like one of Dawn's diseases, where it multiplied inside the Formorians. It'll last decades, if not centuries." Toxic pointed out. Then again, that was new information to us, since we had no way of knowing that.

"It'll hopefully decelerate now that you're no longer contributing more poison to the mix." I said, feeling like a traitor for making a point against the "Disaster" team.

Still. I had strong notions about fair play and discussion, and it'd be unfair for me to not bring it up.

"At the same time, it would probably keep accelerating for some time, as the poison builds up and reaches critical mass." I said, trying to give the other point of view.

"Also, while women might not want their families poisoned, it's usually the Patriarch of the family who's making the decision." Bulwark pointed out, in what was a fairly diplomatic manner.

Still had me somewhat annoyed. Also, Bulwark was obviously not married.

"You think that the Patriarch's wife doesn't have his ear, and can't twist it as needed?" I asked him, in that soft tone that let him know that he was on dangerous, thin ice.

Bulwark looked at me, heard my tone, and decided to shut up and concede the minor point.

Night spent most of this looking thoughtful.

"Toxic. How difficult would it be for a Classer with the right skills to remove your efforts, and restore the place to its natural state?" He asked.

Arthur sucked in air through his teeth.

"Decades, if not more. It's spread far, it's spread deep. It's spread all the way to the Formorian lairs, it got deep inside their hive."

Brawling slipped in another 'innocent' question.

"Can't you just grab it with your skills and be done with it?" He asked, wide-eyed and 'innocent'.

If even I had caught onto his act, I doubt it was fooling anyone else. It did give a nice avenue for Toxic to expand.

"I'm not a Poison mage, I'm a Poison ranger. I create, enhance, and spread, I don't manipulate or anything like that. I can't go around and grab my poison; I can't pick it back up. That's the purview of a different class."

Toxic frowned.

"It doesn't help that I built a poison that wouldn't degrade naturally. We thought it'd take a lot longer for this to have an impact."

I had a moment of inspiration.

"Remember how Brawling sprayed water everywhere earlier?" I asked, getting some nods and side-eyes as people tried to figure out where I was going with this. "Imagine a week later, a month later, coming back here and trying to pick up every drop of water that he sprayed. That's the problem with Toxic's poison. It's had time to spread out and travel. It's not easy to just wave a hand and fix it."

We continued the discussion and argument for hours more, Destruction waking up and joining in the later half. He was mostly lost as to what was going on, and kept mostly silent.

"Right." Night said, once we'd all had a late dinner, having spent way too much time on the matter. "I believe I have an acceptable compromise, which I would like to bring forth as a proposal for how we shall move forward on this matter, and how we shall advise the powers that be to act on the matter."

"First. The location should be turned into a town. Economic realities demand it."

I was throwing Night a sour look, which just bounced right off of him.

"However, the matter of Toxic's work can not be ignored. Those wishing to come here shall be well-informed of the matter. Additional healers will be well-incentivized to come, potentially being paid for by the governor. After all, they are providing a constant service to all. That particular point may need some negotiating with whoever ends up taking command of the area. Lastly, we will need dozens of men with the appropriate classes and skills to come, and work on purging the land itself, freeing it from the insidious toxins that have come to rest in it."

Interesting. Between my upcoming work with Hunting, the impending civil war, this area being somewhat safe and needing some healer's presence, I saw the possibility that I might be here for quite a few years. Maybe bouncing back and forth between here and the capital. I'd still want to see my family.

I reluctantly nodded my approval at the plan.

"I don't like it." I said. "I'd rather *nobody* died, and the area was closed off until it was totally purged. But...." I trailed off, looking around. "There's no way I'm getting that, is there?"

The looks I was getting suggested that, no, I wasn't getting that.

"Fine. But I'd like to make a minor suggestion. Advertise *heavily* that I'm against it." I said, crossing my arms, trying to throw Night another pointed look.

Everyone else had more suggestions, more little modifications to the plan that we pitched in and added.

As everyone was talking, a realization *dawned* on me.

Long term planning. The frontlines, probably going to be turned into a town – tentative name Feronia, although we didn't decide that – was going to be a ghost town for some time. People would need to move, immigrate. A governor would be needed, etc. Shame that the camp followers were all 'gone', if they weren't they'd be the perfect start to the town. They just wouldn't leave, and boom! Roaring town.

Anyways. The long and the short of it was, there was large amounts of land for extraordinarily cheap prices here, right now. Over time, over decades and centuries, if all went well, the town would become populated, squeezed by the walls, and real estate prices would rise.

I had wagonloads of money. Ok, technically, as the law saw it, my dad had wagonloads of money. He knew better than to try and argue it with me. He'd tried *once,* and mom had given him such a telling off, then made him sleep in the vestibule for a week. Anyways.

Sentinel pay was lucrative, on top of my healing business. Sure, I only got a tiny fraction of what I could be getting, but I was still pulling two large, generous incomes. I was probably going to find myself living in Feronia anyways, to help with the poison. Night's example of 'how to become fabulously wealthy as an immortal' was still in mind.

I grimaced to myself. I was about to be a massive hypocrite wasn't I? "Don't move to Feronia! Ignore the fact that I'm purchasing huge swaths of land here!"

The optics were subpar to boot.

Although... everything being in my dad's name to the rescue! I wouldn't be buying it, oh no. Marcus Elainus Cato would be buying it, and generously allowing the Sentinels to base out of the estates while any Sentinel is in town. It was long-term *excellent* for me, it worked short-term, it just made me feel a hair icky.

Blah. The more I bought, the more expensive everything else would be. The whole thing was a messy, convoluted circle, and I had perfect entry-level theoretical knowledge on the subject, courtesy of **[Pristine Memories]**, from having read a book on the subject decades ago. Didn't mean I knew how it'd turn out, nor *which* theory would be correct and apply.

A problem for future-me. I should get in the habit of reducing the number of future-me problems.

We *finally* came to a consensus on how we Sentinels wanted to handle the question of the new town. Of course, we'd need to convince the powers that be – the Senate, in this case – to our viewpoint, which meant convincing command, the endless meetings with Senators. Which had me come to a realization...

"Ocean's going to hate us for this. His input would've been great." I lamented.

That got a few chuckles around the table, which quickly turned into roars and howls of laughter.

Brawling was wiping a tear from the corner of his eye.

"He. He he. Yeah. I'ma buy him a beer then break the news to him. You should all come watch. Make bets how far he sprays it."

Night was also chuckling.

"Sadly, I do not believe we will all be present for such an event. Bulwark. I believe with our current plans, that you have work that you should do. Is there anything that would prevent you from deploying here?"

Bulwark cocked his head, spending a moment drumming his fingers on the table.

"Not that I can think of. Let me know how long you can spare me, it'll let me know what's priority to build, and how much effort I can spend on it."

Made sense. He couldn't just blink and be done; he had a ton of planning to do. A one-man civil engineering department. If he only had a week, he'd probably do slap-dash repairs on the walls about to fall over. If he had a month, we'd get a solid grid of roads to go with it. If he had a year, the foundation of a dozen homes and businesses would be laid, temples and marketplaces laid out, with the city divided into planned grids, ready for people to descend upon it.

If he had a decade, with all the resources at his disposal and no pesky people in the way to slow him down, he'd build the framework of a city that would last for centuries.

Of course, if he was told he had a decade, then three weeks later got pulled to a critical hotspot, none of his work would be usable. He would've spent the entire time measuring and planning.

There was a long pause as Night thought, juggling hundreds if not thousands of things in his mind. The more I saw of Night the more impressed I was. Not only was he a peerless fighter, arguably the strongest we had in spite of Destruction's new class, but he was also a brilliant administrator, inspirational leader, and learned mentor.

"Eight months. I believe you can be away, here, for eight to fourteen months, depending on how the flow of the whole mess occurs. This is predicated that there is not another incident like Massalix which threatens to have us lose an entire city."

Night got an angry look on his face as he thought of that, and angrily spat out.

"I do not wish to speak ill of the dead, but Sky, *that moron,* has left us in a critical bind. Not only have we lost the *Pegasus,* but Sky himself is dead, unable to assist us with rapidly deploying into critical locations."

Night spent a few more moments thinking, as we all traded awkward looks with each other after his outburst.

The silence was only awkward if we made it awkward, and oooooh boy, did we make it *awkward.*

"Right." He said after a moment, breaking the silence. "I am exercising my emergency powers. We have a quorum of Sentinels present. Does anyone object to Ranger Falerius being promoted to Sentinel?"

I was not as up to date on the potential Sentinel candidates among the Rangers. I wasn't going to throw wrenches here and ruin it though. I indicated that I had no objection, along with the rest of the Sentinels.

"Ranger Falerius is hereby promoted to Sentinel, title Maestrai. Brawling, his team should be approaching Deva. You are tasked with retrieving Ranger Falerius, informing him of the good news, and heading towards the capital with him."

Brawling saluted.

It was going to suck for his team though. "Hey, yeah, one of your stronger Rangers? We're yoinking him. Good luck not dying on the rest of the round!"

"Bulwark, as we just discussed. You will be staying here, working on turning the encampment into a town."

"How many squads can I take?" Bulwark asked.

Night frowned.

"One Century." He said. "Be careful to only take a Century from a general who declares himself to be entirely neutral. Elsewise, we risk being accused of subtly sabotaging one faction or another."

Bulwark saluted his understanding, mouth twisting in distaste. *Politics.*

"Hunting." Night said, dishing out orders rapid-fire. "I apologize that we did not get a chance to thoroughly discuss this in-depth. I need you to scout the Formorian lands, and *hunt* down any remaining Formorians. We need certainty that the threat has been terminated, once and for all. Investigate their lairs, burn their home, crush any eggs you find. Dawn will accompany you for support purposes, primarily to mitigate Toxic's poison should it prove to be at a sufficient quantity to cause issues once you are so deep within their territory."

Hunting didn't salute, just gave a weary nod.

I saluted, having enough self-control not to give Night a knowing look. "Did not get a chance to discuss this in-depth" I was totally interpreting as Night deliberately putting the item last on the agenda, then rushing it through. Didn't want other people digging too deeply into it. Maybe he'd let the others know once we were gone.

"The rest of us shall return home, to respond to any problems that have arisen in our absence. If there is nothing else…?" Night trailed off, giving us a chance to say anything. A series of shaking heads confirmed the non-answer.

"Dismissed." Night said.

Chapter 24

Heading Out

The meeting had gone on fairly late, and in spite of sleeping half the day, I was able to instantly fall asleep the moment my head touched the pillow.

A dreamless night I was oh-so-thankful for, followed by waking up in the morning. Hunting and Destruction were still asleep, and Night was semi-dozing on a stool, half slumped forward.

Did he even sleep?

Either way, I got up, and somewhat reluctantly, shucked off my armor and gear. I was down to just my filthy tunic that I wore under it, but such was life.

I found a cloth, along with the other implements needed to maintain my gear, and with a heavy sigh, started to work at it.

Weeks of non-stop fighting and sleeping in the mud had done terrible things to my armor, and I was about to spend days, if not weeks, more in the wilderness with Hunting. It wasn't that I dreaded going or anything, just – I wanted a hot bath. Clean clothes. Less dirt under my nails, hair that wasn't greasy and matting.

I grabbed a lock and looked at it.

I gave an overly dramatic sigh, before taking out my knife and giving myself a haircut, grumbling under my breath about it. Albina was going to half murder me for this. Hope I didn't miss the baby.

Speaking of Albina, I should write her a letter to let her know what was going on. Should write mom and dad a letter as well. Probably Themis and Autumn to boot. Definitely going to send one to Artemis.

Except – problem. I looked around at the tent. The military tent. The tent we'd hijacked. The supplies of "emergency fight now."

The pen was mightier than the sword, but when Formorians were attacking we elected to use swords and spears. They were strangely unreceptive to our pleas and eloquent words. Hence, letter-writing supplies were in short supply.

Blargh. I'd need to hunt some supplies down. I put my armor down for a moment, and popped my head out of the tent.

Excellent. We had a pair of guards, basically bouncers so nobody would bug us without it being important.

Or, as I thought of them, future minions.

"Heya. Can you grab me some writing supplies?" I asked one of the guards, arbitrarily picking one.

He saluted.

"Sentinel. With all due respect, it'll be difficult due to-"

"Great!" I cheerfully interrupted him. "See you soon!"

Rank hath its privilege. In this case, sending soldiers on likely unreasonably difficult tasks, and expecting them to get done.

I was doubly thankful that I wasn't the one running around looking for writing supplies, not when he had mentioned how hard it was. No idea why it was hard, which had me extra-happy I wasn't the one trying to track it down.

I went back into the tent, and kept working on my gear. I looked around, and embarrassingly, in a manner that was entirely unsuited to my station and experience, realized I was missing some of it.

"Toxic!" I yelled at him. "Where'd my spear go?"

I'd given it to him back at the grove where we were fighting the Formorians, since he'd snuck over without his. I'd been blasting ever since then, not bothering to retrieve my theoretical main weapon.

Losing, when I was in the perfect position, a one versus one against a Formorian Soldier had soured me on even trying to use a spear against them, let alone a weapon less suited to killing things. In theory, I could probably dance around a Formorian and poke it full of holes and slowly kill it, but honestly, that was a pathetic way of going about it. After all, I could flicker a beam of Radiance through it and just kill it that way.

Still. It was my weapon, and I wanted it back. If nothing else, I didn't want to have to explain to the Quartermaster that I'd lost my weapon, and I needed a new one issued. I'd get an earful from him.

"Spear? What spear? Don't try to steal mine when you lost yours." Toxic said, shooting me a dirty look.

My mouth opened in outrage, and I pointed a finger at him, planning on giving him a pint-sized lecture.

"You dick! You-"

"Nah, just fucking with you. Here you go." Arthur said, grinning like crazy and holding the butt of the spear out at me.

I grabbed it, then punched him in the arm.

It was ok, because with my measly strength, and Arthur's vambraces and thick skin, I couldn't hurt him anyways. No harm, no foul.

I kept working on my gear as the rest of the Sentinels did their own thing. Hunting eventually got up, and after some moping around, plonked down next to me as I kept maintaining my stuff. With a deep sigh, he stripped his gear off, and started to use the maintenance equipment I wasn't using to work on his own gear.

We spent some time in companionable silence, working on our stuff as the other Sentinels popped in and out, doing whatever they believed needed doing.

"We're going to need a lot of food." Hunting eventually said, the first words I'd heard out of him all day.

I bit my tongue, closing the floodgate of words that wanted to pour out of me. I wanted to ask him all sorts of things, like how was he doing? Was he ok? Did he want to talk about it?

I'd let him know I was available to chat soon, then leave him be. If he wanted distance, I'd give him distance. If he wanted an ear, I'd give him an ear.

Not literally though. I could regrow my ears, but I was rather attached to them. Plus, peeling off body parts as a party favor was just icky.

"Yup. Should try to grab as much as we can before the soldiers get to it." I agreeably added.

Hunting grunted.

"Shame Acquisition isn't around. He'd have a dozen sheep outside our door by now, ready for the slaughter."

Unbidden, the ghost-aroma of fresh mutton filled my nose, making me want to drool. I could feel my salivary glands activating in response. So unfair. Food. Good food. Oh, how I missed tasty food.

Well, soldier rations were better than Formorian.

"Yeah, that'd be nice." I agreed.

"Or pigs. Could go for some nice ribs right about now." Hunting said.

I *wanted* to encourage him on this train of thought, I really did. His mind was slowly going off of Katastrofi, and onto other topics, like our survival in the near future. Survival was good. Planning to survive was better.

Pork, however, I'd sworn off of ever since I blew off Kerberos's head, and his roasting body had smelled exactly like pork. I couldn't even think of it without the memory rising up in my head, **[Pristine Memories]** backfiring slightly as it gave me perfect recall over the situation and the details.

Details that I could now see and remember in all their gory detail, that I had missed the first time. Details like –

I quashed the memory. Nothing good came out of going down that route.

"Fresh fruit." I added in.

"Carrots."

We kept trading foods back and forth, things we'd love to have. Slowly, oh so slow, Hunting was brightening up. Thinking of other things. Sure, a large shadow was still being cast over him, he was still in darkness, but I was making him look towards some light.

One could even say I was having him look at distant light on the horizon.

Our banter was interrupted by one of the soldiers entering the tent.

"Reporting! A Sentinel requested writing supplies?" He announced to the tent in general, saluting with one hand while carrying a banged-up satchel in the other.

"Ooh! That was me! Thanks!" I said, hopping up and getting the supplies from him.

"While you're here, we need a month's worth of food and supplies for two Sentinels." Hunting ordered.

A look of despair flashed over the poor minion's face, before he schooled his expression and reluctantly saluted.

"As you command..." He said, turned on his heel, and practically fled before we could give him more unreasonable requests.

Well, they sounded reasonable to us, but we were lofty and on high, not having a great grasp of the greater situation in and around the camp. I knew intellectually that food supplies were running dangerously low, and that there were constant noises of squads of soldiers running around the camp coming from outside our tent.

Not my problem.

I put aside the last of my gear that I could fix, and picked up the writing satchel. I sat down at the table, got out the blank scrolls, frowned as half the charcoal had been turned to dust and was getting everywhere, and laid it all out in front of me.

"Just checking, nothing we've done or are doing is top-secret, right?" I asked, speaking to nobody and everybody at once.

"Rebellion." Night said a single word from where he was dozing on his chair. I wasn't completely sure how to interpret that, but I decided that meant to stay entirely mum on the subject.

Of course, I wasn't going to risk my friends and family getting blindsided by it. They were worth too much to me.

Lots of wiping – my filthy tunic now had a dozen black streaks going through it as I didn't have anything better to use – and careful writing with what little charcoal I had left, and I had a few letters to send back home.

Artemis!

Big fight, killed a bunch of Formorian Queens, wild party. I'm OK, Night's OK. Sadly, it looks like I'm going to be stuck out here for awhile. More Sentinel stuff to do. Don't know when I'll be back – it's a mess out here. I'll try to write lots!

On a different note – why didn't you tell me about you and Julius!? I'm so happy for you two! You've got to tell me everything when I get back!

Well, not everything.

Almost everything!

Things, for reasons I can't say, might start getting real crazy and hectic near you. **Stay safe.** *Keep your students safe. If everything starts going crazy, hunker down and protect yourself. There's no reason to go out and get involved in nonsense. Not allowed to say anything more.*

I classed up! Got my next healer evolution! **It's so exciting!** *I can't wait to get back and tell you all about it! It's the best thing ever! I have so many cool tricks now!*

Cheers,

Elaine

I looked at the letter, satisfied. Artemis could read between the lines. She wouldn't know exactly why, but she'd figure it out quickly enough once rumblings started.

Hey mom! Hey dad!

I'm safe and sound at the frontlines, after a whole big mess. We defeated the Formorians!! I'm needed for a secondary mission, but it's low-danger. No big healing mess, no disaster, I just need to help out another Sentinel as he pokes around the former Formorian land.

There was a lot of poison used, and I'm just making sure he stays safe and alive.

On that note.

There's going to be a new town founded here, and I suspect I'm going to be spending a lot of time here. While I should be back really soon, the land grab might start before I'm able to travel back, and I could be hijacked for more things, if not outright told to stay here and deal with the fallout. Two requests.

1. Can you make a large purchase of land out here happen

2. Don't come out here yourselves. It's not worth the risk. It'll get cleaned up eventually, at which point the land purchase will pay off

3. Tell as many people as you can not to come out here. I'd hate to see more people die because of it. Arthur keeps getting notifications about the poison killing people, and it's tearing him apart.

Anyways! I got my healer class to class up! It's super strong now! I can't wait to show you all the neat stuff I can do with it! I can even preemptively heal people! In theory. Haven't been able to test it out yet. Should be good for sparring.

*The food out here is **terrible.**I even had to eat Formorian! I can't wait to get back home and eat your delicious cooking again.*

There might be some messes coming down the line. Dad, you should probably take a long vacation once you start hearing about things. No, seriously. Take the vacation. Bring mom and Themis with you. Maybe stay at Artemis's place for a few weeks or months, show the arrogant squirts at the Academy how guards handle unruly mages.

Lots of love, can't wait to see you again!
Your loving daughter,
Elaine

I was less than thrilled that I'd asked for two things, then ended up writing three, but that was life. The bamboo was so smeared and half-ruined already that experience said that I couldn't make the spot-editing work, not without running dark charcoal smears throughout the entire thing.

Dad being a member of the Praetorian Guard had me worried. They were the most likely to be in the line of fire when all this went down, the only physical protection the Senate had once the Generals were removed from the equation, or assumed to be hostile. If armed soldiers tried to forcefully break in, the Praetorian Guards were the only ones who would stop them – which would end with a lot of dead guards. My only hope was there'd be such overwhelming force that it wouldn't turn to violence.

Better for everyone if mom and dad were on vacation. Preferably with Themis, so nobody had the half-baked idea of throwing all the guards and guards-in-training at whatever nonsense was going to happen.

I'd hopefully be back home before that happened, and able to physically defend my family myself. Barring that, the other Sentinels could help, but given that they probably wanted to protect their own families, they might be stretched too thin.

Between "Protect my own family" and "Protect my friend's families" and "Protect my co-worker's families", I knew which one was getting the short stick.

Albina!

Hope you're doing well! Hope the baby's doing well! I'm safe and sound, although duty calls. I'm going to be out here for some time, doing Sentinel work.

*You might hear about a new town being founded out here. Whatever you do, **don't move out here.** There are problems with toxins in the water, the ground, and more. It's a slow poison, it'll take time to notice, but it'll kill off a baby quickly. Don't come.*

There might be a spot of bother heading towards the capital. Close your doors, keep your head down. Knowing me might not be positive in the upcoming mess, so maybe don't advertise it heavily, or rely on it for protection.

Maybe it will help, what do I know about politics?

I'm a complete wreck from this trip though. I'm going to want you all day once I get back – or as much time as you can spare if the baby comes first.

I still hope to make it for the baby though! I can't wait! So excited for you!

Cheers,
Elaine

I didn't want to seem like I was one-upping her by mentioning my class up. There was a strong chance Albina would never get 256 in her lifetime.

Unless I managed to level up fast enough, and start putting my thumb on the scale.

As I started to – well, *pen* would be the wrong word to use here, given that charcoal sticks I was using – write a letter to Autumn, my mouth twisted in a wiry grin. My recognition of the real estate opportunity here was only thanks to Autumn's relentless chattering about money, and her endless rules on how to get lots of it.

Autumn!

I'm safe and sound! They didn't pay me extra, but I found a way to make a few extra coins anyways. Buying land in a new town. Should be profitable.

I hope you're keeping up with your studies. I'll be checking when I next come back!

*You might hear about a new town popping up. **DO NOT MOVE HERE.** The land's poisoned, and that's bad for business. Also, you're a Light healer, and while I shouldn't need to remind you, I just know you're seeing coins and rods, and ignoring my warnings. You're a Light healer, which means your ability to deal with toxins and poisons that are here are practically non-existent. Trust me.*

*Even if you class up first, **wait for me.** I need to check that your skills can handle this, it's a nasty one. You won't realize a problem until you need to spend dozens of rods on a cure.*

With that being said, guard and soldier supplies are likely to spike in price soon. Might want to get ahead of the curve on that. Food might also become more expensive, although sticking around the capital might be a poor choice.

265

Best of luck. Stay safe until I can get back! Study hard. Poke Markus or Caecilius if you have any questions, they should be able to help you.

Cheers,

Elaine.

Honestly, the only way to get Autumn to listen to me was to threaten her pocketbook. Saying "don't do it, it's dangerous" would probably have her disregard my advice in favor of more coins.

"Don't do it, it'll cost you money", on the other hand, was the perfect tool.

I sat back and looked over my letters. I nodded with satisfaction to myself.

Perfect.

Chapter 25

Let's go fly a kite

We spent the rest of the day getting ready, and I was woken up bright and early by Night.

"Dawn. Good morning. We are meeting in a few minutes. Please prepare yourself." He said.

[Sunrise] continued to be the best skill ever, as I was awake almost instantly. Groggy to bright-eyed and bushy tailed in *seconds*.

I spotted the packs that Hunting and I had prepared for our trip, visited the latrine, found some more rations, and was sitting at the table with a huge grin as everyone else woke up, in various states of groggy.

Brawling somehow had boundless energy, and he was awake, while Destruction was half-huddled under some blankets, with a mug of something warm in his hands, taking the occasional sip.

I *could* make everyone else bright and cheery, alert and awake. It was almost more fun not to though, to be the obnoxiously cheerful one in the morning. I'd suffered annoyingly awake people often enough. My turn!

"Good morning." Night said. "Enough time has passed that I believe a return to normalcy is in order. I have not been made aware of any incidents that would require a Sentinel's attention. Does anyone have any other business?"

We all shot Night a look that would promise swift death for interrupting our sleep for... a meeting that did nothing. Blowing a hole in the roof of the tent might let enough sunlight in fast enough to disable Night, letting us pile on before he could retreat to the shadows...

Then again, there was something to be said for returning to a somewhat normal state of affairs. The apocalypse was over, time for business as usual. Vacation days were extraordinarily rare in this line of work, generally a few days around the Ranger Convocation. That was only because, with all the Rangers in the capital, we wouldn't be hearing about any critical problems.

Unless Ranger Command noticed a pattern from everyone's after-action reports, and sent a Sentinel to deal with the problem.

It still didn't stop me from trying to plot Night's demise as the meeting went on. It was significantly more fun than participating, ignoring the fact that **[Oath]** would never let me act on any of it.

"After action analysis?" Brawling suggested. "While it's still fresh in our minds?"

"While we're still all here?" Toxic added.

Night nodded, and Destruction groaned.

"Need more sleep. I did my part to the letter." He said, stumbling away from the table, and collapsing onto his cot.

I swear, he was asleep before he was even done falling down. He still had a serious sleep deficit from being up for weeks on end.

We all glanced at him, then looked at each other. I shrugged.

"I believe that Destruction performed admirably, and may skip this meeting." Night tactfully said. Better to grant permission when the outcome was the same anyways. Stopped his authority from being undermined.

"I'll start, I guess." Toxic said. "We should've had a plan in place for if we killed a Queen, and they counterattacked. We were caught with our tunics down."

There was some muttering of agreement around the table, and I was nodding my head.

"On some accounts, you are correct, on others, I find myself disagreeing." Night stated. "We previously had plans to account for such an occurrence, however, after hundreds upon hundreds of years of planning and drills, without a single event occurring, I determined that the time spent planning for such an event, along with constantly needing to re-work said plan in the face of a changing number of Sentinels and their abilities, to no longer justify the small risk of the Formorians changing strategy to an all-out assault. Yes, we were caught unprepared. However, I do not believe preparation for every single contingency is a proper use of the limited resources we have. Indeed, Toxic was not the first attempt at a similar strike. Why, I remember..."

I tuned out Night's history lesson, and listened with half an ear on the rest of the after-action report. Most of it focused around the decisions around who was brought, and what they'd done.

The stickiest point was if Toxic should've been part of the strike team or not. The rest of the Sentinels spent almost an hour discussing it, while my mind wandered as my eyes drifted around the tent, tapping a foot impatiently.

I just wasn't in the mood to analyze the fight that'd killed a number of us in great detail, especially as I hadn't been part of it. It was too fresh, too raw a reminder that I'd never see Sealing again. Never hear one of Sky's quips. Never ride Katastrofi again.

The only contribution I had was when the question of if I should've been in the strike team or not was brought up.

"I hate to say it, but no. It was right for me to return to the walls." I reluctantly said. "From what I've heard, I'm not sure I could've stopped any of the fatalities, I would've slowed you down, and I saved dozens of soldiers here, and got hundreds or thousands more back into fighting shape."

Endless bloody discussion. I wanted to just get up and leave, walk away, but that'd be rude. I don't think my vacant look and lack of contributions went unnoticed, but eh. I was trying. I had half an ear out listening, and if I thought I had something, I'd contribute.

I wasn't pulling a repeat of ignoring my parents at Kerberos's place. Just... an almost repeat.

After far too much discussion on the topic, we wrapped up, and went our separate ways.

"Hey Hunting!" I called out, as he was double-checking everything. "Do you think we've got time for me to class up quickly?"

I hadn't intended to class up my **[Ranger-Mage]** class anytime soon, but with the huge boost in stats from **[The Dawn**

Sentinel], along with the achievements for killing the Royal Guards and Queens, I felt like I might just be ready. I had a suspicion that my mage class would overtake my healer class though, which would change my eyes from Celestial to Radiant.

As petty as my desire to keep my eyes Celestial was, as much as I wanted them to stay starry, cold logic dictated that I should probably class up. We were in a relatively safe spot, about to go out and explore unknown lands, and I felt comfortable with my achievements, levels, and stats. I didn't think I could improve my offerings too much more at this point.

Blah. Classing up now would also mean no reading time, which sucked. Who knew how many decades it would be before I got a chance again?

Hunting looked at me thoughtfully.

"Do you think you can finish classing up in an hour?" He asked.

I thought about it. There was no way I was going to gimp my future prospects by rushing my class-up, not when the class might stick with me for the rest of my life. If I got another chance like the Celestial class up, where I got to build my own class? I was going to take it.

Ignoring that, I was going to carefully and properly look through my options. I wasn't going to rush it.

"No." I honestly said. "No way."

Hunting nodded at me, seemingly satisfied.

"Right, then let's get moving. Night mentioned that it's about a two-week trip to the lair. Now, that's with him only being able to move at night, and fighting through a Formorian horde, so it should be faster with just us."

"I'm a slow poke." I pointed out. "I'm not nearly as fast as you or Night. Night, walking through the horde, only at nighttime, is still faster than I am on an open road."

Hunting looked down at me and frowned.

"We'll figure something out. Come on, gear up. I want to see the carcasses of the Queens while it's still light out."

I gave him a bit of a glare, letting him know that I didn't need him telling me what to do when it came to preparing to get out there. Still, he wasn't wrong. It just rankled.

"What are the odds of me getting a halfway clean tunic in my size?" I asked, picking at the filthy fabric.

Hunting eyed me.

"Didn't you get a spare one in the care package we were sent?"

I hit my forehead with the palm of my hand. Yes. Yes, I did.

I tore into the package, and got a clean tunic. One of my favorites – mom knew me well. I happily changed into it, grimacing slightly as I felt clean cloth pressing against filthy skin.

The worst part was feeling the cloth pressed tight against my skin once again as my armor was snugly fitted over the tunic. It was clean though, which was an improvement from my prior state of being.

I'd totally go toe-to-toe with a Royal Guard for the chance at a hot bath.

It took me significantly more time to get ready than when Brawling had barged into my room, what, a month ago or so? Felt like a lifetime ago.

Mostly because I wasn't fueled by a liter of raw adrenaline coursing through my body, and also because I was double and triple checking every strap and buckle, jumping a few times experimentally to make sure everything was properly secured.

One last check through my bag and gear, making sure I had everything, and Hunting and I were off!

Armor on, helmets off. Spear and tower shield attached to our massive packs, short swords at our waist.

Technically, the helmets should be on our head. They were off as a concession to both comfort, and visibility. We wanted our full range of vision, since we wanted to see things. We didn't think we were getting into fights. I wasn't concerned that some angry mage would try to put a rock through my head.

We walked a long way through the camp, seeing some soldiers drilling, and others packing up their tents and gear. It

271

was clear that large-scale movement operations were about to begin. I trailed slightly behind Hunting, since he looked every inch what people imagined a Sentinel should look like. Apart from his head, which had a fine layer of fuzz as his hair was regrowing from his 'rip the Royal Guard apart from the inside' misadventure. Either way, his commanding stride, appearance, and badge prominently pinned on his chest resulted in soldiers getting out of our way with a respectful "Sentinel" and a salute.

If he was 20, 30 years younger he might've been interesting.

Still. It was quite a long distance to get to one of the still-operational external gates. We could've just gone over the wall directly, but I guess this gave us a bit of time to shake down our stuff, realize we'd forgotten an extra pair of socks of something.

I half-stumbled catching myself. *Dammit!* I did forget an extra pair of socks! I wasn't about to suggest we turn around just for socks though.

We found a gate, and paused for a moment, one last final check before we were out and about.

"Hang on, before we get going, can I try a new skill on you?" I asked Hunting.

He shrugged.

"Sure, why not?"

I tapped him, putting a **[Solar Infusion]** on him. There was no obvious indicator, no lit up halo or anything. I was a little disappointed. Sure, that had been an offered perk that I hadn't taken, what with how each point of starlight being super important. Still. I'd kinda hoped to get a freebie.

"What's the skill supposed to do?" He asked me.

"Preemptive healing." I replied. "Heals you like I'm touching you while I'm nearby."

If looks could kill, Hunting would've just murdered me. His eyes, pitch black like the void, bore into me.

Guess whatever he was doing had been enough to get his mage class above his fighter class.

"You didn't think to mention that this was a regeneration-disabling skill before you put it on a mage!?" He yelled at me. "It's a damn good thing I've got curse breaking skills! This is how you get a teammate killed Dawn! *Think!* Mages need all the mana they can get, and you know I'm a spellspear!"

I looked down, and mumbled "I did ask for permission."

Hunting either didn't hear me, or didn't care enough as he stalked off, through the gate. I scampered after him, grumbling as he peeled away at his pace, leaving me in the dust.

Blah. I guess I hadn't fully and properly thought through the reactions of mages to the skill. Like, it was a great boon towards physical classers. They hardly used their mana regeneration in combat. They might, on occasion, use their mana pool.

I had thought about the "stop people regenerating, and potentially be able to be less lethal as a result" aspect.

I just hadn't quite put the pieces together that Hunting, who was a physical Classer, would get pissed off because I was screwing with his magical side. Yeah, he was right, I hadn't thought all the implications all the way through.

And worse – I hadn't even gotten a level out of it!

Blasted physical classers and their blasted speed. Ugh.

I made it through the walls, and there must've been some enchantment or inscription on them. The moment I stepped through, the *smell* hit me, and I looked out upon the field.

The black field, filled with dead Formorian bodies. Around the base of the walls and some distance away the bodies had been cleared up, and soldiers were working in teams to throw Formorian bodies onto huge pyres. Dead bodies continued out, almost as far as I could see.

It was a good thing they were burning all the bodies. I was fairly certain that the army knew that leaving a bunch of bodies around was a recipe for disease, and who knew what nastiness the Formorians could brew up when dead? Still, it was being handled, which meant that I wouldn't need to throw a wrench in the plans by insisting we cut back early as a plague-prevention measure.

"How..." I asked, trailing off.

"Trampled over the bodies to get to the next row. At a point, they just stopped moving, and stood to fight."

I eyed the bodies. I looked at the clear sky.

"Welp, I'm going to fly over all this mess." I said, barely keeping the glee out of my voice.

"Won't you run out of mana in like, an hour?" Hunting asked me.

I gave him a mad grin.

"Not anymore! I can fly forever!" I told him, as cheerfully as humanly possible. "I restore almost 64 mana a second, and even with all this gear and equipment on, it costs me about 23 mana a second. I can fly forever!" I joyfully repeated, stepping up into the air.

"As long as you're outside, in the sun, with no clouds, or a Classer who can interfere." Hunting said, ticking points off his fingers. "Come on, let's get a move on."

Hunting took off, and I immediately struggled to keep up. Didn't matter that he had to wade through bodies. In spite of his bulk and equipment, his dexterity was on full display as he gracefully bounded from body to body.

To contrast, I wasn't much faster with [Talaria] than I was normally. Sure, I could step up high like I was walking up stairs, then dive down and try to redirect some of that speed, but it barely counted.

However, I was struck with inspiration.

"Hunting! Hey, Hunting!" I called down.

Hunting looked up, and I mentally thanked the Quartermaster for modifying my standard leather skirt into a skort.

"What?" He asked.

I tossed down a rope, holding onto the other end.

"Pull me along!" I called out, trying and failing to restrain the glee I was feeling. This was going to be so much fun!

I tied the rope off around my waist, as Hunting grabbed the other end.

He looked down at the rope, back up at me, shrugged, and started to walk, slowly accelerating into a run.

I clamped my mouth shut, as I was buffeted around like a kite on a windy day.

This was so much fun!!!

I had to find ways to convince Hunting to do this with me more   often.

Chapter 26

The Formorian Lands I

I had a pretty good view, although I was a bit lower to the ground than I would've liked. I had to keep stepping up to maintain height, because Hunting's pull was downwards as well as sideways. Wasn't quite able to "air-ski" through the sky, although now I was hoping an evolution of [Talaria] would permit that.

Hunting moved at an incredible pace, barely noticing the changing, shifting terrain below him. A testament to the usefulness of dexterity.

He'd occasionally just leap over a large crack in the earth, a permanent reminder of the massive spell that Destruction had channeled and unleashed on the Formorians.

I didn't have to do anything. I just enjoyed myself. Front flips, backflips, twisting myself up and pausing to let Hunting unwind me like a top, "belly-surfing" and more! I was having the time of my life up here, never mind that we were on a mission. I didn't have a good view of Hunting's face from where I was, but little hints suggested that he was entertained by my antics, as much as he tried to keep a "stern and serious" face up.

After far too short of a time – like, four hours of being a kite wasn't nearly long enough for the novelty to wear off – we approached the enormous bodies of the slain Queens. I dropped down. I'd like to say I dropped to the ground, but there wasn't enough ground left to stand on. Just bodies.

I coiled the rope around one shoulder after landing. I didn't want to have to bother retying it later.

Formorian Soldiers. Shooters. Worm-like creatures I suspected were Spitters. Small hills of Royal Guards.

Cruel red splashes on pure white wings, angels crushed and brought low. Broken swords and shattered halos.

I eyed the massive bodies of the Queens.

"They're absolutely, totally, completely dead, right?" I asked Hunting.

He nodded at me.

"I'm looking at all three notifications for them now." He confirmed. "Had the same thought as you."

I looked around.

"I know you want to poke around them, but no way am I camping here tonight. No way. Not happening." I said.

Hunting looked around.

"Surprised scavengers haven't gotten to this yet. Hang out here, I'm going to get a close look at the Queens. Don't touch them, might throw a wrench in one of my skills."

I had no desire to touch the Queens. Even in death they terrified me, an errant twitch enough to crush Hunting to paste, let alone me.

How the hell had the strike team managed to finish one off!? Even with angels helping, even with an earthquake launched on top of them, they were massive behemoths. Like, put me on top of the main part of the crab-like body, give me six months, and I'm still not sure I'd even hit anything vital, let alone kill one.

I decided to take a look at the fallen angels. There'd been all sorts of idiomatic expressions involving angels, along with the occasional 'fairy tale' about them – like when that centurion had called me the angel of his group – but it hadn't quite *clicked* for me how and why angels would be known on Pallos.

Of course, there were stories about angels because angels existed. I'd heard no stories about demons, but they were now high up on my "to be concerned" list.

Then again, I'd heard nothing about "evil" gods, or anti-gods. Even Xaoc and Thanatos, responsible for Chaos and Death, were revered as proper deities. Sure, chaos and death weren't popular deities to worship, and people who did occasionally got the stink eye from more superstitious fellows, but it wasn't like they were considered evil or some nonsense. Death was a part of life, like chaos was a part of order, and vice-versa.

Still. Note to self. Be on the lookout for demons. "How to recognize, infiltrate and destroy a cult" wasn't a Ranger

Academy lesson, which made me think cultists in dimly lit basements weren't all that likely.

Heck, if there was a way to summon demons, I bet Night would've summoned a dozen of them and unleashed them on the Formorians. Or had a droning, 6000-word essay on why it was a terrible idea.

Normally I'd be telling myself at this point to *focus,* but I was on standby, with instructions to *not* screw with the Queens. Distraction away!

I decided to look at the angels, likely a once in a lifetime opportunity – even with my massively expanded lifespan.

While they looked human with magnificent white bird wings from a distance, nobody, not even someone who only had a rough sketch or idea of what a human looked like, would confuse us. On top of the unnaturally good looks and fine features, even in death there was something *more* about them, something Divine. No creatures would look at an angel and think they were anything other than a heavenly being.

I'd had a half-baked thought of getting a few angel feathers, but something about them gave me pause. Even broken and bloodied, coated in mud and left to rot, I didn't dare desecrate their bodies. It just felt wrong. I couldn't tell if it was something divine causing the feeling, or just my own sense of ethics rearing its head, but I didn't want to touch their body, not even to bury them or to arrange them into a pyre. Burning the body where it had fallen felt equally wrong, and I left them there, untouched. For all I knew, there was a deadly curse unleashed on anything messing with their bodies. Or something. I wasn't a priest, heck, I barely stepped into a temple.

I should probably reconsider that policy.

However, a number of feathers had broken off 'normally', and were scattered around. I entertained myself by hunting down a dozen intact feathers, each one a foot-long and pristine white.

I carefully pressed most of them into my pack, and tied two to the haft of my spear. I wanted to tie one into my hair, but it was too short right now for that. Couldn't wait to get back to the capital, and have Albina grow it back out. She'd probably have fun with the angel feathers to boot. Could get me a cute look with them.

Before I did that, I should probably check with a priest that I wasn't going to, like, annoy all the gods and goddesses by doing it. Then again, the lack of the strange feeling when I touched the loose feathers, versus the bodies of the angels, was suggestive.

Either way – I was keeping myself well entertained while Hunting did *whatever* it was that was taking so much time.

If I was a betting girl – which, with the right situation, I totally was – I'd bet that he'd found Katastrofi's corpse, and was busy saying his goodbyes, his final farewells. He'd probably also legitimately find whatever he was looking for, but eh. I'd just keep upping my feather stockpile. I wasn't picky for the first few, but now I'd only accept the perfect, unbroken ones.

One body, however, didn't give off the same feeling as the rest. Like a magnet, pushed away from everything else, I was naturally pushed to it.

I looked at the body, perfect flesh and heavenly features.

I practically jumped a foot in the air as the body shuddered, taking a breath.

Holy! The angel was alive!

I sprang into action, activating **[Wheel of Sun and Moon]** to immediately start the healing process. Wounds closed, and wings straightened out, feathers regrowing in a flash.

I walked closer, and knelt down.

I froze as I reached my hand out, less than an inch away from the angel's flesh. I had no idea what would happen if I actually touched the angel. Bad things, maybe? I eyed my mana.

Zero.

Somehow, I'd completely drained all of my mana on this already. Sure, I had a distance penalty with **[Wheel of Sun and Moon]**, but I didn't think angels were so far from humans as to entirely drain me on relatively minor injuries, and still not be completely healed. Although, he looked almost entirely healed. There might be something else wrong, something that I couldn't see. Would have to give him another shot.

The decision to start pulling from my Arcanite and heal the angel or not was no decision at all. I'd never leave another intelligent creature in pain. I had plenty of the stuff.

As I pulled some mana in, I reflected that this could be a perfect way to trap me if needed. Just throw injured, innocent people at me until I was out of mana, then attack.

I mustered my courage, and leaned forward to touch the angel, healing him again. This time, my mana didn't drop all the way to zero, but it was low.

"low." Ha. It was more mana than I had total five years ago.

The angel opened his eyes, and they were captivating. No other word for it.

No, literally. They were indescribable. I couldn't even tell you the color, the shape of the eyes, the type of pupil, nothing. I'd locked eyes with something distinctly Other, in spite of the similarity in bodies.

He sat up, and without a word, with a single beat of his powerful wings, was fly-floating right above me.

I was entranced. I couldn't take my eyes off him.

He leaned forward, and while I should've felt fear, I didn't.

I did have the presence of mind to **[Identify]** him, which... had no result. It was like trying to **[Identify]** a rock. Just didn't register to the skill. Maybe that's why it had taken so much mana to heal him?

"Thank you." He said, after an indeterminate amount of time. His voice was like his eyes, with no words in any language I knew being able to even start to describe what I was hearing. Leaning forward, he placed a chaste kiss on my forehead, and simply *vanished*, leaving behind nothing but a few motes of divine flame.

I just stood there like an idiot, rubbing my forehead where the angel had kissed it.

I felt robbed though. Healing an angel, which required my entire mana pool and then some, an entirely new experience, repairing wings, and so much more – and I didn't level!

Maybe it had something to do with the fact that I couldn't **[Identify]** the angel?

An indeterminable amount of time later Hunting came sprinting out. That didn't look good. That wasn't the steady jog of "I just want to get from A to B", this was a full-out sprint.

I dropped the coil of rope around my shoulder, letting it fall to the ground in a theoretical neat pile as I quickly repacked my backpack and swung it back on. Naturally, rope was rope, and it promptly tied itself into a half-dozen knots, in spite of my careful efforts. I then started to fly, climbing high while the rope uncoiled under me, knots tightening into annoying lumps in the middle of the rope. I had no idea what was going on, but Hunting clearly wanted to move *fast*, and I was going to make it easy for him.

He slowed down as he grabbed the rope, making sure to not jerk it hard enough that it'd break. Neither of us had a skill like **[Strong Rope]** or **[Unbreakable Line]** or anything like that. Well, I didn't know all of Hunting's skills, but it was a good bet. Unlike Ocean. I'd bet he had a skill like that.

Either way, we were off like one of Artemis's famous pebbles, and as the sky darkened, I instinctively looked up, a trained habit ingrained in every kid since they were little.

A flock of Ornithocheirus darkened the sky, and I cursed as they started to circle the Formorians. One dove, then a second, and with a flurry of wings and cries, they all dove down onto the bodies. Fresh meat for them! Bonus – it didn't fight back!

I cursed, while Hunting just kept speeding along. A few headed our way, and I made the snap decision to shoot them down.

Usually we didn't want to kill them if we were attacked. It'd just increase the amount of food nearby, which would get more of the flock attacking us. However, this time, the entire flock was already coming down, off to eat the tasty Formorian bodies. Killing a few would make no difference.

Three dived at me, the tasty, shiny morsel being tangled tantalizingly on rope, nice and high in the air just for them. I tensed, watching them dive, needing them to be close enough before my Radiance was able to reach them.

Blasted magic. The light from Radiance could travel forever, but the burning, destructive aspect had a limited range.

Fortunately, **[Nova]** wasn't as limited, and I unleashed four low-powered **[Nova]**'s as the Ornithocheirus got closer. With their speed, angle, and twisting way of diving, I wasn't quite sure I'd be able to hit them with a single powerful **[Nova]**, so I elected for a wide coverage, guaranteed to hit and do some damage instead of being a poorly stacked coinflip of maybe killing them, or totally missing.

[Nova] hit, one of the birds tumbled down, while the other two were singed, and then they were much closer, **[Bullet Time]** activating and giving me clarity and time to think.

More precisely, it gave me time to *aim*. Otherwise, trying to hit the twisty, high-speed fliers would be difficult.

The easier one I eyeballed, and threw a **[Nova]** directly at it, fairly certain that it'd connect. The harder one I just drilled a beam of Radiance through its open mouth, stopping when I saw the wings no longer flapping, and a flash of light from behind it.

Two notifications let me know that the two Ornithocheirus were dead, and I had a brief moment of elation before realizing that **[Bullet Time]** hadn't stopped.

I mentally swore as I realized what was happening. The Ornithocheirus had been on a perfect intercept course, dive-bombing from above. Now that they were dead, their gravity assist was the only thing moving them, and one was on a direct course to land on me, dead or not.

I threw up **[Mantle of the Stars]** between me and it, dropped **[Talaria]** to let myself fall faster, then snaked out my arm to grab onto the rope, tensing and pulling it with my entire body's worth of muscles. The combination of movement and shields proved effective, as the body slid off of **[Mantle of the Stars]**.

It all happened so fast, I needed a bunch of small moves to properly move myself enough to have the Ornithocherius bounce and slide off instead of a direct hit.

Then we were out, far away enough from the flock that we were no longer interesting. Or, putting it another way, the massive almost literal mountain of dead flesh was far more appealing than we were.

Didn't stop Hunting from making amazing time across the Formorian lands, going deeper and deeper, still jumping over the occasional crevice from Destruction's work. There were fewer of them now, as his earthquake only went so far.

I'm not sure that an expert tracker was needed for this. The Formorian Queens weren't exactly subtle about their movements, and a three-year-old could've followed their tracks. Hard to miss the divots they imprinted into the earth with each step of their monstrous crab-like legs.

Hunting ran for hours more, and when the sun set, he grumbled, picked me up in a princess carry, and continued to make good time.

Wasn't a huge fan of the princess carry, but given that I was wearing a large pack, full of sharp pointy bits, and he was wearing a large pack, our options were limited.

Eventually we got to where Hunting judged to be far enough, and I watched in fascination as he built an entire small campsite underground, voiding out large portions of the ground to make a narrow entrance that expanded into a tiny enclosure that barely supported the two of us and our packs.

I put my stuff down and uneasily looked at the ground above us. If that came down on us, we were so dead, and it wasn't like we had support beams or anything. Just being in this cave made me nervous, forget sleeping in it.

Still, Hunting seemed like he knew what he was doing, although I dreaded a repeat performance of this.

We grabbed dinner together, no fire. We did close off the entrance with some tarp, and I used my Radiance to make the inside nice and warm and toasty. Some comforts of home.

"What were you looking for?" I asked Hunting.

"Eggs." He replied. "Wouldn't surprise me if the Queens laid the foundation for a new generation as they were dying. Especially the first and the last one. They died slowly, and would've had enough time for a last-ditch desperation egg. Wouldn't be the first time something like that happened."

"And we stopped because of the Ornithocheirus attack." I reasoned out. "Because if there are any eggs, they'll just eat them."

"Exactly. Saves us the trouble of trying to burn the area clean, saves the soldiers the effort of needing to come out and burn all the bodies one at a time. It'll be a pain if they decide that this means food lives here, and they frequently return, but that's a future problem."

I frowned.

"This is going to suck." I said.

"How so?"

"They were loaded up with Toxic's poison. Now they're going to fly all over the damn place while the poison concentrates inside of them, and drop dead in random places. It'll just keep spreading, and spreading." I said.

Hunting grimaced.

"Ouch, really?" He asked.

"Yup."

"Can't you cure or fix it?" He said.

"Only when it's in a human – or near human – and only if I know about it. Some Ornithocheirus drops dead near a village, a wolf eats the body, a farmer kills and eats the wolf, well, I'll never know about it."

"Nasty stuff." Hunting commented.

"I was against the whole idea." I grumbled.

He gestured around the tiny cavern.

"Worked, didn't it? We won. A few people dying here and there of poison's a small price to pay. Heck, I bet fewer people die of poison than would die on the front lines. That's a net benefit, right?"

I just grumbled bad-naturedly to myself, not saying any words but letting Hunting know my feelings exactly. I didn't have a strong logical argument to what he was saying, just an emotional one.

Urgh. The whole thing reminded me that I had no idea what happened when Arthur's toxin was burned. For all I knew we were aerosolizing the crap out of it, and everyone in the camp was going to be breathing it in.

What a mess.

[Name: Elaine]

[Race: Human]

[Age: 19]

[Mana: 153790/153790]

[Mana Regen: 133517 (+98425.6)]

Stats

[Free Stats: 51]

[Strength: 293]

[Dexterity: 347]

[Vitality: 2176]

[Speed: 2176]

[Mana: 15379]

[Mana Regeneration: 15379 (+9842.56)]

[Magic Power: 7897 (+106609.5)]

[Magic Control: 7897 (+106609.5)]

[Class 1: [The Dawn Sentinel - Celestial: Lv 305]]

[Celestial Affinity: 305]

[Cosmic Presence: 231]

[Solar Infusion: 1]

[Center of the Universe: 285]

[Dance of the Heavens: 305]

[Wheel of Sun and Moon: 271]

[Mantle of the Stars: 256]

[Sunrise: 4]

[Class 2: [Ranger-Mage - Radiance: Lv 256]]

[Radiance Affinity: 256]

[Radiance Resistance: 256]

[Radiance Conjuration: 256]

[Shine: 111]

[Sun-Kissed: 256]

[Blaze: 256]

[Talaria: 256]

[Nova: 256]

[Class 3: Locked]

General Skills

[Identify: 151]

[Pristine Memories: 200]

[Pretty: 152]

[Bullet Time: 268]

[Oath of Elaine to Lyra: 270]

[Sentinel's Superiority: 305]

[Persistent Casting: 189]

[Learning: 280]

Chapter 27

The Formorian Lands II

I'd be lying if I said the night was restful. Hunting and I traded watch shifts, with **[Sunrise]** being a lifesaver. Getting a few levels out of it to boot didn't hurt.

Still, sleeping was a terrifying experience. As little ground as was above us, I could still imagine it coming collapsing down onto me, hundreds of pounds of rock and dirt burying me alive. Didn't make for restful sleep, and as little as it'd help if the worst happened, I slept wrapped up in **[Mantle of the Stars]**, with **[Persistent Casting]** letting me maintain it. Sure, I'd still get buried alive, but I'd get a few more seconds to curse Hunting to eternal damnation before I died.

Fortunately, Hunting knew his stuff, and I survived the surprisingly chilly night. I suppose it was almost winter, and we'd been heading steadily south-west. I probably took a bit longer on watch than was strictly fair, but while on watch I didn't need to be in the jaws of the deathtrap. I was woken up by Hunting as the first light of day broke over the horizon, and with only a bit of fumbling did we get the entire campsite broken down and packed up.

"Right." I said, mentally cursing to myself at Hunting's bizarre knot arrangement. "New plan. I set up my stuff, you set up your stuff, and we both take down our stuff, and our stuff only." I proposed.

I got a stink-eye from Hunting, which I didn't feel was warranted.

"I mean, I did set everything up last night." He fairly pointed out.

"Yes! I'll cook, you dig a hole in the ground, it's fair?" I tried to reason, knowing it wasn't that fair.

I got some grumbling noises from Hunting.

"Look. We each like our stuff done a particular way. Yeah, you're doing most of the work, both during the day and to dig stuff out. But, like, it just makes sense for us to arrange our own stuff. Look, I'll handle the rest of the communal activities?" I offered. "[Sunrise] pick me up?" I said, sweetening the deal.

I got a grumpy noise of assent, smacked him with [Sunrise], and got a level up notification.

[*ding!* [Sunrise] leveled up! 7 -> 8]

If my old [Medicine] skill and general human knowledge hadn't contradicted it, I would've believed that the System released happy chemicals to everything that leveled up. As-is, I knew the happy feeling was pure me. The joy of a low-level skill – I got to watch it rise rapidly.

Hunting and I started the day off jogging in a direction that he'd divined. Sun wasn't high enough yet for me to start flying, and being towed along like a kite had some downsides. Namely, it was hard to talk when I was going that fast.

"How would you manage if you were solo?" Hunting asked me as we started to move along.

"I wouldn't." I bluntly replied. "My skillset is primarily handling other people, which generally implies civilization. Worst-case, there'd be trees or bamboo and such to base a campsite off of, which I could then use to build a light structure or something. Middle of nowhere? I'm useless, and I know it."

I decided to change the topic, before Hunting started to dig deep into my skillset, and realize I was entirely unsuited to be here. Dude was smart, and the gears would start turning, and he'd be right back on thinking about Katastrofi.

Then again, when a part of your life as significant as that is torn away, it's hard to think about other topics. Rather, it's easy for any topic to lead back to the subject.

Watching how Hunting was coping, the grief still marked around his eyes in spite of his attempts to be stony-faced about it, was having me think twice about a companion. Especially if I was going to pull a Night, and live thousands of years.

When I bonded to a creature, I'd probably extend their lifespan. In a perfect world, I'd bind to something that increased *my* natural lifespan. That would give me more time to hit whatever obscenely high level I needed to get **[The Stars Never Fade]**. I hoped I'd unlock it at level 400. Most people, heck, most Sentinels didn't make it that far in their lifetime, but I was already over level 300 before I was 20. An obscene leveling pace, no matter how it was sliced, and participating with the Formorian assault just now should give me a solid leg-up. Even if I only got one level a year, I was on track to hit level 400 before I died of old age.

Granted, in the line of work I was in, "death by old age" was a literal joke we told each other.

However, even if I could extend and expand a companion's lifespan with the mere act of bonding with one, there was no guarantee that they'd last long enough. Say I found the best kitten ever. I could expect a cat to have a 20-year lifespan, baseline. Their skills could extend it out to 30, 35 years, and I might be able to even double that to 60, 70 years. Might not be level 400 by then though.

The joke, of course, being a cat becoming a companion to anyone. Cats didn't have owners, they had staff.

Which, if I was doing this the slow and careful way, would mean waiting until I got the immortality skill first, before finding a companion. Opportunity was knocking right now though, and I'd be foolish not to answer its call. Heck, answering opportunity when opportunity came knocking, was how I got here in the first place. That, and *making* my own chances and luck.

Figured I should make some more conversation while I was down here though, and leave the deep philosophical thinking to when I was flying.

HA!

Who was I kidding, I'd be too giddy with delight to be thinking about stuff.

"How's it going?" I asked Hunting, shaking myself out of the thinking pit I'd found myself in.

I got a look that basically asked if I was a moron, and I shut up. Hunting was usually nicer than this, but grief did strange things to everyone. In Hunting's case, it just seemed to make him an asshole, when he was usually nice. Which, quite honestly, was a totally understandable reaction. I didn't like being on the receiving end of it, but if it helped, well, I could tolerate it for a few days more. Or however long my patience lasted for.

"Do you still have your healing touchstone skill?" Hunting asked me after an awkward pause.

I shook my head.

"It's a combination of skills that requires some prep work." I told him. "Haven't gotten the chance to re-do it yet."

"Might be worth doing while we're moving today." Hunting 'observed', seemingly giving me an order.

I wrinkled my nose at that.

"I'll give it a shot. It won't be nearly as good as it was before. Less time, distracted, and last time I did this I had a third skill that helped with this, that I no longer have. **[Medicine]**. Better than nothing though." I worked out, thinking out loud as I went.

Well, I wasn't doing much else when flying. Might as well do something semi-useful. I wouldn't be nearly as efficient – I needed to find a solid multi-day period to recreate my image – but it'd be better than nothing.

"Nothing", of course, being the absolute time of my life as I was able to fly-surf freely through the air. I should totally get Julius to do this with me when I got back to the capital. Who was going to stop us?

For that matter, it was going to take me a lot longer this time to properly recreate the image, without the crutch of **[Medicine]**. I could replicate everything without the skill, I was just eating inefficiencies everywhere. I'm sure I'd be eternally grateful for it once **[Solar Infusion]** started to get some good use.

The sun rose a little higher, basking us in the morning light. I promptly tied a rope around my waist, handed one end off to Hunting without a word passed between us, and took off!

Flying! Flying never got old. I was starting to think about what I wanted from **[Ranger-Mage]** evolving, and **[Talaria]** upgrading and losing the light restriction was high on my list.

For that matter, I hadn't done a lot of thinking on what I wanted my next evolution of **[Ranger-Mage]** to look like. It had been, what, level 210 a month ago? When I didn't spend that much time blowing stuff up if I could help it? Yeah, I thought I had a few more years before I was ready to class it up, and that I'd had the time to think about what I wanted and needed, and for my experience to shape my wants and needs from the class.

While I'd rocketed up to 256 in **[Ranger-Mage]**, I didn't feel like I had the deep, rich well of experience that I had with **[Constellation of the Healer]**. Heck, I'd had **[Constellation]** for literally twice as long as I'd had **[Ranger-Mage]** for. It was kinda unfair, how much faster combat and fighting classes could level up, given the right conditions.

... I complained, having boosted my own healing classes multiple times in deadly situations. From plagues to tsunamis, from Formorians to volcanic eruptions, all the way to Destruction knocking over walls as a side-effect from his earthquake and crushing people, I'd zipped around all over the country healing people, and getting serious experience for it.

I kept thinking about **[Ranger-Mage]** and what I wanted out of it when I got the chance to class it up as the sun rose high in the sky, and started to fall again.

I couldn't recommend trying to eat while being towed along like a kite. Almost choked on my rations, and drinking? It'd be easier to drink and run. Maybe we could've stopped for lunch, but I was already feeling like a burden – literally, I had to be kited along – and I wasn't going to suggest stopping.

After an early, early lunch, I decided to start working on my new image, linking **[Dance with the Heavens]** up with **[Persistent Casting]**. I didn't have the greatest focus, basically needing to be walking on a treadmill the entire time I was trying to focus on my entire knowledge of medicine, recalled through **[Pristine Memories]**.

It helped that I'd done it before, and I simply recalled the last time I did this. Problem was, I didn't have as much time, so it was more like skimming a book than a thorough, in-depth read, occasionally being jolted out of my thinking as Hunting stopped for a moment, and I kept going, only for my leash to get yanked as I drifted too far.

Still, progress was progress, and my efficiency was improving. I'd want to completely re-do this when I got the chance, but something was better than nothing. Also, a lack of efficiency wasn't bothering me too much, as I'd just increased my mana pool to a ludicrous degree. Ideally, I'd have perfect efficiency – my own pride in my abilities demanded I go for it, before I even touched practical considerations – but for now, this would have to be 'good enough'.

We made solid time, with Hunting occasionally stopping to check on something. I wasn't sure what, since there were clearly no eggs, and the path the Queens had taken could only be made more obvious with a giant neon sign, and even that would've only improved it slightly.

I was also continuously amused by Hunting pulling me along. As he pulled me along, I pushed up. As I pushed up, he was also pulled up just a bit, creating a strange bobbing effect. Basically, I was lifting some of his weight as well. Fun stuff!

We spent a few days traveling like this. Death-trap of a campsite, some chit-chat in the morning, traveling through the lands, finding a spot at night, some more lighthearted chit-chat, a quick pulse of [Dance] to make sure we weren't being secretly poisoned by Arthur's poison, and back to the death-trap.

One day, I spotted some ugly, brownish-purple hills in the distance as we continued to make good time. One hill was whole and intact, while the other three were broken and shattered into pieces.

"Hey Hunting! Pause a moment!" I yelled down to him, dropping with [Talaria]. I could drop faster, but why bother?

"What?" Hunting asked me, short, but not rude. He'd slowly, oh so slowly, been coming round and being slightly nicer and more reasonable the past few days.

Good timing as well, because I'd been getting close to blowing up at him. There was only so much rudeness and mean-spirited remarks I could take. Heck, if I hadn't been paranoid that I wasn't quite emotionally stable yet from losing **[Center of the Galaxy]**, I'd have blown a gasket already. Only the fear of being painted as "emotional" kept my temper in check.

"That way." I pointed in the direction we were already going, feeling somewhat lame about it. "Strange mounds."

Hunting gave me a sharp nod.

"Probably the lairs and nests themselves."

He looked up at the sun. Mid-morning.

"Right, let's head on over." Hunting declared.

On one hand, I wish he'd asked for my input. On the other, I was wildly out of my depth and I knew it. It *was* faster and more efficient to just follow the lead of the massively experienced dude with almost 200 levels on me.

Hunting had done well for himself in the leveling department, fighting all the Royal Guards and Formorian Queens. Being able to single-handedly fight a Royal Guard when we were together was great experience, and I bet he'd killed more on the fight against the Queen.

We continued jogging over – I wasn't taking the risk in the air, not when Shooters could still be around, some last rearguard on the hive – and in roughly 30 minutes, crested over a little hill, to see the hives in all their grotesque glory.

[Name: Elaine]

[Race: Human]

[Age: 19]

[Mana: 153790/153790]

[Mana Regen: 133517 (+98425.6)]

Stats

[Free Stats: 51]

[Strength: 293]

[Dexterity: 347]

[Vitality: 2176]

[Speed: 2176]

[Mana: 15379]

[Mana Regeneration: 15379 (+9842.56)]

[Magic Power: 7897 (+106609.5)]

[Magic Control: 7897 (+106609.5)]

[Class 1: [The Dawn Sentinel - Celestial: Lv 305]]

[Celestial Affinity: 305]

[Cosmic Presence: 231]

[Solar Infusion: 1]

[Center of the Universe: 285]

[Dance of the Heavens: 305]

[Wheel of Sun and Moon: 271]

[Mantle of the Stars: 256]

[Sunrise: 11]

[Class 2: [Ranger-Mage - Radiance: Lv 256]]

[Radiance Affinity: 256]

[Radiance Resistance: 256]

[Radiance Conjuration: 256]

[Shine: 111]

[Sun-Kissed: 256]

[Blaze: 256]

[Talaria: 256]

[Nova: 256]

[Class 3: Locked]

General Skills

[Identify: 151]

[Pristine Memories: 200]

[Pretty: 152]

[Bullet Time: 268]

[Oath of Elaine to Lyra: 270]

[Sentinel's Superiority: 305]

[Persistent Casting: 189]

[Learning: 280]

Chapter 28

The Formorian Lands III

The ground had transitioned to hard rock ages ago. Centuries of Formorians marching over the ground, trampling any growth that might occur, had long since scoured the ground to a bare nothing.

The brownish-purple hill was visible, with two shattered remains of similar hills on one side, and a third destroyed hill on the other. A hill for each Queen. My bet was the Queens had been holed up inside, and when one died, the other three burst out of their lairs, and went on their rampage.

The wind shifted slightly, and the stench of mountains of flesh, rotting in the sun for weeks on end, hit us. Hunting pulled a disgusted face and leaned back, while I retched. That was just an ungodly terrible smell.

"Whole or broken first?" Hunting mused out loud, voice strained as he kept his throat clamped shut.

"Broken." I said, not wanting to come face to face with a dead, rotting Queen, the source of the stench so soon. I wanted to work up to it. I *needed* to work up to it.

"Should do the whole one." Hunting said, rubbing his hand over his stubbly chin, face twisted in an unhappy look. Clearly the prospect of going into the whole lair didn't amuse him either. "See what a normal lair looks like, before we see one that's been ruined."

"You're the boss." I went for a neutral tone, but didn't quite manage to keep the disgust out of my voice. Not at him, not at the situation, but at the stench.

We approached the hill, seeing a half-dozen large tunnel entrances in front of the hill.

Rather, I was strongly suspecting that they were tunnel *exits,* designed for legions of newly-hatched Formorian Soldiers to exit, continuing their endless march towards humanity. Some were probably entrance holes, designed to permit Formorians carrying food back into the hive.

I voiced my thoughts.

"Some are probably entrances, some are probably exits. Is it worth figuring out which one is which?" I asked Hunting.

He shrugged.

"Not right now. Let's just pick one and see what's there." He said. "Once we finish one, if it's not obvious, we'll take a look and see if we can find the other."

Plan sounded as good as any. We picked a random tunnel entrance, one that vaguely looked like it led to the intact mound, and headed in.

The tunnels were deceptively large, and we entered into a tunnel that sloped downwards, large enough that a Royal Guard could've moved through it – although with barely any clearance. Which was still an absurdly large size.

"Be on your guard. The entire fight, we never saw a Spitter." Hunting reminded me. I nodded. For all the talk of the worm-like acid-spraying creatures, I hadn't seen a single one. Part of that might've been because of Sealing's work to prevent them from attacking us from below. But it was entirely possible that they were just too slow outside of the lairs to come along on the attack, and had been left behind.

I was just starting to wonder what to do about lighting – I was probably going to use my skills – when Hunting *moved*.

He lunged towards a wall, jabbing it quickly with his fist. It was so fast I couldn't follow his movements, although I did notice the telltale whisps of darkness behind his movement.

With a yank, he pulled a long worm out of the wall, and threw it to the ground with disgust.

"Spitters."

I looked down at the Spitter. There was no head left for me to examine, just a clean cut that started halfway down the body. There was a long, slimy-looking grey body, leaking orangish blood from where Hunting had neatly severed it.

Not terribly interesting.

"I didn't detect that at all." I said after a moment of examining the Spitter.

"Not in your skillset, is it?" Hunting asked.

I shook my head.

"Illusions and mirages I can handle, no problem. Straight stealth, I've got nothing. Well, apart from lighting up the whole area. Won't spot them swimming through rocks or whatever these things do though."

That settled the lighting question for me. I made myself **[Shine]**, as strong as I could reasonably make it without draining my mana horribly, and felt somewhat pleased that Hunting needed to at least squint to look at me directly. The tunnel was lit up, brighter than the outside was, and we continued on.

Hunting would dart from place to place, jabbing the walls and killing Spitters. Now and then he'd kneel down for a punch, or jump up to superhuman heights and hit the ceiling.

Fortunately, he stopped pulling the Spitters out of the walls. No need to step over bodies. It might've clogged the tunnels they were moving through, or something. Heck, for all I knew they could swim through rock like it was water. I knew nothing about these monsters, and my knowledge of what was and wasn't possible with magic was constantly challenged. At this point, I should assume everything was possible.

Although I hadn't seen or heard of any time travelers, and in theory those should be super obvious. Like, one would've come to visit by now? Right? That only ruled out backwards time travel though, said nothing about forwards.

Thinking about it though – we were always time traveling. Forwards. Usually at one second per second. The thought made me crack an amused grin, although I didn't laugh. Wasn't the time or the place, and Hunting would think I'd lost my marbles.

We kept traveling like this, going deeper and deeper into the endless tunnels. Side-branches started to show up, then more and more, creating a dizzying labyrinth.

After the third tunnel, Hunting grabbed his spear, attached to his backpack as was Legion standard, and walked with the butt of the spear dragging on the ground. His skills were on full display as the end of the spear cut through the ground like putty, leaving a strong, obvious line behind us, the path to get back out. A ball of yarn for the labyrinth.

I could only hope there were no minotaurs.

We could legitimately get lost forever down here without the marker. Fortunately, it wasn't like something marked on a wall or anything. It was almost impossible to miss the deep furrow in the hard stone that Hunting was making.

It was funny to see it suddenly wildly zig-zag all over the place as Hunting would dash to a wall to kill another Spitter. A violent history, written as a squiggly line.

I was honestly not doing much, besides being a bright, portable light source. Hunting seemed to know exactly what he was doing, and quite honestly didn't seem to need me.

Then again, he was totally in his element. Flipping it on its head, it'd be like me in a triage tent. Sure, Hunting could act as one of the guards keeping things going smoothly, but it wasn't exactly in his wheelhouse. He'd feel just as useless there as I felt useless here.

That's what I told myself, to not feel as bad.

Hunting kept his head on a swivel, and at one point suddenly stopped, and took three steps backways, head snapping to the right.

"Dawn. Look." He pointed down one of the side paths, which immediately opened up into a massive space.

I looked at it, I looked at the main path we were on. Seemed close enough.

"Yeah, we should totally take a look." I said, heading that way.

We got to the room, and "big" didn't start to cover it.

It obviously wasn't one of the Queen's resting places. It was like a massive cylinder, going up higher than my light could easily reach, and dropping deeper than we could see. The air was warm and moist inside the shaft.

On every wall grew huge mushrooms, covering every surface. The only surfaces that weren't touched were dozens –

hundreds – of other tunnel entrances that also opened up into the room.

Hunting grunted.

"Well, guess this is how they were getting enough food. Will probably want to burn it on the way out."

I looked around. Some of the mushrooms looked hale and hearty, but others had telltale signs of rot, black edges to their earthy brown tones. I had to wonder if Arthur's poison had reached out to the extent where it had even poisoned their food supplies, creating a lethal cycle where his poison just stayed and accumulated, until it overwhelmed the Formorians.

We backed out, and kept going.

I honestly wanted no part of burning food sources. I could do a lot in the name of self-defense. There were large stretches of activities not covered by "Do no harm."

But burning the food source of the Formorians, when I knew a young, intelligent, baby Formorian Queen could eat it?

For whatever reason, that was beyond the pale for me. I'm not sure if it'd trigger **[Oath]** or not – my bet was no – I just couldn't do it. I didn't feel the urge to stay, or to try and clean the poison out, but burning food was a step too far for me.

Hunting turned and started walking back, while I took a moment more to admire the food cylinder. It was quite the structure, a monument to insectoid genius. It was a heck of a lot easier to admire when I knew that most of them were dead, and weren't busy trying to kill me.

I headed back to the main tunnel where Hunting was waiting for me, when a spray of green acid came out of the ceiling, hitting me full in the face.

"Argh! Fuck!" I screamed out, clawing at my face. While my trusty helmet had taken the brunt of the attack, some had slipped past and got covering my left eye, eating my face. The smell of dissolving flesh hit me, a sharp contrast to the ever-present rotting smell of the dead Queen, while I heard my flesh sizzle.

Hunting blurred as he leapt over me, stabbing the hole the Spitter had come out of.

301

I ripped my helmet off, cursing Spitters, cursing **[Bullet Time]**, cursing the whole damn mission.

One eye was blind, and with my other hand I furiously tried to wipe the acid off my face.

I cursed as most came off, but some stayed behind, adhering to my face and eyes.

"Gods dammit all!" I swore, clawing at the stuff, peeling it away in strips.

Hunting was looking at me with a disgusted look on his face as I finished getting the last of it off. I tried to blink to clear my eye, except after my eyelids closed it wouldn't open up again.

"Why is this sticky!?" I screamed. "Fucking eye!" I swore.

I had nothing for dealing with problems "outside" of my body, like dirt. Or in this case, stuff that was sticking to me that wasn't actually causing "problems", as the System seemed to define it. Good to know that gunk traps were a potential problem before I walked into a gunk pit or something.

I dunno, I wasn't thinking too clearly, blasted gunk in my eyes.

"Here, hold still." Hunting said. I held perfectly still, as his hand approached my face.

"You can heal just about anything, right? Including eyes?" He asked me.

"Yeah, but-" I started to say, only to feel fresh air against bone for a brief moment, before my eye regrew itself.

"Blah." I said, getting over the brief moment of not having an eye, then my vision popping into 3-D again as it regenerated.

Hunting was still looking at me with a strange look.

"What?" I asked him, all sorts of pissed off over the completely harmless attack having slowed me down so much.

"Never saw anyone peel their own face off before, that's all." Hunting said, in that carefully neutral tone I recognized as "oh that was so gross but I don't want to show it."

"Yeah, yeah, that's me. Can heal from most hits, but I generally have to eat them first." I grumbled. "Also, that attack just seemed irritating. I thought these were a big deal?" I asked Hunting.

He kept giving me a look, and knelt down to the floor, where some of the acid was still puddled. Some of it was green, the rest a nasty yellow. He delicately put his finger into the green portion, and I was met with the sound and smell of sizzling flesh again, as the tip of Hunting's finger vanished.

He promptly touched me, healing himself back up.

"Dangerous stuff, but my guess is you just heal too fast for it to do anything." He said.

"Except for having it turn to annoying goop sticking to my face." I grumbled, running a hand over my hair. Still had it all, although there was a sticky matted section.

Albina was going to get so much of my money to fix all this.

I looked at my helmet, pitted with marks from where it took the brunt of the attack. I gave a melodramatic sigh.

"I have a skill that warns me about dangerous attacks, but I guess it didn't activate because the attack isn't dangerous to me in the slightest. Just incredibly annoying." I griped.

Hunting pursed his lips at me.

"No offense, but why don't we head back, and make a camp. You can hang out there, while I go exploring. It'll be faster without you, and at this point I'm doubting there's anything here that can threaten me."

"Can't hurt me either." I pointed out, kinda wanting to go back but being stubborn about it. I didn't want to feel like I was being sent home while Hunting went out to play, but it kinda felt like that.

Hunting pointed to my helmet.

"Yeah, but it can wreck your gear."

Excellent. A beautiful excuse for me to get out of here.

"Welp, the **[Quartermaster]** is probably throwing all manner of fits over the entire expedition already. Let's not make it any harder on him than it needs to be." I said with far too much cheer, already walking back along the incredibly-obvious furrow that Hunting had left behind.

"No, we wouldn't want that." Hunting said, letting humor color his voice. "Come on, let's go."

I happily followed Hunting back out of the lair.

I could see why Night had such a hard time assaulting the place. A Royal Guard could completely block the tunnel, and as I had first-hand experience with, they were much tougher from the front than one of the sides.

Add in Spitters shooting from any direction, and Soldiers pouring around from all directions, and I could see an assault being problematic, to say the least.

Then, with a bit of intelligence, a second Royal Guard coming in from behind? Yikes. An attacker better hope they noticed before all the side tunnels were cut off.

"I've been thinking." Hunting said as we jogged out at a good clip. "I've got access to my third class, like Destruction and Night. I've had success so far with picking two completely different classes, and making them complement each other. I saw it with Brawling, and seeing it again in action now, well..."

Hunting shrugged as he trailed off. I seized on the chance though. Anything to distract him. Get him thinking about the future. I dunno, I wasn't a damn therapist, I was entirely the wrong person to bring this to.

"I assume you want all the healing tricks, not just some of them?" I asked him. Hunting nodded.

"Right then. The System likes to enhance classes off of your other classes, and more so off of your elements. I still have no idea what your fighting element is, but if you want everything in one class you'll want Celestial. With that being said, you'll want a Light starting class, to bounce off of your Void mage class, and get a stronger Celestial evolution. At the same time, you can't just snap your fingers and become a healer, unlike a mage. It requires significant study and education. Let's arrange some classes together once we're back in the capital."

"Aren't you going to be stuck out here?" Hunting asked me.

"Eh, maybe. Worse-case, read my *Medical Manuscripts*. They've got most of what I know in them. You just won't be able to ask me clarifying questions, and they're not exactly geared for beginners to just pick up and read."

"Also, don't other advanced elements have everything?" Hunting asked me.

"Yeeeeesss…" I dragged it out. "But I know Celestial inside and out. I can recommend and suggest stuff off of it. Fair warning. Light healer is incredibly difficult to level at lower levels, and it's not the most useful of elements to start with. I do think it'll pay off long term though, which is why I suggested it."

"What are my other options for all-in-one healing elements?" He asked me.

I shrugged.

"In theory, I think Radiance can do it all, but I haven't seen it and I don't see you getting a strong evolution into Radiance. Basically, you want a Light-aligned class with a destruction-aligned class, which is why Celestial is so darn good."

I paused a moment, thinking.

"It's more work, both learning and maintaining, and I know almost nothing about it, but you could also try the alchemy and potion-making route."

Hunting grunted assent.

"What other classes have you been thinking about?" I asked him, curious.

"Speedster. Make myself faster than even Night. Flier. High mobility, drop things from on high. Ranger. I don't have the ability to hit things well at a distance. Crafting. Make my own gear, possibly take an Inscription class. Like that potion making class you suggested. Hell, just settle down and take a hobby class. I've got some mosaic designs floating around in my head that I'd just love to put down in clay. The added stats alone would improve my combat capabilities, and I already have enough kill-things skills." Hunting enthusiastically told me about all his cool plans.

Boys and their toys. Never got old.

I suppose I got that way about certain topics.

"Fighting style is pretty set to boot." I added in. "I'd love to see what kind of mosaics you could make!"

I clearly touched a button, as Hunting went onto a long outpouring of his ideas. Behind those pitch-black eyes was, to my great surprise, the soul of an artist. Our relationship had always been friendly, but professional, and even when we hung out we usually talked about Katastrofi, his great love and passion.

Hunting kept talking as he dug out another campsite with his Void skills, making it larger than usual. I kept hearing about clay types, and how they impacted the final product. My eyes were glazing over like Virinium's clay, which apparently was the best, as the sun set.

Fortunately, I was saved from Hunting's tirade as the light dipped over the horizon.

"Crap! I gotta get back to scouting. Thanks for listening! Leave a message if you need to leave." Hunting said, starting to head back.

"What if I get attacked?" I asked.

"Then blow something up, or make it obvious there was a fight or something." Hunting replied back, starting to vanish back into the tunnel.

I shrugged. What else was I going to do?

Being strongly support-aligned was a bore at times. It was rare, but it happened. Like now.

I settled down into the larger, cozier version of the camp Hunting usually dug out of the hard rocks. Void was super duper convenient for that.

With everyone else grabbing and thinking about third classes, and my hopeful-immortality coming, I should start thinking about a third class. Plan it out ahead of time, instead of stabbing blindly like I'd done up until now.

The thought of classing up briefly flitted across my mind, before I dismissed it. I wasn't safe, not by any stretch of the imagination.

Upgrading and re-doing my [Persistent Casting] with [Dance with the Heavens] was a much better use of my time though.

I settled in, and started to focus.

[Name: Elaine]

[Race: Human]

[Age: 19]

[Mana: 153790/153790]

[Mana Regen: 133517 (+98425.6)]

Stats

[Free Stats: 51]

[Strength: 293]

[Dexterity: 347]

[Vitality: 2176]

[Speed: 2176]

[Mana: 15379]

[Mana Regeneration: 15379 (+9842.56)]

[Magic Power: 7897 (+106609.5)]

[Magic Control: 7897 (+106609.5)]

[Class 1: [The Dawn Sentinel - Celestial: Lv 305]]

[Celestial Affinity: 305]

[Cosmic Presence: 231]

[Solar Infusion: 1]

[Center of the Universe: 285]

[Dance of the Heavens: 305]

[Wheel of Sun and Moon: 271]

[Mantle of the Stars: 256]

[Sunrise: 13]

[Class 2: [Ranger-Mage - Radiance: Lv 256]]

[Radiance Affinity: 256]

[Radiance Resistance: 256]

[Radiance Conjuration: 256]

[Shine: 111]

[Sun-Kissed: 256]

[Blaze: 256]

[Talaria: 256]

[Nova: 256]

[Class 3: Locked]

General Skills

[Identify: 151]

[Pristine Memories: 200]

[Pretty: 152]

[Bullet Time: 268]

[Oath of Elaine to Lyra: 270]

[Sentinel's Superiority: 305]

[Persistent Casting: 189]

[Learning: 280]

Chapter 29

The Formorian Lands IV

With Hunting gone for the next couple of days, there wasn't much to do. Sure, I re-did my **[Persistent Casting]** with as perfect of an image as I could get. I played with my new skills, pushing **[Mantle of the Stars]** as hard as I could, weaving a series of complex images and pictures. Re-doing the **[Persistent Casting]** took me two days, and I felt that they were well-used. With a small amount of luck, it'd last me for *years*.

[*ding!* [Persistent Casting] leveled up! 189 -> 190]

Honestly, the skill leveling up was kinda useless. My mana regeneration was large enough that I literally couldn't tell that **[Persistent Casting]** was using some of it.

While it was hard to set up, I also practiced throwing out my **[Mantle]**, and grabbing and "pulling" stuff slightly. I wasn't going to be able to pick anything up off the ground, but if someone came at me at a glacial pace, I might be able to foul a spear strike.

Of course, at the speeds I was working with, I'd just be better off doing practically anything else under the sun or moons. It was like throwing a cape underwater. Slow to start with, then magic nonsense kicked in and seemed to make it even slower. In a world of stats, of physical classers, supersonic rocks, and poisoned gas, the trick wasn't going to get me very far.

But I was boooooooooooooooooooooooooooooooored. Sitting here all alone, with nothing to do. Being a soldier, being a Ranger was boring work half the time. However, we were a team. We found ways to entertain ourselves, usually by playing games with each other, or sparring, or self-improvement of one sort or another. Almost none of the activities were solo activities.

I did a solid amount of exercise, but I was no fanatic. I couldn't do that all day. I mean, I had skills to be the ultimate bodybuilder. Between [**Sunrise**] granting boundless energy, and [**Dance with the Heavens**] able to heal anything, it would be way too easy to lift heavy rocks, get stronger, and lift even heavier rocks with absolutely no cooldown whatsoever. I could get close to the physical fitness of an Olympian in just a few days.

I had no desire to be Olympic-class. Although, the games were starting again this summer, and I did want to watch.

Oooh, wait. I could totally be a trainer for one of the contestants.

I spent a few hours fantasizing about being a trainer for an athlete, instead of, well, becoming a grade-A athlete myself. Beyond a strong baseline that I felt I needed to have to be a proper Sentinel, I had no desire to push myself further. It was a heck of a lot more fun to imagine finding some poor kid off the street, and being the "gruff young mentor" who took her from zero to hero, dominating the entire Olympics! Every event! Gold to my student! I could even play up the "crazy person in the shadows" persona.

I was crazy bored, and imagining stuff was entertaining.

However, there was only so much playing with myself that I could do.

I wanted to bemoan the lack of books, but there was nobody to complain to. I tried to see if I could conjure up Librarian to talk with… although, upon reflection, that might be more that a little nutty, talking with myself like that.

I was going nuts staying in the underground campsite, with only the light from the entrance showing the passing of time.

I did what any incredibly bored person did.

I took a walk.

I wanted to leave Hunting a note, but we didn't have any writing supplies. It's not like we were expecting to send letters from the middle of the wilderness.

I tried to carve a little message into the hard walls of the campsite with my Radiance, but burning light versus stone?

Yeah, the stone kicked my ass.

I shrugged, and leaving my pack behind, making sure I still had my sword, I crawled out to get some sunlight, warmth, and fresh air.

I still reeked, having spent more than a month away from a bath at this point. I'd literally kill for a bath, and only feel a little bad for it. Add in me staying inside the cave for a few days, and whoof. It was bad in there.

I emerged from my cave, and shielded my eyes as natural light hit them. I hissed at the sun, briefly pretending I was a vampire.

"Ack! Away with you, vicious day-star! I curse your brightness! Go bother someone else!" I said, covering my face with my arms and rolling around on the ground.

… look, I was bored.

Having had my fun pretending to be a vampire, I decided I was now Elaine, Explorer Extraordinaire! Off to map strange new lands!

I looked around me, trying to decide what way to go. There was the lair, back the way we came, or the two other directions. I arbitrarily picked one, and started walking, then flying. Didn't go up too high, the sun was still in the air, but the day was moderately cloudy. Didn't want to get knocked out of the sky. Sure, I could probably survive any fall at this point. It didn't mean it was pleasant to fall screaming out of the air.

Plus, the Spitters were still around. Who knew if there were some Shooters or not?

I went on a little flight, making sure that I could always see the hive. Basically, I ended up doing a great big circle around the lair, keeping it as a landmark to make sure I didn't get lost.

That'd be incredibly dumb. I always made sure I knew exactly where the hive was located. It was right… over…

There. Phewf. Close one.

I flew back towards the hive with some relief. Elaine, the Explorer was ready to become Elaine, the Indolent. At least for like, another day or two.

Making it back to the lair? Easy mode.

Finding the relatively small hole that Hunting made, a basic level of disguise towards our little campsite underground? When everything around the lair looked the same?

That took me until the sun set, and even then I spent another two hours walking around with **[Shine]** on, cursing that I hadn't made an obvious marker or packed myself a lunch or anything.

Still, I did manage to find it, and happily tucked myself away. I hadn't appreciated how warm the campsite was, especially after a bit of focused Radiance work to heat it up, nor how nice the bedroll could be, or food! Hunger was the best spice.

I wrapped myself up in the bedroll, stealing Hunting's supplies to bulk up my blankets. It was getting awfully chilly at night, a combination of the southernly direction we'd traveled, and it being early winter now.

I closed my eyes and happily drifted off to sleep, wrapped up safe and sound in my **[Mantle of the Stars]**.

My nightmares decided to stomp all over my happy time. The Formorians were now working with the pirates and bandits.

Somehow made the nightmares a bit easier to handle.

"That was ugly." Hunting said, somehow managing to speak clearly in spite of shoveling food into his mouth at top speed.

"Tell me more." I said, not at all interested. Anything that a Sentinel was calling 'ugly' I wanted no part of, but at the same time, we were a team. We were the only real support network for each other, the only people that had some idea of the trials and tribulations we faced.

Elaine, the Good Listener was here! Hunting had shown up the next day, looking exhausted. Going for days on end, no matter what stats one had, would do that to a person.

Hunting had gone back into the lair, navigating through the twisting labyrinth, killing Spitters as he went. He did some damage to a few of the mushroom pits that we'd seen, but eventually gave up on trying to ruin them all.

"Then, I..." He said, trailing off with a thousand-yard stare. He shook his head.

"Never mind. Let's rest up. The Formorians are no longer a threat."

"We going to head back?" I asked, unable to keep the eagerness from my voice. Baths. Food. More baths.

Screw it, I was going to turn myself into a prune when I got home. Just spend a week inside the baths. I'd let Night know where to find me if there was some emergency or another, but I was going to get *clean*.

Mmmm. I had Autumn as an official apprentice. I'd make her do the fetching and carrying to keep me well-supplied when I was in my week-long bath.

I was so deep in my own fantasy world that it took me a few seconds to process what Hunting had said.

"Excuse me?" I asked incredulously.

"No, we're going deeper." He said.

"Because....?" I tried to keep my tone neutral, but some of my aggravation must've slipped through. We'd been on a long mission.

"Because I want to get a sense of what's on the other side. I want to get some idea of why all the Formorians came towards us. They only had the four Queens. Why did they risk them all on an attack? Why didn't they scatter, to make sure some of them survived? It smells." Hunting said.

I wrinkled my nose. I hadn't quite gotten used to the putrid stench, although I could kinda ignore it.

"Sooo... you want to take a peek, and see what happened?" I asked him.

"Yeah basically. For all I know, the ocean wraps around and they were trapped by the water, with no other place to go. Maybe there's a canyon, or mountains that they couldn't pass. Either way, the biggest danger is our food running out."

"How are we going to mitigate that?" I asked him, only to get a look in return.

Arms held out in a particular way, which could only mean one thing.

Ugh.

"I hate being carried." I muttered under my breath.

We sprinted through the lands at top speed for three days. Hunting had been humoring me before, when he kited me along on the end of a string. Now I was seeing what a physical Sentinel, over level 500, could do when he wanted to.

He was moving so fast, I could barely see what was going on. Not that there was anything to see, just endless beaten rock on one side, cloudy sky on the other.

I'd totally try to take a nap if it wouldn't be super awkward. This was somehow even more boring than being in the campsite. I needed skills to amuse myself.

Or, like, a portable library. Full of books.

I needed to convince people to start making books first. My attempts had failed miserably, mostly on scrolls being superior in most ways currently.

I'll confess, I half-dozed. At least Hunting was staying super-healthy, as he was constantly touching me and getting healed.

Then Hunting came to an abrupt stop, jolting me out of my semi-slumber. He never stopped like that, and I went from 20-100 instantly, half-jumping out of his arms at the same time that he dropped me, landing gracefully, ready for whatever was coming.

Well, what we were facing was dreaded by people and armies, not only in this world but on Earth as well. They had stymied thousands, and broken hundreds of spearheads against its bulk. A towering colossus, colored a dark reddish-brown, its length reached from horizon to horizon, and it was over two dozen meters tall. It cast a long shadow, reaching and stretching out, grasping at us.

It spoke of timeless strength, a menacing strength that promised to crush all those who came at it. A strength, so close to being a fundamental force of the world – of the worlds – arrayed against us.

314

Walls. Wooden walls, stretching as far as the eye could see. While there were clearly more than one log that had gone into building the structure, there were no obvious breaks or changes from piece to piece.

Well, not from this distance.

Wooden walls – not built by any human. At least, not any humans we knew of.

Hunting was busy getting his shield and spear ready, and I geared up, sliding my sword out of the scabbard into my hand.

"Careful. Let me do the talking." Hunting said. "Don't do anything unless you absolutely have to."

I nodded my assent, not wanting to contradict Hunting, even though I didn't quite agree with him. There were quite a few things I'd want to do preemptively, like running away, shielding, and more, but this wasn't the time or the place to argue, or make decisions by committee. Hunting was more experienced than I was, and was one of the top-ranking Sentinels, in spite of our theoretical equality.

Best to present a united front in the face of whatever this was.

We spent a few tense moments looking at the massive wall, before silently looking at each other, shrugging, and starting to walk towards it.

A bearded face, made tiny by the distance to the top of the wall, popped out and spotted us.

Under normal conditions, I wouldn't be able to hear what he was saying, but he was so loud, and there was nothing else making noise or between us and him, that I was just able to make out what he was yelling.

"Attack! Attack! The Formorians are attacking!"

Chapter 30

Dwarves I

Hunting and I looked at each other with concerned bemusement. On one hand, the call to arms from the wall was *mildly worrisome* to put it gently. On the other, we just couldn't get over being called Formorians.

The call to arms went on for a few minutes, Hunting and I awkwardly trading looks between each other then the wall, before a number of bearded faces popped over the walls.

I was not impressed with the response time. At all.

I was significantly more impressed – and concerned – when panels in the wall started to slide apart, and huge arrows, powered by massive ballistas, poked out of the walls.

I promptly ignored Hunting's instructions to not do anything unless absolutely needed, and raised my hands.

"Whoa! Don't shoot!" I yelled at them, getting a withering look from Hunting.

I shot him a "Are you fucking serious" look as he started to hunker down behind his shield.

"Hold! Hold fire!" A different voice called from the wall.

More inquisitive faces popped over the wall – along with a bunch of crossbows. I heard a loud curse, and some of the faces vanished.

I'm pretty sure we weren't supposed to hear what was happening, but the dudes were *loud.* Also, I'm pretty sure the guy wanted all his minions to hear the dressing down.

"Thofur Krelur the 93rd! You worm-ridden cheese-for-brains *idiot!* Do those look like Formorians!? Are they large, menacing ants!? Is that an unbreakable, unending tide? What was that? I didn't hear you! That's what I thought! NO!"

More faces popped up, took a look at us. Vanished again to discuss, this time at a quieter volume.

"Are you sure you're not Formorians?" Another head popped up and asked us.

We looked at each other.

"Think we should say we killed them?" I whispered to Hunting, only 60% confident that they couldn't hear us from a distance.

Hunting looked at me, clearly weighing my words in his mind. He eventually shook his head.

"They clearly seem hostile towards the Formorians, but what if they consider us to be a bigger threat because we killed them? Nah, we can always let them know later."

Wasn't going to argue with that.

A number of the ballistas withdrew into the walls, which would've been more reassuring if the three that were pointed towards us had also gone back in the walls. No, those ones turned to aim at us, which I didn't consider to be an improvement at all.

Eventually a door in the wall, so cleverly done that it was impossible to see that it was there at all, opened up, and a very nervous-looking, very short man with a massive beard walked out. Trembling somewhat, he walked towards us.

The penny dropped.

They weren't human.

These were dwarves.

He had on armor, but it was strange. I was somewhat biased from my experiences. I expected metal and leather, same as what we had. Instead, everything seemed to be made out of a shiny wood.

No – varnished wood. But it only looked like wood. I had enough experience with armor to see that it didn't move like wood at all, in spite of it obviously being wood.

It didn't look slapped together either. It was strong, solid, and had that polished look to it that high quality crafted goods tended to have.

"Hi! I'm Elaine! Nice to meet you!" I said, waving cheerfully at him. Everyone liked cheerful!

He got close enough for me to identify him.

[Warrior]. Around level 280 or so?

How was someone so damn high level so scared? He should be a fearless warrior.

He was clearly **[Identify]**ing us as well, as he bowed towards us.

"Healer. You grace us with your presence, and I wish to invite you to break bread and share salt with us."

I glanced at Hunting. That was an encouraging start to things!

"Thofur Krelur the 93rd! Sheep have more sense than you! Stop extending hospitality to them until we know more!" The voice from the wall yelled down.

"She's a healer! Tradition demands that we extend hospitality!" He yelled back.

That statement caused a lot of muttering on the wall, and more than a bit of yelling. Not enough to get anything concrete, but it seemed that when "Tradition" and "Border Security" collided, there was a strong question of which one took priority.

"Fine! Healer! You grace us with your presence, and I wish to invite you to break bread and share salt with us!" The command dwarf yelled from the wall.

I glanced at Hunting. He shrugged, and whispered to me.

"Seems to be an in. Let's take it, see what they're like. This tradition of theirs seems strong, and you're unlikely to get hurt by it."

I nodded, grinning.

"Everyone likes healers."

Thorfur Krelur the 93rd suddenly turned, and ran screaming back into the walls.

"Void mage! Void mage! He's a Void mage!"

And it had been going so well to boot.

Thorfur Krelur the 93rd – it only seemed appropriate to say his entire name, given that every time we heard his name it was the full thing – was running screaming back to the wall, and the ballista all came thundering back out of their holes. More holes in the wall opened up, and large gemstones, surrounded by glowing lines and Arcanite, popped out.

Naturally, they all turned and pointed at us.

I had no idea what skills were stored in those gems, but I didn't want to find out.

"Void Mage! You have six seconds to leave!"

"Six!"

Hunting and I looked at each other, briefly at a loss for words. If they'd attacked immediately, we'd be on the move, shielding and shooting and getting the heck out of here. The countdown starting at six, and not ten to boot?

Weird.

"Five!"

That got us talking, mostly over each other.

"I should stay."

"You should stay."

I tilted my head, letting Hunting take the lead, and the reins.

"Four!"

"They like you, they're clearly traditional, you're unlikely – scratch that, impossible – to be harmed. Plus, you could easily fly out if needed."

"Agreed." I said.

"Three!"

"They should have writing supplies. Get some. Take notes, lots of notes, on anything and everything. From the people you meet to the food. Get it all. I'm going to head back, and get a real team sent out here to relieve you."

"Two!" Our time was running out.

"Hopefully Night and Ocean, at the bare minimum. Maybe more. Anyways. Good luck, and when in doubt, shut up and don't do anything." Hunting said, continuing to give me the crash course.

"ONE!"

Hunting mock-groaned.

"I can't believe the architect of the *Pastos* incident is being used as a diplomat. What did I ever do wrong in life? We're all doomed." He said.

"Good luck." Were his parting words, as he vanished so fast it made my hair whip around.

I stared at the wall, the ballistas and glowing arrays of gemstones armed, primed, and pointed at me.

I held up my hands again.

"Please don't shoot."

"Hold! Hold! Withdraw!" Commander-dwarf was yelling and shouting. One by one, then in a sudden wave, the various arrays and ballista were withdrawn, folding back into the wall in such a seamless manner that I couldn't tell they were there.

With a bunch of muttering, most of the dwarves vanished off the wall, while I stood outside, awkwardly not moving.

Was I supposed to say something? Walk up? Stay here?

The awkwardness of the moment just made the seconds stretch out, longer and longer. I was just starting to think I should turn around and try to catch Hunting, when a door in the wall opened up, and Commander-dwarf showed up.

"Sorry about that." He said, before straightening up – hilariously, shorter than me still – and going all formal on me.

"I am Tilruk Falvim the 91st." He said, then stopped, staring at me expectantly.

"Um, hi. I'm Elaine." I said.

If the area wasn't a complete disaster, we would've had tumbleweeds. Tilruk Falvim the 91st's eyebrows started to climb a bit. I got some divine intervention, and the penny dropped for me.

"No, really. Elaine's my full, entire name. We don't do numbering. Well, some people number their kids, but they do it as their name, not as an add-on. Like Septima. She was super nice. Helped me at the river, kept reminding me when I lost stuff. Or like Octavia. She was the 8th kid. Got the name eight. Yikes, I haven't thought about Octavia in ages." I said, wincing as I remembered her fate.

Almost mine.

I was completely punting this, wasn't I? First human contact with another intelligent, reasonable civilization, and I was blathering.

I didn't count goblins as intelligent or reasonable, and selkies were inexplicably murderous. Although, I had somewhat worked with that one tribe…

Focus.

Tilruk Falvim the 91st seemed to mentally struggle for a moment. I could see his beard twitching every which way, as different parts of him went to war. No idea what that was, reading normal people was hard enough, let alone dwarves. before relaxing and deciding that what I said had been good enough.

"Greetings, Healer Elaine… how old are you?" He said, half-bowing, adding the last part sort of as a question.

I saw no reason not to answer that.

"19." I said, which got an eyebrow quirking up in surprise.

"19, 19… that'd put you in the 94th generation…" He mused out loud.

"Greetings, Healer Elaine the 94th" Tilruk Falvim the 91st formally said *again.*

I had this feeling that I was about to deal with a large amount of formality and repetition. My sanity was going to be in question at the end of this.

"Sure, Elaine the 94th, why not." I said, agreeing amicably. I wasn't about to go into titles and alternative names, not until I had a better grasp of what was what.

Also, I had a feeling that explaining what a Sentinel was wouldn't turn out great. Maybe they'd respect me for mentioning I was recognized as one of humanity's best. Maybe they'd be unhappy that I was in an organization full of "kill stuff dead" people. Maybe that'd strip the respect for my healer title away.

Not like I was hiding it, not with my armor on and weapons obviously visible on my waist and pack.

I just had no idea about anything.

Which, honestly, was par for the course when it came to anything *social.*

I'd gotten a blessed reprieve ever since Pastos.

I threw a quick **[Identify]** onto Tilruk, and got back a **[Leader]**, around level 340 or so.

When in doubt, use a mirror.

"Greetings, Leader Tilruk Falvim the 91st." I said, a heck of a lot more confidently than I felt, and bowed back.

"Healer. You grace us with your presence, and I wish to invite you to break bread and share salt with us." Tilruk said, giving the formal-seeming invitation a third time. My theory of 'lots of repetition' was confirmed to boot.

"I'd love to. What next?" I said, figuring I'd try the direct route.

Maybe it'd be easier to be so far off of their normal traditional route, than to try and mimic it? Instead of trying to sing their song and being horribly off-key, I wouldn't sing, and I'd just talk instead. Or some logic like that.

I dunno. I didn't do social stuff. I'd call this a win if I managed to get out of this without starting a large-scale war. Small war, sure. That was a win in my book.

He hesitated, then gestured, a near-universal 'come on in, the door's open.'

"Come! Follow me." He said, and I walked through the door in the wall.

I got a close, close look at the wall. I'd mentally marked where one of the ballistas had retracted into the wall – right above the door I was about to enter – and no matter how close I got, no matter how carefully I looked, there wasn't even the line of a seam.

I stepped through the door, and it was like I'd been drowning, and I'd come up for air for the first time in my life. Light had touched my face, when I'd lived in darkness. Water, quenching a thirst I never knew I had.

[*_ding!_* Congratulations! [The Dawn Sentinel] has leveled up to level 305->306! +3 Dexterity, +24 Speed, +24 Vitality, +170 Mana, +170 Mana Regen, +48 Magic power, +48 Magic Control from your Class per level! +1 Free Stat for being Human per level! +1 Mana, +1 Mana Regen from your Element per level!]

[*_ding!_* [Celestial Affinity] leveled up! 305 -> 306]
[*_ding!_* [Dance with the Heavens] leveled up! 305 -> 306]
[*_ding!_* [Sentinel's Superiority] leveled up! 305 -> 306]

"Whoa!" I cried out, hand over my heart, breathing rapidly.

"Are you ok? Is something wrong?" Tilruk said, looking concerned and worried, eyebrows furrowed.

"Ok? Ok!? I feel better than ok! I feel great! I feel wonderful! This is magical! Amazing! Fantastic! What did you _do!?_ What is this? An inscription? Wow! It's one heck of an inscription! I've gotta know how to do this!"

Tilruk was looking at me like I'd gone mad, which, in retrospect, wasn't an unfair assessment.

Slowly, like he was talking to a child, like he couldn't believe what he was asking, he spoke.

"Hang on. Are you talking about the feeling of leaving the dead zone?" He asked.

[*_ding!_* [Learning] leveled up! 280 -> 281]

"I dunno! If you mean that fantastic feeling just now, then yes!" I said, before my brain caught up to my mouth.

"Wait, what do you mean, dead zone?"

[Name: Elaine]

[Race: Human]

[Age: 19]

[Mana: 155500/155500]

[Mana Regen: 135176 (+99520)]

Stats

[Free Stats: 52]

[Strength: 293]

[Dexterity: 350]

[Vitality: 2200]

[Speed: 2200]

[Mana: 15550]

[Mana Regeneration: 15550 (+9952)]

[Magic Power: 7939 (+107176.5)]

[Magic Control: 7939 (+107176.5)]

[Class 1: [The Dawn Sentinel - Celestial: Lv 306]]

[Celestial Affinity: 306]

[Cosmic Presence: 231]

[Solar Infusion: 1]

[Center of the Universe: 285]

[Dance of the Heavens: 306]

[Wheel of Sun and Moon: 271]

[Mantle of the Stars: 256]

[Sunrise: 13]

[Class 2: [Ranger-Mage - Radiance: Lv 256]]

[Radiance Affinity: 256]

[Radiance Resistance: 256]

[Radiance Conjuration: 256]

[Shine: 111]

[Sun-Kissed: 256]

[Blaze: 256]

[Talaria: 256]

[Nova: 256]

[Class 3: Locked]

General Skills

[Identify: 151]

[Pristine Memories: 200]

[Pretty: 152]

[Bullet Time: 268]

[Oath of Elaine to Lyra: 270]

[Sentinel's Superiority: 306]

[Persistent Casting: 189]

[Learning: 281]

Chapter 31

Dwarves II

Tilruk continued to stare at me as the doors closed behind us, a soft teal light emitting from strips against the wall in the tunnel.

"You didn't come through the dead zone?" He asked me.

"I have no idea what that is." I repeated, confused as hell.

"Tis the place you just left." He said.

"The Formorian lands?" I asked him.

"Yer, that's part of the dead zone." He confirmed. "The other side where you live shouldn't be dead."

"How would I know if it was part of the dead zone or not?" I asked him.

I got a strange, pitying look from Tilruk.

"You would know." He simply stated.

"I clearly don't!" I said in frustration.

"Maybe you call it something else." He reasoned out. "Where do you start to get that feeling that nothing's right? Where once you return from it, it feels like the rich smell of trees and wood have returned, and all's right with the world?"

I gave him a blank stare.

"The feeling I got when I came in through the walls was the first time in my entire life that I've felt that." I said.

"But – but you're over level 300 before you're 20!" He sputtered out as we started to walk down the tunnel again.

"Thank you! I worked hard for it. Almost died. A lot." I said, shuddering at some of the memories. "Plagues, earthquakes, wars, volcanoes, tsunamis, Formorians, monsters, run of the mill dinosaurs, kidnappers and more!" I said, ticking them all off my finger. I'll admit, seeing him go slightly green was quite fun.

He stared at me in open-eyed shock and awe.

"Ye realize the dead zone eats experience, right?" He slowly said.

I stopped and stared at him.

"What?!"

The whole story slowly came out, as we were both too stunned by the other's revelation to keep walking through the tunnel.

In short, according to the dwarf's traditional history, which all dwarves were extensively educated on, the Formorians had tried attacking them once upon a time. A brief mental comparison against Night's recollections of events suggested that they had attacked the dwarves harder than humanity at first, which made sense if they knew about the dead zone.

However, once the dwarves had driven the Formorians back, and discovered the dead zone, they basically said "fuck it." What was the point of trying to claim "dead" land? If people felt miserable inside of it, and got significantly reduced experience, what was the point?

So, they carefully measured exactly where the dead zone started, and built a massive wall around it. The Formorians had attacked quite a few times, but as time marched on, they had stopped.

Still, *tradition* demanded that the wall was manned, guarded against Formorians or whatever other threat the dead zone generated. Not that they thought anything could be a threat, not with the large experience gain imbalance.

It did make me wonder though – what, exactly, could be 'eating experience'? That had terrifying implications. There was some grand force out there that could interfere with everyone's System access.

The existence of one suggested, but didn't promise, the existence of more than one. Although maybe it was the land itself, and not some creature, artifact, plant, fungus, elaborate curse, disease, godling, or other being that was eating the experience?

Like. Did vampires radiate a dead zone around them?

That... didn't quite make sense. Not with how Night and the other vampires moved around, and with how precisely the wall was located on the edge of the dead zone. With Night being on the frontlines, I'd expect the dead zone to have moved somewhat. Given the precision and timelines involved, I would expect that it was stationary, whatever the problem was.

Or the zone was just dead, and it was a quirk of the world. I'd need to try and find out one day.

I seriously doubted it was the Formorians. They were dead, and after all, the "living" zone was at the edge of their territory.

I needed to tell Night all about this. Probably the Senate as well.

There were a billion implications to this.

I was practically fuming by the time I'd heard it all.

"You're telling me, my entire life, through all my struggles, I've only been getting half the experience I should normally be getting!?"

It wasn't fair of me to yell at poor Tilruk. Don't shoot the messenger and all that. I. Was. Furious.

"Or less." Tilruk whispered.

I punched the wall. It was an unrestrained punch, with all my strength and weight behind it, with all my anger and frustration behind it. A trained punch, one I'd thrown thousands of times.

My low strength, high vitality, and persistent healing all stopped my hand from being rightfully broken. **[Center of the Galaxy]** even killed any pain I might've felt. All in all, a completely useless punch.

Did make me feel a bit better though.

"Whoa! Easy there!" Tilruk said.

"Sorry." I apologized, instantly feeling bad. In a minor win, my feelings of shame and regret flooded over me hard enough that I was no longer feeling terrible about having lost half my lifetime experience. Or more.

"Just. Friends of mine have died because I was too weak. People I've known and cared about are gone because my level was too low. Hearing that it was because I lived in the dead zone? That sheer blind bad luck probably caused it? That I should be level 600 instead of 300? It's deeply upsetting." I said.

Tilruk patted my arm, and we kept walking.

"If it makes you feel any better, you should only be about 50 or 60 levels higher, not 300." He said, without a lot of conviction.

I rolled my eyes, and composed myself.

"I apologize for my outburst." I said again, this time with more feeling.

"It's understandable. Hey, thinking about it, you probably spent a lot more time working on each class. Your class quality should be higher as a result." He said, and shot me an inquisitive look.

"Yeah, my healer class is dark green." I said. Sure, it was probably super-secret "don't let them know how strong you were" information, but screw it, I was never great at keeping secrets.

Tilruk let out a low whistle.

"That's a mighty powerful class you've got there."

"Thank you! Do you mind if I ask…?" I trailed off, not really wanting to ask. "Don't tell people about your stats" was still deeply ingrained into me, which had asking about stats and skills being equally rude.

"Orange." He said, with obvious pride, then deflated.

"I worked my axe to the handle a dozen times, and Orange was the best I got." He said, a strange mix of pride and unhappiness mixed together.

Heck, if my 256 class was Orange, I'd be pretty upset as well. Then again, I did just show him up massively.

"Maybe it's because life in the dead zone is harder?" I suggested, trying to claw back some benefit to having had most of my experience eaten.

"Aye, and since it takes more time for you to level up, you've got more time to get achievements." Tilruk added in.

Did I just successfully pull off some minor diplomacy!?

I pinched myself, before rolling my eyes at **[Center]** completely killing off any negative aspects of the pain, just letting me know I'd been pinched. How could I check if I was in dreamland or not if pinching didn't work?!

Tilruk abruptly changed the subject.

329

"What were you doing traveling with a Void mage?" He asked me, all curious. "For that matter, you're not also a Void mage, are you...?" He looked at me warily, hand wavering madly between his side, and itching towards his sword.

I didn't want to find out where "hospitality" and "kill the Void mage" landed.

"Nope! Radiance is my second element!" I said, letting myself **[Shine]**. I suppose that it didn't show I was Radiance, that I could be Light, Brilliance, Mirage, or something else similar – but either way it demonstrated I wasn't a Void mage.

[*ding!* [Shine] leveled up! 111 -> 112]

I pursed my lips in how damn unfair leveling up seemed to be all of a sudden.

"What's up with Void mages anyways?" I asked him. "Sure, Hunting's super strong, but why the concern over them?"

I got another long look, as the end of the tunnel through the wall approached.

"The long-horned pansies keep telling us they randomly explode, taking out a city at minimum with them. Doesn't matter the level of the Void mage, level 30 or level 3000. Boom. The pointy-eared bastards are a right pain in the rear, pardon my expression, but when they swing by to warn us of stuff, they're usually right." Tilruk grudgingly admitted.

"They're shit at working with wood though." Tilruk added in, seemingly needing to regain some pride back.

That... was a ridiculous amount to unpack.

"We're here." Tilruk announced, as we made it to the end, right before the door leading out.

I decided to aim for some last-second flattery. All the talk about wood made me think they considered it important.

"I'm impressed." I said, waving my hand around, gesturing at the wood all around us. It was impressive. Dozens of different shades of wood, and not a single obvious joint, join, or break in the wood. Also, some of it was glowing, providing light, without any obvious inscriptions. Those pieces of wood were some master inscriptions. I was about as subtle as an elephant in a library, but eh. It *was* impressive.

"Ah? At what?" Tilruk asked me.

I gestured around me.

"This! All this wood, so beautifully crafted."

I could hear the smile in his words. "Aye. We dwarves are masters of wood. From finding good places to plant trees, to creating the perfect soil, nurturing seedlings, to growing giants. We're masters of it all."

Pride and admiration colored every word he spoke.

"Then the cutters, in the right season at the right place come along, chopping the tree down and removing branches." He said, and his voice was significantly less respectful when mentioning them, but then it yo-yo'd right back.

"The sawyers remove the bark, season the wood, and cut it into planks as needed."

Tilruk's tone took a reverential tone, the sort that was usually reserved for priests. Heck, with the way he was talking, it almost seemed like a religion.

"Then the carpenters get the wood, and oh! What wonders they perform! From the [**Grand Wall Carpenter**]s that made this wall, all the way down to the [**Living Armor Carpenter**]s who made my armor," Tilruk took a moment to beat his chest with a single fist, a sharp knock telling me just how sturdy it was. "the carpenters make everything that we use to live."

"Cool." I said, not having anything better to say. I'd clearly hit a spot of pride. *When in doubt, shut up.*

Note to self: Compliment whatever dwarf I was talking with on whatever wood-related thing he or she seemed to have going on.

"Anyways, letting you know about them now. They outrank us, and there's further complication depending on what type of wood they work on. Don't worry about that, although don't offend anyone who works on redwood or higher. Anyways! Let's go!"

331

Tilruk Falvim the 91ˢᵗ opened the door, letting the bright light in. I squinted as I got my first good view of how another country, another civilization, another species lived.

Wood. Wood everywhere.

I'm not sure why I was even slightly surprised.

It was clear that the posting next to the dead zone wasn't one of the plum assignments, and that most, if not all, of their budget went to maintaining the actual wall. Oh, nothing was in disarray, but it was clear that things had been built properly ages – maybe decades or centuries ago, I had no idea what they could do with wood – and just sort of left there. A few dwarves were sparring, axes and swords and spears flashing and hitting wooden shields with solid *thunks,* but even more dwarves were just spectating, lounging around and watching with a mug of what I assumed was beer in their hands.

The buildings all gave off a strong militaristic vibe, and even though we'd just exited the tunnel in the wall, I could already see where the tightly packed buildings abruptly ended, edging against a forest.

Militaries were similar the world around. I would've needed to be blind, as well as deaf, to miss the sparring ring. The large number of many-windowed buildings that all looked exactly the same had to be the barracks. The large, boring-looking building was a warehouse of some flavor. Armory or granary, I had no idea. I didn't want to poke around, and be accused of spying.

I mean, in a sense I totally was spying, because everything I saw would eventually end up in front of Night, and, unless another Sentinel showed up in a hurry, I'd probably end up in front of the Senate.

No reason to give the dwarves a sense or idea that I was hostile, or give them a reason to try and kill me.

I'd go down fighting, but there was no question that I'd go down.

Then again, I had to remember – even Tilruk, a commander, only had an orange-tier class. The difference in tier was starting to become more significant than the raw levels would suggest, and the people I was looking at were weaker than I'd expect them to be.

Still. I didn't want to get into a fight. Heck, throw me into the infirmary, and let me work my magic!

Speaking of, there were a few more unique structures, with slightly more polish than the other ones. I was out of my depth guessing what, exactly, they were. Did the Quartermaster get his own building? The armory? Spare gems for the arrays? The infirmary, like I was wondering about? Was that a stable for some sort of exotic creature? A central place to control arrays and the ballistas?

Only so much guessing I could do, but one building was all too obvious, and it was the one Tilruk started to take me towards.

"Come on. Let's go meet the commander of this section, and break bread." My dwarven companion said, leading the way to the fanciest building, one with a flag on it. Green Oak against a blue field.

At least, I assumed it was an oak. I hadn't paid too much attention to trees in my survival lessons beyond "this one's poisonous" and "The wood of that tree will ruin anything you cook."

Wood was wood, and would all burn.

Anyways!

The   headquarters!

Chapter 32

Dwarves III

Tilruk escorted me towards the building I had to assume was the headquarters. A pair of stout, slightly more serious looking guards were at the door, wooden helmets open enough to allow their intricately braided beards to flow down.

I eyed up the beards and spent a few moments thinking.

Normally, the Rangers considered long hair to be an impediment in a fight. Easy to grab and pull, and I'd gotten good at cutting my hair short, as much as I wanted it long. I swear my hair was like a yo-yo at times. Long, short, magically long again, burnt off.

Anyways. The coarseness of the beard, along with how it was tied with little pieces of wood and beads woven in made me think that trying to stab or slice through said beard would end poorly, and it did make for a strong neck guard.

Wood was still the name of the game, and the building, while large and fancy and headquarters-like, still somehow gave off a strong "log cabin" vibe. I don't know if it was the neatly stacked logs making up the walls, the wooden shutters, or sloped roof that was making me think log cabin, in spite of the huge size, but there it was.

"Tilruk Falvim the 91st" one of the guards saluted and respectfully greeted him.

It was a little unsettling. Rangers and Legionnaires saluted by thumping our right hand in a fist over our heart. The dwarves saluted by smashing their fists together, gauntlets and all. Sounded like someone knocking sharply on a door once.

"I am here to meet with Briga Glof the 90th on a matter of moderate importance." Tilruk said.

I mentally gave him the stink eye as I was only of 'moderate importance'. I liked being the super-important person that got things done. I would've hoped that being the first contact from a civilization within the dead zone would be enough to jump me up.

Ah well. Couldn't have it all.

The guards eyed me up.

"Healer." The second one respectfully said, bumping his fists together in salute.

"Who's she? Some dwarf from the metal clans who isn't even old enough to grow her first beard who wandered over?" The guard grumbled unhappily into his beard.

Idiots. They existed the world around, and no culture or race seemed to be immune to them.

Then again - I was short enough to be a tall dwarf, and we didn't seem to look that different. Being slightly generous to Grumpy, as I was nicknaming him, his line of thought was reasonable, if off.

Also, the revelation about metal clans? Oooooh, I wanted to know *more*. Heck, this entire thing made me want to know more about everything. How they got wood to do all the things I saw them doing with it. Maybe I should ask for a tour at some point? Get a list of magical woods and what they could do?

I was totally getting ahead of myself.

"Visitor from the dead zone." Tilruk eventually answered. "Figured Briga Glof the 90th was the person to bring her to."

The guards glanced at each other and shrugged.

"Not our place to say if your reason's good or bad for seeing Briga Glof the 90th" Grumpy said. "Might want to leave the weapons behind though." He added, eyeing up my spear, still on my backpack, and the sword on my hip.

I frowned at him, and nothing more was said on the subject.

My estimation of their martial prowess was rapidly plummeting.

Another round of knock-on-wood salutes, and we entered the building. It was nothing special on the inside, although all the ceilings were lower than I was used to in Remus. I imagined there were no Arthur-sized giants roaming around.

A hop, a skip, and a jump later, and we were knocking on the door to who I assumed was Briga Glof the 90th.

"Enter." A contralto voice called out, making my ears twitch in surprise.

We entered into a large wooden room. This one was a bit fancier and better decorated than the previous militant hallways we'd gone through. There was a fancy painting on the wall, a number of tiny dwarves working industriously around a large tower. Upon closer examination, the "painting" was actually just a large number of tiny wood chips, each one carefully painted and placed together, like a large puzzle.

Six different potted plants - saplings - were neatly tucked into corners, with two more flanking a large, elaborate desk. The desk itself was a work of art, looking like it'd been carved out of a single piece of wood, with a different dwarf having been carved into each of the legs, and a picture of a heroic battle of dwarf versus *something* was carved prominently in the front.

If the enemies were goblins, I couldn't tell. The artist seemed to have deliberately made them as ugly and awful as possible. No points for guessing how they felt about said enemy, even in victory.

The rule of "Armor got more ornate and decorated as rank went up" seemed to hold true for dwarves as well, with Sentinels still being the only group of people who went for simple armor.

Except our capes. And our badges. And the silly amount of Arcanite and gems woven into our armor. And - ok, fine, we just did ornate a different way.

Behind the desk was a large flag, same as outside, and a bookcase.

I locked eyes with the dwarf I assumed was Briga Glof the 90th.

"Briga Glof the 90th." Tilruk said, saluting in the same strange knuckle-clapping way.

"Tilruk Falvim the 91st." Briga Glof the 90th said from behind the desk, saluting back. A benefit of their salute – it was easy to do while sitting down.

My brain caught up to my eyes, and I barged forward.

"Whoa, is this a bookshelf!? You have books!?" I said, ignoring the stunned look from Tilruk and the glare from the commander.

I grabbed the first book I could see on the bookshelf, and read the title out loud, savoring every word.

"Playing with his wood: An in-tree-mate guide."

There was dead silence at what I said. I felt heat rush to my cheeks as I realized what, exactly, I was holding and I'd read.

"Um, yeah, I'm going to just put this back..." I said, only for a skill to take the book and rip it out of my hand.

"YOU!" Briga Glof the 90th roared at me, and I felt a skill grab me and violently move me, placing me into a chair at high-speed in front of her desk. "What are you doing!?" She screamed at me.

"And you!" She yelled, pointing at Tilruk. "What are you doing bringing this cretin before me!?"

Tilruk was shooting daggers at me, which I suppose I deserved. He saluted, in the most polite "Get me out of trouble" military manner I'd ever seen.

"Tilruk Falvim the 91st reporting. Healer Elaine the 94th came out of the dead zone with a Void mage. Claims to be part of a civilization living inside the dead zone. Offered her hospitality, as tradition demands for a healer, and brought her to see you, so that we may all break bread together." He said.

80 coins said he was leaning on tradition to bail himself out of trouble. Another 200 coins said that tradition demanded he get punished anyways.

Or rather – that Briga Glof the 90th would say that tradition demanded he get punished.

I got the stink-eye, which I couldn't meet. Embarrassment flooded through me again, and I looked down at the floor.

Nice paneling.

"Hi I'm Elaine nice to meet you." I mumbled.

"Tell me, Healer Elaine the 94th." Briga Glof the 90th said with a dangerous voice. "Is pawing through others personal belongings normal from whatever backwater place you come from?"

"No ma'am." I mumbled to the floor, still embarrassed.

"What made you think it was appropriate to go through my *personal* belongings?" She asked again.

"Sorry! I love books a ton, and it's been almost 20 years since I last saw one! I just wanted to read..." I said, putting a pitiful, plaintive note in my voice at the end.

"You have great taste?" I tried to rectify the situation somewhat.

Nope. More evil glares.

I matched it, letting the shame fade away.

I locked eyes with her, feeling some of my confidence return.

Screw being Healer Elaine the 94th. I was Sentinel Dawn, and I had the class, skills, stats, levels, and experience to back it up. No two-bit commander on a semi-neglected fortification was going to stare *me* down.

Even though I had read the cover of her smut book.

Out loud.

In front of her minions.

She gave an amused grunt after some time.

"Not entirely spineless after all. Tilruk! Bring us bread, for the three of us to share. In the Willow room, if you'd please." She ordered.

Tilruk saluted and hurried off.

I got another side-eye, followed by a sigh.

"Come. Let us break bread and share salt, and I'll listen to your tale." Briga Glof the 90th said, getting up from behind her desk.

I followed her as she exited her office, and we made it to another room.

I expected a picture of a willow tree as the door, or something.

No. Of course not.

They had a fully grown, miniature willow tree inside the room, branches reaching up to the ceiling then forming a graceful curtain around the edges of the room.

A sturdy, ornate table dominated the room, with chairs around said round table.

"Come! Sit!" Briga Glof the 90th said, gesturing around. "Feel free to put your pack down by the wall." She pointed to a spot, where I happily shucked my backpack.

My strength and general fitness usually made it a non-issue, but it was still awkward to lug around, plus I did get tired.

Also, sitting in a chair with a big backpack on? I'd look *ridiculous.*

After my bookshelf fumble, I was being a hair more careful. I looked at the table. Completely round, no hints there.

The chairs though, each one was seemingly made out of a different wood. Or had a different color at least. I had a sneaking feeling that a "proper" dwarf could look at the chairs and instantly identify which one came from what type of tree, and the "right" chair to sit in, if any, depended on the wood.

I skipped a reddish-looking one, and sat on a pale chair. Birch? Was this birch? I hoped so. I think that was low on the wood totem pole? Probably wouldn't cause offense by sitting here.

Unless TRADITION demanded that the healer always sit in the third chair from the left, or the maple tree was always reserved for the healer.

Shit. There was probably some tradition like that. I should've asked instead of just sitting. My plan of "just do whatever and don't try to follow tradition" might backfire when there was a distinct way of doing things.

Tilruk came back, with a simple tray of bread, and a small bowl of salt. Without hesitation, he served me a small loaf, then looked at me expectantly.

Time to *ask,* and stop guessing at shit I had no idea about.

"What's the traditional thing to do here?" I asked him, gesturing. Behind him I saw Briga Glof the 90th crack a grin, then quickly suppress it down.

Score!

"Dip the bread in the salt, and take a bite." Tilruk said.

I did exactly what he said, chewing thoughtfully on the bread as Tilruk moved on.

He served Briga Glof the 90th the second loaf, and himself the third. Both of them performed the same ritual, dunking the small loaf of bread in the salt, and ritually eating it.

I felt like I was expected to say something here, and, just blind guessing, I figured I'd go with my "do something sincere and hope it panned out" plan.

"Thank you for granting me shelter, food, and hospitality." I said, deciding to just check off all the boxes. "And letting me in. Talking with me. Meeting with me. Helping me level. Educating me..." I said, ticking the items off my fingers.

Briga Glof the 90th gave Tilruk a significant look, who made himself scarce.

"Speaking of educating, I'd love to know more about where you're from, and what you are. Do you *really* live in the dead zone?" Briga Glof the 90th asked.

That was a big question. I figured I'd tackle it one at a time.

"As far as I know, yeah." I said, stretching in a luxurious manner. The *feeling* I'd had the entire time I'd been in dwarven territory was fantastic. The intrinsic happiness and completeness that I hadn't known was missing. "I'm in a group of people that are some of the highest-level humans Remus has, and we just barely got the first of us to hit level 500, which is a rarity. Only managed *that* after killing the Formorians. Dozens of Royal Guards at level 750, and the Queens, over level 1000."

Tilruk came back at this point, wheeling a trolley loaded with food.

Including apples! And pears!

"What are those called?" I asked, pointing to them, totally side-tracked. I could eat an apple again! I could taste a sweet, juice pear once more!

Sure, I hadn't been the biggest fan of pears back on earth, but a chance to try them again! Oh my heart be still.

"Apples." Briga Glof the 90th said in the standard language we all spoke, pointing to the apples. "Pears. They're tasty, you should try them."

"Thanks! It's been ages since I last had one!" I said, happily accepting the apple from Tilruk and biting in, closing my eyes in delight as an explosion of flavor erupted in my mouth.

I got a *look* for that.

"How have you eaten them before without knowing the name?" I got asked, with a tone of genuine curiosity.

I froze, juice dribbling down my chin. I chewed slowly while I thought about it.

I was *not* having another interview with government vivisectionists. I wasn't going to go over the whole reincarnation shtick, not again. This time, I could bail, and was going to.

I also didn't want to lie to them.

Think. Think. *Think!*

"Um. Long story?" I said, happily starting on the pear. "What other questions do you have?"

"Does nobody have a beard?" Tilruk blurted out.

I smiled. Easy question!

"Men can grow beards, women generally can't. However, with the exception of one city, culturally, men shave in Remus." I answered.

"Wait – they voluntarily shave!?" Briga Glof the 90th asked with surprise. "And you can't grow a beard at all?" She said, with a tone of extreme pity.

"I'm so sorry to hear it." She said, moving her hand as if to pat my shoulder.

Briga Glof the 90th opened her mouth as if to ask another question, then closed it.

"Tilruk. Can you please get Quartermaster Dwen Flidi the 90th, Executive Officer Kolran Dem the 91st, Head Builder Khelvem Kroku the 91st, and Captain Dwen Flidi the 92nd here? I believe they should be present for what Healer Elaine has to say."

A quick shuffling around, a delicious lunch eaten in relative silence – I had no idea what the steak was, but it had a delicate, sweet, and juicy note to it. Didn't have that strong flavor I associated with most dinosaur meat, but who knew. They probably had radically different dinosaurs here to boot!

I wanted to know more. I wanted to know everything.

Four more dwarves filed in, three of them with a book and quills. The better to take notes, I guess? Or read under the table during yet another "boring" meeting. Heck, I totally would've read under the table during most of the Sentinel meetings if there had been any books to read!

I *had* to get as many books as possible from the dwarves. I also needed to import the book technology. Heck, forget spending my money on artwork or real estate. I could manufacture books instead!

Wait, shit. That would require authors and writers to make stuff to print.

Hmmmmmmm.

I'd need to import it from the dwarves then. Might be a bit of a pain, but if I was going to be living in the border town anyways, might as well get some trade started.

Assuming there wasn't going to be a war.

… I could totally see Night trying to redirect the generals into attacking the dwarves over having a civil war though. For all that he was espousing neutrality, I could see him seizing the chance for relative stability, especially against an opponent who showed no interest in invading back. Humans were warlike enough, and tribal enough, to jump at the chance to boot.

I was going to get a massive headache from all of this.

Chapter 33

Dwarves IV

Four dwarves filed into the room, without Tilruk. Shame. I liked him, and hoped he'd stick around.

Briga pointed to each in turn, and repeated their names, making introductions. I had so many new things today, and life was so strange, that they all sadly went in one ear, and out the other.

Ok, sure, I could probably recall the names with **[Pristine Memories]**, but nicknames were just easier.

Instead, I mentally labeled them "Braids, Beads, Woven, and Messy", depending on what their beard was. Braids had long braids on the side of his beard, Beads had a bunch of beads in her beard, Woven had a complicated, intricate pattern in her beard, and Messy required no description for his beard.

Not that one would be easy to give.

I tuned back in after Briga went over the names.

"Everyone, this is Healer Elaine the 94th. She's had an interesting journey to get here."

There were mutterings of greetings around the table, and four almost-identical offers to share bread and salt.

Oh, for fuck's sake. I'd already shared bread and salt!

I had a feeling I was going to be thoroughly sick of bread and salt by the time I was done here.

Maybe that's why they venerated healers so much. Nobody could tolerate the constant "tradition", and nobody signed up to be one.

"She's a... actually, what are you?" Briga asked me, seemingly realizing she'd never asked.

"Human. I'm a human." I said.

"Human." Briga said, savoring the word. "We're dwarves." She said, giving me the standard name for the species in the Pallos common tongue.

"How do we even speak the same language?" Braids asked.

We all turned and looked at him.

I blinked.

That was an *excellent* question.

"We're speaking our traditional language." Beads muttered into her beard. "How did you get our traditional language?" She asked me, peering at me suspiciously.

"I have no idea." I replied, thinking about it.

We spent a few moments pondering quietly about it, before I snapped my fingers.

"Night!" I exclaimed.

I got puzzled looks around the table.

"Sorry. Night. My boss. He was around during creation. Told me language got dumped in his head. He's been around, for, well, forever, as I said. You mentioned you're speaking your traditional language, so, maybe not too much linguistic drift. Night, and the other vampires, have probably stopped our language from drifting too far."

That... was a hell of a feat thinking about it. It'd been almost 5000 years since creation. Neither language had drifted at all? We could still understand each other, when it only took a few hundred years for languages to change to an unrecognizable state?

I suppose massively increased lifespans probably threw any number of wrenches into linguistic drift, and it'd take thousands more years for languages to properly diverge.

Or they never would. What did I know, I was no linguist.

"Your boss?" Messy asked, while everyone was looking at me like I'd grown an extra head. "What do you do?"

That seemed to snap them out of whatever funk they were in. Briga smacked him upside the head.

"You know someone of the first generation?" She asked me, with a reverent tone.

"Um. I guess? No idea how your generations work though." I answered, more than a bit confused.

"How could they have someone from the first generation though?" Woven asked, a frown being magnified on her beard.

"Entirely possible that this Elaine has gotten it wrong. The time involved..."

She shook her head.

"Close to impossible."

Briga shot Woven a look.

"Proper respect is due to our guest that has accepted our hospitality." She rebuked Woven.

There was some more bickering over Night, before Briga raised her hand.

"Enough. Healer Elaine. You said he was your boss? What do you do?"

"Oh, I'm a Sentinel. Sentinel Dawn." I said, putting a smile on my face and pointing to my badge.

"What does a Sentinel do?" Briga asked. "Is it an organization of healers?"

I laughed. I wish we had some of those!

"No, military." I said, getting a bunch of hostile looks in return.

Mmmmm.

I kinda deserved that didn't I?

"How does that work?" Briga asked me.

That kicked off a long, long conversation between the six of us. I dimly recognized that I was being pumped for information, just like I was trying to get some information out of them.

If it was a game, I would've totally lost. By a huge margin.

They were fascinated by the account of the end of the Formorian war, although they were entirely disinterested in the gods and the angels, practically waving them all away. Not terribly religious. They venerated their ancestors, and placed great stock on what generation someone was in.

I couldn't quite keep a lid on Destruction being able to create massive earthquakes, although I probably played it up a bit. Oooh humans! Super scary!

I was honestly trying to not start a war. I have no idea if what I was doing would backfire or not.

... why did we think this was a good idea again?

At the same time, nothing I told them was exactly *secret*. Most everything was standard knowledge, like the fact that Remus has a Senate, and that Rangers existed in teams of eight.

Things like average level, class quality, how many Sentinels there were and what our jobs were?

I kept a lid on all that. I wasn't going to tell a clearly military force the details of our top-end.

I was bad at diplomacy; I wasn't terminally stupid.

We talked for hours, and I got to know some of how they were structured.

Their country was called Nolgrod, and there was a second country of dwarves called Khazad. That bit of information they were a little reluctant to part with, but it mainly seemed like some sort of bad blood, or rivalry, between the two. Not out of any concern for the information.

"What do they do?" I asked, trying to channel Brawling a bit. 'Innocent, naïve questions.'

"They rip up the earth." Messy said with a frown. I was getting good at reading beards! "They grab and they take stone and metal, which will never be restored, and build their own monstrosities with them."

"Plus, they're all wrong on the generations." Beads grumbled. "They're on the 41st right now, which is all wrong. Not at all what our ancestors wanted. This is the 94th generation!"

Translation: When the guard dwarf had asked if I was from the metal clan, that was a derogatory way to ask if I was a dwarf from Khazad. Also, those were the dwarves that used metal, while the Nolgrods used wood.

Which started an hour-long propaganda speech on the superiority of wood versus metal, with all of the dwarves happily patting themselves on the back about how they were soooooo much better.

Which got more than a few dirty looks thrown at my equipment, which naturally got my hackles up.

"Like take Healer Elaine's vambraces." Beads said, gesturing to me. "Sure, the metal's plenty hard, but the moment it gets a scratch, she'd need to return to a metal crafter just to get them fixed! Every time! Living wood's much better, it'll just repair itself."

I was beyond cranky. The shots weren't deliberately at me, but, well, they hurt, and I'd just spent a bunch of time in Hunting's unhappy company.

"Sure, but can vambraces made out of living wood do this?" I asked them, taking it off, and flipping it around. Showing them the dozens of gemstones interwoven into the armor, that normally pressed against me.

I smirked as they all looked avariciously at my gemstones.

Wood is superior my ass. I smugly thought to myself. Maybe they were just ragging on the Khazad because they were jealous of all the gems they probably got from mining?

Then again, they had many hundreds of valid points as to why making everything out of wood was good. I wanted to know more – a lot more – and hey, I might be getting a third class one day. I should start doing some light thinking about it. Maybe there was something to be said for wood, carpentry, and making things out of wood? A hobby, combined with making my own armor that could adapt to me and repair itself?

Magic was *so damn cool.* I still held onto that girlish excitement. There was so much I could do with it! Unlimited potential, endless possibilities! An open third class that I could properly plan for, while having maturity, and experienced advisors, was the most exciting thing *ever!*

I'd been a frog in a well when I'd picked my first second class – **[Student]** – and I'd been fairly haphazard with leveling and classing it up. Thankfully it merged into my first class, but then I'd grabbed a **[Firebug]** without having knowledge or experience to back it up.

Now I could see a third class coming down the line, and-
Wait.

I wanted to hit my face, I felt so dumb.

Dead Zone. Eats experience.

I totally needed to do healing and leveling stuff **OUTSIDE** of Remus! I'd level so much faster!

347

And I got more experience by doing new things…

I wonder if the dwarves needed a strong, free healer?

I should be paying more attention to what they're saying about my vambraces. Damnit! Totally the wrong time to have an epiphany.

"Are those all your gemstones?" Beads was asking, a note of disbelief and longing in her voice.

Yesss. Everyone liked shiny stuff, and a quick mental review had that what I'd missed was mostly the dwarves asking rapid-fire questions. The only other thing I'd missed was every dwarf protesting that, yes, gems could fit into wood just fine. I could *totally* gracefully re-enter the conversation here, and it wouldn't look like I'd missed anything.

Bless **[Pristine Memories]**. While it didn't help me focus, it mitigated the heck out of getting distracted.

"Nope! Got more… all over really." I said, realizing that I might've said just a hair too much. I didn't want to give away all of my armor and gear's tricks. It'd be possible to extrapolate that the rest of the Sentinels were geared in a similar way, and I'd already established that Sentinels were THE elite fighting force of Remus, the absolute best of the best. I didn't think I wanted to give them a good look into what our top-end could do.

Heck, mentioning that Night was a vampire was probably going too far to boot. I was a little surprised that they hadn't asked about the word. Were there more vampires around? I'd need to let Night know. They knew we had some floating around, and he couldn't do mysterious strikes, hit and runs with total confusion.

I wanted to stop examining everything through the lens of a war. It was painful, and saddening to think about. Trade, and the exchange of ideas is what I wanted. Peace and harmony.

Still. I was being looked at differently. Like I'd shown them I was a walking arsenal.

Which, to be fair, I was. I puffed up slightly at the realization.

I hadn't *quite* put it together, but I had almost single-handedly taken out a level 750 Royal Guard. I wouldn't deny that Sealing had helped, not only trapping, but probably weakening the Royal Guard, in a 1v1 combat that was his prime – but I'd done the damage in the end.

I was fully charged up, and had used almost none of my other gems. Only **[Feather fall]** was out of commission, and given how rare it was for me to fall out of the sky, I didn't have more than the one. Usually because I could see clouds coming, break my own fall with **[Mantle of the Stars]**, and I ended up back at Ranger HQ often enough to recharge the gem if I did end up using it.

Gems were expensive, and **[Feather Fall]** barely pulled its weight in the first place. The price to reward ratio on additional **[Feather Fall]** gems simply wasn't there.

Of course, I'd just jinxed it, and I expected to see myself getting blown out of the sky any day now.

Focus.

Holy shit my focus was bad today. Too much time around people and being diplomatic had destroyed my ability to properly focus. I was an introvert, dammit, and I needed recharge time.

The topic veered off into some more light chit-chat, as nature decided she wanted to give me a ring. I'd been going for hours non-stop after all.

"Excuse me." I asked politely. "Could someone point me to the restroom?"

The dwarves glanced at each other.

"Commander Briga Glof the 90th." Woven said, formally. "I request permission to have leave, and get back to my work. I can show Healer Elaine the 94th where the bathrooms are."

Briga thought about it for a quick moment.

"Granted."

Woven got up from the table, beckoning me to follow, which I happily did, leaving my backpack behind.

Everything important was on me, after all.

A twist and a turn, and Woven pointed down one last hallway.

"End of the hallway, turn left, they're right there. Impossible to miss." She said, and I thanked her, heading down the wooden hallway, turning left.

Impossible to miss, yes.

Impossible to figure out as well.

Two heavily stylized trees were on two doors, each one clearly a restroom. It probably made *perfect* sense to the native inhabitants which one was the men's room and which one was the women's room. Naturally one of the trees was *obviously* male, and the other *obviously* female.

Pretty sure trees had a sex. Nature would know for sure.

Heck, Nature probably could easily guess.

Just how had I ended up here!?

There was *no way* I was going back to the meeting room and asking for help with the *bathroom*. No way on Pallos was I going to embarrass myself like that.

Well. 50-50 chance, and I picked one at random to enter.

Thankfully, it was a single-person bathroom.

Less thankfully, it was confusing as hell.

There were two holes in the wall, and one hole on the floor. A chain from above, a slider, a button, and a lever met my eyes.

What.

The.

Fuck.

45 minutes later, I opened the door a crack. Seeing nobody around, I quickly darted out, and closed the door, briskly walking away from the scene of the crime.

They'd probably be able to figure out it was me, but I wasn't going to stick around for someone to point a finger at me. Time and distance and all that.

The building was laid out in a logical, military manner, which made navigating the paneled hallways easy. I went back to the meeting room directly, kinda surprised that they just let me wander around without an escort. Either they were incredibly lax, or hospitality was taken incredibly seriously here. Perhaps, because I had accepted their hospitality, it was assumed I wouldn't do anything bad to them?

I needed to know more.

I made it back to the room. Tilruk had come back, and everyone else had left. My "short break" had been anything but. I couldn't really expect everyone to hang around for me, although they'd probably gotten a strong chance to talk about me or something.

Why did they even have a lever for that?!

"Healer Elaine the 94th." Tilruk said. "Commander Briga Glof the 90th would like to see you in her office."

More wooden navigation. I was spending so much time around wood I was starting to see subtly different shades in the color of the wood that made up the building. It probably meant something.

We made it back to her office without incident, where Tilruk knocked on the door.

"Healer Elaine the 94th to see you." He announced me.

Briga looked up from her desk, as my eyes ended up locked on her bookshelf. I know I should probably be looking at her, but *books!* At long last!

I had to figure out a way to get a few.

"Healer Elaine the 94th." Briga politely greeted me, standing up from her desk. "It was a pleasure to meet you."

"Likewise!" I said.

"We had a discussion about you, and would like to propose a plan, if it suits you." She said.

"Sure, what's the plan?" I asked.

"You coming, and the existence of, ah," Briga quickly flipped through her notes on her desk. "*Remus,* is a much larger event than I'm prepared to handle."

I nodded. Made sense. If I didn't have the Sentinel title, it would be entirely outside of my ability to handle.

Ok, fine, it was totally outside my ability to handle. My Sentinel title only gave me some legitimacy. I could, somewhat, a little, speak for the government.

The Senate would throw a hissy fit if they knew, but Sentinels had a *lot* of leeway. We could get yelled at, pay docked, but, end of the day, if Night thought we'd acted somewhat rationally, we were protected.

What were they going to do, lose one of the guardians of the Republic? Not have the right people when the next disaster hit, one so large that a Ranger team couldn't handle? Especially after we'd just lost a number of Sentinels?

Nah. "Don't start a major war" was the bar I needed to clear, and it wouldn't be too hard if I shut up, stayed polite, and figured out how the bloody heck those bathrooms worked.

"We'd like to send you to the capital with a strong escort, so you can talk with someone much more important than I am." Briga said.

I thought about it a moment. It seemed like a totally reasonable request, and while it might be awkward getting back, having talked with someone important seemed like a win.

Although, maybe I should stay? Wait until a [Diplomat] or someone showed up? Then again, what [Diplomat]s were there, anyways? It wasn't like Remus regularly engaged in foreign relations.

I suppose inter-city conflicts counted. Or guild conflicts. Or...

Ok, fine, there were probably a bunch.

Still, the pros outweighed the cons. Like, be polite, be nice, go along with what they wanted for the most part. They want me to break bread, dip it in salt, and eat it? Sure! They want me to use a confusing bathroom? Why not! They want me to travel to the capital to meet bigwigs? I see no reason not to!

I think? I wasn't the right person for this *at all*. Less likely to start a war by agreeing to just about any reasonable request though. "Give me all your stuff//tell me all of Night's skills//Give us your all-access Sentinel badge" – hells to the no, and I'd fight them if they insisted.

But "Go meet a bigwig" seemed totally fine.

I wished I had some way of contacting Hunting, or whatever other person showed up, and letting them know what was going on. Thinking about it, it was unlikely that they'd send Hunting, not with the way the dwarves had tried to react with extreme violence towards him, just for being what he was.

"I should probably leave a letter, explaining where I've gone if anyone else shows up looking for me." I said.

"How will they know it's from you?" Briga asked me.

I shrugged.

"Don't you have a **[Scribe]** who can make authentic signatures or something? They know what my signature looks like."

I'd shoved enough *Medical Manuscripts* in the Sentinel's faces, and I'd authenticated more things besides. It wouldn't be too hard to prove it was me.

Some quick arrangements later, and I was writing a letter, awkwardly standing in Briga's office as I did so.

To whom it may concern,

There is a 10,000 coin reward for getting this letter to a Sentinel.

I, Sentinel Dawn, am journeying deeper into the dwarven land. They'd like me to meet with some of their leadership, just as an initial meeting of sorts. I don't see any reason not to. I've been well-treated so far, and believe a friendship is in the future.

From what I've found out so far, the dwarves are strong traditionalists. Following along with what they want to 'traditionally' do makes them happy.

We live in something called the 'dead zone', which 'eats' experience. We've all been getting dramatically reduced experience our entire life. I've been leveling up like I was level 80 ever since I got here. Worth exploring the edges of the dead zone, and getting out.

With us being in the dead zone, the dwarves have no desire to expand towards us, or be in conflict with us. However, their defensive position is powerful enough that, according to them, the Formorians gave up entirely on attacking them.

With that being said, the guards on the wall here have the level of an experienced Ranger, although I suspect they don't have the same quality or richness of experience that a Ranger would have. Being in the dead zone means that we take significantly longer to level, which means we have more achievements by the time we class up, which gets us better classes, which has a positive accumulation effect that the dwarves lack.

They are masters of wood, able to carve and shape it however they please. I strongly recommend attempting to form polite relations with them, and trade with them. They're fascinated by the gems I have, and given their complex relationship with mining, I suspect gems, like moonstones, would sell extraordinarily well here. By the same token, they've found a way to cultivate and grow all sorts of magical woods, which we don't have in Remus.

I'll be doing my best to get back after meeting with some of their leaders back in the capital. Leaving this letter to let you know that I'm ok.

Let my family know that I'm OK.

Cheers!

Sentinel Dawn
Elaine

"Moonstone" was my way of saying "Yes, everything is totally ok." "Sunstone" was my "Problem" word, AKA I was being forced to write the letter.

Including neither would just cause confusion. On someone like Hunting, we'd assume the letter was being dictated to him.

With me, Night would probably just assume I'd forgotten.

We each used the gems corresponding to our elements. It'd be totally natural for me to mention that I'd blown through half the **[Nova]**'s in my Sunstones, for example. Which would let them know not all was kosher.

Which didn't matter, because everything was kosher.

"All set?" Briga asked me as I signed with a flourish, the **[Scribe]**'s skills giving my name the distinct signature.

I opened my mouth to say "Sure!", then closed it, and eyed Briga's bookcase.

"No chance I could get a few books for the road, is there?" I asked   with   an   impish   grin.

Chapter 34

Dwarves V

Briga had quickly realized that, given enough books, I would happily stay in the room I'd been given and not cause mischief.

Even me wandering around caused mischief. Not only did Briga decide that I needed a full escort of guards, it wasn't quite clear who was being guarded.

The crazy human wants to wander around? Ok, sure – but what to do when the crazy human wants to poke her head into the armory, out of sheer, bored curiosity?

Do we say no, and risk a diplomatic incident? Do we say yes, and risk her killing herself?

All in all, bored, curious, and enough firepower to level a building was a *bad* combination, and for the low, low price of a few of Briga's less-loved novels, I was out of everyone's hair. I get books, Briga avoids headaches, hurray!

And oh, to read books again! Tasty, delicious morsels to devour, sweeter than any mango. Lasted longer to boot. I could read again!

I wasn't a careful, patient reader. I wanted to read the books, and I wanted to read them *now*. Briga had lent me five books, probably figuring that it'd take me a day per book, with a few extras for me to have some variety and choice.

However, I was a well-rested Radiance mage, which meant that even when the glimwood dimmed as the sun set, I could turn on my own reading light, and read far into the night.

Unfortunately, that also had a chef profusely apologizing to me, as I neglected to eat the food that had been brought to me.

"Oh generous Healer Elaine, are you most certain that the food is to your liking?" The chef – whose name I missed in his rushed introduction – wrung his hands nervously.

"No, no, it's totally tasty!" I protested, around a mouthful of cheese and bread.

Fondue. They had *fondue* here! Tasty, delicious, decadent cheese, with little cuts of bread on dippers! Dip in the bread, swirl it around, and mmmm! Delicious! Magic kept the timber bowl both warm, and unburnt. There were some spices in the mix that I couldn't quite identify, and it was sheer bliss.

I swallowed, and continued on.

"I'd just been so busy reading, I totally lost track of time, and meals." I said, raising the book I'd stubbornly kept in my hand while eating one-handedly.

Look, it took time to get a bookmark, put the book down, then pick it back up and find the page again. Time that could've been spent reading instead!

"Are you sure?" He asked again. I wanted to sigh, roll my eyes, and throw him out of the room so I could eat fondue AND read at the same time in peace. Instead of placating the chef.

However.

Politeness, social niceties, and being diplomatic, AKA not starting a war, meant that I had to talk with the dwarf, and reassure him that, yes, everything was AOK. I was fairly certain that snubbing the chef wouldn't result in a war, but then again, Pastos had started over something almost as small.

I was already in the history books for *Pastos.* I wasn't going to go in the history books as the starter of "The Great Fondue War".

Small talk and ego management it was!

I hated ego management. Especially when the thrilling adventures of Carpenter Durin awaited! He was currently imprisoned deep in the orc's dungeon, but had a tiny amount of wood that he'd smuggled in. I was pretty sure he'd be whittling a tiny key to escape with, but who knew! He could've come up with something even cleverer to escape with!

I finally got the chef to leave me alone by asking him for a dozen pots of fondue for the road, which seemed to properly reassure him that everything was good, and I was happy.

Back to Durin!

The foolish and slovenly orcs had left him a bed and a bench in his cell, naturally made out of wood, which he carved into a full suit of armor, weapons, and a shield. He then carved the tiny chunk of wood that he'd smuggled in into a pick, to pop the hinges of the jail and break out, slaying all the captors, and rescuing the girl with the bushiest, best-groomed beard.

The quality of writing wasn't that great. Like. Why did he need to carefully bring in some wood if half the cell was made out of it? Did the author really expect me to believe that orcs were so dumb that they put the hinges inside the cells? However, I wasn't going to complain. It'd been so long since I'd read any book that I'd take a child's book using less than 50 total different words.

However, it was a *fascinating* insight to how dwarven culture worked. Nothing spoke more strongly to a culture, and what they believed was right and wrong, than their popular works of art.

Oedipus was a great example from the Greeks, and the values they espoused. Similarly, I was getting glimpses of dwarven culture and values from reading.

Of all things, **[Learning]** leveled up from all my reading. I'd also gotten a **[Persistent Casting]** level, just from my already-on casts, and keeping **[Shine]** on in the evenings when I was reading.

Which had leveled up. Three times.

It was absurd how easy levels were coming to me again. It was completely and totally unfair. I'd spent my whole life on hard mode!?

If nothing else, the dead zone information was critical. I was happy I'd written the letter to Night, although I hoped the Senate didn't get the idea in their head to try something dumb like invade.

[Sunrise] had leveled up a good amount, but that was probably more because it was low level and I was spamming the heck out of it. Still hadn't gotten a good chance to practice **[Solar Infusion]**.

"Hey, go get yourself hurt" could easily end poorly, and I was trying to avoid problems.

Either way, I needed to be practically dragged away from my books when the time came to leave for the dwarven capital.

I made my way out with my gear, to a large, open-air wagon, pulled by two massive yaks. There were seven dwarves in total, all of them as tall as I was, but twice as thick, stocky, and covered in various degrees of wooden armor. Some had what I'd consider to be "heavy" armor, while others were lighter. Seemed like a case of convergent logic, where both humans and dwarves had a level of agreement of how much armor should be on what type of Classer. I saw Tilruk, and six more dwarves I didn't recognize.

Tilruk was back, doing the introductions.

"Everyone, this is Healer Elaine the 94th. Saying this once more. She's a high-ranking member of her government, and your mission is to safely escort her to the capital, so she can meet with the clan leaders. Healer Elaine the 94th, these dwarves will be your escort. They are one of the best teams we could assemble. First, the leader is Lule, the 89th."

"Charmed to meet ya." She said, extending her hand out. I shook it, giving her a critical look.

Frizzy red hair hung around a warm, smiling face, a pair of gentle brown eyes with the strength of a mountain behind them, dominated what little of her face could be seen behind her beard. She was showing up as a mage, and a strong one to boot. I wasn't quite sure, because I didn't quite have the experience needed, but I was guessing around level 380 or 390.

Obviously, they were taking this seriously, and bringing their A-game.

"This is Warrior Fik the 86th." Tilruk introduced the next dwarf. My eyebrow quirked up in surprise at hearing the low generation number. It was something like every 50 years or so was a new generation, which meant he was, what? 8 generations behind me? Like, 450 years old or something?

Wow.

Unkempt silver hair framed eyes that made me think of Arthur's, which made me think he was a Forest element. His gear spoke towards expecting heavy fighting, like he'd be in the thick of things. His beard was just as messy as the hair on his head, and he gave me a polite, formal bow.

"Healer Elaine the 94th." He stiffly said. "You grace us with your presence, and I wish to invite you to break bread and share salt with us."

Lule rolled her eyes at him.

"Healer Elaine will be sharing lots of bread with us, I'm sure. Is this the time or the place?" She gently rebuked Fik.

He glared back at her, and sniffed.

"Tradition is to be maintained at all times." He said, practically with his nose in the air.

Oookaaay then. I've found the dwarf who knows all the traditions, and seems to be super-traditional even by dwarfish standards. If I have any questions on traditions, I should ask him.

If I can ever figure out the traditional way to ask.

"Fik, I know you're retiring this run, but can you just... keep it simple for this?" Tilruk asked, somewhat pained.

More sniffing.

"I suppose there isn't a traditional method to handling... *humans*... I shall endeavor to create sensible traditions."

Everyone else in the circle groaned at that. I mentally bumped him up a few notches in my "pain in the rear" chart.

He was a **[Warrior]**, around level... 340? Hard to estimate. Went down a few notches, comparing his generation and level to Lule's generation and level.

Although maybe Lule was an outlier?

"Moving on!" Tilruk said, clearly trying to regain control of the conversation. "Warrior Drin the 89th. Scout Glifir the 90th. Mage Toke the 90th. Healer Ned the 92nd." Tilruk said, pointing to each in turn, probably not wanting a repeat of the prior derailment.

Or just wanted to get his job done and to get out of here.

Drin was up first.

[Warrior], with the gear to support that assumption. "Normal" blue eyes, in so far that not having an element present was "normal" at his level. At roughly 380 or so, not having an advanced element on his highest class seemed weird to me, although Ned didn't have an element either. Had his entire beard and hair in braids.

Maybe they knew something I didn't about advanced elements?

He was the first one to talk with me after Tilruk's introduction.

"A pleasure!" He said, shaking my hand. "Long shot, but you wouldn't happen to have any bugs from Remus, would you?" He asked me.

I was no **[Diplomat]**. I couldn't carefully school my expression, not when thrown a curveball like that.

"What?" I asked, somewhat stupidly.

"Bugs, you know! Little critters, beautiful things. Usually have six legs and wings."

I stuck my finger in my ear and rubbed it around. I was *sure* I was mishearing him. Or there was a language barrier, or linguistic drift that I was encountering for the first time. Language had been flawless up until now, but there was always a chance.

Lule buried her head in her hands.

"Ye lot couldn't have kept the lid on being weird for half a day? A quarter of a day? No?"

I looked at Lule in confusion. She gave me a pitying look back.

"Aye, he's that mad about bugs."

"Yeah, see!" Drin said, pulling out a jar, and popping the lid open. A golden substance met my eye. "Tree sap's great for preserving bugs in! I've got a whole collection!"

Well. I had encountered a lot of bugs on my travels, and this seemed like a chance to make some sort of connection. I smiled at Drin.

"We've got the Kadan Jungle, with almost endless types of bugs. Maybe you'd like to travel there some day?" I asked him.

"Sounds fun!" He answered back.

"Scout Glifir!" Glifir happily butted in. "Got a map of Remus?"

Glifir's eyes were glittering and reflective, in a subtle way. I initially guessed Mirror, but quickly revised my guess to Ice

361

after a few moments. A **[Ranger]** was his **[Identify]**, and crazy high to boot. Around level 400? A hair under?

Hard to tell. I didn't have a lot of experience **[Identify]**ing people that high level. I should check if tradition allowed me to ask, and get better at figuring out high level people.

Hey. Some elements were tricky to work out. Like Maximus's now-infamous mixing up of Hesoid's Miasma and Decay eyes.

"Nope!" I said. "Might be able to draw you one though." I said, then instantly regretted opening my big, fat mouth.

[Pristine Memories], combined with a map back at Ranger HQ meant that, yeah, I could make a damn good effort at a full map of Remus. Except giving a full, detailed map of everything might be a bad idea. Be good for leveling up **[Pristine Memories]** though.

I was going to *murder* Hunting when I got back. The longer I stayed, the worse the idea of me acting as a diplomat/first contact seemed.

Hopefully I could show off my healing. Everyone liked healers.

Fortunately for me, I'd never practiced drawing. My map was going to make a 3-year-old with crayons look like an artistic genius.

"That'd be great!" Glifir grabbed my hand and enthusiastically pumped it.

Mage Toke came to my rescue.

"Healer Elaine! Wonderful to meet you! I'm looking forward to this trip together!" She said, taking my hand and pumping it furiously. Her blue eyes, set narrowly within their sockets, contained a murky darkness, and her brown, wavy hair was pulled back into a neat ponytail. She'd gone for the "woven" style with her beard, and at some point I needed to ask what the different styles meant.

If anything.

If I could somehow find the traditional way to ask.

Whoever the Senate eventually sent over was going to need the patience of a saint, and the memory of an elephant. This was crazy.

Then again, I suppose that's what I was for? To get a rough feel of things, and let people back home know what was what?

Either way, Toke was a **[Mage]**, and from the looks of it, roughly in the middle, around level 360 or so.

I turned to the last member of the group, Healer Ned.

"Greetings, Healer Elaine the 94th." He mechanically (woodenly?) said to me, saluting with the strange half-clap.

"Greetings, Healer Ned the 92nd." I replied back, mentally giggling. I was the same level as he was! And he didn't have fancy eyes!

[*ding!* [Identify] leveled up! 151 -> 152]

While it was nice to level **[Identify]** up, gaining an extra half a meter on the range didn't seem like it'd do much for me.

Blonde, shaggy hair was under tight control, while Ned's beard was neatly combed, but otherwise unornamented.

"Right! Reiterating a bit, Healer Elaine, our sole mission is to escort you to the capital. Please, come and take a seat, permit us to be your protectors and wardens." Lule said, the last part in a ritual tone of voice I was coming to recognize as Tradition, with a capital T.

"Why thank you, I'd be delighted to have you as my protectors and wardens." I said, climbing up into the open-air cart.

The cart not having a top felt all manner of *wrong* to me, grated at every instinct I had. Still, when in Rome…

Ned took a seat opposite to me – clearly, being a healer had some small privileges at least – and Fik took the reins of the yaks.

Yaks. Still couldn't get over that.

With a sharp snap of his wrist, the cart started to move, with the remaining four dwarves – Leader Lule, Mage Teko, Warrior

Drin, and Scout Glifir taking positions around the cart. It was clear that I was the VIP, with a comfy seat and no work to do.

I could get used to traveling in style.

We almost immediately went from "military outpost" to "deep forest" in like, 40 steps. It was quite something.

Glifir looked to Lule, who nodded at him. He jogged off into the woods, scouting I assumed. The remaining three dwarves changed how they were walking, moving to form a triangle around the cart.

The rest of the cart had chests and crates of supplies, and a medium-sized package literally had my name on it.

I decided now was as good of a time of any to mentally review what equipment I had, and what was in the package with my name on it. My bet was tasty, tasty fondue. I had promised the chef I'd take some with me.

First off, most importantly, was my armor. Vambraces, containing my gem supply. I was out my **[Feather Fall]** gem, but I still had dozens of utility gems, and dozens more **[Nova]**'s. I felt confident in my ability to handle most single-monster threats with them.

Attacks by multiple powerful creatures, I was less sure about, but then again, I wasn't exactly a fearsome combatant. I'd probably just try to fly away.

Among my utility gems, I'd had some time to review, revise, and otherwise swap gems out slightly from the standard set. I'd dumped **[Light]** ages ago – I was a Radiance mage, I could make my own light – but kept **[Gust]**, **[Water Conjuration]**, **[Shocking Paralysis]**, **[Watery Manacles]**, **[Brilliant Barrier]**, **[Mana Void]**, **[Tracks-be-gone]**, **[Tripwire Alarm]**, **[Summon Knife]**, **[Cast Scream]**, **[Invisibility with eyeholes]**, **[Muffle]**, **[Amplify Voice]**, **[Wall Buster]**, and **[Curse Breaker]**. I'd also dropped **[Revealing Radiance]**, since it was **[Shine]** with a different name.

Instead, after my massive success with **[Invisibility with eyeholes]**, I'd picked up a few more gems, and gotten Magic to charge them.

Which made me want to use them all the less. It was one of my last mementos of him, physical proof that he'd existed.

I could probably trade out **[Mana Void]** for something else, now that I had **[Solar Infusion]**. Which I needed to practice.

I also needed to chat with Ned, trade medical knowledge. I'd like to think my knowledge was unmatched, buuuuut I could be wrong.

Nah. Secretly I was hoping for the chance to show him up massively, and demonstrate who the better healer was. Both of us at exactly the same level? I *had* to compare notes. My class quality was probably better, but he had two whole classes dedicated to the art, while I just had the one. I was pretty sure I'd win – the powerful, top of the class healer wasn't sent to the boring frontlines, while I was the pinnacle of humanity, but hey! I could be wrong.

I wasn't usually this competitive, but... eh.

Moving onto the rest of my gear. Lamellar vest flowed into a tough leather skirt, studded with metal. Most of my Arcanite was woven into the chest piece, easy to access and pull from. Also easy to remember where it was, when I needed to maintain my gear. Shin guards protected my sandals, which was super important. No sandal meant no flying, and I'd still found few threats that could properly take down a flier.

I had a helmet, which had helped block a Spitter's attack. It wasn't looking in great shape.

All of my armor had inscriptions running through them. Inscriptions for strength, for speed, toughness and dexterity. It boosted me, and was unnaturally difficult to damage.

In theory.

In practice, anything that was able to get to me, and meant me harm, could probably shear right through it. Then again, it did stop and help with minor attacks, usually of the overwhelming variety. It was good for dealing with a boulder exploding near me, and a hail of pebbles raining down on me. The armor would neatly deflect most of it.

For that matter, while I'd worked out most of the kinks, there was only so much I could do, and the armor still had dozens of scrapes and dents from when I went sky diving out of the *Pegasus*. I was going to keep my mouth shut about that, so the dwarves wouldn't laugh themselves silly and tell me about how wood was oh-so-superior.

Weapons. Sword at my hip, spear attached to my bag. I didn't have my knife, because when Brawling had burst in my room informing me that it was GO TIME, I wasn't exactly grabbing my full kit – just my "fight right now" kit. I hadn't drilled with the sword and the spear since coming here. Didn't want to give anyone the wrong idea. Was my weapon of last resort, although it worked decently as a threat. If I pointed a finger at someone, they'd just laugh, or not get it.

Pointing a sword? Universal gesture. Could also help in a desperate situation. Like if a Mirror monster attacked me.

Heck, a level 60 Mirror monster would give me trouble. Hence backups.

My bag had rope, a trowel, my horribly abused shield attached to it, packages of field rations and water bottles, half eaten down from the trip across the Formorian lands. A bedroll, a canvas, a small metal skillet, and some fire making supplies helped round out my gear. I was fully confident in my ability to survive in the wilderness for extended periods of time, especially when it was forest, with wild animals that could be eaten and such, and not a barren wasteland.

Lastly, the pendant mom had gotten me for my awakening day. I'd worn it basically non-stop ever since, although I'd needed to replace the leather cord a few times now. I knew more now, and while I knew it didn't have any sort of inscriptions or anything, I still kept it and wore it. For luck. For protection.

I opened up the package addressed to me, to round out my supply check. Six large sealed wooden containers met my eye, clearly the chef's fondue in easy-travel-mode. I noticed Ned giving them a jealous look.

I'd share one, and see if he'd open up.

Shame we didn't have one more – I could give one to everyone. The way to the heart was through the stomach, after all.

No pesky sternum in the way.

At the bottom, there were a few more books. Briga had clearly seen how effective keeping me entertained was – completely out of trouble – and had gone the extra mile to keep me entertained, and out of trouble, while I was heading back to the capital.

They would have a lot of trouble trying to explain to Night that they'd misplaced me. Ooooh, Night would *not* be happy to learn that they'd lost one of his precious Sentinels. There would be more than a few violent words at that.

I glanced through the titles of the books Briga had sent to me, my cheeks burning up as I read one of the covers.

Oh.

OH.

I don't think she meant to include *that* one!

Chapter 35

Dwarves VI

The seven of us traveled along the dirt road, deeper into the forest, and deeper into the dwarven country. The trees only grew bigger, and the forest became denser as we made our way along the ever-winding road.

I'd been a Ranger, and a Sentinel, far too long. My instincts were constantly reminding me that, with the poor light filtering in through the canopy, that my regeneration was likely cut, and that I wouldn't be able to fly around if needed.

I eyed the sunbeams again, mentally amending the statement.

I'd need to jump from sunbeam to sunbeam, like a spider swinging from one part of her web to another, if we got into a fight. Also, a stiff breeze would make it all go haywire...

I should just stick to the ground.

I wondered what Nolgord was, what the system of government was. SOMEONE had to be in charge of making the roads, after all, and traditionally it was a government that did it. Pooling resources to do stuff no one person could do and all that. Roads were *the* classic example.

Kingdom? Empire? Republic? Clans? Some other form of government that I was unfamiliar with? I should find out at some point. Some basic, simple questions like that I hadn't bothered to ask, but now found myself wondering about.

Speaking of roads, their roads were significantly worse than Remus's roads. I didn't ask, because I didn't want to seem to be showing them up, but if I had to guess, the dwarves' border wasn't exactly high priority, and wood rotted and decayed over time. The sheer expense needed to make the roads out of wood and maintain them would be ruinous, and the money could be better spent elsewhere.

That, or they just didn't care, not with the excellent craftsmanship of the wagon. I'd take the dwarves oh-so-comfortable ride on the dirt roads over the Ranger's wagon on Remus's stone roads.

I eyed a root in the road, carefully watching it as the yaks pulled the cart over the root. I didn't feel a thing! If I hadn't been carefully watching, I would've never known it was there.

All of the dwarves except for Ned were busy scouting around, guarding the cart, and generally gossiping with each other. I tried briefly to listen into their conversation.

"… thought she could order me around! Me! When I'm of the 87th generation, and she's of the 93rd!" Fik said, working himself up.

"Not even a carpenter. The audacity of it all." Drin muttered into his beard, to nodding heads all around.

Ooookay then. I had absolutely nothing to contribute to the conversation, although I'm sure I'd learn a ton from listening in.

Ned was sitting in the cart with me, which I was guessing was special treatment for healers. I hadn't seen him and Lule discuss anything about what he was supposed to do, he just jumped right into the cart like he belonged, and she hadn't said a word about it. I assumed it was because he was a healer.

At the same time, nothing about him screamed that he was wealthy. Almost every healer I'd met – myself included – could be described as upper class, by sheer virtue of our class and skills. Even I still looked wealthy, having an entire set of armor, woven with dozens and dozens of gems and Arcanite crystals.

There were no such signs on Ned. My first guess was that since he was stationed at the border wall, he was part of the military. Since he was part of the military, he wasn't being paid as well, or wasn't able to properly display his wealth – just like healers at the frontlines.

However, the veneration, respect, social standing, and how they were letting him get away with doing almost nothing, made me think that he was being "paid" with social standing and status, instead of money.

Which was an interesting way of doing it. It meant that every dwarf could access medical care and attention, for the price of some politeness. It would explain why the dwarves all seemed to be on their best manners around me. Not only was I acting as a de facto diplomat, but I was a healer to boot.

"Hey Ned." I called out to the other healer.

I got a stinkeye, and a stare.

"Healer Elaine the 94th. Is there something I can help you with?" He asked me.

I blinked, taken aback.

"Um. What's up?" I asked him, somewhat lamely. I just wanted to try making some small talk.

"Trees." He curtly replied, crossing his arms and looking at me like I was a moron.

Fine, fine. Either he didn't like me for some reason – entirely possible – or I'd screwed up some tradition thing, and he was mad about that.

Like… oh shoot, I hadn't said his title or his generation when I called out to him. All other conversations started with that.

Mentally facepalming, I made a mental note to do that every time I started a conversation with one of the dwarves. I wasn't about to try and restart the conversation though.

"Healer Ned the 92nd." Lule said, with an unamused voice. "Be polite to our guest." She rebuked him.

Which had him looking even grumpier.

Well. There wasn't going to be a conversation here. There wasn't anything for it, but to dig into the new books Briga sent me.

I put the extra-special book to the side – no way was I reading that in front of everyone – picked up *A Tale of Two Trees,* turned on a small **[Shine]** and tied it off with **[Persistent Casting]** to have permanent light, and started reading.

I was only reading for a moment, and the cart was already coming to a stop. I turned off **[Shine]**, and looked around me, blinking as I tried to adjust to the much darker light levels.

I glanced up, seeing the dusky sky high above. There was no way I'd been reading that long, right…?

I glanced down at my book. My now 3/4ths read book.

Whoops.

I hurriedly packed it away, and got up.

"Hey, Leader Lule the 89th!" I called out, carefully making sure I gave her title and generation.

She turned to me, axe in one hand.

"Healer Elaine the 94th." She politely said. "Is there something I can do for you?" She asked.

I half shrugged.

"I mean, I'd like to help. Just tell me what you need me to do!" I said, years of experience with the Rangers and training at Academy prompting me. Everyone pitched in, barring unusual circumstances, like injury, sheer exhaustion, or any number of other factors. None of which seemed to apply here, and many hands made light work.

Lule looked at me with a frown on her face, tapping one foot against the ground.

"On one hand, we're supposed to be doing what you want, within reason." She slowly said, clearly thinking out loud. "On the other, it's all sorts of wrong to have you work on this..." She said, trailing off.

I thought fast.

"Because of Tradition?" I asked.

"Aye. And who ever heard of the VIP digging a latrine?" She agreed amiably with me.

"Would it be easier for you if I... didn't help?" I forced the heretical words out of my mouth, in the interest of having things go easily, and keeping everyone happy.

Well, everyone but me. I was willing to sacrifice a bit of happiness to keep everyone else happy though. Greater good and all that. Was kinda built into me with how I picked up healing as my vocation. Probably should double check that I wasn't being too selfless at some point.

Still, I didn't want to step on their honor or their pride or I-don't-know-what by insisting I help and awkwardly inserting myself into their system. So, I sat in the cart and watched.

It was *fascinating.*

Rangers would've set up tents, a perimeter, a campfire, and a watch. The dwarves were setting up a campsite as well, with one notable, major difference.

They were building a lean-to, on the spot. It seemed way too big for us though.

Drin and Fik were doing the heavy lifting. They went out into the forest with their axes – the same ones they'd kept near them all day as they escorted me – and with a mighty crash, a medium-sized tree was felled, and they got to work. Branches were hacked off, Glifir further measured and cut, and Lule, despite being the team leader, followed Teko's directions when and where to put logs roughly into position. Once a log was in place, Toke worked some of her magic – her second element obviously being Wood – and the log would bind to its neighbors.

Ned just stayed with me in the cart, practically with his nose in the air.

I didn't like Ned much.

The lean-to – now much closer to a full cabin – sprang up over the course of almost two hours, as I watched with open-jawed amazement. A careful fire was lit, and at that, Ned left the wagon and seated himself around the fire.

He was sitting on the ground, and I figured I'd just mirror what he did. Seemed to be safe, we were both healers.

Also, I was glad that the impromptu carpentry seemed to be limited to walls and a ceiling. I don't think I could've taken it if they made chairs, tables, the whole works. That'd just be blatantly unfair.

Ned looked around, muttered into his beard, and with great reluctance, went back to the cart, grabbed some rations and a skillet, and started cooking.

I eyed him somewhat doubtfully. I couldn't tell if Ned was lazy, and reluctantly performing his task. I couldn't tell if he 'Traditionally' wasn't supposed to be cooking, and was bending for the sake of expediency. Or if he was just plain hungry, bored, or something else.

It wasn't like I could ask him. "Hey Ned, are you super lazy or what?" No, better keep my mouth shut.

Soon enough, everything was built, and I started to make small talk with the rest of the dwarves as they came in one by one, having finished their tasks.

Lule looked around, hands on her hips, standing above the rest of us while we ate and chatted.

"Good work all of ye." She looked around the place. "Goin' to be a wee bit cramped in here though."

I looked around. The place seemed cavernous enough. All of us would be able to sleep with our arms out, and not touch each other. What could...

"Drin the 89th." Lule said, and with a grimace Drin got up and left.

My confusion vanished as the yaks were brought inside, along with the wagon. Guess this is why it was more like a lean-to, with a fairly open side. Let the yaks in. I wrinkled my nose as their pungent smell hit me again.

Well. I see why this was going to be cramped.

Also, yak fur closeish to fire? I hoped the yaks had a fireproof coat.

Still, the food was good! Ned's cooking was solid, and as much as I disliked him, I had to give him props for it.

"Mind if I go hunting tomorrow?" Glifir asked. "Get something fresh for the pot?"

"Aye. Just make sure ye keep yer ears open. Don't go harryin' off, and forget about us." Lule responded after a moment's thinking.

Glifir got a huge grin on his face, and bumped his knuckles together in the way the dwarves saluted.

We wrapped up dinner, and the evening entertainment began!

Namely, me.

"Trade you a story." Toke offered.

Stories! I could totally do stories.

I had *so many stories.*

Actually – I had a challenge for myself. I wanted to out-story all the dwarves.

Combined.

"A long, long time ago, in a land far, far away..."

Being the VIP was good, and bad.

Good: I avoided the scut work like digging the latrine, and *yikes,* did the dwarves take their temporary latrines seriously. Not needing to dig one out though? A major win in my books.

Bad: Lule insisted that herself or Toke escorted me to the latrine. Which was six different shades of embarrassing. At least it was a hole in the ground, and not one of their six-stage contraptions.

I had figured out how the dwarven plumbing worked. Step 1 was to pick the right gender's bathroom. Steps 2-6 were natural results of that.

Why dwarves decided that vomit needed its own hole, I'll never know.

The latrine was bad enough. It was worse when we were on the road.

"Could I have some privacy? Please?" I begged Lule, Toke, and, for some reason, Ned.

"We've gotta protect ya." Lule said, a slight note of sympathy in her voice.

"Never know when a purlovia's going to get you. Or a raptor. Or a hellhound. Or a vermillion bird. Or a..."

Lule smacked Ned over the head.

"Stop scarin' her! If a vermillion bird attacked, we'd all be dead anyways." Lule rebuked Ned.

Which didn't stop the three of them from looking at me, looking around, as I squeezed my legs together.

Cursing myself ten thousand times for removing the privacy aspects from **[Mantle of the Stars]**, I still threw it up around me. Since it was now a mantle, and now somewhat flexible, I tried to layer it back on itself, like folding a piece of paper. Again. And again. And again.

Then I said fuck it, and blasted a powerful **[Shine]** all around me. Sure, it sent up an "Elaine's peeing here!" beacon for the whole world to see, but nobody could actually *see* me.

Which only slightly mitigated the problem.

[*ding!* [Shine]has leveled up! 112 -> 113]

Chapter 36

Dwarves VII

It only took a week for me to suspect that something was up. As a Sentinel, I was used to rapid, *rapid* deployments from A to B.

Even as a Ranger, we quickly moved from place to place when needed.

The lower level dwarves had similar levels to experienced Rangers, although the class quality and combat experience was less. Either way, the problem remained.

We shouldn't be going this slowly!

Yaks weren't exactly known for their high-speed moves, but as undignified as it was, there were a billion ways to go faster. Like, plain running. Or jogging.

I decided to politely ask about this.

"Hey Lule." I asked one morning, as the dwarves were bustling around getting everything packed up. To my great confusion, they completely took down the lean-to as well, letting it "return to nature."

To each their own, but it did explain why there weren't a million lean-tos in various stages of decay all over the place.

"Healer Elaine the 94th." Lule responded back, taking a few steps to be closer to me.

I looked around, seeing the other dwarves. I refrained from sighing. No way would we be getting some privacy. I'd try to be discreet about it though.

"Why are we moving so slowly?" I asked, mentally patting myself on the back for not accusing Lule of nefarious means. Diplomatic win!

I got a long stare, followed by her shoulders slumping.

"Ah, you got us." Lule said, cheer returning to her voice. "We could've moved you faster, that's true."

Goosebumps rose all over my arms, as I mentally marked where each of the dwarves was, and their capabilities.

Ideally, I'd hit Ned first, and hit him hard – except I couldn't, not if he wasn't attacking me. The shadows meant that flying was almost impossible, although my higher regeneration was on.

Toke was almost literally in her element, those being Dark and Wood. Being in some dark woods, well…

"We just wanted to show you all the good things we have in Nolgrod! More practically, the faster we move, the harder it is to give you a proper escort, and proper protection. It also," Lule lowered her voice into a conspiratorial hush, as I leaned over to hear better. "let us send a runner ahead to the capital, and give people more time to prepare for your arrival."

She thought a moment more.

"We can try to pick up the pace, if you'd like?" She offered.

I relaxed massively at that, and stopped cataloguing threats. That was all perfectly reasonable.

I thought about it a moment, then shook my head.

"I leave the choice in your capable hands, Leader Lule the 89th." I smiled at her.

If there was something more nefarious at hand – I felt well-equipped to handle it.

Seemingly satisfied, Lule moved on.

"Hey Lule. Can you tell me about a Tradition of yours?" I asked her. "I'm trying to know more, and I figure this is a good time to ask."

"What do you want to know?" She asked back. "Usually takes us decades to figure them all out." She said, chuckling at some private memory.

I shrugged.

"I dunno. Anything?" I asked.

She looked thoughtful for a moment.

"I expect we're going to be hunting at some point. We usually bury the head of the creatures we kill." She said. "Shows respect, and helps them return to the cycle of nature."

"Cool." I said, not having much more to add.

We seemed to speed up a bit after that conversation. Our breaks were a little shorter, and we pushed a little further on both ends of the candle. Nobody seemed to mind.

The trees were starting to change though. First was the largest tree I'd ever seen. All seven of us touching hand-to-hand wouldn't be enough to get around the girth of the tree, and it soared ever upwards, into the sky. Impossibly large, and yet, entirely mundane.

A redwood tree.

Of course, later that day, the tree was immediately replaced as "the largest tree I'd ever seen" when I saw an even larger redwood tree.

And they just kept getting *bigger*.

The hills that we were going over became larger and larger to boot – so slowly I hadn't quite noticed it – but when we reached the top of one particularly large hill, I saw where we were heading.

A huge, sprawling mountain range was in front of us, coated with redwood trees.

No bets where we were headed!

Three days later, a miracle occurred. It started to snow!

Huge, lazy flakes started to come down from the sky, dancing on subtle breezes. They teased, swapping and exchanging positions, before gently and gracefully landing on the forest floor, where they quickly melted.

Tradition be damned, I'd only seen snow once since coming to Pallos, when it had been a particularly cold winter in Aquiliea, which was already near the southernmost portion of Remus. With a shout of glee, I hopped out of the cart, and started chasing snowflakes around with an open mouth, greedily trying to catch them with my tongue.

Some of the dwarves chuckled as I bounded around, intent on catching ALL THE SNOWFLAKES.

It was fun, although my gear got mud splattered all over it. Didn't care! There were snowflakes to nom! Delicate structures to catch on my nose, and look at cross-eyed for a brief moment before it melted!

Snow!

Shame that it was the first snow of the season, and none of it was going to stick. I would've loved to make a snow angel.

The thought of grabbing an Ice class for my 3rd class, whenever it happened, briefly flitted through my mind before I dismissed the idea. It would be a ton of fun, but "fun" wasn't the primary goal of a third class.

Or... maybe it could be?

What I needed to do was get a scroll- or a book! - and start writing down all of my ideas for a 3rd class. Then talk with Artemis – and Night, Julius, and the rest of the Sentinels I guess – about it, and see what they thought.

Either way, even if I didn't get Ice for my 3rd class, a vacation home somewhere snowy, where I could have snow if I wanted?

That sounded like a solid goal!

The pitfall of snow that I always forgot – cleaning up. Also, wet mud rapidly became cold mud, and while I loved snow to bits, I was, at heart, from a tropical and sub-tropical climate. Vitality helped, but I didn't exactly have tens of thousands of points in the stat. As such, with my relatively lightweight gear, designed more towards keeping cool than staying warm, I wasn't the happiest of campers.

Or I wouldn't be, if it wasn't for MAGIC! My armor had inscriptions woven throughout, and a relatively minor one that I'd forgotten about was some minor heating. Sure, it'd burn itself out soon enough, as all Inscriptions did without maintenance, but it'd help me stay warm.

Being a Radiance mage also helped me stay warm, as with some fine control, I carefully dried out most of my clothes. I could also use it on myself to try to get warm, although my **[Radiance Resistance]** made that a little difficult.

A muffled scream escaped my throat as I burned a hole through one of my socks though.

One of my socks – that I didn't have a spare pair to replace it with. I'd been wearing them with sandals – HERESY! - because it was bloody cold, and comfort came before fashion.

Welp. At least I'd be fashionable now.

"Healer Elaine the 94th. Everything alright with ye?" Lule asked me, having heard my muffled scream.

My cheeks were red from the cold, which hid the blush of embarrassment. I just lifted my sock which had recently found religion, staring at Lule through the hole.

"Everything's perfectly fine." I said in the most monotone voice, as my eye stared at her through the hole.

She just laughed and walked away. Better than most reactions I could've gotten.

I spent the rest of the time drying out my stuff, and peeling dried mud off, cursing my decision not to go back and get my spare pair of socks when we'd left camp.

"Purlovia! We're eating purlovia tonight!" Glifir eagerly bounded into the lean-to we'd set up for the night, a furry beast slung over one shoulder. From the angle I was at, it was hard to tell what the creature looked like.

He heaved, and with a thump, the body of the purlovia landed on the floor.

Fik was frowning intently at Glifir, who noticed his look and rolled his eyes.

"Yeah, yeah, I was getting to it." His voice took a ritual tone, one I associated with Tradition.

"The hunter has come back with his prey! Yet, this could not have been done without the strength and support of the clan. As such, I give this back onto you. Who wishes to join me in this feast?"

"I wish to partake." Fik said, way too fast.

"I wish to partake." Each of the dwarves said, one at a time.

Welp. This one seemed to be easy mode.

"I wish to partake." I added in, getting looks of approval all around.

Score!

"Do you have a skill to purify food?" Ned asked me.

I did a double-take.

"A food purification skill?" I repeated, somewhat dumbly.

Ned got that annoying superior look on his face that made me want to punch it.

"Aye. A skill that makes food safe to consume, no matter who eats it." He smugly informed me, going over and touching the purlovia.

Ned was somewhat of an annoying git. He loved finding things I couldn't do, then somehow mentioning that *he* had the skill, and would occasionally explain to me in excruciating detail how it worked, implying the whole time that I was a bad healer for not knowing it.

I had no idea why he treated me like that. Oh, there was nothing I could obviously point to, but we were never going to be good friends.

Maybe it was because of the generation thing? Ned being in the 92nd generation made him at least 50 years older than me, and probably a lot more. Could be as much as 149 years older than me – and I'd gotten to the same level as him, while being in the dead zone. Maybe he was just jealous?

Either way, I'd tolerate him for now, and hopefully wouldn't see him again after this trip.

Toke took the purlovia outside, and started to skin and prep the meat.

There was no real rhyme or reason to who did what. It wasn't like there were assigned tasks, although the dwarves fell into various roles naturally. Some of the dwarves stood out in my mind more than others.

Lule was, to no surprise, the organizer, making sure it all got done.

Fik avoided doing anything that wasn't directly assigned to him.

Ned pitched in whenever Tradition let him. My estimation of him went up slightly – he wasn't lazy, just hidebound.

Gilfir loved roaming around, and I was hoping he'd supplement our rations more often.

Toke always seemed to be in the right place, at the right time, for the highest-visibility job.

Drin was flat-out a hard worker. Did keep his mouth running permanently though.

My role was storyteller and VIP.

"Ever had purlovia before?" He asked me, and I shook my head.

"It's OK. Pretty good for a game animal. Spicy." He happily told me.

"Spicy!?" I whipped my head towards him, in complete disbelief.

"Aye. Spicy!" Drin happily told me. "Supposed to attract Snow Moths. Been trying to get one for my collection. They only come out in winter, with the snow, and I'm usually on border duty when it happens. Why, twenty years ago I had my chance! Almost managed to get one. You see, the problem I had was…"

Drin liked to talk. I was perfectly content to get him started on something, and just let him ramble along. However, there was one point that annoyed me to no end.

"…and best of all, Lightning can stun people!" Drin said, a trail of purlovia grease skating over his beard.

"I mean, sure, stunning someone is great, but why not just kill them?" I asked, more than a little skeptical – and wanting to defend Artemis's methods. I did somewhat approve of his fanatical appreciation of Lightning though.

Given how long Drin would take to answer, I had enough time to get a nice, solid purlovia bite. I teared up at just how damn spicy it was, snot running out of my nose. However, after a literal lifetime of relatively bland food, even gamey food that was spicy was *amazing*.

"I mean, I do kill them!" Drin happily tapped on his axe, still at his waist. "But making someone completely stop for a moment or two takes almost no power or mana!"

"Ya still need a boatload of control!" Lule added in.

"One stat instead of four!" Drin retorted.

"Does it do no damage?" I asked, getting curious. It sounded a bit like what I'd suggested to Artemis ages ago – rip out the Lightning from the nervous system, and just stop someone dead. Quite literally.

"Doesn't need to." Drin muttered into his beard. "Wears off over time, good for spars."

I noticed he didn't mention taking prisoners, and with how much he loved to talk about the benefits of his method of fighting, there's no way that was an oversight.

My bet? In spite of his high level, he'd gotten it the slow way, hundreds of years of sparring and minor conflicts, maybe some fights against beasts. Not a lot of experience trying, or needing, to kill other intelligent creatures.

"I'm kinda curious about it now. Can you disable me?" I asked.

Lule looked nervous at that, but I had everyone else's attention.

"I'm warning you, it's not pleasant." Drin said.

I grinned at him.

"Oh go on, let me see!" I said, offering a hand.

He looked at Lule, who buried her head in her hands.

"Do what you must." A pained noise came from her.

There was no winning from her point of view. Either she tries to ruin my fun – telling the VIP "no, don't do that relatively harmless thing" – or the VIP is, technically, attacked by a teammate.

Drin touched my hand, and I rapidly pulled it back as I felt like I'd been zapped.

I waved my hand in the standard "that smarts" move. Mostly for show, because **[Center of the Universe]** killed the pain.

Drin was looking at me bug-eyed.

"How'd you stop it!" He asked, somewhat outraged.

"Wait, that was it?" I asked him.

"Yes!"

"Try again?" I offered my hand back to him. Another zap, and I was still completely mobile.

Ned started laughing, and in a strangely familiar move, threw an arm around my shoulders.

"Drin, I've told you! Doesn't work on us healers." He grinned at me.

"Well, good healers." He amended.

My happy thoughts towards him turned into mental daggers. He hadn't said anything because he'd assumed I was a bad healer!

"Why don't you lot pipe down? We're arriving in Lundar tomorrow." Lule said, relief on her face.

"Healer Elaine hasn't even told us a story yet!" Toke protested.

I winked at Lule.

"Alright! One story!" I said, searching my memory for a nice, short story. Everyone wins!

Chapter 37

Dwarves VIII

We rolled into Lundar the next day. Tall wooden palisades surrounded the town, taller than most of the walls I'd seen in Remus. Advantage of living in a redwood forest and making everything out of wood – it was easy to supersize things that needed to be supersized. Redwoods were giants, with their biggest downfall being how long they took to grow. Add in skills and magic, and poof! A fantastic material to make everything out of.

I was becoming sold on wood being a superior material to stone. Then again, I doubted that wood could turn into an instant wall. Bulwark was good at turning ground into an instant wall if needed. However, that was something of a niche use, compared to the insta-cabins the dwarves built every night.

Then again, it might not be fair to compare the two. All of the dwarves had the level of a Sentinel, if not necessarily the raw stats to back it up.

Lule wandered over to me as we approached the gates.

"Leader Lule the 89th." I politely greeted her.

"Healer Elaine the 94th." She responded back.

Traditional greeting over – I was getting sick to my stomach of Tradition – we could now start the 'real' conversation.

"What do you need from me here?" I bluntly asked.

"Normally, we'd just spend the night, then move on." She said. "However, with you being around, we should pay our respects to the mayor. He'd be offended if we didn't."

Ego management. Yaaay.

"Any chance of getting a bath while we're in town?" I asked.

Months. Literal damn months since I'd been able to get halfway clean. I swear some Formorian guts were still in my ear canal, having been baked, then frozen, then I don't want to know what. I'd burn half the town down if it meant getting clean.

Lule looked me up and down.

"Slim... but we've got a..." She said a word I'd never heard before. This was happening a bunch on this trip. We spoke the same language, but some words we'd used in Remus out of necessity, while the dwarves had invented stuff of their own.

The start of the languages drifting?

"A what now?"

"Big room, hot rocks, pour water on the rocks, bunch of steam. Sit in the steam." Lule said, using the smallest words she knew. "A sauna!"

It wasn't a bath, but I'd take anything.

"Cool! Any way you could wrangle a visit?" I asked, deciding to throw my dignity to the wind and give her my best puppy eyes.

She threw her head back and laughed.

"Of course! We'd all like to!"

On one hand, I didn't want to share. On the other – sharing was a lot easier than burning half the town down.

Welp. When in Nolgrod, do as the Nolgrodians.

Getting into town was easy, we were practically waved in. Lule went forward to meet with the mayor, while Toke led the rest of us to the sauna. She dropped back to me once we got there.

"Elaine!" She cheerfully greeted me. "I'm guessing you've never been to a sauna before?"

"Nope! Looking forward to it!" I said, practically drooling.

"Right, so they're a very traditional place." Toke started to give me the run-down. "You take your clothes off in the antechamber, grab a towel, and enter the sauna proper. With your gender, generation, level, and occupation, there's a specific area where you should sit. Don't worry too much about the rules determining it – I'll just point you to the right spot. When you've had enough, leave through the door on the other side, jump in the pool, then the door will lead you back to the antechamber, where you left your stuff."

I froze at that, doing some mental calculations.

"No chance I can bring my gear with me? Like, in a bag or something?" I asked Toke.

She made a disapproving hmmmmmmmmmmmmm.

"Probably not. But! Nobody would dare touch your stuff! The sauna is practically sacred. It'd be against tradition." She said, trying to reassure me.

I eyed Toke skeptically. It was probably traditional not to rape and murder, but I'd bet every single coin I had that it happened anyways.

I went deep into the think tank.

Option 1) Take the risk, strip my gear off, and get blessedly clean. Run the risk that nobody decides to snag the unique and extraordinarily expensive gear that I had.

Option 2) No risk, no sauna. Stay filthy, but safe.

The decision was no decision at all.

"Sorry Toke. I think I've gotta pass." I said, steeling my voice.

Fik patted my arm, before hustling his bustle through the door.

"You've got the right idea. You never know when thieves are about." Ned helpfully told me. "Or murderers. Why, 700 years ago, there was a murder in a sauna! Can you believe it!"

I blinked at him. I had no idea if he was trying to reassure me that I'd made the right choice, or was mocking me.

"Was it someone important?" I asked, having no idea where he was going with this.

"Nah." He said dismissively, as everyone else went in. "Just two woodcutters having a disagreement."

"In 700 years." I said, rethinking things as I looked at the sauna. Tradition was *that* strong?

"Aye. Was a huge scandal at the time. Still. Can never be too safe. That's why I'm going in!" Ned said, cheerfully going through the door.

I was *so confused.* Was he saying I was smart for not going in? Or that it was safer to be in the sauna than not?

Where was Ocean when I needed him? Or anyone else, for that matter?

"I'll protect you." Glifir said. Long experience with Arthur stopped me from jumping up when he showed up. That, and he wasn't as good as Arthur. I'd noticed some tell-tale whisps of Mist hanging around, which was a fairly good indicator that Glifir was about.

"Thank you Glifir." I politely thanked him.

Toke looked like she was going to give me a sour look, then her shoulders slumped.

"I'll stick around until Ned and Fik get back." She grumbled.

"Sorry. It's not that I don't trust you, it's that…" I let my voice trail off.

Inspiration struck me. Mostly true!

"It's traditional for Sentinels not to leave their gear when in the field." I said, mentally pumping a fist at that.

I got a bit of a side-eye for that, followed by a grudging nod. It was only a lie in technicality – a Sentinel in the field didn't leave their gear behind. Heck, even when traveling incognito I kept it on under whatever cloak or tunic was acting as a disguise that day.

Truth was, I didn't trust them entirely. There was no history between us, no connection. I was a 'diplomat', and they were the escort. A purely transactional basis. They hadn't gone through Ranger Academy, they didn't have the same bonds forged. I hadn't grown up here, I wasn't a dwarf. I wasn't steeped in tradition like they were, and I did keep stepping on toes.

It's why I hadn't classed up. I didn't trust them to guard me for the day. Silly, when I was letting them guard me every day – but there was a difference between being awake and alert and guarded, and being completely helpless.

Eh, I'd class up when I got back. All this stuff I was doing was going to help my evolutions. Plus, I'd be damned if I got skunked out of my reading time again.

Speaking of reading time – no privacy had meant I hadn't gotten a chance to read the special book. Oh well.

Toke snapped me back to reality.

"You don't feel secure being away from your defenses." Toke said, giving me a solid excuse for all of us to be happy.

"Exactly! I've been in enough nasty situations to be paranoid." I happily latched onto her answer.

Glifir gave me a Look.

"Yeah. Your age, your level, the dead zone?" He said, and whistled. "Don't worry your pretty little head here though! Glifir's got it."

It was a good thing Glifir was the scout. He was so overprotective I could strangle him if I was exposed to him for too long. I could protect myself.

We kept making some small talk for a few hours while the rest of the team enjoyed the sauna. Even Lule showed up briefly, saw that I was hanging out, seemingly happy, and made her way in.

Being the boss had its benefits, and she was the last one out – even after Toke and Glifir had a full trip.

"Ah – Healer Elaine the 94th – was the sauna not up to your standards?" She asked me.

I grimaced at her.

"Didn't want to spend too much time separated from my gear." I answered back.

She stroked her beard thoughtfully.

"Let me see what I can do. It wouldn't be right for you to miss out on a sauna!"

The rest of the team murmured in agreement.

"Aww, you don't have to." I said, hoping that Lule would manage to make it happen.

"Nonsense! We'll figure something out!" Lule promptly replied.

I decided *not* to mention just letting me bring my stuff in with me. Tradition seemed to be so deeply ingrained into the dwarves that they literally couldn't think of just... breaking the tradition.

"Anyways, the mayor would like to have a feast with us tomorrow evening. It was the fastest he could make it work." Lule said.

We were given a small cabin inside the town walls for the night – courtesy of the mayor. It had a cozy fireplace and everything! Super nice, and I was feeling extra-bad, being the only grimy one while everyone else was fresh and clean. It was nice, being inside with a fire, with a howling cold wind rattling the shutters.

Lule came back, letting a cold blast of air in with her. There was much yelling to "close the accursed door already!", which I might have participated in.

"Aye, pipe down you lot, I'm closing it as fast as I can." She yelled back, stomping her way in.

"Healer Elaine." She said, cutting off my generation. No idea if that was a familiarity thing, or just getting lax.

I'd noticed as time went on, everyone was being less and less formal about titles and generations. I was suspecting it was a familiarity thing.

"Leader Lule." I said, trying to mimic her.

"Still interested in trying out the sauna?" She asked me, getting right to the point.

"Yup!" I had a feeling that she'd pulled some strings for me, and I wasn't about to throw her hard work out the window.

"Great. I've solved your issue." She said. "Toke. Join us?" Lule gave a standard 'suggestion-that-was-actually-an-order' to Toke.

Toke said nothing, just got up and joined us by the door. We huddled up, and headed out into the night.

The wind went straight through my gear, biting me to the bone. Fortunately, the town wasn't gigantic, and we made it to the sauna.

"How's this going to work?" I asked.

"Well. I figured if nobody else was around, you could have a private session, by yourself, and not have to worry about your fancy armor. The sauna's usually closed at night, but we got you in. I'll be showing you around, and Toke can look after your gear. Now go! Enjoy!" Lule followed me in.

I was touched. The lights – more glimwood – were still on, and I was finally in the sauna.

I had a brief moment of hesitation. I was, after all, going to be trusting someone else with my gear. What if something happened to it?

At the same time, I hadn't gotten this far by taking no risks – although this seemed to be a superfluous risk, one that I didn't need to take.

Or was it?

Alright, let me work through this at lightning speed.

I slowly started to unbuckle and strip my gear off. The leather skort was easy – it had to be, for prolonged time in the field – but everything else was a maze of straps. I didn't even need to think about it, taking my gear off and putting it back on was second nature, but it burned time while I thought.

First – the dwarves seemed to feverently believe that the sauna was sacred, and nobody would try anything.

Second – Toke would be guarding my stuff. Throughout the travels, the dwarves had given no signal that they meant me any harm. A random dwarf might try something, but if the team I was with wanted to hurt me, it'd be better to just ambush me as a group of six, instead of letting me know the jig was up in a two versus one situation.

Third – I was going to be meeting with some important person or another. I *reeked*. I'd kept my armor clean and maintained – as well as I could – but there was no helping my tunic, my hair, etc. At the very least, I shouldn't smell so offensively that they're put off their food.

Fourth – I just liked being clean. I didn't think a sauna would be nearly as good as a real bath, nor did it seem like I had a chance to do proper laundry, but it was *something*.

Fifth – Lule had gone through some effort for me. Showing that I could follow along with the Traditional stuff would probably earn me brownie points in her book. I had no illusions that she wouldn't be whisked away by the dwarf's version of vivisectionists, and relentlessly interrogated about her interactions with me, and what she thought of me. It'd probably be an insult not to.

I was getting a headache.

Fine.

Sixth – my stuff vanishes? I didn't *need* it. I was trained as a Ranger, and I was a mage, not a warrior. The town was in one spot. While the dwarves were much higher level on average than I expected, I had full confidence in my ability to fight – or, more likely, run away – if push came to violent shove.

On the downside -

I'd be fighting naked. Not that it was a problem, although the cold might get to me.

The sun was down, which meant my extra regeneration and flying was down and out for the count. At least until sunrise.

I was horribly outnumbered.

The extra Arcanite was nice. The [Nova] gems were my trump card. The utility gems could get me out of almost any situation. The armor turned blows away.

I was a total badass even without them. I believed in my abilities.

I finished stripping down, leaving my gear in a well-organized fashion, with Toke looking somewhat admiringly, somewhat enviously at it. Wasn't doing much for my confidence, but hey.

"Right! Here's a towel." Lule said, throwing me a large, fluffy towel.

She then walked into the steam room, and I followed.

The room was like a giant corner – two walls, with tiered, wooden seating around a stout iron container. A large basin of water was next to it, and a pile of firewood on the other side. A ladle was sticking out of the basin.

I kept a smirk off my face. For all the talk of the superiority of wood, when push came to shove the stove was made out of metal, and the fireplace back in the cabin was made out of stone.

Lule was stroking her beard, and after a moment's thought, pointed to a seat.

"It'd be proper for you to be seated there." She said, and having no reason to object, I put my towel down, and sat on it.

Some arcane muttering, a log thrown into the stove, and a ladle of water over the top later, and the room filled with hot steam. Far hotter than I'd expect, with far more steam.

Skills or Inscriptions at work. My bet was a few powerful skills by the owner.

I relaxed as I let the steam wash over me, and as I started to sweat buckets.

I simply didn't have the experience with a sauna to be able to tough out the hotter steam, nor did I have a monster amount of vitality to throw at the problem instead. I threw in the towel – well, not literally – after only twenty minutes.

[*ding!* [Pretty] leveled up! 152 -> 153]

I had sweat pouring down from me as I called out to Lule.

"Hey, sorry, I think I'm done. I'm just not built for this." I said to her.

She looked... disappointed?

"It was wonderful, don't get me wrong!" I said, making my way to the exit – not the same door as the entrance. "I just have terrible vitality, and it's my first time. I gotta work up to something this hot."

"Ah, no worries. Come on, onto the next part." Lule said with a grin.

I was relieved. I thought she'd be disappointed that I'd called it quits so fast.

Then again, passing out because I was trying to prove something would be even dumber.

We made it to the next room, which was a large pool.

My eyes went as wide as saucers. I could try to get clean here!

Without a word to Lule, ignoring her predatory grin, I cannonballed into the pool, only to come up spluttering and shivering.

"Why is it so bloody c-c-cold!" I yelled at Lule while holding myself and shivering, who promptly doubled over in laughter, wheezing and pointing at me.

"The look on your face! Going right in like that! Ha!" She said, not answering the question but clearly enjoying my misery.

As deep as the cold was biting, as much as I was risking serious damage to my teeth – not that any damage would *stick* – the desire to finish getting clean overcame any other objections I might have, and I rinsed in the magically-below-freezing pool, teeth chattering and fingers going blue by the time I hauled myself out.

Still, I was a clean little ice cube, and with Lule's help we were able to find someone who could magically make the non-armor parts of my outfit clean.

Missing the stench that could raise the dead, in a clean and presentable outfit, I felt "armed" and ready to do the deadliest battle yet since coming to Nolgrod.

A *social* event.

Chapter 38

Dwarves IX

"Ok, one more time Lule." I said, as the seven of us were walking to the Mayor's house. "Let's go over what I should and shouldn't do."

"Aye, I've told you. Just relax! Yer an honored guest. Yer fine." Lule tried to brush me off.

I was having none of it. Proper prior planning and all that.

I was coming round to the dwarves Tradition. They had rules for everything! Rules for how to talk, how to eat, how to walk.

All I needed to do was learn ALL THE RULES, and I'd never set a foot wrong! No awkward blunders! No putting my foot in my mouth!

Some were easy, like "respect the ancestors." They had some serious ancestor-worship going on, which was why they were mostly unfazed by gods, religion, angels, and the like. On one hand, I kinda saw their point. Their day-to-day lives were built by the work of their ancestors, and they all believed they were standing on the shoulders of giants – errr, normal-sized people. Giant by dwarf standards. Anyways!

Some were harder, like the winter solstice traditions, or the exact calculation of where a dwarf was located in dwarvish society – or where to sit in a sauna! While I'd gotten the information in theory, I'd yet to succeed putting it into practice.

Sure, the rules could grate on me somewhat, like the endless invitations I got, but that seemed to be a small price to pay to remove awkward moments forever.

I ignored Glifir's protests that I didn't need it down perfectly.

"Right! When I come in, I say 'I thank you for your gift of hospitality, for sharing of hearth and home?', right?" I asked Lule.

She sighed and rolled her eyes.

"Hearth, home, and bread." She replied.

"Hearth, home, and bread." I repeated to myself.

[Pristine Memories] should be helping with this, but it took time to properly dig through all my memories to find the right lesson. I was working and practicing with Lule to make it second nature, habit, so that when it came time to give the right response, I didn't stand there for 20 seconds trying to find the right memory.

[*ding!* [Pristine Memories] leveled up! 201 -> 202]

We kept talking, reviewing the rest of the greetings and potential customs I might encounter. Lule was a treasure, a veritable font of knowledge, and in spite of her belief that I didn't *need* to do all this, was happy to entertain my requests for knowledge.

We made it to the door, and knocked, four times in a Traditional pattern. I only knew there were a bunch, but only knew the one that Lule knocked.

"Invited guests have arrived."

There were more complex and formal variants on it, I'd been told, but they were for ~extra fancy~ occasions.

The door opened, and we were led to a large banquet hall, tables forming a T-shape.

A small dwarf with a magnificent red beard, looking like it was made of fire, greeted us. If not for Lule's lesson, I might've mistaken him for a greeter of some sort, and not the mayor himself.

"Ha! Healer! You grace us with your presence, and I wish to invite you to break bread and share salt with us!" He enthusiastically greeted us – mostly me.

I glanced at Lule, and put my game face on. Big smiles! Can't be too big, no grimaces.

"I thank you for your gift of hospitality, for sharing of hearth, home, and bread." I replied, mentally patting myself on the back for landing it.

Or wait. Shit. Was this a case that I should've used the healer counter-greeting instead? No time to check, better cover my bases.

"And your sharing of salt. Yes." I said, refraining from facepalming as I somehow punted it horribly.

All that prep work. Why did I try?

Right. The dude's happy grin, as he passed me a loaf of bread and a small bowl of salt. I dipped the end of the bread in the salt, and took a big bite.

"Mayor Dibo Birber the 88th, at your service." He said, politely giving me a half-bow.

I glanced at Lule. Host first, then the guests, in hierarchical order. Lule's combination of Leader and 89th beat out my combination of healer, diplomat, and 94th, via arcane rules that Lule had explained to me, and I somehow failed to properly execute in practice.

However, I did know that "non-dwarf" was one of the rules, and it counted against me.

"Leader Lule the 89th." She said, doing the same half-bow.

"Healer Elaine the 94th." I said, finishing the formalities.

I got a great big grin from Dibo.

"Come! Sit! I've heard that you're not a dwarf! Is that true?" He asked, peering at me intently.

"Um, no. I'm a human." I said, taking a seat on his left at the head of the table. The honored guest position.

"Would I bring a nameless to you?" Lule asked, with amused exasperation.

Nameless? What? I looked to Lule, then the rest of the dwarves, with a question in my eyes, but none of them would answer me.

Glifir mouthed "later" though, which was nice. The five other members of the group saluted Dibo, one at a time, in their own ranking order, then went to the lower tables to find a seat.

Sitting down to eat, I noticed, was a much less structured affair, and more a massive free-for all. Glad not everything was rigid! Could you imagine? Everyone needing to shuffle seats every time someone new showed up?

Lule sat next to me, and I noticed with interest that there was a dwarf wearing metal on Dibo's right.

"Who's this beardless lass? You're not playing one of your games by putting a nameless above me, are you?" He grumped, and I promptly didn't like him.

Still. *Diplomat. Social.* Time to be polite.

With a smile that didn't come close to reaching my eyes, I went through the introduction ritual.

"Healer Elaine the 94th." I said, giving him a half-bow. "Human! I'm from Remus, a country inside the dead zone."

"Miner Thabo the 35th." He eventually reluctantly said, clasping his wrists with his hands. "What're your people doing, sending someone so young here?" He grumbled at me.

I had this brief moment of whiplash as I thought the dwarf was over 3000 years old – more than half the time Pallos had been around, by all accounts – only to remember my travel-mates muttering about Khazad dwarves screwing up the generational count, and doing it totally different. Must be one of those.

I shrugged.

"I was available, and I get the sense that we're a much shorter-lived race than dwarves are. I was traveling with a Void mage, and, well, the border guards didn't take kindly to him."

The hall fell silent, and I got stares from just about everyone.

Ah screw it. It's funny seeing their reaction.

"Bluebeard's not so bad. Nice guy. We hang out a bunch." I said, letting a manic grin slowly unravel on my face.

The conversation slowly started to resume, as Thabo shook his head at me.

"You lot sound crazy. Which is good!" He said, hurriedly realizing what he'd said. "We're looking for crazy."

"Why's that?" I asked him.

"Well, we've located Lun'Kat's lair, full of every type of treasure imaginable. From raw mithril to growing ironwood, diamonds the size of eggs to actual eggs from creature of every shape and size, strange objects which defy all knowledge to magical herbs, the dragon's a huge collector! We figure all we need to do is evict her, and we'll be rich for generations!"

It was my turn to stare at him, pale and open-mouthed.

"What's wrong?" Mayor Dibo asked me, with no small amount of concern.

I swallowed and mentally reset myself.

How do I say this?

Hmmmm.

The awkward pause dragged on, as I struggled to find words. Finally, a bad analogy came to mind. Hopefully it'd work.

"Like you're scared of Void mages, we're scared of... well... what you were talking about. We have a belief that they can hear us when we say their name, and it's taboo." I got out, carefully phrasing my words so I didn't say the D-word.

I got looks like I was crazy.

"Lun'Kat flies overhead every few decades or so." Dibo said, with the careful tone of voice one used on a skittish horse. "She's given us no problems so far."

I wasn't about to get talked down so badly.

"You're planning on poking her in her home though. I've known Bluebeard for a decade, and he's had decades of service more. No problems from him either." I bit back.

"That's not the same!" Lule argued.

"Peace. Peace!" Mayor Dibo said, interrupting everyone. "Let's eat, and discuss happier topics. Healer Elaine, what can you tell us about your hometown, and where you were born?" He said, steering the conversation somewhere wildly different.

I didn't mind the change of pace, and I started to talk about my hometown as food came out.

"Well, I was born in a mid-sized town called Aquiliea. It had a river going through it, and it was on the shores of the Nostrum sea, a great big sea in the middle of the Remus Republic, connecting most of the towns to each other. Growing up, I..."

I took the occasional mouthful as I talked about my town and history. There was some pork mixed in with the bread and beans, and I mentally cursed. I hadn't checked what the food was, nor did I mention my aversion to eating it.

It only took half a thought to remember the smell of Kerberos's burning flesh in the arena. There were some memories I treasured, and would carry forever, like Artemis dancing with Lightning. Others? Others I wished I could erase.

I picked around it, hoping I wasn't causing some great offense, as the discussion continued. Some tankards of ale were brought out, and I carefully sipped on mine. They were ok, but nothing spectacularly amazing. I felt slightly let down, but I didn't let it show. There was more to come.

After the whole dragon-Void mage spat, I was feeling more relaxed. The dwarves didn't seem to take arguments all that personally, and it was looking like it'd be hard to say something offensive enough to start a war over.

The meal was finally over, and I sat back with a full stomach.

"Right! Time for the good stuff!" Mayor Dibo shouted, and a huge keg was rolled in.

"Healer Elaine! This stuff's so strong, it'll put a beard on your chin!" Mayor Dibo happily shouted to me.

"Ah, let me see!" I yelled back at him, getting in the spirit of things.

Right! Traditional message!

"I'll drink your beer here! I'll drink your beer there! I'll drink your beer anywhere!" I said, to a few approving grins.

"Drink till ye drop!" Lule said, happily taking a huge mug of frothing ale from one of the dwarves who was pouring mugs off the keg.

I got passed one, and started to tip it into my mouth, getting it in just in time to hide a wicked, evil grin.

This wasn't the first time people had tried to get me terribly drunk for one reason or another. Usually with impure motives.

For *some damn reason,* people kept trying to get a *healer* drunk. I could instantly purge myself of alcohol in an instant, and it was always amusing to drink people under the table by blatantly cheating.

I was no good at cheating at cards, dice, or other games, but drinking?

I considered it mostly fair game, as I was tagged [Healer]. They had their chance of knowing. I wasn't going to advertise it.

We all clanked our mugs together, and bottoms up!

The fact that **[Bullet Time]** activated as I brought the mug up to my face gave me a moment's pause, but I mentally shrugged, made sure **[Dance with the Heavens]** was busy healing me, and started to down the mug.

Strong didn't begin to cover it, as my throat seized up as the powerful brew burned all the way down. I couldn't manage it all, and came spluttering back up after just two mouthfuls.

All it tasted like was tingly alcohol, like I was drinking a strong spirit directly, and not some sort of ale. Still, the alcohol was purged as it hit my system, and I wasn't about to show defeat after two drinks, not when everyone else was going bottoms up.

Bottoms up it was! I kept a half-eye on my mana, seeing it occasionally flicker a few points away, only to be instantly refilled. Strong stuff.

At the end, I could see the bottom of the mug, but why was it spinning? It shouldn't be spinning. Spinning was baaaaad.

I put the mug down on the table, frowning.

They never told me this was a fun room! The table kept tilting back and forth, and I stuck my tongue out and bit it in concentration as I tried to carefully put my mug back down on it.

Which, with much effort and concentration, I managed.

"Yay!" I said, throwing my arms up, feeling all sorts of tingly and happy all throughout my body.

There was a roar of approval – and quite a few more laughs. The room was spinning in several directions, the tables going one way, the walls another. The windows were happily spinning in place on the walls, and there were bright sparks of color going off.

What fun! I needed a cool room like this for myself! Wonder how much it'd cost. I could afford it! Being rich was AMAZING.

"Alright! I'm immune to alcohol! Bring me the next one, so I can drink you lot under the table without you realizing anything!" I yelled, getting another round of laughter – and more than a few drinks sprayed, as some dwarves tried to laugh and drink at the same time.

Lule carefully put her hand over my mug.

"You've probably had enough." She said, as Thabo said. "Lightweight."

"Hey! I am not a lightweight! I'll prove it! Gimme another!" I said.

"Healer Elaine. You are drunk." Lule said. "Our ale has a lot more than just alcohol in it. We put in tingle-weed, which has magical properties that work just like being drunk. Otherwise, none of us would be able to ever properly enjoy ale once we'd leveled up some."

That sobered me up real fast. There was a world of difference between not realizing I was drunk, and being forcefully made aware of it.

I looked around the room, still spinning somewhat, sparks of color going off.

I could no longer tell reality from fiction, and my fight-or-flight reflex was going off full blast. I could feel a cold calmness overtaking me, ready for the worst.

I started to walk, trying to leave before someone attacked me or something, promptly hitting the table in front of me and half-folding over it.

Danger.

Danger.

NO!

No danger. Just drunk. Badly drunk. Don't start blasting. Do no harm. Don't murder a house full of happy dwarves because I couldn't hold my liquor. That'd start a war.

Prooooooooobably.

Wars were bad. Bad was bad.

I felt someone grabbing my arm. Pulling me back. Going to – oh wait, it's Lule. Lule was ok. Right?

Hang on, her mouth was moving. I should listen to her.

"Elaine! Are you ok?" She asked again.

I thought about it. Was I ok? Well, I'd gotten ripped to another world, but I'd adapted. So OK there. I'd escaped an arranged marriage, so I was OK there. I was a Sentinel, which was mostly OK, but I didn't sleep well at night. Which wasn't

OK. So did that make me OK in the end? Or did my problems end up-

"Elaine!" Lule said, bringing my attention back to her.

Ah right. She wanted to know if I was ok right now.

I shook my head.

"Not ok." I said. "Gotta leave." I tried again, and tried to stumble out.

"You sure?" Lule asked, supporting me.

I nodded, trying to dampen down the rising panic. I jumped as a nearby dwarf suddenly raised his hand, preparing to attack me.

A shot through the head would be fastest, but I didn't want to kill him, plus the angle was bad – it might hit someone behind him. A joint shot would be better, plus it wouldn't ki – oh wait no, he was just getting a drink. Not attacking me.

"I have to get *out*." I repeated to Lule, stumbling forward.

Fuck it.

I closed my eyes, and let Lule guide me out. I opened them again when I felt the cold air blasting on my face again.

Lule kept me steady as we staggered down the street.

We made it back to where we were spending the night. Bless having my own room.

"Beard Lule the 700th." I said, madly giggling after. She had a beard! I was totally being polite with giving her a TITLE! And a generation! 700 seemed right.

I got a frown back, and I remembered what I wanted to say.

I got a little more serious.

"Lule. For real. I'm super drunk. I already struggle when I sleep. I'm alone, in a place with no friends at all, and I've been in more fights and seen more people die than you'd believe. Whatever happens. DO NOT DISTURB ME. I almost attacked three different people thinking they were trying to hurt me in there. Someone walks in, and I can't promise I'll tell they're friendly before I start shooting. Just. Leave me be."

I didn't wait to see or hear her reaction. I just curled up under the blankets, and tried not to cry.

403

I was a healer. I wanted to help people. I hated that I was on a hair trigger. I hated that I had nightmares. I hated how I'd developed a reflex of blasting first, and asking questions later.

Was it too much to ask for a simple life? Was it too much to just have things be easy?

Why me?

I woke up the next morning with a *pounding* headache, that no amount of **[Dance]** could get rid of. I closed my eyes, wishing the pain would go away, would go bother someone else. My head being super-foggy wasn't helping.

When was the last time I'd had a headache? One that I couldn't magic away?

It was....

Argh.

Thinking *hurt*.

Thinking bad.

But.

Hurty no go away if no think.

I *probably* needed water. Then again, this was a magical hangover, caused by more whatever-the-fuck the dwarves used to make their ale more potent.

With a groan, I rolled over, and got out of bed.

At least I'd de-filthified, and whatever potent blend of herbs the dwarves used didn't want to involuntarily exit. Bless the small things in life.

At the same time, embarrassment, shame, and remorse flooded over me.

I'd gotten *so drunk*. "Couldn't-t-stand-up" drunk. "Needed-to-be-carted-out" drunk. At a fancy, formal function.

I tried to remember what I'd said last night, and as soon as I remembered, I wanted to crawl right back under the covers and hide away, until nighttime when I could sneak out. With any luck, Lule and the rest of the team would be too busy looking for me before the *real* diplomats could arrive, and make a better first impression than I had.

The real question was – hide in the ground, under a rock? Or high up in a tree?

The dwarves were short, and low to the ground, which made being under rocks a little trickier as a hiding spot. At the same time, they loved and venerated the gigantic redwoods, so they were probably looking up a bunch.

Neither was a winning move.

Maybe I could play it off as "getting totally sloshed was the human way?"

That might save some face, but it didn't help the embarrassment I was feeling in the moment.

Bleargh. Lying here and wallowing wasn't going to improve my situation, nor my headache. I needed to gal up, and face the music. The sooner I tackled this, the sooner it'd be done.

I stumbled out of my room to see Fik sitting at the table, idly moving three pebbles in an orbit. What was interesting was the way they wavered and wriggled as they moved near each other. Which, assuming he wasn't deliberately trying to do that, meant that either he was an Earth mage of some sort, or more likely, he had some other element that he was using to manipulate stones as if he was an Earth mage.

"Healer Elaine the 94th!" He happily greeted me from where he was sitting. "You're up! Heard you downed an entire mug. Good job! I didn't think someone your age, without a beard, could manage it. Why, I remember my first mug, when I became an adult! Sprayed half of it across the room! Barely got any of it down my throat, but eh! Better than Drin. He was actually sick, can you believe it? Oh! Right! Hangover cure's right there." He pointed to a drink, still not getting up, and I thankfully stumbled over and downed it.

Sure, it was probably brewed for dwarven anatomy, not human, but my head was murdering me, and Fik enjoyed nattering on. If I didn't know better, I'd say it was deliberate.

"Thank you." I forced out, wincing as each word sent a spike of pain through my head, like an icepick through the eye.

I thankfully grabbed and downed the hangover cure. How did medicine always taste awful the world around?

For that matter, I hadn't needed to properly drink medicine for years and years. My healing was just that good for just about everything.

My head started to feel better – then worsen. Still, the fogginess was gone, and with a few extra braincells working, I realized I might've made it worse.

Medicine was *complicated.* There was a reason I'd gone into the easy "touch and heal" style of medicine, rather than the ridiculously complicated field of trying to brew potions. There were some benefits to being an alchemist, but one of the downsides was just how damn tricky it was.

A gross, massive oversimplification worked like this. See, if I had not enough of, say, insulin, and I got a shot of insulin, happy days! I'd live! However, if my blood-sugar levels were already fine, and I got a shot of insulin, I'd go dangerously hypoglycemic. In short, if the problem didn't exist for the medication to counteract, it could cause just as much harm as the initial problem itself.

I'd happily purged myself of alcohol, so when I'd drunk a magically-brewed cure that handled residual alcohol and intoxication, along with whatever magic drugs were in the ale, I'd screwed it. I'd already purged myself of alcohol hours ago, so the "counteract alcohol" and "counteract alcohol derivatives" portion of the brew had nothing to properly work on – and was doing goddesses-knows-what to my body.

I gave the empty hangover cure the evil eye, scrounged up food and drink, and retreated back to my room.

Chapter 39

Dwarves X

Two days later, we were back on the road, winding our way up a mountain to a "great vantage point."

"It's a bit of a detour, but I'd thought ye'd like to see the best view in Nolgrod!" Lule enthusiastically told me.

"I'd love to see it!" I said, distinctly feeling on the back foot. After the utter disaster that had been meeting the Mayor, I was down to do anything Lule thought was a good idea. I'd like to be back in her good books. Anything to get a good word in with the important people on the other side.

"Ah! When the sun hits just right, it's like the entire mountain sings!" Drin enthusiastically entered the conversation.

"Are there any good bugs to be found up there?" I asked him, having finally caught onto the way to butter him up.

He shook his head.

"If anything, it's a bad spot. Not too many bugs live on the peak." He told me.

"Oh." I'd almost assumed there was some sort of super-duper rare bug living in the highest reaches of the mountain. A fun little diversion as we tried to catch it, only to be outwitted in the end by something with a brain the size of a speck of dust. Nope. No such luck.

"It's great for seeing the stars though! Lusebalt Summit has no trees on the top, and at night, the sky just opens up!" Fik told me. "I've been dying to show you the constellations, but the trees keep hiding them from us. Now I can show you the Carpenter, the Anvil, the Firefly, and my personal favorite, the Lyre!"

"Sounds like fun!" I told Fik, only for Glifir to hurry back from scouting, concern on his face.

"Leader Lule, we've got a problem." He said, and his tone caught my attention, while the lack of a generational honorific caught everyone else's attention.

"Report." She said, as weapons were drawn.

"We've got a Chupacabra stalking us." He said. "Probably wants the yaks. Wanted me to see him."

Lule's beard creased in a way that I associated with frowning. Helmets started to go on heads, and I grabbed mine as well, getting it strapped onto my head.

No need to get my armor on, I lived in it.

"It's trying to wear us down. Catch us off-guard when we're exhausted." She finally declared.

"Toke. Ned. Rest. Sleep if you can. Drin. You're on stare-down duty for now. Keep eyes on it permanently. It shouldn't attack while it knows we're watching. Glifir. You're still on scouting, let us know if anything else is coming. Nothing else should want to mess with a Chupacabra, but it might have a mate, and be trying something tricky. Fik. You're with me on guard duty." Lule rapidly assessed the situation, and handed out orders.

"What do you need me to do?" I asked, feeling somewhat left out. "I have a skill to restore and energize, which could help if it's trying to exhaust us."

I got a quick glance from her, a weighty look.

She gave a curt shake of her head.

"Nothing. It is our pride to protect you." She said.

I shut up, although the moment the Chupacabra came into view, I wouldn't hesitate to heal everyone, or take some shots of my own.

Wonderful thing about Radiance was the travel time – or lack thereof. I was unlikely to foul anyone's shot with my attacks, although I'd announce it.

Should probably lay off the [Nova]'s. Especially in a forest.

The Chupacabra took that moment to growl, and reveal itself through the trees.

It looked vaguely like a large, mangy dog, with a row of sharp spines down against its back. It growled at us, loudly, making sure we knew it was there – then spat a sizzling glob of something orange at us, which arced up high, then broke into a fine rain. The Chupacabra promptly faded back into the trees after its attack.

Toke lazily waved her arm, and shimmering darkness spread above us, shielding us from the acid rain.

"No problem to shield this, but this is going to be a pain." She said with a frown.

Lule sighed.

"No rest for the hard-working." She muttered into her beard.

I was inclined to agree.

Three attacks later, and I'd had enough.

"Oi! You little shit!" I yelled at it, jumping up and hitting it with a cone of **[Shine]**. I walked towards it, eyes promising murder, as the light stopped it from slinking off too far. I threw a **[Nova]** after it, but it was gone before it landed.

So much for "not throwing **[Nova]** into a forest". That hadn't lasted long, although with the colder, wetter weather the odds of starting anything bad were slim.

I went back to the cart, muttering.

"Any reason we're not doing more to annoy it?" I asked Lule, stomping back after the Chupacabra ran off.

"No point in getting ourselves riled up." Lule answered me after a moment's pause.

"Mmmm. It might think we're not quite as soft anymore though." I said.

"Yeah, but if we never do anything, we say we're so strong we don't care about it." Drin joined the conversation.

"We need to block its attacks already. Not exactly a show of strength." I grumbled.

"Fine! I'll help ye on the next trade." Lule said.

Which is exactly what she did. Next time the Chupacabra showed up, Lule did her best Artemis impression, and threw a few rocks its way. Nothing landed, but it was taking longer and longer between harassments.

We stopped earlier than usual, to set up camp. The Chupacabra lurking about made it take twice as long as we needed to move more carefully, and avoid getting picked off.

Watches were arranged, three pairs of two, and in spite of my volunteering, I wasn't assigned to any of them.

"I've got a shield though! I can help!" I protested.

"It would be improper." Was all Lule replied to my protestations.

I settled in, fully expecting to be attacked in the night. I didn't lie down at all – I just half-slumped against the wall, helmet on, shield on my arm and spear in my hand.

I slept fitfully, jumping at every shift change, at every loud snort, every cracked twig.

I was practically awake when the call came.

"Attack! Hellhounds! Attack!" Drin yelled, and I was on my feet in a flash, as Ned ran into the lean-to, with Drin taking a position in the entrance.

The entrance was way too large for him to block by himself though.

First thing first – see what was going on. I used **[Shine]**, bright enough to light the area up, but not so bright that a dwarf looking at me would go blind. It was a good trick to make it super bright and blink it when not working in a team. In a team though, I needed to be considerate.

Ned was out with Drin, and there was already a shimmering connection between the two. As the rest of the dwarves were roused and exited, Ned hooked them up.

As for the hellhounds themselves, they were like mid-sized dogs. Bigger than a small dog, smaller than a medium-sized dog, they were a weird size. They barked and leapt and bounded over each other, a shifting, whirling mass of animal that was hard to get a good number on. I'd wager over thirty, what they lacked in individual size they made up for with individuals.

Some had smoke trailing out of their mouth, others seemed to leave ash in their wake. A few didn't seem to have any obvious elements, although most of the pack being casters didn't speak well for us.

Then, as if my light was the signal, they charged, and everything became a chaotic mess.

With a dedicated healer on the team, I went on the offensive. I started by throwing three [Nova]'s at the mass, trying to break them up. Then, when I saw an isolated hellhound, I'd try to drill a beam of Radiance through their head.

I felt a bit like I was a one-trick pony at times, but hey. It was a good trick.

The hellhounds were fast, but I was able to just *barely* track them, which let me carve deep into their flesh when I had a moment.

Fik joined Drin near the entrance of the lean-to, and Toke and Lule each worked their magic, closing the entrance somewhat. Toke had extended the walls a hair, closing the entrance, but leaving herself small slits to shoot out of. Lule did the same on the other side, but instead of wood she used stone. I mentally winced at that, because the sheer volume of conjured stone would've had a major impact on her mana pool. Artemis had done similar tricks – with a wagonful of Arcanite fueling her.

It was good, because now we were properly safe and secured inside.

Bad, because now I didn't have a clean shot to hit the hellhounds.

Mist spread across the battlefield, and Glifir seemed to fade away. Not quite invisible, but *blurred.* He walked right past Fik and Drin, and scooted around, out of view. Given the hellhounds weren't violently ripping him to shreds as he walked past them, he'd probably concealed his scent somewhat. Or there were other skills at work.

Still, they made a solid team. Toke and Lule on the flanks, protected by the lean-to's walls and their own protections. Fik and Drin in the middle, Ned, having healing connections on everyone but me. Glifir in the Mist, an occasional icy blade flashing down to kill an isolated hellhound, then fading back.

Drin hadn't shut up about his method of stunning and killing, and mentally I'd been poo-pooing it. It hadn't stopped me for even a moment, and I'd thought he was all talk.

Well, I got to see it in action. A hellhound would leap at him, mouth full of flames, and he'd block with his shield. As he blocked, a loud *crack* echoed, and the hellhound would fall, stunned.

Drin would then swing his axe down.

Honestly, I felt bad for the hellhounds. They were literally stunned immobile, defenseless, as Drin hacked them apart with one or two blows.

I noticed that he never went for the vitals on the first blow, and while my estimation of him and his tactics as a warrior went up, my belief of how good of a person he was went *way* down.

I was slightly concerned about his shield, constantly warding off flaming attacks while being made of wood, but every time it was scratched, the wood regrew, keeping his armor looking pristine, never mind that he was in the middle of a bloody battle.

I had a brief debate of "wagon or yak", before deciding on the wagon. I climbed up onto it, and, half-hunched over due to the ceiling, looked back towards the battle.

Yup, between the top of Drin's head, and the ceiling, was a gap wide enough for me to comfortably throw Radiance beams through, although I didn't want to risk a **[Nova]**. I stifled a chuckle – I was in the *exact* position and pose Artemis had been in when we got attacked by goblins, back when I first joined up with the Rangers.

From my angle, I wasn't able to hit anything in the fighting, but I could hit some of the hellhounds that were skirting around near the back. Generally not lethal, but I stung badly enough that most of them limped away, licking charred flesh.

Lule was a heck of a lot stronger than I gave her credit for. She was holding a little hammer, and swinging it up and down, behind the protections of her barrier.

A much larger hammer made out of stone was outside, and with every swing of her hammer, it came crashing down,

412

crushing hellhounds with started yelps of pain... only for the gory hammer to rise again, continuing its bloody work.

The hellhounds weren't taking this lying down. Seeing the first few waves get smashed, they backed up a bit – right into Radiance laser range. Still, a few of the ashen hounds seemingly exploded, coating everything in thick ash, with small bits of burning embers dancing through the air. They burned and scorched when they landed on small bits of exposed skin – but fortunately for me, I didn't have a lot of that. Not that a minor burn would slow me down.

The ashen veil hid their attacks though, and spears made out of glowing ash shot out of the darkness, with us only being able to see and react to it a moment before it connected. [Shine] was amazing against Mirages, but physically filling the air with ash was a different story.

However, the ash neatly ate up my Radiance. Sure, I could probably try to burn through it, but that'd be a large waste of mana. Instead, I decided to survey the field, to see if there was anything else I could be doing.

I looked at Drin and Fik, and briefly considered throwing up shields near them, to help them deflect attacks. They looked like they had things under control.

I had no idea on Glifir, who was either enjoying the added layers of confusion – or had been knocked out of his Mist by it. Either way, I wasn't going to run out and break the formation when I didn't know if he was even in trouble. It'd just cause more problems.

Now, if he called out for help, or made some noise that indicated he needed healing, we'd have a problem.

Ned still seemed to have the healing well in hand, Lule was still doing hammertime, and Toke –

Toke didn't seem to be doing much, although she had one hand on the lean-to, and another on her barrier. Maybe she was reinforcing the wooden lean-to against the hot ash, preventing us from getting trapped in here? Maybe making wooden spikes on the outside, to stop a hellhound gnawing on the wood? Shooting wooden balls out?

I had *no idea,* but she looked fine. Not all skills were flashy.

Last were the yaks, and my eyes widened as I threw a **[Mantle]** over both of them.

Luxurious fur + burning embers + multi-ton beast of burden = disaster.

Welp. There wasn't much else I could do at this point, besides provide overwatch as the fight continued. I briefly debated trying to finish off the hellhounds that Drin was stunning, but that would require shots between his legs. His rapid footwork meant I could never be sure that he wouldn't step in front of my beam, which had nothing like a friend or foe identification system. Hamstringing my ally wasn't a great way to endear me.

So here I stood, Sentinel Dawn, healer, Radiance mage, being a wet blanket so the yaks wouldn't catch on fire and murder us all. Not exactly my finest moment, or the best display of my combat abilities. The dwarves just worked so damn well as a full team though.

I did occasionally dismiss and re-form my shield when a flaming projectile came in, catching it and making it roll to the ground before it could hit something delicate and wooden, but Commander Briga's assurance that she'd gotten a capable team to escort me was proven in fact as they defeated the hellhounds with strong teamwork.

Without fanfare, without notice, there were no more attacks, just angry barking fading away.

We stayed there for quite a while longer, as the wind slowly blew the ashes away through the trees.

Lule's arm dropped, and with a *thud* that shook the entire lean-to, her massive stone hammer dropped as well.

"Well, that was quite something." She remarked. "Anyone got a flavor of hellhound they prefer?"

Some of the dwarves shouted their preference, while others did their own thing. Glifir showed back up without a scratch.

I just shook my head, and after checking that the area was somewhat secure, laid back down in the wagon and tried to get some more precious sleep.

Chapter 40

Dwarves XI

I bolted awake as I heard a branch break, slamming against the side of the wagon, peering over, ready to do battle again.

Blasted hellhounds interrupting my sleep again, why I –

Oh wait.

It was Fik, coming back with an armful of firewood.

Nothing to see here... I figured I should check my notifications from the battle before.

[*ding!* [Mantle of the Stars] leveled up! 256 -> 257]

System? Hello, System? Are you there?

I flopped over in annoyance. SERIOUSLY!? One measly level for a life or death fight?! Out of the dead zone my ass. I should've gotten a lot more for...

Wait.

I was an idiot.

Of course I wasn't getting any levels. **[Ranger-Mage]** was capped out, and I still hadn't gotten a chance to evolve it. The attack by the hellhounds just reinforced my decision to hold off on classing up – I wasn't safe here. Sure, I had my escort, but I didn't quite trust them enough to look after me for days on end while I was potentially classing up.

I'd done practically no healing to boot. Just a few embers on my arm, and if *that* had been enough to level me up, I'd be stripping and jumping into a fire again.

The rest of the dwarves were waking up, and breakfast was soon being cooked – fresh hellhound.

"That was a right mess." Drin said, to nodding heads all around as we chowed down. The hellhounds tasted smoky, and it wasn't a particularly pleasant type of smoky. More like they'd been caught in a bad fire.

Yet, Glifir was, if anything, undercooking them. It wasn't an issue with the chef, so much as the source material. Hey, who was I to complain? At least it was novel.

"Aye."

"Yup."

"I hate my sleep being interrupted."

"We going to make it to the peak today?" Toke asked Glifir.

He paused his cooking a moment to check the map.

"We should..." He said, trailing off, glancing at Lule. "Unless you've got other plans?"

She shook her head.

"Nah. Let's make it up there, and camp for the day. Enjoy the view. Have a break after that nonsense last night." Lule said.

The small talk resumed, and I was frankly shocked. No after-action analysis? No consideration of what went well, what went wrong, what could've been done better? No mention of the yaks nearly igniting?

I restrained myself. Maybe they just did things differently here. Maybe it was Tradition to wait a day before doing an after-action analysis or something. I wanted to speak up and start a conversation about the battle, who did what, what worked, and everything – years with the Rangers had ingrained the habit in me, and even as a Sentinel we went over each other's combat once the Sentinel was back.

Sure, those were less useful, given that each Sentinel was literally at the top of their game, but the conversations helped, cross-pollinated ideas and information if nothing else. We didn't consider ourselves too good for it.

Still. I was mindful that I wasn't the best diplomat, and I wasn't about to say or hint that the dwarves were bad, or wrong, or something else.

Plus, I didn't see it mattering all too much. Their team was their team, and I was just a hanger-on. I could do an after-action analysis on my own actions, some quiet introspection while we traveled.

I had to say – I could totally get used to not needing to do anything, and being carted around.

Right!

This was going to completely, and totally, ignore the diplomatic repercussions of my actions. Gods and goddesses, I missed being in Remus, where all I needed to worry about was not looking corrupt, and not making Sentinels look like they were easy targets.

From a combat perspective, my first mistake was not making my capabilities clear to Lule and the team. I hadn't insisted that we drill together, I hadn't insisted that we work out tactics and how to integrate me into their formation. For example, if Lule's and Toke's barrier had been a little skinnier, Fik and Drin could've been a bit further apart, and I would've had room to be more actively engaged, instead of taking potshots over their head from the wagon.

Or the lean-to could've been wider, to accommodate the same. Alternatively, Drin and I could've worked on our tactics, and made room for me to kill hellhounds that he stunned – or other monsters.

Right. That was the pre-combat analysis.

During the fight, what could I have done better?

Shielding the yaks was critical, and if I hadn't been there to do that, we would've been in serious trouble. I should've talked with Toke though, and seen if we could've shared a shooting hole, especially since Toke didn't seem to be using it all that much. Could've stuck a finger out, and blasted [Nova] from it.

Right! After-action analysis complete!

I looked around. The dwarves were keeping a steady eye on the forest around them, obviously not completely ignoring last night. Nobody was talking, seemingly to better hear what was going on around us. Ned was his usual stoic self, which left me to my own devices.

I could re-read a book, and I probably would, but first! How would I have handled the attack if I was solo?

Well, based on their appearance, I was guessing that they had a good sense of smell. My [Invisibility with Eyeholes] gem would've been less useful, so I would've needed to pair it with my [Tracks-be-gone] gem. I would've blasted a path to the tree,

417

and tried to climb it in the confusion. Once I was high up in the tree, I would've been safe enough to wait for them to go away – or for daylight. Once daylight hit, I'd just fly away, after climbing the tree enough.

I eyed yet another redwood. That would've been a *lot* of climbing.

The plan B would be to get my back to a tree, shield my sides, and judiciously blast away with **[Nova]**, both the skill and my gems, and use Radiance beams to handle individual hellhounds that survived. Use my **[Gust]** gem when the ash hellhounds filled the air with ash. Use the spear and shield for anything that got too close.

Actually! Thinking about it! With how **[Mantle]** worked now, I could try to hold a weak monster back with it, and stab it with my spear.

Satisfied that I'd done a proper after-action analysis on my own abilities, I grabbed my book and went back to reading.

"Hey Glifir?" I asked him, as he was on scouting break.

"Elaine! What can I do for you?" He asked me.

"Are you familiar with thunderbirds?" I asked him, figuring if anyone knew about him it would be Glifir.

"A little, why?" He asked me.

"Well, frankly, I've been thinking about getting a companion, and part of the reason we headed this way was to see about poking around a pair of thunderbirds we saw heading this way." I confessed.

Glifir shrugged.

"You lot are probably quite a bit different than we are, but we don't believe in 'looking for' a companion. If it happens, it was meant to happen. No sense in trying to force it." He said.

Fik was making some strangled noises.

I opened my mouth to keep prodding him about it, then closed it. I had time, I might as well continue to try and be diplomatic. The dwarves had relaxed somewhat, but were still somewhat touchy around me. "No sense in trying to force it" and Fik – the stout traditionalist – making unhappy noises made me think the subject might be a touchy one for the dwarves.

Right then. Operation sneaky Elaine hunts for a thunderbird egg begins!

Maybe I could ask for an egg as a present? Not say what it was for?

Ooooh! Maybe there was some sort of market where I could buy one! It wasn't unheard of in Remus for eggs to be bought and sold, although usually it was some of the more common dinosaurs being bartered. I was game to barter some of my gems away for a thunderbird egg. The Quartermaster, and the rest of the Sentinels, would totally understand. Heck, it'd probably even be a steal, trading something replaceable for something almost irreplaceable!

Right then. Operation "sneaky egg acquisition" had a plan!

We reached the top of the mountain, and the view was to die for.

I could see why we'd decided to detour over here, even though climbing the mountain with the yaks and the wagon was one heck of an ordeal, and probably added a few days to our journey.

A gorgeous, sprawling vista met my eyes. Mountain after rolling mountain, all covered with redwood trees, banks of mist hiding in the shadows. A few breaks in the canopy in some of the valleys suggested towns that the dwarves had carved out, chopping down the trees for space.

If I looked the way we came, I could, in the distance, barely see the walls the dwarves had built to hold back the Formorians, and marked the end of the dead zone.

Then, like a needle in heaven's eye, a defiance of the gods and whatever creatures ruled the skies, rose a wooden tower. Even from the vast distance, several mountains away, it was visible to the naked eye.

"The Sierra Obelisk." Ned pointed, obvious pride in his voice. "Our greatest creation. Generation after generation of dwarf has worked on, labored upon, the tower, reaching far into the heavens, a demonstration of dwarven ingenuity. It is our temple and our pride, our seat of government and our inerasable mark upon this world."

"It's amazing." I didn't even need to pretend to be amazed. I couldn't imagine the years – centuries – of effort needed to erect such a tower, nor the engineering ingenuity required, the maintenance, replacing old timbers – it just boggled the mind.

Bulwark would *love* it. Heck, he'd love everything about the dwarves, from their "structures on the go", to the tower, to the wall, to *everything.* I should totally recommend that he make his way over, spend some time comparing notes with their engineers.

I should put that on my to-do list! "Get Bulwark a meeting with someone as nerdy as he is".

We spent the rest of the day drinking and goofing off. I spent a bunch of time just staring at the incredible scenery, just blown away by my tiny size in the grand scheme of things, the vastness and majesty of nature.

There was one small mar to the fantastic scenery – a small ventilation shaft, made out of stone. Fik kicked it grumpily.

"Bloody Khazads." He said, as I wandered over, wondering what he was doing. "We work so hard to keep nature pure and pristine, for there to only be traces left of us when we intend it to be so. That's why we take down our lean-tos. That's why we build out of wood. When we leave a place, nature can reclaim it, for future generations. We remind ourselves that we have our bounty due to our ancestors with our generation numbers, and remind ourselves that we need to preserve for our future."

Quite the rant coming out of him.

"But?" I prompted, and he kicked the ventilation shaft again. It was fairly large, with a narrow entrance that was just a hair too narrow for me to squeeze myself through.

"Khazads don't believe in that. They believe the earth and stone is theirs to take and shape. When they're done, they just leave things behind, and build strongly enough that nature almost never reclaims what is hers. They scar the earth, forever." He said, pointing to the shaft.

"This mountain top was pure! Pristine for generations of dwarves to visit and enjoy! Then the Khazadian mine expanded underneath, and they built a shaft here, to get air down in the mine. Nature is trying to warn them, suffocate them for their insolence, but do they listen? Noooo. They just mar her further, blasphemy on top of blasphemy. Now everyone who visits this mountain needs to look at their ugly, temporary work." He said.

I had absolutely nothing for that. Fik was sounding like a True Believer, and there was no reasoning with those.

"Ale?" I offered him a mug of blessedly not as powerful stuff.

He took the mug from me, and downed it in one angry go.

"Ahhhhh, that's the stuff. Right! Let's get back to it!" He said, heading back to the group.

I headed back as well, noticing with a little giggle that Glifir was trying to draw a map of the area – but staying far, far away from the edge.

"You know, it's easier to see and map if you go right to the edge!" I cheerfully called out to him, only to get a death-glare in response.

Heh! Who'd ever heard of a map-maker who was scared of heights?

The rest of the day went well, setting up a lean-to, setting a watch, and going to sleep after a long session getting the constellations explained to me.

Chapter 41

The Dragoneye Moons I

Most nights I expected to be attacked in my sleep, and my dreams were a constant reminder of the threat I was under. I was trying to get better, to improve, to heal myself of the problem, and was getting less jumpy when woken up by surprise.

All that improvement went out the window - not that there was a window anymore - as I was woken to a world-splitting roar, and our lean-to exploded, wooden logs transforming into a hail of deadly shrapnel.

[Bullet Time] activated and adrenaline kicked me awake, making **[Sunrise]** redundant. I used it anyway.

[*ding!* [Sunrise] leveled up! 45 -> 128]

Holy shit *what?!*

The levels were wildly distracting. I disabled System notifications. I had no time for them, especially since the huge level gain told me that whatever was going on was dangerous. More lethal than anything else I'd been near, by a wide margin.

I refocused on staying alive, thanking **[Bullet Time]** for having given me the extra thinking time.

The wooden splinters were already tearing through the dwarves, and I reflexively coated myself in **[Mantle of the Stars]**, entirely out of position to aid them.

I activated all the Inscriptions in my armor. Speed, strength, toughness of my flesh, hardness of my armor. Perception and reflexes, Sentinel armor had almost everything. I had no idea what was going on, and I wasn't holding back.

Seeing the barrage incoming, I started to dive behind my backpack, with the tower shield I'd been lugging around the entire time on its side. I almost never used it, and had mentally cursed it a dozen times. Now I was grateful for something to try and hide behind.

Basic math was my enemy. The splinter assault was moving at incredibly high speeds, whatever force that had destroyed the lean-to launching the projectiles at high velocity. I had jumped up when I heard the explosion, and I was still on my way up, trying to cross my arms over my face, when the splinters crashed into my barrier.

[Mantle] held for a moment, stopping a few of the larger wood shards, and a dozen of the smaller ones. Then it shattered and the rest of the splinters slammed into me.

Most of the shards that hit my armor just bounced right off. A few left minor dents, but the superiority, wisdom, and paranoia of always wearing armor - even in my sleep - paid off massively.

My leather skort got pin cushioned, but it held, keeping my thighs safe. Likewise, shin guards and vambraces protected my extremities.

No, where I was in trouble were my hands, elbows, knees, and worst of all, my head. My arms weren't going to make it in time to guard my face, and desperate times called for desperate measures.

I launched a [Nova] point-blank from my mouth, trusting that it'd hit some splinter and detonate in my face. I'd much prefer large-scale burns over my body and face to a splinter through my head.

I knew I could heal full body burns.

In theory I could recover from a splinter through my head. I wasn't eager to test that particular theory. Being wrong would be fatal.

[Nova] did indeed blow up in my face, washing me with Radiance. [Radiance Resistance] helped me, but not my clothes, gear, or bag.

My angel feathers bit the dust, only the ones in my pack safe.

I healed just about as fast as I took damage, and even before my vision was restored, I blindly reached out with [Wheel of Sun and Moon], trying to slap healing on the dwarves. They were busy picking themselves up off the ground, having been rudely woken up.

Death by wooden splinters was, generally, a relatively slow, painful way to go. Worse-case was a splinter through the eye or heart, but death by a thousand cuts was likelier. Nobody was dying on my watch though, and I'd like to think I was faster than Ned.

Not that he'd ever admit it.

I took a stance, ready to run, fight, heal, blast, whatever had caused the problem.

Also, where was Drin? He was supposed to be on watch - why hadn't he warned us.

I looked around, and spotted Drin. He picked himself up off the floor

"It's Lun'Kat! Lun'Kat the dragon!" He was yelling and pointing, running back to the cabin.

"Lule! Toke! Talk to me!" He screamed, grabbing logs and heaving them away.

I glanced at him, tied off **[Wheel of Sun and Moon]** with **[Persistent Casting]** into a permanent, if terribly inefficient, heal aura, and took stock of the situation.

Drin had pointed me in the right direction. I had a great vantage point from the mountain summit we decided to stay on, and could see for miles in every direction.

I could barely make out the massive walls down on the plains, but in the opposite direction I could see the Great Tower the dwarves had built. Were building? They weren't entirely clear on it. Either way, it marked their capital, their pride and joy. I could tell there were two towns by the large gap in trees, nestled into a pair of valleys. A line of flames blossomed and split the mountains, from beyond the horizon to far past where I could see, like a sword of fire, leaving a trail of flame and devastation. Even as I watched, the flames grew, grasping hold of the forest and growing greedily.

They didn't care that it was cold and winter. They didn't care that it had snowed recently, and that everything was supposed to be wet.

They were dragon's flames, magical and all-consuming.

And there, high up in the sky, far and only just barely visible thanks to my vitality, flying with deadly, sinuous grace, was the living catastrophe. Black, iridescent scales, powerful wings, legs that ended with claws as long as swords, and a mouth full of teeth like curved daggers. Billowing flames poured from her mouth, burning all in their path.

Lun'Kat, the dragon.

I cursed the idiot dwarves. The Khazad dwarves, the metal and stone workers, who had tried to recruit me on their inane quest to "evict" a dragon and loot her lair.

No guesses how *that* had gone, and it seemed like Lun'Kat was taking it out on the dwarves. The *wrong* dwarves, but that distinction was probably lost on her. If she even cared.

She spent a moment, high up in the sky, looking down. Not at us, thankfully. I don't think we would've survived the attention. Then, she vanished, leaving a trail of fire descending from above, and I saw a shockwave rippling outwards.

"Brace! Incoming!" I yelled, looking around to find some sort of shelter. The first blast had half-wiped the summit clean, while making more of a mess at the same time. The shattered ruins of our lean-to, a few trees that were toppled over and blown towards us, and the top of the old mine ventilation shaft were the only things up here with us.

The yaks were flat-out gone. I suspected they'd fled in terror, not that any of us could try to do anything to stop them, not when we were too busy trying to survive.

I didn't want to be near the logs, so I turned and ran towards the mineshaft.

I was moderately quick. 2200 points in speed, and solid physical fitness.

While I was quick, and while it took almost fifteen seconds for the sonic boom to hit, the summit was large, and I wasn't quite able to make it to the shelter of the mine ventilation shaft before it hit. I threw **[Mantle]** up, and braced for impact.

It wasn't worth blowing one of my gems on. It was just going to hurt like hell.

Naturally, **[Mantle]** got shattered, and I was picked up and slammed back onto the hard, rocky ground. I felt my ears pop again, as they were broken and restored in almost the same moment. I pushed myself up, only to feel one of the dwarves grab my arm, and start pulling me.

"Come on healer!" Fik said, pulling me up. "Got to get you to safety!"

I let a bitter laugh escape. Safety? What safety? Nowhere was safe when a dragon was rampaging above, merrily burning the countryside to the ground.

I looked around as we scrambled over to the vent shaft, a tiny outcropping of stone. Built sturdily enough that the sonic boom hadn't knocked it over.

Good stuff.

The rest of the dwarves were there, huddling around what little shelter we had. There wasn't one without significant bloodstains on them, but that was the only mark they had of the damage that had been done. Their living armor, combined with Ned and I, had kept everyone alive.

"Elaine! Good! We need to get out of here!" Lule shouted at me.

I looked around. The mountain was half-ruined, with trees flattened all around us. Getting down would be an obstacle course over broken trees that could shift at any moment, crushing us under their bulk.

A second burning line cut through the mountains, a second slash making a cross with the first. Smoke was rising, and the dragon was high up in the air again.

Vanished again.

"Incoming!" Half of us yelled, as we all scrambled to get to the other side of the stony shaft before the shockwave hit us.

Toke threw up a large barrier of darkness, and I added in my own **[Mantle]**, having no faith that her shield alone would protect us.

They didn't, but between the two shields, and the ventilation shaft, we were almost entirely fine. My ears popped *again*, and I noticed with some concern that my mana had been dropping fast.

Between the shields and the constant healing from the bone-rattling not-even-intended after effects of Lun'Kat simply moving around, my mana was getting chipped away.

The last slash had created a wall of fire vaguely behind us, but now it was all too obvious - nowhere was safe. Part of the second flaming slash looked like it was awfully close to one of the towns. I hoped the dwarves, with all their love of wood, knew enough to handle a forest fire.

Even if it was magically generated.

Lun'Kat stayed high in the air, looking down at the country.

Looking specifically at the tower, the dwarves' pride.

Fik grabbed Lule's arm, and pointed up.

"Look! The stars!"

We all looked up. It took me a moment to notice, to realize what was going on.

It looked like the sky - no, every star in the sky - was falling, coming down to earth.

An entire sky's worth of stars, now significantly larger, started to rain down across the entire mountain range, causing devastating explosions wherever they landed. Giant redwoods jumped and snapped like twigs, and the entire mountain shook with the devastating impacts, as stars spent minutes - that felt like an eternity - raining down from the heavens, causing explosions and destruction where they landed.

We were lucky that none landed directly on the summit, although some were close. I felt thankful that I'd been knocked over, as a fallen redwood went spinning over our heads, as if it was a tiny boomerang, and not a hundred-meter giant of a tree.

Still, one of the branches casually scraped my leg. Not only did the force grab me and send me tumbling, but the flesh and muscle sheared off and bones broke – only for my healing to instantly kick in and re-knit everything. **[Center of the Universe]** kept the pain at bay, keeping me alert and aware, and not having pain wracking my body and interfering with my thoughts.

I'd be so dead if I wasn't a healer.

On one hand, the stars falling was an illusion, revealed as the real stars rapidly reasserted themselves in the sky. Then again, a skill that actually ripped the stars out of the sky would've probably ended the world already.

At the same time, the spell was of apocalyptic proportions, destroying and devastating the countryside. It was plenty powerful enough.

I picked myself up off the ground again, noting the relatively small chunk of my total mana needed to survive that attack. Bless my massive mana pool.

I was also debating the wisdom of getting back up when it was likely that I'd just get immediately knocked over again.

Blah. I was getting wrecked here, and I wasn't even the target of the attack. I was getting badly hurt by tertiary effects of attacks.

Human lands were to the north, while the dwarven capital was to the south. Mountains stretched far to the east and the west, as well as continuing south.

The dwarves tower? Their great pride?

It was gone. Entirely annihilated.

Several mountains away, a lone redwood remained standing untouched among the broken remains of its fellow trees. In spite of craters indicating that several stars had landed on or near it, it stood tall, defiant against the attack.

I squinted my eyes at it. It didn't quite seem like it was staying in one place, but the distance made it hard to judge.

No, no, I was right. It was moving.

It was a treant, not a tree. Disguised as just another tree in the forest, this one was anything but.

It took a few moments to speed up. And up. I realized that I was seeing visible, rapid movement from a giant of a tree, several mountains away. Nothing that big, that far away, should be that quick.

[*ding!* **You are in the presence of Guardian Yurok, The Plague**]

428

I glared at the System notification. I'd disabled them, damnit! Obviously, the System didn't care about me disabling notifications.

Also - wait. Guardian? Like Etalix?

The notification also explained something I'd never thought of before.

How *did* we know the name of a dinosaur?

If Yurok was anything like Etalix, the answer was now obvious- a System notification.

Clouds of red gas poured off of Yurok, flowing towards Lun'Kat in the air.

No bets what it was, when gas came off of something with the title "The Plague."

With a derisive flap of her wings, Lun'Kat blasted a wave of wind through the gas, dispersing and scattering it to the winds. Some landed on the hills, trees crackling and dissolving as it hit.

Some were blown towards us on the hill.

"Shields!" Toke yelled, and I threw mine up behind hers.

While I intellectually knew that the shields were helping, it didn't feel like it as both were shattered. **[Bullet Time]** activated, giving me all the time to think. Not wanting to try and tank the deadly spores from a monster powerful enough that there was a bloody System announcement about it, I rapidly ran through my list of options, before cracking a grin.

The gem I'd never used, which had always been an afterthought, saved our collective ass. **[Gust]** summoned a blast of wind, blowing the spores away from us.

Until about twenty minutes ago, I would've called the blast of wind powerful. Having seen Lun'Kat's sky-shaking blasts as she casually traveled from place to place, my idea of the pecking order of the world was entirely upended, my place right at the bottom of the totem pole reaffirmed. I was the ant with the best healing power, but that didn't make me any less of an ant.

The wind tore through the cloud, pushing most of the spores away, with some at the edges wildly spinning around in a circle.

One tiny spore was ejected from the whirling wind, and in a split-second decision, considering how much harder it'd be to

429

heal Toke than myself, I pushed Toke out of the way, taking the hit myself.

I instantly crumpled, vomiting blood and black bile, as my arms blackened, necrosis setting in and racing up along them, withering first my blood, then skin and muscle, sending it sloughing off my bones before they too were liquefied, the vile black goo which had moments ago been attached to my body splashed onto the ground, so toxic that the stone beneath me discolored. And yet it wasn't done, as the toxic plague invaded my chest, blackening and rotting my organs. It was only my instantaneous healing which kept me alive, organ puree being replaced by intact and healthy flesh, only for the cycle to repeat as I flickered between "healthy" and "on the brink of death." Necrotic flesh filled my body displacing what was left of my torso and forcing me to cough up what toxic sludge hadn't spilled out from around my armor. On my hands and knees, I spat out more blood and bile, and wiped my mouth.

"Why did you do that!?" Toke yelled at me.

"Healing myself is more efficient." I groaned back, looking at my mana.

That one spore had taken a 30k chunk out of my roughly 150,000 mana pool. I shuddered to think how much it would've cost with a cross-species penalty.

Someone would've died.

Chapter 42

The Dragoneye Moons II

I felt someone smack my head. I stood up and glared at Lule, who was giving me the stink-eye.

"We're here to protect you! Let us do our jobs!" She yelled at me. "We have Ned, who can also heal us!"

I noticed that there were thin, shimmering lines between all of the dwarves and Ned. I bowed my head at Lule.

"Sorry." I said, meaning it.

Ned and I healing a dwarf was *probably* more powerful than me just healing myself.

Maybe.

"Ned, I *need* to know, what's your magic power?" I asked him.

He looked at me with wary eyes, saying nothing.

"Tell her!" Lule yelled at him.

He sniffed.

"Over four thousand." He said, with the most pompous voice, like there was no way I could possibly beat that.

"Four thousand? *Four thousand!?*" I yelled at him. "What the fuck do you think you're going to do with four thousand magic power?! I'm sitting at over *one hundred fourteen thousand* magic power when I heal, and I could barely manage that attack! That took me thirty thousand mana to manage, and it still almost instantly killed me! *Four thousand* power is just going to get everyone killed!" I couldn't help but say that last part contemptuously.

Fuck letting one of the other dwarves tank an attack. Ned didn't come *close* to making up for what I'd lose in efficiency.

Ok, so yelling at them wasn't exactly *fair,* but I wasn't in the mood to go through this carefully. Something about watching my flesh writhe as it disintegrated only to be restored was doing a number on my mood.

The dwarves were looking at me like I was a monster. I realized I might've screwed up a bit, and quickly backtracked a hair.

"I did mention I was *the best* healer humanity has. That means something." I pointed out.

Nope. Was still getting looks like I'd grown seven extra heads.

The awkward moment was interrupted by an earth-shattering *roar*, my eardrums popping again as they got blown out and instantly healed.

The rest of the dwarves were grimacing, and I noticed that they all had blood running out of their ears as well. I dunno if my healing or Ned's (ha! Like he was doing much with his low-powered healing, compared to the **[Wheel of Sun and Moon]** I had going on them!) was keeping them up, but either way we were all in deep shit.

From the east, a dinosaur, eight times the size it had any right to be, a behemoth of a monster, crested a mountain, roaring in challenge. It was bipedal, hunched over with a long, crocodile-like jaw, dark green scales, and a massive fan on its back.

A cascade of Lightning sparks leapt from the Mist-wreathed titan as it moved.

I'd seen that dinosaur, that Spinosaurus, before. In front of every temple, carved out of the finest marble. I'd grown up on stories of him, of hearing how he was the guardian.

Well, I could see him in the flesh now.

[*ding!* You are in the presence of Guardian Etalix, The Storm].

Etalix bellowed once more, the night sky turned greenish, and in a single moment three tornadoes formed out of the sky and descended, whipping up debris, coalescing into spinning, lethal forces of nature.

Unlike Destruction, who clearly could barely manage a small tornado after weeks of channeling, and couldn't control it once unleashed, Etalix had perfect control over the three large tornadoes he'd instantly summoned. They worked in tandem, harassing and chasing Lun'Kat, whirling dervishes of indiscriminate destruction.

Yurok wasn't standing still either. It was constantly releasing multi-colored clouds, and given how much we'd struggled with just a single spore, I was keeping a wary eye on them – and paled as the tornadoes sucked some of the gas up, becoming colored instruments of destruction and plague. Lun'kat soared over Yurok, strafing it with dragonfire, but Yurok wasn't taking it lying down. A disk of blackened wood surrounded him, as some large skill was cast.

Even Lun'Kat didn't seem to like whatever Yurok was doing, as she roared and twisted aside.

Yurok was burning though, dragonfire crawling through its branches. The treant shuddered, and the layer of burning bark shed, restoring the treant to its natural state. Solid skill, that.

Or was it just a natural ability all treants had?

I should be running. I should be hiding, fleeing, doing what I could to survive.

Instead, I stood entranced, hypnotized by the battle of the titans I was witnessing. In a moment of insanity, I wanted one of the guardians to pass close enough that I could [Identify] them.

Then, in one of her many passes over the mountains, continuing to burn and fight with the guardians, Lun'Kat stopped one of her attacks near the mountain we were on.

Close enough for me to [Identify].

[Lun'Kat, the Stygian Deceiver].

Seeing it gave me a massive, pounding headache, and I felt liquid - blood - ooze out of my eyes, ears, and nose. One of her eyes twisted and locked onto me.

I immediately dropped to the ground and prostrated myself, saying nothing, remembering that Night had said the dragons didn't seem to like worshippers talking to them. For all I knew he was wrong about that, but challenging, running, or defying Lun'Kat all seemed like ways to end up dead via a casual flick of her wings, and prostrating myself seemed like it might have a small sliver of a chance for survival.

I had no shame in admitting that Lun'Kat's direct attention terrified me to the point where I peed myself. The ability to *drop the sky on a country* as an *opening move* was enough power for me to be properly scared.

And yet, even as my face was pressed into the hard stone, my only chance at survival being Lun'Kat ignoring me, the memory of her eye was burning in my mind, filling my thoughts as I mentally chanted prayers to every god and goddess I knew to keep me safe.

I'd seen that eye before.

I mentally cursed the dwarves who were making a clamor, although from the sound of it Lule was stopping them doing anything terminally stupid, like attacking Lun'Kat.

I swear, if the dwarves got me killed, I was going to spend the entire afterlife haunting them. I'll ask to be reincarnated as the most annoying creature, specifically to pester them in the next life.

Notice of my short-term survival arrived as another shockwave, significantly stronger than any other, washed over me, cracking my head against the hard stone.

Bless my healing.

Heat started to rise from the latest batch of dragonfire brought forth by Lun'Kat, as she'd set our mountain ablaze.

With us still trapped on the summit.

The dwarves were doing *something* near the mineshaft, but I couldn't tell what. I was too entranced by what I was seeing.

The clouds crackled with green lightning, a lightning bolt jumping from cloud to cloud, coming from the distant north. I saw the bolt pause a moment, seemingly thinking, then descend down to earth – wreathing the mountain we were on, forming a curtain of green lightning all around us.

Fortunately for us, it didn't hit the top of the mountain, and the lightning reformed itself. A gigantic serpent, clad in rainbow scales encircled the mountain, facing Lun'Kat and hissing, with such power that my teeth rattled together.

[*ding!* You are in the presence of Guardian Galeru, The Rainbow].

Bonus! It happily landed on the burning wood, crushing it, and formed a nice barrier between us and the flames!

Of course, it also meant we were trapped on the mountain.

There was a brief shimmer, then a half-dozen more snakes were on a half-dozen of the surrounding mountains

Large coils wrapped around the mountain, as green lightning seemed to arc constantly from Galeru - and the copies - towards Lun'Kat, a steady stream of power and damage from Galeru and her clones, enough to fry a city in a heartbeat. It filled the air with enough static electricity that my hair was wildly dancing about.

Lun'Kat seemed to simply shrug off the attack, barely noticing. She simply exhaled an inferno of Pyronox, bathing Etalix in black flames. He vanished beneath the flames, a huge explosion of Mist expanding in every direction.

I seized the chance to **[Identify]** the massive snake coiling near me.

[Guardian Galeru, The Rainbow] I got back.

Had no idea if the **[Identify]** was black because of its high level, or if guardians had a black **[Identify]**. Either way, it seemed to be on the same tier as Lun'Kat - although the way Lun'Kat was simply shrugging off its attacks made it clear who was superior.

Looking around, the Mist that Etalix had exploded into was reforming on another mountain, and the dinosaur's massive shape was becoming clearer. Neat trick, that, being able to turn into Mist and just be completely invulnerable for a time. Maybe. I'd need to get the skill itself and see what it did.

Never thought that Mist would be high up on my to-acquire list, but hey! Learned something new every day.

The tinkling of windchimes came to me, starting off slowly, then steadily getting louder until each noise was like a high-pitched gong going off in my ears.

[*ding!* You are in the presence of Guardian Asura, The Destroyer].

I looked, and running on the wind from the north, light radiating from behind it, a beam of Radiance coming from its horn, was a unicorn. Pure white fur, a mane of silver and golden hooves that galloped on nothing but air.

The beam of Radiance from its horn went straight through Lun'Kat, and my heart leapt into my throat. Did Asura just kill the dragon?

That would've been too easy. Lun'Kat shimmered, then shattered like a mirror. I put one and one together - we'd been getting our asses kicked by an illusion, a Mirage.

Heck, we hadn't even been the subject of the attacks. The mere shockwave of Lun'Kat's illusion moving around was enough force and power to knock us on our asses constantly.

Asura's Radiance washed over the mountains - and us - breaking and shattering all illusions. The many clones of Galeru also broke, which led me to think that the guardians didn't exactly have strong teamwork.

However, Lun'Kat's true body was revealed, and the guardians shifted their attacks, which started to land.

Runes drawn in massive, mystical light formed behind Asura, spitting forth dozens upon dozens of different types of attacks. Magic missiles and arrows, beams and chains, small bolts and arcing lightning were just some of the attacks that spilled forth from the mandalas being instantly drawn behind Asura. There was even an extra-large Mandala that took time to charge, then unleashed a powerful beam.

Far more attacks than skill slots alone could account for, each of them aiming at Lun'Kat – who ignored the arrows, broke the chains without noticing they existed, and dodged the charged attack with a twist of her wings.

Asura wasn't the only one ramping up their attacks. Yurok had stood still for some time, but moved again - together with the entire downed forest around him. Trees stood once again and

436

each one began to launch branches at Lun'Kat, a veritable avalanche of wood heading her way.

No snowflake thought it was responsible for the avalanche, but it was like when the lean-to had turned into a splinter attack. One splinter was harmless, but when massed, it could be problematic.

These "splinters" were the size of normal trees, given that they were the branches of redwood giants, animated once more.

Etalix's tornadoes were both helping and not, as they sucked in some of the barrage, and flung them back out at high speeds. Some were accelerated towards Lun'Kat, others shot to nowhere.

Some entered the plague tornadoes and vanished, presumably consumed and corrupted by the poisons Yurok was emitting.

A few shot towards some of the other guardians, who either dodged, blocked, or disregarded them. They didn't seem like intentional attacks, just a force of nature being a force of nature.

Lun'Kat expelled another black blaze, seemingly into the air, but instead of attempting to burn anything, dozens, hundreds of little dragons spawned from the black fire, flying down onto the controlled trees, and attempting to burn them with their own black Pyronox.

Some got sucked into the tornado, never to be seen again.

But the forest was burning even harder. Lun'Kat's initial passes, her deadly red streaks of fire were growing larger, smoke creeping across the sky. The miniature dragons she summoned were spreading pyronox flames, and it was with no small amount of concern that I saw they were sticking to rocks - and continuing to burn.

Dragonfire. Didn't seem to care about the normal rules of what was flammable - it just burned everything.

"Don't get hit by the flames!" I yelled to the rest of the dwarves, who had taken up a defensive position.

I got a "no shit" look back.

Drin. Fik. Lule. Ned. Glifir. All in a semicircle around me, backs to the shaft, all with their shields out.

"Hang on, where's Toke?" I asked.

I got a glare from some of the dwarves. Lule just pointed to the old ventilation shaft.

"She's gone in, trying to use her Darkness magic to widen the passage enough for us. We're trapped here otherwise." Lule said.

Given that Galeru was about ten meters wide, and wrapped around the entire mountain, trapping us on the peak, that made sense. I didn't think even an entire mountain would be enough to keep us safe, but it was better than being out in the open, tornado winds whipping around, needing to constantly shield against random splinters, colorful gases, and stray lightning bolts.

Speaking of, my pack was gone. Entirely. Somewhere in the mess it had been picked up and blown away, and I was thanking my lucky stars that I hadn't fallen to temptation, and I'd always slept in full gear, as uncomfortable as that had been.

No idea what happened to the yaks either. I'd bet money on their souls, if they had them, busy queuing up for reincarnation by the time dawn arrived.

Chapter 43

The Dragoneye Moons III

The battle continued, the six of us on top of the mountain partially shielded by Galeru - partially put in the line of fire because she was there.

Lun'Kat soared up high, so high that I could barely see her. Then, wreathed in flames, she descended like a meteor onto Etalix.

I didn't think there was a skill involved – just sheer bulk, speed, stats and physicality.

Etalix exploded into Mist again, but the mountain he'd been standing on was annihilated by the sheer force of Lun'Kat's impact. "Small" rocks the size of villages went flying everywhere, the earth shook from the impact, and a boulder the size of Ranger Headquarters came spinning towards us.

Galeru lazily flickered her gigantic rainbow tail towards the boulder, shattering it.

Causing thousands of high-speed stones to rain down on us, deadlier than any skill Artemis could produce.

I tried to shield and dodge the best I could, but end of the day, it got ugly. Drin and Fik took up a defensive stance, shielding the rest of us, and Fik used his magic – which I now recognized as Gravity – to grab and haul the worst offenders out of the way.

I threw up a complicated [Mantle], woven with dozens of holes in it. My goal was to block the largest pieces of stone still flying at us, even as Fik frantically moved them out of the way.

Between Drin and Fik's physical shields, my magical shield, and Fik deflecting the majority of the deadly projectiles, we were "only" rained on by the "little" stones.

Enough rocks to kill a normal person by stoning, but none of us were normal. We all had armor on, and between my healing and Ned's meager contribution, we survived. Broken bones were almost immediately re-knit, and some large dents in our armor was the only evidence left.

We survived the side-effects of a Guardian deflecting the after-effects of a dragon's purely physical attack.

Toke needed to dig that hole *faster*. Although, the evidence was clear – not even an entire mountain was enough protection, not if Lun'Kat decided to remodel.

It was a little hard to see the sky, because of Galeru's constant green Lightning attack. Lun'Kat roared again, and beasts and monsters from myth and legend peeled off of her. Griffins and Wyverns, Rocs and Vermillion Birds, all made out of constellations, bright, starry, and shimmering, all were summoned with every flap of her deadly wings, and engaged the Guardians.

Asura simply released a beam of Radiance from her horn, piercing the constellations sent after her, while a fan of Lightning came from Etalix, disintegrating his attackers. The griffin and other entities sent after Yurok somehow, in spite of being made out of stars, seemed to age, sicken, and die, while Galeru's tail went from rainbow-colored to a shimmering mirror and slapped an attacking flock of wyverns, returning them to sender. The wyverns tried to attack Lun'Kat, but they were all killed in a single burst of dragonfire.

Still, the attack had distracted the guardians, forced them on the backfoot. Lun'Kat used the moment of distraction to devastate the country, burning and razing as she pleased.

To say she held a grudge was understating it a hair. I was all on Team Guardian at this point – Team Dragon seemed to want nothing more than to devastate everything she saw, while Team Guardian seemed to be "stop that."

A rift tore open the sky, and high-pressure water sprayed out, directly hitting Lun'Kat, slamming her down. All manner of fish, sharks, and other deep-sea creatures poured out through the rift. There was even a small kraken, who immediately started to struggle and flail as it went from the bottom of the ocean, to the middle of a mountain range. I couldn't help it. A manic giggle escaped my lips.

Heh. Fish outta water.

[*ding!* You are in the prese-]

A System notification was aborted as Lun'Kat summoned a shimmering ribbon made of an Aurora Borealis, and whipped it around, slicing *through* the rift, forcing it to collapse. The Aurora-whip continued on, barely slowing from destroying the rift, and sliced clean through a half-dozen mountains, forming brand-new passes all throughout the range. Skinny, narrow, impossible passes - but the fact that I could see them from mountains and miles away suggested they were significantly wider than they seemed.

I had no idea it was even *possible* to abort a System notification. They'd always seemed to instantly show up for me, but the evidence in front of me suggested otherwise.

With a speed that was unbelievable for its huge size, one of the mountains that had gotten cut by the Aurora-whip, much deeper in the range and hardly touched otherwise by the epic battle that was occurring, *stood up.*

I could see the ripples race through the earth as the local part of the planet rearranged itself to a mountain standing up, tectonic plates shifting and stone splintering as a secondary shockwave traveled behind it.

Not again.

A creaking groan, the sound of the earth itself standing up, washed over me as the soundwave hit. I braced myself with some of the dwarves, and managed to stay standing up.

The giant looked *pissed,* and given that some of the starfall bombardment had hit him, I would be too. With three steps, each one shaking the earth hard enough that I felt it from mountains and miles away, he stepped from mountain to mountain, striding to Etalix. Instead of helping him, he gave Etalix a mighty kick - one that went straight through him, as he turned into Mist and reformed himself on another mountain.

The giant wasn't done though, as he turned on Lun'Kat, and with a hand the size of a town, *swatted* her out of the air, down to the ground.

With that, the sky flickered.

I looked up.

The moons.

Winked.

Out.

The baleful red of the moons no longer washed over the battlefield. The ominous eyes no longer stared at me. Instead, two pale orbs hung where the moons were. One pale yellow, the other a pastel blue.

The pieces clicked.

The dragon's familiar eyes.

Mirage and Celestial elements.

A title of "The Deceiver".

The Dragoneye Moons *were an illusion, cast by Lun'Kat!* A mirage, coating the moons. A casual display of immense power, a flex, demonstrating Lun'Kat's superiority, how she was always there, always watching, an apex existence.

I stared down, at Lun'Kat, who was recovering on the ground. Bleeding.

With a scream, raw and primal, loud enough that once it hit from over a mile away it still blew my eardrums - again - Lun'Kat flew up at the giant.

I didn't know much about dragons, but she looked *pissed.*

She opened her mouth, and shimmering, silvery flames exploded out like a lance, burning through and bisecting the giant, who dropped like a sack of potatoes.

A mountain-sized sack of potatoes that took 15 seconds to fully fall, sending waves rippling through the earth, destabilizing our footing, causing us to grab onto each other to stop ourselves falling.

Fortunately, our mountain hadn't gotten knocked over yet, and I couldn't quite believe that was a real problem we had to be concerned about.

The giant's arm weakly came up as he was lying down on the ground, filling in a valley with his bulk.

I cursed as I realized he wasn't dead.

My fucking [Oath] was going to get me killed, wasn't it? This was the end of the line for me.

I started to run down the mountain, ignoring Lule's cries for me to *stay with them.*

I had never hoped for another intelligent, living creature to die when it wasn't trying to harm me before. Even as I reached Galeru, and her wall of shimmering scales, I was praying that the giant would die, pretty please, and free me from my self-imposed and totally futile obligation to help.

Even with all my mana, with all my Arcanite, there was no way in hell I could save the giant. There was no way I could even *get* to him in time, not with needing to cross a mountain and change before he bled out. I couldn't start to heal on the scale of the injuries. Maybe if it was, like, missing a fingertip or something I could help.

And, of course, Galeru was wrapped around the mountain, the massive rainbow serpent another obstacle. It only took a few minutes of running at top speed, dodging falling trees and jumping over secondary fires, to reach the first set of coils that I'd need to cross to reach the giant.

I looked at the wall of flesh and rainbow scales, trying to figure out how to get over them, hoping that Galeru didn't shift or get hit, which could easily crush me under her. She wouldn't even notice.

A pillar of starlight came down from the skies, roughly where the giant had fallen. I felt relieved. The giant was likely dead, and I was free from my attempt to heal him.

I eyed Galeru's massive body.

443

Fuck it. It was likely I died here, but if not, I was going to get myself some *crazy* experience.

I dashed forward, touched her body, and with the worst image possible, applied a **[Solar Infusion]**, then pushed a **[Dance with the Heavens]** through her.

I also flickered **[Shine]** briefly, figuring with all the illusions running around I might randomly hit one and get some experience. At the same time, I didn't want to attract attention, hence only doing it when sheltered by Galeru, where it could just be another twist of her scales causing the light; where it'd be drowned out by her lightning.

My mana instantly zeroed out, and I was hopping back and running up the hill, refilling my mana from my Arcanite reserves.

Lule met me as I was jogging back up the hill.

"Fool! Why!?" She yelled at me, grabbing my arm and pulling me along, back up the hill.

"Have to heal." I gave a curt answer.

"Even if it costs your life!?" She yelled back.

"Yes."

My answer was calm, serene. I'd accepted my fate. With my lifestyle, with how I acted, with my impending immortality skill, there was only one way my life would end.

Dying as I ran to heal someone.

When accidents were removed, when old age, disease, and cancer were gone, the only end for me was a violent one.

Or a really, really complicated accident. Given my lifestyle, violently was where a smart girl put her money.

Well, I wouldn't. I wouldn't be able to collect, not unless there was *another* accident with my soul and I got another do-over.

We made it back to the summit, and my eyes were drawn to Etalix, shrouded in a rapidly expanding swirl of rain and clouds.

"Hurricane!" I yelled, as the swirl *exploded* into a full-force typhoon, stretching to blanket the mountains, blinding us with winds going hundreds of miles per hour and battering us with sheets of freezing rain.

"Get into the shaft!" Lule yelled, and the rest of the dwarves started clambering feet-first into the mineshaft.

No idea if Toke was done expanding it enough for us to fit, but at this point, being stuck in a mineshaft seemed to be safer than staying on the summit. The dwarves slipped through one at a time, Lule helping them through, acting as the rearguard. Boldly making sure that all of her charges were safe before getting to safety herself. A true leader.

[*_ding!_* You are in the presence of Guardian Ho-O, The Conflagration].

I could see white bursts occurring deeper in the storm, and Lule got bowled over by a chunk of ice hitting her square in the head.

It was just us two on the peak - the rest of the dwarves had already bailed down the shaft. I ran over, cursing Etalix and the clouds for hiding the moons, preventing **[Wheel of Sun and Moon]** from working.

I really needed to remove all my restrictions on my healing.

At the same time, **[Cosmic Presence]** was doing work. There was almost no bleeding, and I slipped on the icy, slick rocks, arriving at Lule's side.

I threw more healing into her, **[Dance with the Heavens]** still a solid touch-skill, and she groaned as she sat up.

"Move!" I yelled at her, and we supported each other as we tried to get to the shaft.

Something had inserted a crapton of Ice into the fight, and since magic was magic, instead of dispersing, the hurricane was now throwing around freezing water and ice, which was adhering to, and freezing, the slick rocks on the summit.

Somehow, I doubted that anything called The Conflagration was responsible for Ice. Then again, I couldn't see what else could be causing it.

The storm blew one of the Pyronox dragonlings into us, and it squawked, seeing prey. It breathed Pyronox flames on us, even as I tried to blast it apart with **[Nova]** and beams of Radiance.

Damn storm ate half my attacks.

Ice cracked as Lule ripped stones from the mountaintop and threw a barrage into the black flames. The stones just rippled through… and a moment later came right back to pelt us as the storm grabbed and redirected them.

Normally, I'd just tank lightly thrown stones and let myself heal. A bruise, a broken bone at worst, wasn't worth the mana cost of shielding.

Problem was, with the icy, slippery footing, I was concerned about slipping, falling, at which point I'd lose all control.

I [Mantle]'d it, at the same time the dragonling blew Pyronox flames at us. Two birds, one stone!

Except for the flames sticking to the [Mantle], and my mana starting to drop at an alarming rate. I canceled the [Mantle], expecting the flames to vanish.

No. Of course not. These were dragonfire, derivative or not. Something as mundane as being in an icy storm, with rain pouring on them and lacking any fuel source wasn't enough to stop them. They surged forward, blown by the wind, onto Lule and I.

Onto just Lule. She moved at the last moment, pushing me out of the way and throwing herself in front of the flames, getting coated by them. Just like I'd jumped in front of Toke. Then the dragonling continued, blown past, and was gone, out of range, out of reach, of the two of us.

The black flames started to surge and spread, greedily devouring Lule's armor and spreading to her beard and face as she stoically tried to beat the flames out.

"Strip!" I yelled at her, making the snap call to thrust my left arm forward and touch her, pumping healing mana into her.

Lule grabbed at bits and pieces of her gear, throwing burning chunks of living wood everywhere. I was careful about the flaming pieces and [Mantle], only briefly flickering it up to stop a piece hitting me.

Yet the black flames spread across her body, over her head, down her legs.

Touching my hand, starting to spread up my arm.

I looked at my hand through the flames, seeing that it was still whole, still perfectly intact - even though my mana was dropping rapidly, as the flames consumed my flesh, only to be instantly restored.

They started to lick forward, hitting my vambrace.

My vambrace - full of gemstones.

There was a *snap,* a crackling of energies, and a **[Nova]** exploded out, impacting and immediately exploding on my arm as the Pyronox ate into and destabilized the gem. It wasn't a full explosion, it wasn't as strong as it could be, and it was one of my smallest gems, located on the edge.

Still, it made it clear that my gemstones were now a liability, and I fired off all of my **[Nova]**'s with the wind, making sure they wouldn't blow back and hit me.

The wind and icy rain extinguished them rapidly, a brief moment of heat the only remnant.

"Go!" Screamed Lule. "Leave me!"

"No!" I yelled back.

She didn't answer, but collapsed to the floor, screaming and writhing as she was consumed.

She clawed at her face as she screamed, her flesh soft and melting like putty. Her thick fingers were able to dig deep into her flesh, and just pull chunks of her burning face off, flames rushing to fill in the gap even as my mana healed and restored the lost flesh.

She tried to levitate stone from around her, to encase herself in rock. More than a few stones tried to get through me, and I was once again thankful for my armor, even as my arm got crushed by her manipulation.

I ripped my arm free, once again free of dragonfire, and restored my hand. I didn't hold it against Lule at all, she was trying everything to survive. Given how my hand was now free of flames, it had a strong shot of working.

Then again, everything on fire had been amputated, which helped.

For a moment it looked like her self-created tomb worked, that she'd smothered the flames. Then brown stone turned black, and the flames burst forth once more, casually consuming the rocks.

There was a *pop* as fat in her abdomen finished liquifying, then the water boiled over and exploded out of her. Sizzling filled the air, so loud I could hear it over the flames, and I redoubled my vow to *never ever* eat pork again.

I went to a knee, putting a hand on her, trying to burn through the flames with Radiance, seeing if I could *somehow* combat them. I drained the mana out of my Arcanite, pushing things longer, further.

Trying to smother the flames with **[Mantle]**.

Rolling her on the ground. Awkward, when I was only using one hand. I refused to let my other hand catch fire.

It was only when my mana dropped to nothing, and Lule stopped moving did I get up. I felt terrible. All I'd managed to do was prolong her suffering. What would've taken seconds had instead been a prolonged session of torture and agony, as I made her burn alive – and consciously – for far longer than was needed. However, I would need to mourn her properly another time. I looked down at her with sorrow, then turned to myself, and the black flames that were now past my elbow.

No idea why they'd gone slower on me than on Lule, but I wasn't going to complain. Maybe it was a limitation on the skill? It had generated dozens, if not hundreds, of the little Pyronox dragons, who were breathing deadly cursed flames all over the place, each of which resisted everything that could be thrown at them. Perhaps poor chaining was the reason the entire world hadn't burned down already.

Healing hadn't worked, time, cold, water, starving it of air - nothing seemed to work on these cursed flames.

The only thing that had given them pause was amputation.

Welp. Nothing for it.

I turned off my **[Persistent Casting]** of **[Dance]**, and drew my sword. I looked at my arm, breathed in once, twice, steeled myself, and swung, awkwardly trying to hack my arm off at the bicep.

The bad angle, a short sword meant for stabbing, with no real edge to it, and my low strength relative to my vitality made it an ugly, ugly job. That was before the mental aspect of "I'm cutting my own arm off!" started to yell at me. I was starting to feel woozy and light-headed from the blood loss, as I added yet another problem to the storm.

The bone was extra-hard to hack through, and I'd been contemplating trying at the shoulder, where there was the joint, when I managed to make it through.

Still, with my arm off, I'd regenerated enough mana to do a small heal, closing off the wound, and restoring my blood.

I was going to need every drop of mana for what came next.

I gave one last regretful look to my arm, picked up and tossed by the wind, and turned towards the mine ventilation shaft. I sheathed my sword, and one-handedly picked myself up, preparing to drop down the shaft.

Then the wall of the hurricane passed, and I got a brief moment in the eye of the storm.

Lun'Kat was still high in the air, superior, dueling flames with a bird-like creature made out of pure flames.

A Phoenix. Ho-O.

Yurok was continuing to emit gas, tendrils of the noxious poison reaching out like hands to grasp Lun'Kat, who casually ignited it with normal flames. As "normal" as dragonfire was anyways. The flames roared down the poisoned spores, back to Yurok, causing explosions the entire way down.

Ashen spears rained from the Phoenix, magical missiles fired from the Unicorn, surrounded by mandalas, green Lightning arced from Galeru, and icy missiles descended with alarming regularity from the sky, striking indiscriminately.

Lun'Kat shrugged off nearly every attack, elements sliding off her shimmering black scales, roaring dominance. Flames roared and consumed as far as my eyes could see, from the walls in the north to beyond the horizon in the south, heedless of the pouring rain and cold. A burning hellscape, brought to Pallos, choking and smothering with the thick smoke being poured into the atmosphere.

It was like the world had ended.

In the eye of the storm, in one of dozens of areas cleared out by the fight, a pyramid of sand rose. Taller and taller, until it was almost the size of one of the redwoods. Then it crumbled and collapsed, and a strange creature was revealed.

It was a gigantic turtle, but instead of a tail, there was a viper. Both heads were locked onto Lun'Kat. It was at least 40 meters tall, and significantly longer before the snake half came into play.

A Xuan Wu. Just as legendary as a phoenix, just as mythical as a dragon.

[*ding!* You are in the presence of Guardian Hebai, The Mountain].

My hair rose around my head, as a pillar of Lightning, nearly as wide as a town, descended from the sky, directly onto Lun'Kat, blinding me.

Deafening me.

Without the ability to see or hear anything, and having been *strongly* reminded that I had no business there, I dropped down the shaft that Toke had made, only for local gravity to increase an insane amount.

I could only hope that the shaft led to safety, and that the rest of the dwarves had made it to safety.

Chapter 44

Minor Interlude – Autumn

The Letters I

"Healing! Free healing!" Autumn yelled into the crowd, cursing the lack of Elaine's presence. Just by being around, Elaine had moneybags lining up down the market aisle, most of the cash-holders wanting to meet the famous Sentinel, with the rest having legitimate injuries that needed tending to.

By herself? Autumn didn't do nearly as well. She was running headfirst into the problem that Elaine had warned her about – low-level Light healers couldn't do much, so coin-dispensers tended not to visit them.

Autumn was trying Elaine's trick. Somehow, she'd stumbled upon a fantastic method for getting the sweet clanking of coins into her jar, all while having the poor former owners of said coins smiling all along.

"Is your healing truly free?" A bounty bringer came up to Autumn, who **[Merchant's Appraisal]**ed her lightning-fast.

A heavy pouch on her waist – but it was all wrong. The little shapes and bulges being made from the contents didn't match the outline of coins at all. Decoy purse! Autumn approved of deceiving thieves, but not merchants. Nooo.

Her clothes were high-quality, but well-worn. A light breeze blew through, ruffling her clothes a hair. One part of her tunic didn't move quite the right way, revealing a second pouch tucked into her clothing.

Yet, that tiny glimpse was all Autumn needed to get a good estimate of exactly how many coins this particular supplicant could bestow upon her.

Autumn would get her purse filled, one way or another.

This wasn't a big fish, but it wasn't a small one either.

First! The hook! Get the tasty fish with the golden scales –
err, purse – interested.

"Yup! Completely and totally free." Autumn said, internally
smiling as she got the sentence out without stammering or losing
her cool once.

She'd practiced saying that with her dad at home, needing
hundreds of attempts and repetitions before she could say it in a
smooth, natural, believable way.

The phrase itself was a violation of Rule 1 – Always, always,
always get paid. Yet, it was needed. Lure the target in, then
shake them down for everything that would rattle loose.

Of course, nobody believed Autumn was giving away free
healing. It boggled the mind of even the most naïve of targets.

Autumn mentally revised that.

Of the most naïve of targets that still had any money worth
getting.

"I'm in it for the experience. Hard to level up my class." She
explained, watching the guardian of the green's face carefully. A
tiny amount of sympathy showed, but not enough.

"My master left on a trip, and abandoned me to my own
devices." Autumn added in, putting on a sad face.

Lying was *bad.* It was a sure-fire way to destroy one's
reputation as a merchant. It didn't matter if the lie was a terrible
backstories, faking freshness, to flat-out selling defective goods.
Autumn could make a few quick coins today – and never make
another coin again, not with a destroyed reputation.

Honesty was best.

It didn't mean she couldn't present things in the best light
possible for herself! Elaine had technically run off again on some
mission-or-another, and she'd been gone a few weeks now.
Autumn wasn't worried....

Ok, Autumn was worried. It wasn't like Elaine to be gone
this long on one of her missions.

The custodian of cash's face took on a more sympathetic
look. *Yes! I've got her!*

"I'm doing this for free in hopes of getting enough levels to
make it on my own." Autumn said. "Also, since I can't promise I

can fix you, it would be wrong of me to charge. However, if I manage, a small donation to keep me going helps. Whatever you want to pay!" Autumn said, inevitably slipping from her "pity story" tone of voice, into her "sales" tone of voice.

She mentally cursed. She was working on it, but she'd been working at keeping the "pity story" tone of voice during her pitches. Ah well, it looked like she was fine.

"Hmmmm. Ok, thank you." The minder of the moola said, turning and leaving.

"Tax collectors!" Autumn cursed as she slumped in her stool. Another one that got away. Her money! Her precious money – oh, and experience – was walking away! Drat.

A heavy hand landed on her shoulder.

"You should probably read some of the scrolls Elaine left for you, hmmm?" Autumn's dad, Neptune, said.

Autumn slumped her shoulders, glancing down at where the scroll she was currently on was.

"I should, but..." She trailed off, not quite sure how to articulate her concerns, why she didn't want to read it right now.

"It's not a betrayal to read them. Nor is thinking she's dead." Neptune said. "Heck, part of her instructions to you, her apprentice, was to read them when she wasn't around. Have you been doing that?" Neptune asked her with a Look that said he knew exactly how much she'd been reading them – or how little.

"Well, I'm still confused about this one part..." Autumn said, trying to defend herself.

"Then read a different part. I know medicine builds on itself, but you can read a different thing, and get more questions for when Elaine gets back." Neptune said. "Think of how happy Elaine will be!"

Autumn frowned, then brightened up.

Yes.

She'd have ALL THE QUESTIONS for when Elaine got back! She might even level!

"Right! I'm on it!" Autumn said, pulling out a different scroll with gusto, and diving into it.

She could try to get some more suckers with silver, but digging into medicine sounded more fun at the moment.

She unraveled the scroll, and started to read.

Impact and Symptoms of each type of organ failure.

Dry stuff – but learning it would bring Autumn one step closer to her goal of a swimming pool full of coins.

"Working hard?" An amused voice said, and Autumn snapped her head up, information about collapsed lungs and breathing patterns fleeing her mind.

"Yup!" She said, recognizing the golden goose from earlier. In tow was a sulky-looking boy, without a single coin on him. Autumn categorized him as "totally broke", then dismissed him from her attention.

However, the potential payment patron was with penniless, so Autumn took a second look.

"My kid hurt his hand. Can you take a look?" The bounty bringer asked me.

"Of course!" Autumn's **[Money to be Made]** skill was alerting her. She'd considered ditching the skill, because it really only went off when it was blindingly obvious that a sale could be made.

Autumn extended her hand, and gave an encouraging smile towards Broko. He slowly unfolded his arms, and presented a slightly mangled hand towards Autumn, who started looking at it with a critical eye.

She didn't have anything for the pain, so she tried to minimize the amount of poking and prodding she did. Still, two of the fingers were somewhat mangled. Autumn sighed in relief. It was something she could handle.

She *hated* money walking away once she diagnosed the problem – and it wasn't something she could fix. Autumn swore she could hear the sweet clanking of coins bouncing against each other when bacon bringers bailed.

"Right, hold on a minute." Autumn said, diving into another pack, and grabbing some bandages."Ok, this is going to hurt a bit." She said, as she 'massaged' the fingers roughly into the right position, keeping a poker face as bone scraped against bone. Destitute winced, but didn't try to pull his hand back.

Autumn grabbed the two mauled fingers - "ring" and "middle" Elaine called them – and wrapped each one with the neighboring finger, before using a skill of hers.

"[Speedy Recovery]" Autumn said out loud, because how else would the Capital Conferrers know that she was also performing a limited, exclusive skill, that would normally cost money?

Autumn felt the fingers in her grip slightly rearrange themselves, and she silently cast the spell a few more times. No need to display that she couldn't do it in a single shot.

After a half-dozen casts, she let go, and put on her sweetest smile.

"Just give it a week of rest in the bandages, and you should be all set!" She said. "The extra fingers are wrapped to give it support, and while it's probably good now, we wouldn't want to stress it and cause a problem by starting too early." Autumn said.

She'd screwed that up once, and it'd *sucked.* The ingrate had come back, yelling and screaming, and the only reason a wrecking ball hadn't gone through Autumn's reputation is Elaine had shown up the next day, back from a mission of hers. He hadn't dared kick up a fuss with Sentinel Dawn sitting RIGHT THERE.

Autumn sighed. She missed Elaine.

Back to the good part!

Payment.

Autumn rapidly looked over her most generous gold giver, rapidly evaluating dozens of factors while **[Merchant's Calculation]** ran, all while speaking to her.

"As you know, I'm a free healing service. Always have been! It's good for my experience. With that being said, a few coins donated towards me helps me keep going." Autumn said, going over her daily-edited and rehearsed speech, modifying it for what she thought this particular loot leaver would like. "If you could donate just 17 coins, that would mean the world to me." Autumn said, **[Merchant's Calculation]** coming back with the number.

It evaluated dozens of different factors that Autumn knew about, from the quality and wear of her clothes, the town they were in, the location in the marketplace, the likely size of her household and family, a blind guess of how generous she was, the goods she was carrying, and most importantly of all, the size of her purse, how many coins were left in it, and a strong guess on how much shopping she had left to do in the day.

It was the moment of truth as the Moola Mom pursed her lips, running her own calculations, looking between Autumn and Impoverished, before giving her a curt nod and dropping the coins in Autumn's eagerly outstretched hand, who promptly whisked them away to her secure coin storage.

"Thank you so much!" Autumn said, playing up the "thankful kid" angle. "Please come again, and tell your friends! I'm good for scrapes you don't want mom to know about." Autumn said, telling the last bit in a whisper to pauper.

Rule 25. "Everyone can get money in the future." Her patient had no money – today. He couldn't donate anything – today.

Future patient? Future Autumn? There could be money there, and sowing good seeds today could reap a bountiful harvest in the future. Autumn was young. She could take the long view.

She happily waved off the pair, as a runner arrived.

"Are you Autumn? Daughter of Neptune?" He asked, looking between a letter and her, confusion visible on his face.

Nobody sent expensive letters cross-country for a *kid* after all.

Not unless you had as much money as Sentinel Dawn, and equally little sense in spending it.

"Yes! That's me! Gimme gimme!" Autumn said, grabbing a handful of coins and thrusting them at the runner. Tips weren't needed, but they were polite, and a good way to get good service, and Autumn didn't care how many coins she spent, not if it meant getting Elaine's letter faster.

456

[Merchant's Calculation] told her that she was handing over 20 coins, but Autumn ignored it. The runner handed the letter over, and Autumn eagerly tore into it.

Autumn!

I'm safe and sound! They didn't pay me extra, but I found a way to make a few extra coins anyways. Buying land in a new town. Should be profitable.

I hope you're keeping up with your studies. I'll be checking when I next come back!

You might hear about a new town popping up. **DO NOT MOVE HERE.** *The land's poisoned, and that's bad for business. Also, you're a Light healer, and while I shouldn't need to remind you, I just know you're seeing coins and rods, and ignoring my warnings. You're a Light healer, which means your ability to deal with toxins and poisons that are here are practically non-existent. Trust me.*

Even if you class up first, **wait for me.** *I need to check that your skills can handle this, it's a nasty one. You won't realize a problem until you need to spend dozens of rods on a cure.*

With that being said, guard and soldier supplies are likely to spike in price soon. Might want to get ahead of the curve on that. Food might also become more expensive, although sticking around the capital might be a poor choice.

Best of luck. Stay safe until I can get back! Study hard. Poke Markus or Caecilius if you have any questions, they should be able to help you.

Cheers,

Elaine.

Autumn's face went through a whole range of emotions reading the letter. Happiness that Elaine was safe. Despair that she didn't get paid extra. Pride that she somehow managed to wrangle some profit out of it anyways – and that clearly her lessons were sinking in, if Elaine was starting to look for profitable opportunities.

Deflected guilt that she'd gotten back to her studies before she'd gotten the letter – *how had she known Autumn was slacking!?*

The rest? The rest was going over Autumn's head, and was far more complex than she was willing to deal with.

"Dad? Hey dad?" She asked, tugging on his sleeve.

Neptune finished up his sale, and turned to Autumn.

"Yeah?" He asked her.

"Elaine sent a letter. Not sure what to make of it." Autumn said, handing the letter to Neptune.

He read it with a frown.

"Right. What do you think we should do?" He asked Autumn.

"Try to figure out what's going on, because Elaine doesn't know business *at all.*" Autumn promptly replied. "For all I know, Elaine thinks there's more food coming, and wants us to buy it when prices are low."

Neptune barked a laugh out.

"That would be like her, you're right. Let's focus on what is here though. A new town. What does a new town need?" Neptune asked, going into tutor mode.

Autumn thought about it.

"People?" She hazarded.

"Yes, and?" Neptune prompted.

"Buildings?"

"Go on."

"Buildings need stone." Autumn said. "But I never heard of stone being bought in large quantities."

"Because it's not. It usually goes from the quarry to the building site, and the front lines have their own dedicated quarries. For that matter, most of the buildings probably will come from those quarries." Neptune said.

Autumn kept thinking about it, pitching other ideas, only for Neptune to correct her, or encourage her.

Finally she snapped her fingers.

458

"Metal! Iron!" Autumn said. "Need it for all manner of tools, and there's going to be a ton of soldiers retiring to become farmers! They're all going to need metal for their tools! Is there an iron mine near the frontlines?" She asked, only for Neptune to give her a huge smile and ruffle her hair.

"Nope! They funnel everything through the capital, where they outfit the soldiers before sending them to the frontlines. They also run supplies through here. Iron's the perfect thing to buy! Also, if Elaine's somehow correct about soldier supplies, metal's a key component. Plus, it's not food! What's wrong with stockpiling food?" Neptune asked Autumn.

Autumn rolled her eyes.

"Rule 31. Don't stockpile anything that'll get you ripped apart by a mob." She recited. "Drugs, dangerous animals, and food in a famine, plague, or drought are all good examples." She continued, going past the rule and reciting part of her teachings.

"Very good! Right, this is your chance. How reliable is Elaine? How good is our information? And how much do you want to put on this?" Neptune asked Autumn.

Autumn didn't hesitate.

"Everything!"

Chapter 45

Interlude

The Letters II

Lightning played over Artemis's body, as she bent over in agony, her muscles spasming as the lightning wreaked havoc on her.

A moment later, she straightened up as she'd grabbed the lightning herself, wrapping it up into a neat ball in her hand.

"Good try." She told Horatio, who was looking concerned.

"Um…" He said, gulping and trailing off as his eyes locked onto the ball of Lightning that Artemis was holding onto.

"Lightning is a fantastic element, as I'm sure you know." Artemis said, keeping half an eye on Horatio, and the other on her students, who were surrounding the area, watching her exhibition duel/lesson.

Artemis took a practical approach to teaching magic. There was practicing shooting earthen plates - then there was practicing fighting another person.

There didn't tend to be a whole lot of earthen plates lurking in the wilderness, trying to kill young mages.

"It's quick. It's deadly. It's versatile." Artemis continued, giving her full attention to her students as poor Horatio threw up defense after defense.

Artemis glanced, and quickly evaluated his defenses. Not enough. Not for the point she was trying to make. She did wish he'd make flashier defenses though. It would make the demonstration stick all the better once she shattered them.

"Horatio's mistake, was trying to use Lightning against another Lightning-element mage." Artemis said, trying to keep how happy and proud she was of Horatio out of her voice.

He'd picked Lightning as his element, in an attempt to emulate her. Elaine had totally been right. This teaching stuff was *wonderful.* She got to see the kids dropped off with her grow and learn, and she longed for the day when one of them properly surpassed her.

Elaine didn't count. She was Sentinel based on her healing abilities, and as much as Artemis took credit for her physical and magical combat prowess, she knew that she was still a better, stronger mage than Elaine was.

"Once it's too far from Horatio, the Lightning he conjured up wasn't under his control anymore. Can anyone tell me what the second issue with using the same element against a mage is?" Artemis asked, looking around.

This was a fairly basic introductory lecture, so she didn't expect anyone to immediately know the answer.

Still, after a moment, with Horatio still frantically erecting defenses, a small flame went up. Artemis insisted on conjuration being used to answer questions, and it helped both with conjuring the element, and controlling it.

"Yes?" She said, pointing at one of the students, and mentally sighing at Horatio. He'd forgotten one of her key lessons - a good offense was a good defense. His fighting will had been broken by how casually Artemis had defeated his first attack.

Artemis overwhelming him right here and now with attacks was a basic lesson to demonstrate the point she was trying to make, but it wouldn't work to solidify his basics. She'd need another student to spar with him, to get that lesson in his head properly.

She quickly ran the students through her head.

Theseus would be a good partner.

"Because you have [Lightning Resistance]?" The student asked nervously.

Artemis gave him what she thought was an encouraging grin.

"Exactly! There are a number of elements which mages get the resistance skill for. Lightning is one of them. Not only was Horatio's attack dramatically weakened by my resistance, but he gave me a nice chunk of Lightning to use for myself. Watch!"

Horatio had *finally* gotten enough defenses up to survive what Artemis was about to do. She took the ball of Lightning, and like an Olympic shot-putter, she threw it back at Horatio.

She added a few low to the ground rocks in the mix. Keep him on his toes, if they didn't remove them entirely. She'd given him enough of a chance to arrange his defenses, Artemis wasn't going to give him any more of a chance than that.

The Lightning ball ripped through his hastily-erected shields, then as it got too far away from Artemis, exploded out in all directions, playing over his flesh. The pair of rocks she'd thrown down low then hit both his shins, and Artemis winced a hair as she heard the secondary crack of bones breaking.

Fortunately, the healer on-hand was already moving, having gotten used to Artemis's methods by now.

"Lastly, Lightning is great because it's so loud, and so bright, that it hides other attacks." Artemis loudly announced, pointing to Horatio who was clutching his leg.

[*ding!* [Teaching] leveled up! 188->189!]

Ha! Yes! Another level!

Artemis loved **[Teaching]**. It gave additional experience to her students when they were learning, and doing stuff at the school she taught at. It gave them a solid level boost when it was all tallied up.

Best of all, it stacked with them if they got **[Education]**, **[Learning]**, or a similar skill!

Horatio wasn't screaming, thank goodness. That was always awkward when a student started yelling and screaming in pain. One of the first lessons Artemis tried to get out of them - screaming and crying did *nothing*. Worse than nothing, it distracted your teammates, and let the enemy know you were hurt, injured, and worst of all, *still alive*. The ultimate "kill me now" signal.

She walked over to Horatio as most of the students muttered to themselves. A few were looking a bit green, and those either quit, or pushed through and became some of the better students, as they drove themselves hard.

"You ok? I hope my performance wasn't too *shocking*." She asked him, leaning over and offering a hand. She didn't mean physically, of course - the medic had seen to that - more of his ego, and mental well-being.

"Yeah. Totally forgot about the rocks." He said, taking her hand and accepting the assist up. Artemis shook her head.

"When have I ever gone easy?" She asked.

"Um. Most days. New students, intermediate students, most of the advanced students." Horatio said, starting to tick off his fingers.

Artemis swatted him.

"Oi! If you've got enough vigor to sass me, you can run laps. Go on! Get!" She yelled at Horatio, trying and failing to keep the laughter out of her voice.

"What are the rest of you looking around for? 10 laps! Get going!" She yelled at the rest of the watching students. "Can't be any good as a mage if your body can't keep up!"

With some muttering - a few of the newer students had come in good clothes, they'd learn soon enough - the students followed Horatio on laps around the Academy.

Artemis still felt like she was an imposter, that she had no idea what she was doing. All she did was a haphazard set of lectures on what she knew, mixed it up with some practical demonstrations, add in some sparring and physical exercise, and that was it!

Well. And sat with each student in one-on-one sessions, talked over their build, and gave them nudges, direction, and advice. Still, it felt weird that people were coming to her for advice.

As the slowest student rounded the corner, out of sight, Artemis saw a delightful sight for the eyes.

Julius!

She kept her expression carefully schooled. They were keeping their relationship under wraps for good reason. Still.

They knew each other well enough to see the tight little lines, mirror gigantic grins on their face barely suppressed.

"Commander Julius." Artemis said, giving him a salute.

"Artemis." Julius said, handing her a letter. "Letter from Sentinel Dawn."

Artemis gave Julius a quick look, then opened the letter, turning herself so only she could read it.

Julius tried to shuffle around to see, but Artemis kept twisting to keep it hidden.

"Hey!" Julius protested.

"Shoo! My letter, from my healy-bug." Artemis said, flapping a hand at him.

"She's my Sentinel!" Julius protested.

"Did she send you a letter?" Artemis asked, giving him a look.

"Well, no..." He said.

Artemis got the smuggest look on her face.

"*My* healy-bug. *My* letter." She said, starting to read it.

Her face went from happy-grinning to serious real fast as she read the letter, and she silently handed it over to Julius when she was done.

Artemis!

Big fight, killed a bunch of Formorian Queens, wild party. I'm OK, Night's OK. Sadly, it looks like I'm going to be stuck out here for awhile. More Sentinel stuff to do. Don't know when I'll be back – it's a mess out here. I'll try to write lots!

On a different note – why didn't you tell me about you and Julius!? I'm so happy for you two! You've got to tell me everything when I get back!

Well, not everything.

Almost everything!

*Things, for reasons I can't say, might start getting real crazy and hectic near you. **Stay safe.** Keep your students safe. If everything starts going crazy, hunker down and protect yourself.*

There's no reason to go out and get involved in nonsense. Not allowed to say anything more.

I classed up! Got my next healer evolution! **It's so exciting!** *I can't wait to get back and tell you all about it! It's the best thing ever! I have so many cool tricks now!*

Cheers,

Elaine

"I haven't even gotten Night's report yet." Julius said with a frown.

"Mmhmmm." Artemis said, with a distinctly unamused tone.

Julius didn't really notice.

"What she's written here implies some sort of large-scale event – one that we'd be better off weathering, instead of trying to fight. So it can't be all bad..." Julius said, his mind working rapidly as it considered and discarded a dozen different possibilities, before finally settling on the right one.

"Can't be monsters, can't be environmental, so it needs to be people. Can't be small, otherwise Rangers, Sentinels, or the 3rd Legion would handle it. It needs to be bigger than all three combined – which is the majority of the army. What could they be doing to make Sentinel Dawn concerned enough to send a letter? A coup's the only thing I can think of." Julius reasoned out.

He paled.

"That might be why I haven't gotten Night's report yet. The runner might've been told to take it nice and slow – or even intercepted. He'll be furious, but what's done is done."

Artemis smacked Julius over the head.

"Never mind that! We'll just take the students on a field trip."

"We?" Julius asked dumbly.

"Yes, we. After you let the cat out of the bag with Elaine!" Artemis yelled at Julius, her face as thunderous as her famous element.

"Oh, um, that. She tricked me!" Julius said. "Implied that you'd told her!" He held up his hands, praying to Aion that he'd get off lightly.

"Elaine. Tricked you." Artemis said, with a tone of disbelief. "Elaine couldn't trick a newborn rabbit, let alone one of the most cunning *Ranger Commanders.*" She said, electricity crackling between her fingers.

Julius tried to bail.

He was fast. A speedster, and high level, with a powerful class.

He wasn't Lightning-fast.

Artemis activated one of the Inscribed Scrolls she had. Cheaper than a gem, but single-use, she couldn't wait for the day when she could reliably get a gem, and charge it with a similar skill.

"Twenty more laps everyone!" She yelled, her voice being amplified throughout the school, as the Inscription burned through the scroll, the material unable to handle the power coursing through it.

Damn cheap things. She cursed as she chased after Julius.

Two weeks later, Julius was in his office, doing scrollwork. Endless scrollwork. If Ranger Command had told him how much scrollwork he would be doing when he got promoted, he might've said no.

Ah, who was he kidding. Julius would've said yes anyways.

He finished off the current report – a request for a Sentinel, to handle a mine that nobody came out of – and leaned back to stretch in the sunlight, coming in through a narrow window.

A smile played over his face as he remembered his latest adventure with Artemis. Gods, she was radiant to be around. Witty, smart, strong. Didn't take shit from anyone – himself included. He wanted to marry her, but knew what her response would be.

Didn't stop him from having a ring tucked into his desk drawer, for a day he thought proposing would work.

A knock came on the door, interrupting his musings. He straightened himself back up – always had to put on good appearances.

"Enter." He said, and the Ranger's internal runner popped in.

"Mail for Command." He said.

Julius rubbed his eyes and motioned him forward. Downside of being the newest Commander – all the scut work was his.

He motioned the runner forward, and took the scrolls from his hand. There were a lot of scrolls, far more than usual, and he narrowed his eyes.

Extensive paranoia was part of the job, and he had a sense that a full meeting of all the Commanders was in the near future.

He checked the dates on the scrolls, seeing that they'd been dated over roughly three weeks. Someone had been tampering with the mail.

First was a missive from Night. Short, sweet, to the point.

Victory. The Formorians have been defeated.

A scroll, dated two days later, gave Julius the full details of what had transpired, including the casualty count.

"Kyros." Julius ordered, the guard in question popping into his office a moment later, saluting.

"Run down to the apothecary. I'm going to need a lot of stamina potions." Julius said, handing over a few coins. He lowered his voice.

"And if you want to get into some good graces, the rest of the Commanders will probably want some once the meeting gets started." He said with a wink.

Everyone won if Kyros was the one pre-emptively helping. If Julius did it, it'd look like he was being presumptuous. If one of the guards did it? Well, they were just being diligent.

Still, potentially promoting one Sentinel was a headache. Now they had multiple open seats, which created a dizzying maze of potential promotions.

The next scroll came in, which detailed Night using his emergency powers to promote Ranger Falerius to Sentinel, title Maestrai. Julius felt the flavor of his headache change. One

467

problem was gone, creating three more in its wake – the inevitable endless arguing over if Night had overstepped his authority or not being the first one.

Julius had spent a lot of time with Artemis. Artemis, who'd been mentored and taught by Night once upon a time. That, combined with what he'd seen of the reclusive leader of the Sentinels, let him know that Ranger Command existed in part because Night didn't want to handle it. He was the power behind the council, the reason Rangers had lasted so long.

Night wanted to promote a Ranger to Sentinel? It was done, and arguing it was a waste of time. It wouldn't stop the fools from the Senate protesting until they were blue in the face.

"Lykos." Julius ordered, his other guard stepping into the room and saluting. "I need Sentinel Ocean here, on medium to high priority. Thank you." He said, dismissing him.

Ocean was *probably* findable, given how reliable he was. He was also hyper-aware that he was the only combat Sentinel left to deploy, and there was at least one festering problem that a Sentinel would usually be sent to handle, that was currently being sat on.

Ugh, and Sealing was dead. He would've been the go-to Sentinel for that particular problem, which meant Night might have to be deployed.

Except Sky was gone and the rapid deployment Sentinel, Maestrai, was brand-new, not even in town or given the shakedown, and...

Julius thanked his lucky stars that there were eight Ranger Commanders, not one. That particular issue was one that would be solid for the entire council to discuss.

Moving on.

Scroll after that detailed the deployment of all the Sentinels. Brawling to fetch Ranger Falerius – pardon, Sentinel Maestrai – and Hunting and Dawn into the Formorian lands, ensuring all the Formorians were dead.

The next scroll extensively detailed an incoming coup, along with each faction, allegiances, strengths, and estimations of how the fighting would occur. Night must've spent *days* working on this, and it included simple instructions.

"Do nothing."

A pain, but full instructions were given. The council would argue furiously over it, and the Senate would then be informed by the Senate Commanders, but that was going to be their headache, not Julius's.

The next scroll was Julius's headache though, and had him reaching for his hidden jug of wine.

Hunting and Dawn had made contact with another civilization! One that built large wooden walls, as far as Hunting could see. His estimation of their military strength was mixed. While the walls were expertly crafted and the weapons second to none, the actual manpower and discipline of the soldiers manning it were severely lacking.

However, they took a shine to Sentinel Dawn, and they'd made the snap decision to leave her there, to make a good first impression.

Julius needed a single stiff drink to get through that particular scroll. He'd been Elaine's team leader, once upon a time. He *knew* Elaine.

Elaine? First contact?

The last scroll confirmed his worst fears.

...Three days before we arrived, the sky lit up in all manner of fantastical colors, and two soldiers on watch claimed the stars and moons did strange things. Still, we carried on....

Julius knew *exactly* what night that had been. Rumors of the moons flickering to a different shade for a brief while were so widespread as to be fact. Heck, one particular Senator with a slightly looney reputation was suggesting changing the calendar to have the "night of the flickering moons" be year 0.

He was roundly laughed at for the suggestion, but it'd been made.

... When we arrived, there were no walls. No civilization. Instead, smoldering buildings, some still weakly on fire, others

469

with warm embers inside, met our gaze. There was a forest and mountains further on, but what was not charred and blackened was still alight, merrily burning away.

We spent days searching, but we could locate no sign of Sentinel Dawn....

Julius read the report over three times before drinking the entire jug of wine, eyeing up the scroll in the room that detailed Sentinel Dawn's exploits.

Including the *Pastos* incident.

Damnit Elaine! What did you do this time?! Julius thought, as he prepared the necessary paperwork.

Sky – Killed in Action.

Sealing – Killed in Action.

Magic – Missing in Action, Presumed Dead.

Dawn –

Here Julius hesitated a moment. He hadn't been there, but he could imagine the scale of the devastation. If Elaine was alive, she would've worked her way back over to Remus.

At the same time, maybe there hadn't been enough time for her to work her way back over? Elaine was tough, almost unkillable. And while the report stated they'd stayed a week, maybe there was something that prevented her from making it back.

Either way, Julius judged that the circumstances of her disappearance didn't merit assuming the worst. He wasn't looking forward to telling Artemis, or the rest of Elaine's family.

Still. It was with a heavy heart that he wrote the words about the plucky girl he'd picked up once upon a time, feeling that in many ways it was his fault.

Dawn – Missing in Action, Presumed Alive.

Chapter 46

The Fall

I dropped straight down the darkened old mine ventilation shaft, pulled extra-hard by whatever Gravity nonsense was going on. The shaft was now wide enough for the dwarves, courtesy of Toke. More than wide enough for me. I needed to get out of here before another stray fraction of an attack came over the mountain peak and my luck ran out.

The dwarves were a stocky bunch, and I immediately tried to twist, pressing my remaining arm against one side of the shaft and my feet pressed against the other side, trying to wedge myself in.

Toke's carving away of the stone with her Dark magic had left the shaft supernaturally smooth. Despite the stone surface, it was difficult to get any sort of traction to properly slow myself down with.

Which, of course, had me rapidly speeding up as I futilely tried to get a proper grip, my sandals burning with the friction. The Gravity was fluctuating as well, letting me know that the fight outside was still going on. After just three seconds, during a pause in the increased gravity, I gritted my teeth, and properly jammed my hand into the wall.

Skin peeled off, leaving a long, bloody streak on the wall as muscle tore, giving me the mother of all rugburns. I opened my mouth in a silent scream as I managed to come to a halt, taking a few deep breaths, and considered my next moves.

It was pitch black in here, only a few small stars in a circle of light above me. An Elaine in a well.

I'd completely emptied my mana in my futile attempt to heal Lule, and I didn't even have any Arcanite reserves left to top myself off with. Given that I associated "Mine ventilation shaft" with "Long, straight, and ends with hard stone", I expected a long, long fall, followed by *splat* that I'd hopefully survive. The rest of the dwarves had also taken the same passage, but Toke would've gone in slow-mode, as she cleared the shaft one length at a time, which would've stopped her from a hard landing. Most of the dwarves were physical-based, which would allow for rough, but survivable landings.

I was worried about Ned, but a healer with a full bar of mana *should* be fine. He might break a few bones, but his level was high enough that I wasn't concerned about his fate. Even if he *only* had 4000 magic power.

Mine? It was dicey. I was going to go down as slowly as possible, to give myself time to regenerate enough mana, so I could un-splat myself at the bottom. That's why I wasn't restoring my arm, and trying to do this one-handedly. If I fixed my arm now, I'd just need to fix it again at the bottom.

Nah, better to go down one-armed, and heal it later, when I had more mana.

Still, **[The Dawn Sentinel]**'s stats were working overtime, restoring roughly 38 mana per second. Ideally, I'd have a full mana bar, and bounce off my shield a few times on the way down to bleed speed, then be able to fully resto-

I cursed as my thought process was interrupted by the small circle of stars seeming to fall, and I recognized Lun'Kat's attack from earlier, where she brought down the entire sky on the countryside. If the skill had a cooldown, it wasn't particularly significant, and I let go, allowing myself to drop.

I wanted a lot more mountain between me and that attack.

Naturally, this would be the exact moment that Gravity decided it didn't want to work nearly as well, and instead of accelerating down at full speed, it was more like I had a lazy slide, right as I wanted to go full speed.

My bet was the Xuan Wu was doing this, since the Gravity nonsense had only started after he'd shown up. He was probably trying to slow down all the stars, and reduce the impact of the stars.

I didn't care about that, I just wanted to go *down!*

Which of course had me rudely yanked at the wrong moment, back to free-falling like somewhat normal.

I did spend a bit of precious mana restoring my rugburnt hand, before trying to slow myself down again, blessing **[Center of the Galaxy]** for letting me ignore the burning pain in my feet. I managed to briefly slow myself to a halt, only for the entire mountain to start shaking as some attack or another hit, dislodging me and causing me to tumble down, into the pitch-dark depths.

I made the snap call that knowing when I was about to hit something solid was worth losing a bit of extra mana, and I used **[Shine]** to project light down the shaft, twisting my neck so I could see.

Nothing but darkness.

The mountain was shaking, not quite as violently the further I fell, but I was picking up so much speed that I wasn't able to wedge myself in the shaft any further. Faster and faster I hurtled down, trying to summon **[Mantle of the Stars]** to slow my fall enough to get a grip, only for my blood-slick feet to fail once again.

I only got a quarter-second warning that I was about to land, but with **[Bullet Time]** activating, that was enough.

It had to be enough.

I tied off the *worst* image possible to my **[Dance with the Heavens]**, linking it to **[Persistent Casting]**.

"Heal the head. Then the rest."

As I did that, I twisted my body such that I'd land feet-first, like a gymnast finishing her routine. I fought the instinct to cover my head with my arm, instead putting it out.

Another support to break before I did.

Hopefully long enough for my healing to kick in.

I hit the ground *hard,* screaming as **[Center of the Universe]** broke, feeling my shins snap, my kneecaps pop off, my femur break. My shin guards snapped, and my leather skort was entirely useless for stopping anything here.

My pelvis shattered, my spine bent and popped, and my arm turned into a triangle.

My armor creaked and broke, small pieces flying off in random directions.

I kept screaming as the pain overwhelmed me.

As I stopped, only to topple over, bleeding from uncountable places where bone had punctured through flesh, my mana dropping to, and staying stubbornly at, 0, as every drop I regenerated went toward healing the massive injuries I'd just sustained.

"Elaine? Elaine! Ned, get over here!" A voice I identified as Fik said, as I screamed and screamed and screamed, until my lungs reminded me that I needed air in them to scream more.

A light came over, four concerned faces looking down at me.

I breathed in. It *hurt*. Agony wracked my body, and twitching in response just caused more agony, causing me to flail and spasm. Wounds that had already closed over thanks to the rapid passive healing from **[Cosmic Presence]** opened backed up, spraying one of the dwarves in hot blood. He reeled back, spluttering and pawing at his beard.

Then – relief. Blessed, cooling relief washed over me, and I could see the red-painted bones sticking out from me slowly retract back into my body, my one arm twisting back into position. It felt like it took an eternity, but couldn't have been more than six or seven seconds.

Made me appreciate my significantly higher power.

"Get ready to catch Lule!" Glifir said, and I was unceremoniously rolled out of the way, still one-armed. I rolled through a few puddles, getting soaked and splattered with mud. I coughed and spat, trying to clear my throat. I tried to get up, only for my legs to fail me, and I faceplanted onto the hard stone, cracking my head hard enough that I saw stars.

Fine.

I was just going to lie here for some time, long enough to recover somewhat. It sucked that one of my legs was in a pool of freezing cold water, but eh. I couldn't bring myself to care enough to move it, not with the energy level I was at.

Being out of mana – and wanting it all for healing my arm – meant no **[Sunrise]**. Downside of being a healer-mage. Out of mana? Out of tricks.

Still.

We were under no threat.

Wait.

A thought slowly percolated to the surface of my thoughts.

Four dwarves?

I cracked an eye open, looking at them. The four dwarves looked *rough*. Even Drin's armor, which normally healed itself instantly, was battered and broken. There were the dents I'd expect from a long fall, but claw marks?

Burns?

I groaned, and turned off my **[Persistent Casting]**. I hadn't knocked myself out, hadn't needed to keep healing going while unconscious. No sense in wasting mana on shit healing, not when the mines didn't seem nearly as safe as I'd first assumed.

That, and I could get a much more efficient heal if I spent half a second thinking about it. Honestly, it was a win all around.

I rolled and pulled myself up slightly, leaning against the wall I could barely see in the flickering light the dwarves had on them.

Wasn't worth using any mana on my own light.

"De-" I tried to say, only to cough and hack again. I licked my lips, wetting them.

"Dead." I managed to croak out.

"What?" Fik asked, glancing back.

"Dead. Lule didn't make it." I repeated, starting to get my voice back, closing my eyes at the memory.

I got an angry snort from Ned.

"So much for 114,000 plus magic power." He said, mocking me.

I creaked open an angry eye at him.

"It was dragonfire. I blew 300,000 mana trying to save her. The dragonfire didn't care." I retorted, curling my hand into a one-finger salute.

My hand was still on the floor, and Ned probably didn't know what it meant. Still. It was the thought that counted.

"Still left yourself enough mana to drop down." Ned sneered at me.

"Fuck you." I said, with as much feeling as I could put behind it. "I dropped with no mana, and no Arcanite."

Saying that exhausted me, and I put my head back against the wall, closing my eyes.

"How much danger are we in?" I asked, getting silence back.

I kept my eyes closed.

"You're probably thinking that you still need to escort me. Yes. Fine. I'm not helpless. I need to know what we're up against." I said, wishing they'd just *understand*.

"We don't know." Drin said after a moment. "We jumped fairly quickly. When we landed, there was no sign of Toke. We got attacked by some monsters though."

"How dangerous?" I repeated myself, mentally running through what resources I had left.

My [Nova] gems were all gone.

My Arcanite was drained, but I still had all of it. It was part of a layer that hadn't snapped off. I was out my shin guard, but I still had my right vambrace – which meant I still had my utility gems. The only one I'd blown was [Feather Fall], although I slightly regretted that I'd brought just one.

Oh well. I survived the fall. I was alive.

"They're not as dangerous as we are!" Drin crowed.

"Oh shut up. They're just as strong as a dwarf, and it'll get us killed not to admit it." Glifir argued back.

That started off rounds of bickering, which seemed unwise given our predicament. I decided to take stock of what I had, while my body slowly finished reknitting itself. Ned had done a lot, but there were minor issues that still needed to be addressed.

My armor was bent, battered, and not exactly in one piece anymore, and my sandals were in dubious enough shape that I doubted [Talaria] would work. Not that "flying" and "cramped tunnel" went well together. I didn't have my pack, spear, shield, or helmet.

I had my short sword.

My lucky pendant.

My talent, training, skills, and System.

Speaking of – I had half a moment to process. I wonder what levels I'd gotten?

[*ding!* **Congratulations!** [The Dawn Sentinel] has leveled up to level 306->355! +3 Dexterity, +24 Speed, +24 Vitality, +170 Mana, +170 Mana Regen, +48 Magic power, +48 Magic Control from your Class per level! +1 Free Stat for being Human per level! +1 Mana, +1 Mana Regen from your Element per level!]

Bloody hell. Healing Galeru, trying to heal Lule, being on the edges of the fight with a bloody *dragon,* and surviving secondary dragonfire off a skill, then surviving the fall, all outside of the dead zone, was good for some serious, serious experience.

[**Learning**] multiplying things probably helped to boot.

[*ding!* [Celestial Affinity] leveled up! 306 -> 355]

I wonder if watching the sky fall helped at all with affinity?

[*ding!* [Cosmic Presence] leveled up! 231 -> 269]

That seemed like a lot. Then again, the skill was sort of subtle. I'd been actively healing just about every injury as it occurred... so really, getting two levels would've been a win, let alone freaking 38.

It did make me think that, since my [**Persistent Casting**] was off, that whenever I took an injury and I didn't need to immediately heal it to save my life, that I should consider letting [**Cosmic Presence**] take a crack at it first. The skill was powerful enough now that it could possibly get some serious experience. A snowball effect, basically.

[*ding!* [Solar Infusion] leveled up! 1 -> 110]

And the winner for biggest level jump in a single occurrence goes to - [**Solar Infusion**]! Previous casts on Hunting had gone nowhere, since he almost immediately broke the skill. Thinking about it, putting it on Galeru might've been suicidally stupid, if the big snake decided it didn't like me.

She probably didn't even notice that I'd done anything.

Welp, the skill now had some decent power behind it, and I'd need to work with the rest of the team on how to best utilize it.

[*ding!* [Center of the Universe] leveled up! 285 -> 355]

I didn't think the skill breaking when I hit the ground had helped a ton, but it killing pain so I could keep healing Lule, then hack off my own arm to save my life?

Yeah. Good experience. Also reminded me that I was completely, totally out of the dead zone, and good experience was the name of the game.

[*ding!* [Dance of the Heavens] leveled up! 306 -> 355]

I half-expected the amount of experience the skill had just gotten to somehow break the skill cap imposed by the System.

300,000+ mana went through the skill, in a combat situation with multiple guardians and a dragon, healing *dragonfire*. Not just regular dragonfire, but *skill-backed* dragonfire.

Ok, so I was letting the myths and legends surrounding dragons get to me. It might not be that special, but it was from a monster at such a high level it caused bleeding just to [**Identify**] it.

Then again.. Galeru hadn't caused that problem.

Money on dragons being stupid good. Or just having some skill like [**Identify-Me-Not**]. I could believe it.

Couldn't wait to get to the skill.

[*ding!* [Wheel of Sun and Moon] leveled up! 271 -> 311]

The constant shockwaves I'd healed the dwarves through paid off with a nice smattering of levels. Sadly, Etalix had clouded the sky, which stopped me from using it later on.

I wasn't going to complain, not with the literal hundreds of combined levels I was getting.

[*ding!* [Mantle of the Stars] leveled up! 257 -> 315]

I'd been abusing **[Mantle]** hard, and the massive jump showed. Kinda wished it'd overtaken **[Solar Infusion]**, but I couldn't win them all. Plus, I'd cast the skill a dozen times, not once.

[*ding!* [Shine] leveled up! 115 -> 188]
[*ding!* [Identify] leveled up! 152 -> 200]
[*ding!* [Identify] has upgraded into [Long-Range Identify]!]
[*ding!* [Long-Range Identify] leveled up! 200 -> 355]

While the upgrade didn't seem all that potent, a quick check told me that I'd more than quadrupled the range, while also being able to identify a group in one go.

I wasn't going to complain about free, more powerful skills.

Especially not when a new record was set, and I got 200 bloody levels in a single skill from two **[Identify]**s after a whole freaking lifetime IDing people to get 152 in the first place.

Ugh. I shouldn't have wasted my time, and just come here in the first place and ID'd Lun'Kat. BOOM! No time wasted, no grinding needed. I'd also have to check, but I might be able to **[Long-Range Identify]** anything that I could reasonably see at this point, barring, like a giant sleeping like a mountain.

[*ding!* [Pristine Memories] leveled up! 201 -> 205]

I had no idea what the skill was doing here, but I'd take it.

[*ding!* [Pretty] leveled up! 153 -> 154]

What. Why?

[*ding!*] [Bullet Time] leveled up! 268 -> 269]

[Bullet Time] not activating as I was plunging to my death was the source of no end of irritation for me. I could've used the extra processing time! I could've tried to heal bone, keep them together to force more of the impact to work on breaking unimportant bones.

Bah. I suppose willingly jumping to my doom didn't count as an attack.

[*ding!*] [Oath of Elaine to Lyra] leveled up! 270 -> 300]

Willingly running to my doom to save another creature, and spending everything I had on Lule was recognized, and rewarded, by the System.

I glanced at my stats and nearly had a heart attack. First, finishing up the rest of my skills, blitz-style.

[*ding!*] [Sentinel's Superiority] leveled up! 306 -> 355]
[*ding!*] [Persistent Casting] leveled up! 192 -> 255]
[*ding!*] [Learning] leveled up! 282 -> 340]

[Learning] oh **[Learning]**, how I loved you as a skill. Steadily increasing multipliers to my experience? It was the only reason I was as high level as I was.

I looked around. A dim light, held by the four dwarves, my only companions down here in the mine. Water, dripping from above. The occasional shake as some powerful attack or another caused the mountains to shake.

My pack, spear, shield, and one vambrace – gone.

I was battered and injured – although that was temporary – in a mine filled with monsters, the only people nominally on my side not all seeming to like me very much. I had no food, it was freezing cold, and the water here was questionable. There was a battle of the titans overhead, and from what we'd seen, "an entire mountain" wasn't nearly enough of a defense. I had no map, no directions, no idea which way was out.

I let a soft chuckle escape my lips.

I'd been spending my time trying to dance and play politics, to be in polite society. It was no surprise that Ned looked down on me, was dismissive almost to the point of cruelty. It was no wonder that they treated me like a slightly dumb flower, to not even let me risk hurting myself as they built camp.

I wasn't a diplomat, and it was a dumb fucking idea to have sent me as one. Hunting and I should've just gone back together.

I was a *Sentinel*. I danced with Black Crow, I flirted with White Dove. I was a tease, coming to the brink of death, wriggling my eyebrows suggestively at them, then laughing as I spun away, out of their grasping claws.

Stealing away a partner, that I'd ripped out of their claws, saving to live another day.

An abandoned mine, full of monsters? Danger around every corner?

I hated acknowledging it, but I couldn't deny it any longer.

I was in my element.

They wouldn't know what hit them.

[Name: Elaine]

[Race: Human]

[Age: 19]

[Mana: 0/239290]

[Mana Regen: 216486 (+153145.6)]

Stats

[Free Stats: 101]

[Strength: 274]

[Dexterity: 497]

[Vitality: 3376]

[Speed: 3376]

[Mana: 23929]

[Mana Regeneration: 23929 (+15314.56)]

[Magic Power: 9997 (+149955)]

[Magic Control: 9997 (+149955)]

[Class 1: [The Dawn Sentinel - Celestial: Lv 355]]

[Celestial Affinity: 355]

[Cosmic Presence: 269]

[Solar Infusion: 110]

[Center of the Universe: 355]

[Dance of the Heavens: 355]

[Wheel of Sun and Moon: 311]

[Mantle of the Stars: 315]

[Sunrise: 128]

[Class 2: [Ranger-Mage - Radiance: Lv 256]+]

[Radiance Affinity: 256]

[Radiance Resistance: 256]

[Radiance Conjuration: 256]

[Shine: 188]

[Sun-Kissed: 256]

[Blaze: 256]

[Talaria: 256]

[Nova: 256]

[Class 3: Locked]

General Skills
[Long-Range Identify: 355]
[Pristine Memories: 205]
[Pretty: 153]
[Bullet Time: 269]
[Oath of Elaine to Lyra: 300]
[Sentinel's Superiority: 355]
[Persistent Casting: 255]
[Learning: 340]

Chapter 47

Major Interlude – Iona

Julie d'Audrey I

Dread Pirate Iona adjusted her tricorn hat as her commandeered ship cut through the waves, flying Iona's personal flag.

The Wakacola sea wasn't the largest sea on Pallos, but it was the one that fell under the Valkyrie's ever-shrinking area of protection. Unfortunately, after the goblin catastrophe and the practical fall of the order, there were less than two dozen Valkyries left, which had them stretched to the breaking point trying to cover everything.

Which meant some problems didn't get the attention they needed. Some problems grew.

Like the rampant piracy problem on the Wakacola sea.

Grandmaster Sigrun was stubborn. She refused to shrink the scale that the Valkyries operated on, or the territory that was under their protection – and that, in turn, paid them. That hadn't stopped other Orders, Sects, nobles, and anyone else who thought they could steal a slice of the pie from encroaching on their territory, luring away towns with promises of prompt protection.

Iona was conflicted on the matter. On one hand, she saw Sigrun's point. The Valkyrie order would come back, one day. By letting it shrink, the size they could grow to in the future, and the speed it would occur at, would be limited.

On the other, if Sigrun had properly reevaluated the size the Valkyries could operate at, people wouldn't have gotten hurt. There wouldn't be pirates on the Wakacola sea. The Valkyries would have more time to train new recruits, although the pool of candidates would be shrunk.

Iona was a full Valkyrie, and one of the extraordinarily rare people to be permitted to have a combat class above 256 without being sworn to nobility. A perk of the order, which the **[King]** of Rolland had yanked once news of their diminished size had reached him.

Not before Sigrun had made absolutely sure that every surviving Valkyrie had classed up past 256 though. There'd been some grumbling over it, but they'd technically followed the laws as written. From what Iona could tell, the lords and ladies were slightly annoyed, and had decided.

They'll die out soon enough. No sense in kicking up a fuss now. Just play the long game.

Which had Iona – and the surviving Valkyries – pissed.

They would not go gently into the night.

Nor would they swear themselves to a noble, and let themselves get absorbed, becoming just another elite unit under some duchess. Their independence was just one small part of their pride.

Which, from what Iona had gathered, was causing some more subtle tensions. Not all the nobility wanted the Valkyries gone. The king, in spite of yanking their ability to have more large classers, had given them some support. Mostly in the form of public speeches and a break in taxes, but it was more than nothing. It wasn't like he was some fantasy **[Absolute Ruler]**, able to do what he wanted. No, he needed consensus, and to get other nobles on his side. Which, in this particular case, he had some. Not all of the nobility wanted them gone.

The only ones that wanted them to stick around lived nowhere close to the Valkyrie's lands, and gained nothing if they were fully eliminated. However, their rivals would gain.

In short, the only people that cared for the Valkyries because they were Valkyries, and not because they stood to gain or lose themselves – were the Valkyries themselves.

Still. There was more territory, and more problems, than the Valkyries could handle, and Iona was given more-or-less discretion to decide which problems she'd tackle.

She unfolded a letter with well-worn creases, which had prompted her to visit the Wakacola sea, and handle the pirate problem.

My dearest Iona

While our time together has been nothing short of extraordinary, I am deeply saddened to inform you that my father has discovered our relationship. He has delivered an ultimatum to me – marry Matthieu d'Baschet of the Baschet Trading Emporium, a most unpleasant man which I have told you about – or join the Abbey of the Guiding Waves.

I always knew that one day I would need to make a choice like this, and my answer was easy – I have elected to become one of the nuns at the Abbey of the Guiding Waves, as a more peaceful life calls to me.

We always knew our time together would be short, a brief fling, two ships passing in the night.

Do not cry for me! I am happy with my choice. My only regret is that I was not able to see you one last time, not able to place one last kiss on your red lips. I was not able to feel your hands along my tail. I was not able to...

The letter got quite a bit more lurid after that point, to the point where even Iona was flushing reading it.

Yours,

Sister Julie d'Audrey.

Well. If it was Julie's one regret that she'd never see Iona again – Iona was going to fix that.

A small voice whispered in Iona's ear that this might not be the only letter Julie had sent out, but that was between Julie and the other letter senders.

It helped that the Abbey of the Guiding Waves was on the Wakacola sea, and Iona was killing quite a few birds with one stone. Handling the piracy problem, seeing her old friend, possibly for the last time, and making sure that the Abbey where her friend was going to wouldn't be bothered by said pirates.

All in all, a fairly neat and tidy arrangement. Sigrun hadn't even raised an eyebrow when Iona had come and requested the assignment, the dust from her old job still on her boots.

Not that any of the Valkyries had time to get the dust off their boots. Too much to do. Which neatly looped around back to Iona's thoughts on reducing their size, and taking the time to properly recruit and train the next generation.

Big, flashy deeds were great for recruitment though...

Iona once again thanked her Patrons for her not being the Grandmaster, and someone else having all the headaches.

"Whatcha got there?" A nasally voice came from over her shoulder, and an embarrassed Iona whirled around, mentally reaching for her armor, ready to slam it into position, and physically reaching for her axe.

It was just Woodrow 'Bird's Eye' Payne, one of the more reputable pirates, if such a thing existed. Iona had started small, and by "small" she meant "quietly requested passage on merchant ships until a pirate ship eventually visited, and murdered nearly the entire pirate crew." It spoke to just how bad the pirate problem was that it'd only taken three trips for her efforts to bear fruit, and not years.

It amazed Iona that anyone was even still trying to ship goods around.

The merchant crew had looked more than a little green as Iona had single-handedly slaughtered her way through the pirates, only sparing a few of the weaker, less combat-inclined ones.

Still, Iona couldn't crew an entire ship by herself, nor did she even have any idea how. Hence, she spared a few of the more cowardly pirates, those without a [Piracy] class or skills, to better sail her brand-new ship around for her.

Iona's ability to look at people's skills – all of them – was quite the boon. It wasn't perfect, but Bird's Eye lacked any fighting classes or skills, which made his story of being gang-pressed into service by pirates believable. The skill helped in fights in other ways.

"None of your business. You should go swab the sails or something." Iona retorted back.

She'd spared him, and a dozen other pirates, to form some semblance of a crew.

And directions.

"You sure? You do spend a lot of time... looking... at..."

Bird's Eye trailed off as Iona's look steadily grew stormier with every word he said. She towered over him, and wasn't afraid of using a little intimidation. Especially not when it came to her personal matters.

"How about I get back to swabbing the deck or looking for ships, eh?" Bird's Eye said, quickly clambering up the line to the crow's nest.

Iona sighed, and turned back to the waves. They weren't moving fast, but the pirates had been working together.

"This is a terrible mistake." Petey 'Cowardly' Paddley said. "Lord Admiral Bloodpyre's going to kill us all." He cried out.

Iona gave him a flat look. Nobody with the name 'Lord Admiral Bloodpyre' was going to scare her.

"Yeah, yeah, you'd kill us faster..." He muttered under his breath, continuing to haul lines as needed.

Iona hadn't threatened anyone – not directly. She'd simply fought and killed most of the pirates, and had started yelling orders out to the remaining pirates, who'd decided not to argue with the one-woman wrecking crew.

Iona was slightly out of her depths here on the ship, and was somewhat regretting her choices. Still, the ship was moving, and with the collective spine of the remaining pirates not enough to support a mannequin, she wasn't afraid of treachery, or them steering her wrong.

No way were they going as fast as they could. Or doing everything properly.

Iona eyed a storm that was starting to brew on the horizon, weighing the chances of the ship making it through intact.

Ah well. Worst-case, she could swim. Being a physical Classer was awesome.

She leaned forward on the bow of the ship, taking a moment to enjoy the spray of the waves, and the rocking of the boat. Iona spent a few moments letting the sea water spray her long hair, then turned around, leaned back, and took in the view of the ship.

She could see most of it from where she was, and it was an interesting angle. Iona took out her notebook and a pencil, and started to sketch the scene, as seen from where she was.

Everyone needed a hobby, and Valkyrie Dusk's was one she could practice on the road. It was somewhat useful to boot, as her practice [Drawing] occasionally came in handy when she needed to sketch out a person's face, or make a crude map.

Mostly, she drew the people and places she'd been. When she came back from a mission, she dropped off her notebook, got a new one, and kept going. It made a sort of travelog of her journey and adventures, snapshots into each of her missions.

One day she'd get a companion, and if nothing else, she'd have more time on the road to sketch.

Less time overall, as companions needed care, attention, and love, but more "on-the-road" sketches.

Possibly new points of view! Most certainly new subjects to draw. She'd have the cutest companion!

Iona finished with a sketch of the ship, and since the storm hadn't quite blown in yet, she flipped the page, and decided to sketch Bird's Eye, high up in the crow's nest.

Interesting view. Iona mused, as she tried to get the line of his jaw just right. Might give him the drawing when I'm done.

Might be good for morale.

Iona continued working through the night, [Gaze of the Galaxy] giving her near-perfect vision.

Fortunately, the storm mostly missed them, and was extremely mild.

"Cave's ahead!" Bird's Eye yelled, which had Iona glance around for a moment before climbing up the ropes to the nest herself.

Yup. That was shore and a cave, just like the pirates had described.

"Full speed!" Iona shouted, pointing towards the cave.

"We are going full speed..." Bird's Eye muttered – not quietly enough for Iona to not hear.

"But we'll crash." Cowardly whined from below.

"So?" Iona asked, giving him a puzzled look. "What do we need this boat for after anyways?"

He opened his mouth, then closed it, a thoughtful look on his face.

It looked completely wrong on him.

They closed in rapidly on the cave, charting a course like a sailor that had four too many beers. The downside of eliminating all the competent pirates when she took over the ship. Iona didn't care too much, as long as they got there, but it was slightly irritating that the pirates would have more than enough time to prepare.

She mentally shrugged. Such was life.

A pirate ship came out of the cave to "greet" Iona and her crew, with Iona's flag clearly indicating her allegiances.

"Not-Pirate."

Iona knelt, and sent a quick prayer to Selene and Lunaris, her patrons.

"Selene. Lunaris. I'm going into battle now. Pirates. It's not going to be pretty. But it'll help the people here. They need protection. Anyways. Going to be in an abbey after this. I'll see if they're cool with me sending you a prayer from there. Talk to you soon!"

Iona stood up, and mentally reached for her armor. With a thought, it flowed from her back, around her chest, down her arms and legs, the Mallium merging and contorting to her form, flowing like liquid before hardening once it was in position.

The final touch was the helmet, the metal climbing up Iona's neck, flowing into position. A small pair of wings sprouted above her ears, the classic calling card of the Valkyrie order.

Her round shield stayed on her back, unneeded for this stage.

Iona had decided to focus on shortbows when everything was said and done. Her initial class had been good for all types of bows, but when the dust settled, the Valkyrie order had found itself poor in people, and rich in materials. It was easy to give Iona a full suit of Mallium armor – all the remaining physical Valkyries had a full suit of armor, made out of magic materials. Iona had opted for flexibility, others had gotten suits with different properties.

The remaining mages of the Valkyrie order were kitted out in gems and Arcanite, able to act like one-woman armies.

In the end, there were a few odds and ends. Iona was already walking the archery path, and with one of the spare pieces being a shortbow made out of Springwood, famous for being able to take the abuse of a high-statted physical classer without needing a corresponding "strengthen bow" skill, Iona had jumped on it.

It was useful with her mixed fighting style as well. The bow neatly tucked on Iona's back, leaving her with a full range of motion when she got in close to fight.

Since specialization came with greater power than being a generalist, and after a disastrous attempt to try and mix longbows with axe fighting, Iona had decided that shortbows were the direction she was taking herself in.

Iona strung her bow, and [Gaze of the Galaxy] was helpful once more, magnifying and improving her vision. She decided to start off with some normal arrows, and wanted to make her first shot count.

She glanced at the ship. The pirates were yelling something, but they were too far away and Iona honestly didn't care.

Iona carefully examined the pirates on the ship, using her divine blessing to read their skills. Not all of them, just the important-looking ones.

Iona spotted the captain, made obvious by his skills, and quickly looked over them. She grinned as she saw that he was more magically-inclined, and without a reflex skill like [Speedster's Perception] that might've bailed him out.

She nocked an arrow, and pulled her Springwood bow taut, the magical wood allowing Iona to bring her full [Vow]-boosted stats to bear.

After all. This action was defending the denizens of the Wakacola sea. It was protecting the merchants, the sailors, and the ports. Most of the Valkyrie's missions were protection details of various sorts – only items like Iona's planned detour after this wouldn't trigger her **[Vow]**'s increased stats.

[Chilled Mind] had a dozen uses, but one that Iona found nice was it magnified her perception dozens of times when she had an arrow fully drawn, making the whole world seem like it was moving in slow motion. **[Shortbow Skills]** stacked with **[New Moon's Dance]**, which was multiplied by both **[Valkyrie's Valor]** and **[Weapon Mastery]**.

It helped guide her hand, read the wind, and make the tiny, subtle adjustments needed. Iona only got one initial shot, one surprise attack.

She finished finding her aim, exhaled to relax, and let go, the arrow screaming across the distance in a moment.

Planting itself directly in the important-looking pirate's eye.

[*_ding!_* You have slain a [Pirate Lieutenant (270 - Decay)]//[Loot Locator (260 – Mantle)]]

Iona let some of the tension leave her shoulders as the pirates started to madly scramble around, raising shields and preparing spells.

A second ranging shot over their physical shields indicated a lack of barrier, and Iona prepared her next trick.

[Ice Arrow Conjuration] summoned a crystal-clear arrow made out of ice, which Iona put on her bow. A benefit of the skill was it also let her fire said arrows, although anyone else trying to use the arrow would just have it shatter on them – ice wasn't made for shooting with bows. Iona aimed high and fired, putting the arrow on a slow, lazy path that would bring it far over the top of the pirate ship.

She rapidly drew and fired a second arrow, letting **[Trick Shot]** guide her. It did exactly what it needed to do, intercepting the Ice arrow when it was above the pirate ship, redirecting it to aim straight down at the pirates.

Then it exploded into a dozen tiny shards, **[Blizzard Shot]** turning the arrow into an icy barrage. **[Glacial Slow]** then applied a chilling cold to all pirates hit, slowing them down. The pirates that had strong strength and vitality basically shrugged Iona's attack off, while more magically and speed-focused pirates were slowed down.

Not that Iona needed the debuff to kill them all. She gave a mental sigh as the skill failed to level. Even massively outnumbered and surrounded, her level compared to the pirates was too high, and the task wasn't difficult enough. She'd need to repeat the process a few more times, in the hopes of grinding out enough experience to get another level.

The pirates weren't taking the attack lying down. Some of the stronger pirates were throwing out attacks on the very edge of their range. Small earthen bullets, throwing knives, javelins, arrows, wooden spikes, and dozens of other attacks came Iona's way. No Forbidden Four classers here today, although it's more likely that the pirates would turn on one themselves, rather than tolerate their presence.

She was careful to twist and turn her head in such a way that nothing got in her eyes, but for the most part she let her armor, reinforced by her [Celestial Armaments] skill, take the blows, returning fire with her own arrows. In one part because dodging everything wouldn't work, in another for the sheer intimidating factor - "None of your attacks matter."

Iona's ship stopped moving properly though, as the various pirates she'd gang-pressed into service had vanished, deciding to risk her wrath rather than be in the line of fire of the rest of the pirates. She eyed the wooden deck dubiously.

Generally, ships had captains, and the System recognized them as such. If anyone on this ship was the captain though, it was Iona, and she had exactly zero ship-related skills. No **[Strong Lines]**, no **[Unbreakable Sails]**, no **[Reinforced Hull]** skills for her. In short, the ship was made out of mundane wood, and acted like it.

Which, given Iona's skill combination and stats, meant that she needed to be a little careful. She couldn't just try to jump the gap to the ships closing in – she'd just punch right through the hull instead. The gap needed to be smaller, or the ship's deck reinforced in some way.

However, Iona could keep screwing with the pirates. Even though they were hunkered down, there was always a little slit that she could plant an arrow in. If there were no easy targets of opportunity, Iona took the time to shoot the lines, causing rope to snap and whiplash across the deck, injuring pirates and making their ship lurch oddly.

Which usually created more targets of opportunity. Rinse and repeat.

Iona could do this all day.

Then the pirates came close enough, and Iona traded her shield on her back for the bow in her hands, then drawing her axe, giving it a few experimental swings. She half-hunkered down, and waited.

If the pirates were exceptionally smart, and wanted Iona dead at all costs, they'd sink the ship slowly, from a distance, then attempt to drown her with multiple water mages and underwater swimmers. Iona would be in one hell of a pickle if that happened, and would probably try to emergency grab [Swimming] or some other related skill to try and survive.

Still, pirates were greedy, and ships were expensive. Iona was counting on them coming close enough to try to board, and capture the ship intact, especially as all resistance seemed to have stopped.

She let a smirk cross her face.

After all, they'd pinned down the only fighter. They had more than enough people to kill one person, even though her level was quite a bit higher than theirs.

They had more than enough people... if [The Dusk Valkyrie] wasn't a dark green quality class, a System reward for surviving the goblin horde. If Iona didn't have a **[Vow]**, strengthening her physical stats seven, almost eight times over.

Frustratingly, that made it harder to level. If a task was too easy, there wasn't a lot of experience in it.

When she was a **[Squire]**, Iona wasn't a fan of Rolland's - frankly, most every mortal country had it - restrictions on combat Classers. The rules that didn't allow **[Warriors]**, **[Rangers]**, and **[Mages]** to go past level 256 without permission from the nobility. Usually that meant swearing service to the noble, and only a few rare, trusted organizations had limited slots for themselves.

Faced with a number of pirates trying to end her life? Being the beneficiary of the rule?

It was *great.*

Most people didn't start off aiming for a life of violent crime. Many people disliked the idea of being restricted in their class, and picked **[Laborer]**, **[Artisan]**, or any number of "better" classes. Only when life got tough did they resort to piracy, and their classes weren't well-aligned for brutal fights.

Sure, it was good enough to hold a sword and point it at some poor merchant, and it didn't matter if a **[Sailor]** was hauling lines on a cruise ship or a pirate ship. But they weren't designed with eight skills focused on fighting and killing.

The true **[Pirates]**, once they got the class, once they made their break from civilization and started killing people, had to start at 256, plus whatever experience they'd banked. Their levels were rarely impressive, and sidegrading a class evolution was rarely as potent as going down the line.

All this to say - as a Valkyrie, the law of the land gave Iona a *significant,* multi-hundred level lead on the pirates, letting her act as a one-woman army. Only if the pirates were given too many years to grow, develop, and level would they be a true threat.

Another Order would ruthlessly crush them before they got that far though, correctly judging that the Valkyries couldn't keep their territory secure, and, well, now it was theirs.

The System allowed anyone with drive to achieve power. It also allowed those already in power to crush those who would challenge them. A balancing act, one that tilted towards those already in power. The **[Biomancer]** who helped Iona out when she was young was an excellent example of ways the powerful stayed in power.

Right when Iona judged them to be close enough, she unfurled from her kneeling position behind her shield, and shot off across the deck, the wooden planks beneath her creaking in protest. As she got near the edge, she took a mighty leap, soaring through the air with a tiny boost from **[Snowflake Drift]**. It wasn't a particularly strong skill, but every little bit helped.

As Iona mostly-hurtled, partly-floated across the gap, her perception sped up, making everything seem slower. It was a strange quirk of the System, and how massive vitality and perception worked. Everyone talked and saw things at roughly the same rate, until they needed the increase in speed. From attacks, to being late, to running fast, to wanting to have a super-quick conversation with someone else with equally high vitality – or wanting to talk deliberately fast to screw with someone.

Either way, however vitality worked, the world now looked like it was moving slowly for Iona, giving her all the time to think and process as she drifted between the two ships.

A great white shark leapt out of the water on an intercept course for Iona, moving quickly – from the perspective of an outsider. For Iona?

She twisted in the air, and with the axe still in her hand, she punched the shark solidly on its nose, knocking it back down into the sea. It wasn't dead, but it was stunned, and whatever pirate was companion to the shark wasn't going to be too pleased – nor was the shark likely to do it again.

Still would be worth remembering. Extra motivation not to fall into the water.

However, the punch completely threw off her trajectory. She was still going to land on the ship, just not in the optimal landing spot.

Oh well. It didn't matter.

Iona twisted again, activating [**Moon's Descent**] to increase her weight, landing feet-first on some poor unfortunate pirate, his neck cracking as Iona's speed and mass was far too much for him.

Then she was in the midst of them, and a wolf among sheep would've had a harder time.

No, she was like a tiger amongst lambs. The pirates moved slowly to Iona's perception, each blade like it was dragging through water. Each shield was too slow to block her, as she simply performed her [**New Moon's Dance**], weaving her axe around their swords, spears, and other weapons. Every slash found exposed flesh, every blow went straight through the pathetic excuses that the pirates called 'armor'.

In contrast, Iona moved like lightning, her axe flashing out to rip out a vulnerable neck, her shield striking forward to crush a skull. The whole time, the pirates moved in slow motion, and Iona didn't need to worry about parrying, blocking – any of it.

Just. Chop, dead, slice, kill. Bloody butcher's work. Man, woman, human, dwarf, orc, beastkin, ogre, young, old. Iona didn't discriminate, she tore through them all.

There was no contest once the Valkyrie closed the distance to the pirates.

She had significantly more respect for the pirate's attacks once she was close though. There were a number of magic spells and skills that had great power, but terrible range.

Iona bit off a curse as one pirate brought to bear some sort of darkness magic, and tried to slice her in half. Her helmet blocked enough of the attack, but it still slashed her nose open horizontally.

She dampened down a flare of concern as she made sure to kill the mage with extreme prejudice. This wasn't the Wobby Pass, it wasn't Goblindeath, as the songs were calling it. It was just a single cut. Iona was roughly half-done with this wave of pirates to boot.

She wasn't going to die screaming like most of the Valkyries had, a thousand small cuts chipping away at her until she had nothing left.

Iona was a blender of death, Celestial and Ice whirling as she slaughtered the pirates. There was a tense moment as one mage, further back than the rest, managed to encase Iona in a watery sphere, lifting her off the ground and cutting off her air.

Iona immediately began to struggle against the attack, thrashing with her whole body in an attempt to break the skill, flickering **[Moon's Descent]** on and off to bobble herself in the water, making it harder and harder for the mage to keep enough control to hold onto her.

Then a pirate, seeing his chance at local fame and a silly number of levels, tried to stab Iona with a spear. Letting go of her axe, Iona grabbed the spear, and used it and the pirate as leverage to finally break out of the watery sphere.

Iona liked axes the most, but all Valkyries had been cross-trained on a wide variety of weapons. That's why her skill was the broader **[Weapon Mastery]**, and not the narrower, stronger **[Axe Mastery]**, or some Celestial variant.

So while it'd been a few months since she last held a spear, much less practiced with one, she still felt comfortable hurling it with all her might at the Water mage who'd bubbled her, the spear utterly annihilating his chest, the planks of the deck creaking under the sheer force Iona subjected them to. The mage wasn't even pinned or dragged along, the sheer force just ripping a massive hole through him without resistance, painting the deck with blood and gore.

Iona caught her axe on the way down, punched her shield through another pirate, chopped a third in half, head-to-groin, and the fight was back on.

She distantly noted a number of pirates abandoning ship, jumping off the sides, but she gave them no mind. She had bigger problems to worry about right now, and if she smashed the majority of the pirates – and more importantly, their ships – the few loose pirates who escaped would barely be a threat.

In a maelstrom of blood and steel, the surface of the ship was cleared, and Iona went to clear the lower decks of the ship.

It went about the same as the deck, Iona bursting into a room, killing pirates waiting in ambush with a single strike, or holding back her blow as a pirate cowered, no longer a threat. The only twist was a kid, no more than 10, trying to stab her in a room.

Iona had a small amount of mercy for plucky kids, running to their doom. Even when said kid was trying to knife her to death. She defenestrated him after checking that he had a **[Swimming]** skill.

Iona did need a new crew for this ship.

It was only when she got to the lowest level of the ship did a painful, high-pitched whine start, causing Iona to bleed from her ears. She grimaced, and looked around.

No pirates here. Normally Iona would assume a "surrendering" pirate would be quietly using a skill on her – more than one had tried something similar – but no, there was nobody.

Nobody *visible*.

Mirage mages. Iona gave a sigh, and rearranged her helmet slightly to catch the blood coming out of her ears, going as deaf as a doorknob. She didn't want the Mirage-Sound mage to see that he was succeeding at hurting her. Right now, Iona's best bet was to make it look like the pirate was utterly failing, and get them close enough for her to handle.

Iona strode back up to the deck, grabbing pirates as she went along.

"Hey! Need you to sail this ship where I say!" Iona grabbed a pirate by the scruff, yelled her orders, and continued up. She would've ignored his protests, even if she'd heard them.

Damn Sound mage. Iona could feel his attack in her teeth.

Iona continued through the ship, gathering up her new crew, entirely, literally deaf to their cries and protests.

She left the kids alone.

One pirate found his courage to try and backstab Iona. His knife just slid off her armor, and she whirled around, snapping his neck with a casual backhand.

She waited a few heartbeats until she got the kill notification, then carried on.

She made it back to the stairs leading up to the deck, and turned back around and faced the crowd.

"Stay here until I call for you!" Iona yelled, then walked back onto the deck.

The ship looked like it'd been rotated a quarter-circle, and while Iona was bad at ships, she wasn't that bad. The mage was obviously creating an illusion, hoping Iona would just walk right off the boat and into the sea below.

Iona had no idea how he was doing it, but the Sound mage was still attacking her, and his weak attacks were starting to stack up and cause her problems. Iona had no idea how he managed to hide in the crowd – probably disguised himself as just another pirate – but since nobody else was clutching their ears and bleeding, he or she probably had line of sight to her.

Iona went onto the deck, the floor slick with way more blood than most people would believe could fit in that many bodies.

Not Iona. She'd seen how much people bled. Had literally seen people drown in blood.

She casually put her axe away at her hip, and slung her shield over her back. This next move would be difficult.

She walked down the deck, doing her best to act natural, like nothing was wrong. It only took a few steps into "open air" for the pirate to drop the "twisted ship" image – it must've been expensive to maintain, and had clearly failed. Iona's acting was fairly bad, and the Sound-Mirage mage was persistent. It'd boggle the imagination that a persistent attack was doing nothing, and both Iona and the unknown mage knew that she was on a timer.

Iona made it to the bow, then carefully walked along the jutting bowsprit, balancing on the thin wooden spur.

She made it to the end of the bowsprit, looking like a maidenhead. Then in a single fluid motion, she took the bow off her back, drew the string back as she summoned an arrow with **[Ice Arrow Conjuration]**, and fired an **[Blizzard Shot]** down the deck of the ship, thousands of tiny ice shards turning the top into a brief blizzard.

Iona was already running down the bowsprit as she fired the arrow, and carefully watched the storm. The icicles weren't moving right in one spot, vanishing into a random space in the air and not coming back out the other side. Iona reached there, grabbed with both hands, felt flesh under her hands, and tore the mage in half.

The infernal ringing in her ears stopped. It wouldn't heal her, or fix the damage, but it was done.

Iona took a moment to compose herself.

Safe. Not going to die.

She needed to spend some time with one of those people who claimed they could heal the mind. Iona was a hair skeptical – after all, most healers were instant, or nearly instant, but mind-healers claimed they needed months or years to work – and needed to be paid the entire time, of course, and made no promises they'd work. Iona was also crazy busy. Still, it was on her to-do list.

Iona shook her head, mentally resetting herself. She inhaled, and yelled down at the pirates cowering below decks.

"Get up here, you scurvy lot!" Iona said, having no idea if they were actually scurvy or not. She knew it was a term healers used now and then, but didn't quite know what it meant. Still, sailors mentioned it constantly, and Iona was trying to communicate with them in a language they knew.

"Right! I'm Dread Pirate Iona, and I'm in charge now! Sail back into the cave!" Iona yelled, literally deaf to the complaints all around her. She simply pointed at the cave, and kept yelling until the pirates reluctantly turned the ship around, fixed the damage Iona had done to the ropes, and got it sailing back the right way.

Iona could kinda see why these pirates in particular had been left to fester until now. The Valkyries, for all their training in a dozen different disciplines, never bothered to cover water travel. The Wakacola sea was the only significant body of water in the area they protected, and even then it was at the edge. There were just too many other useful skills to learn – and Skills.

Hence, the finer points of sailing a galleon were ignored. One or two Valkyries got lessons on sailboats and other small craft – Iona in particular had taught herself how to row a boat, for romantically related reasons – but nothing approaching this size.

However, the pirates put their back into it. The steely-eyed Valkyrie who'd carved through them like a knife through butter was there, completely ignoring every word they said, covered in fresh blood and small shreds of flesh, menacingly stroking the blade of her axe with an armored thumb. They didn't want to find out her method of enforcing her orders.

A [Pirate Captain] would flog them, deprive them of rum, or have other, more cruel and inventive punishments.

The Valkyrie? She'd started off murdering most of the crew, and no pirate wanted to be the first to discover how she handled minor infractions. Not yet. Not when the decks were still soaked in blood, not when the bodies of a dozen pirates were still tripping hazards.

The commandeered ship sailed right back into the cave, Dread Pirate Iona at the bow.

Chapter 48

Major Interlude – Iona

Julie d'Audrey II

Iona's eyes adjusted as they got in, and she was in the middle of a brief look around when massive earthen spikes detached themselves from the ceiling, impaling the ship, dooming it to the depths.

Iona flung herself from the sinking ship, leaving the remaining pirates behind. The ones who hadn't died from the attack would sink or swim on their own merits – mostly swim, the skill was easy enough to get, or to have merged into another skill. Their career had been enough to forfeit any protection Iona might've extended towards them.

Iona managed to make it to rocky ground inside the cave, rolling as she landed, making sure she'd taken cover behind some rocks. She looked up, then around the cavern.

While dimly lit, there were enough torches, and pure sunlight from outside, to see well enough. A couple of holes in the ceiling let some natural light in, with unnaturally large patches of grass and trees near where they landed – the work of some skilled person amplifying what nature was providing. A clever Earth mage had made a number of large stalactites hanging from the ceiling. It meant that with nearly no effort, the stalactite could be broken off, the large mass plunging down on any unsuspecting invaders – like Iona. Given the narrow cave entrance that ships would be forced to use, it was a solid defense.

The pirates had nearly an entire port built inside. Four docks, with one ship left. Iona hoped that the pirates were ambitious, and she wasn't going to miss a fourth pirate ship out and about once she was done here.

There was no way she was going to be that lucky.

A variety of buildings were shoddily built of wood and stone. Even as Iona watched, they creaked and swayed in the breeze.

Animals filled pens, sheep and chicken, pigs and cows. They were the primary beneficiaries of the unnaturally large patches of grass. Naturally, the pirates were the beneficiaries of said animals. They were packed against each other, each animal with practically no room to move. Not a humane practice, but only worth frowning over, possibly tut-tutting over later with a date.

A building looked like a warehouse, another a tavern. The big one was probably where the mayor//pirate admiral administered from, and that one was probably a brothel.

Almost a full, working town.

Iona was briefly starting to reconsider the mission when she spotted the last pen, separated from the rest by a gap.

All the better not to hear them screaming.

People.

Humans, dwarves, beast-kin, all had collars and chains. Even a harpy was present, weights cruelly punched through her wings.

Iona felt revulsion filling her, almost forcing its way out, as the brothel and tavern took on new, ominous light.

As she studied the town, she noticed a detail that she'd missed on her first check, the distance and the light making the bodies swinging on the gallows hard to see.

Left to rot.

Fine.

Iona wasn't quite sure how, but it looked like the pirates somehow thought she was still on the wreck. Perhaps a combination of the light and shadow as the ship passed into the cave, combined with the falling rocks and spray of breaking planks and splashing water had hidden her as she jumped off. Either way, nobody was approaching her hiding spot.

However – Iona had dramatically underestimated how many pirates there were. She believed she could take a ship full of pirates, especially as she could force the terrain to her benefit, and it was harder to surround her and kill her via a hundred cuts.

Hell, she could take them all if it was a hundred one vs ones. She'd trained under Alruna after all.

But she was slowing. She'd taken a few hits, point-blank instant spells cast right as people died, and had more than a few cuts, was bleeding from more than a few places. She kept reshaping and reforming her armor to close any holes, but it thinned her armor. Not to mention, Iona couldn't hear anymore. Missing an entire sense was bad news, especially if she needed to handle so many pirates at the same time.

The Wobby Pass flashed through her mind again. The ratio was similar, and Iona was alone, without even a companion or another Valkyrie to watch her back.

She knew she had limited time. What Iona needed to do was even the odds, and unorganized pirates were a lot easier to handle than organized.

Fire. Fire was the answer. Sure, they probably had a water mage or eight around – it was a good element for mages living on the sea – but it'd cause a distraction. Iona briefly cursed taking Ice, and not Fire for her arrows, before putting the thought aside. There were torches everywhere, and some looked like they were dangerously close to the main building.

Ugh. That would probably end with Iona needing to save the innocents trapped in the buildings.

Perhaps the slaves would participate. It would dramatically change the odds, even if they just acted as a distraction.

Fire. Fire in a lot of places, but none too large. Nothing that would cause uninvolved people to burn alive.

Iona's [Vow] would be pissed, and Iona would die shortly after.

There was an elegant solution. Iona drew her bow, and carefully sighted.

It wasn't the longest shot Iona had ever tried to make, but the size of the target at the range made it one of the hardest shots. About the size of the smallest coin, although blessedly not the size of the tiny bit of Arcanite embedded in every coin that provided its value. And the torch needed to fall the right way.

Iona stilled her breathing, not even hearing her heartbeat in her ears. She sent a quick prayer to Selene and Lunaris, then a second one to Xaoc for good measure.

Selene and Lunaris wouldn't mind. What Iona was asking for was a bit outside of their domain – and entirely in Xaoc's.

She drew the bow to full, and carefully worked on her aim, carefully adjusting for the slight breeze, trying to get a feel for the capricious wind and how it'd grab and twist her arrow.

Iona loosed, and cursed as a gust knocked the arrow off-course. A chicken squawked, but the pirates hadn't noticed her attack.

They had noticed that she wasn't in the water, or the ruins of the ship, and had started to break up, searching the cavern.

A second arrow pulled, aimed, and fired.

Hitting the stone next to the torch.

Iona bit off a curse as some pirates were getting closer and closer to her hiding spot. They were moving in a careful, methodical manner, but Iona was rapidly running out of time.

She pulled one more time, and let the world fall away as she focused, ignoring even the incoming pirates who'd see her any second now.

Aim. Adjust. Observe. Adjust. Breathe. Adjust.

And... relax, the arrow springing forth from her bow like a horse at the races, like a dog promised a cookie. It eagerly crossed the distance, and Iona continued to focus, not moving, staring at the arrow, willing for it to land, to connect.

Which it did. The arrow clanged against the holder, cheap like all the pirates' things. Quality holders had four brackets of metal, this had a single thin one made of wood – not even stone. Their Earth mage had better things to do than arrange lighting, or was a late comer.

Either way, the arrow went through the wood, cleanly breaking it. For a brief moment, the arrow itself held up the torch, a single narrow shaft of wood holding back disaster.

Then the arrow finished its flight, shattering against the wall, as the torch slowly tipped over.

Right onto the hairy pig's back.

The torch fluttered, then caught, flames igniting, then rapidly spreading from pig to pig, trapped haunch to haunch next to each other.

Concerned noises turned into loud squeals of fear, as the fire spread. The shoddily built pen couldn't contain the sheer panicked porcine mass, and the flaming pigs scattered throughout the settlement, letting everyone know in no uncertain terms that they were on fire.

Setting small fires in every direction.

The burning bacon was an excellent distraction, but Iona jerked as a club hit her head, sending her sprawling.

Without [**Moon's Descent**] active, Iona was a regular weight – which, given her size, mass, and equipment was still a few hundred pounds. Light enough for another physical classer to move her with a solid blow.

The pirate's cries went unnoticed, with all the yelling and screaming – not that Iona could hear a word of that.

Her time was limited though. Iona began the second round of bloody work, fighting her way towards the "town". Most of the pirates were running around, trying to deal with the searing swine and the fire. Those seeing the bloody, flame-lit rampaging Valkyrie descending upon them like the Goddess of War promptly decided that they'd rather go chase the burning pigs. The ones waaayyyyyyyyyyyyyy over there.

Their organization broken, panic rising, the pirates broke and fled. Iona quickly went through the buildings, making sure that nobody was about to burn to death, then quickly climbed one of the only remaining upright structures. She unslung her bow, preparing for the next stage.

The first shot was a weak [**Blizzard Shot**] fired straight up, then raining back down on the town. Iona felt somewhat green as a few shards of ice rained down on recently released prisoners, her [**Glacial Slow**] hitting them and [**Vow**] being unhappy about the collateral damage. Still, it was for the greater good – smothering the last of the fire so nobody was at risk of burning alive.

Some would say that it wasn't quite sporting or honorable to shoot fleeing pirates in the back.The Valkyries - and Iona - only had those notions in a dueling arena. Alruna was all about being out in the field, and getting stuff done. She had no time or

507

patience for showy fights that got nothing done – and as a result, neither did Iona.

Arrows in the back of the head it was.

Iona had dropped a dozen pirates, before needing to jerk her head out of the way. A flaming blue sickle passed where her head was, only for the flaming chain it was attached to suddenly stop, and jerk to the side, wrapping Iona up with burning flames.

Has to be Inferno. Fire wasn't solid. Iona thought, and let herself get pulled off her fragile ledge, **[Celestial Armaments]** flickering madly as it tried – and failed – to stop the attack from burning her armor.

She landed to the ground with a thud, and saw her attacker. A demon, one hand holding onto the chain, and the other hand ending in a wicked hook – also made out of burning blue flames. She sneered at Iona, full of confidence and looking all-too-smug.

Iona could see the demon's foul mouth moving, forming words. Probably. Iona was still stone-deaf from earlier.

It was *rare* to see a demon here. They were Immortals, after all, and the Treaty of Kyowa mostly banned their presence in mortal lands. Not that it stopped criminals, and this demon was young, and low-leveled. Not strong enough, not causing enough of a disturbance to get the Wardens called.

Iona wasn't into banter, so she quickly scanned the demon's stats. [Blue Flames], [Weapon Creation], and [Move like a Wildfire] were the important ones, and Iona noted that the stat distribution had the demon like a speedster more than anything else. She flipped up, yanking the demon closer as she overcame her stance and weight, then grabbed the chain, flexing to break the bonds.

The demon's mouth briefly opened up in surprise as Iona yanked the chain, bringing the demon along for the ride. Small flames erupted around her feet, but while in the air there was nowhere to jump off of, nowhere to go.

And Iona was faster, thanks to **[Vow]**.

Iona finished reeling the demon into her grasp, and she quickly and efficiently broke her neck, letting her drop to the floor as the kill notification dinged.

System notifications were extra-weird when Iona couldn't hear anything else.

Before Iona could even take a moment, a high-speed knife appeared directly in front of her, right into the small gap in her helmet exposing her face. Iona leaned back, narrowly catching the knife in her teeth.

She kept the movement back going as more knives appeared, but it was only the first one that gave her trouble. She spat it out, and looked around as she ducked and weaved, constantly moving in strange ways to not run eye-first into another knife.

She saw him then. A pirate, gaudily dressed, on the last ship in the port. She gave him a quick look with her blessing.

[Captain of the Black Shark] – Wood
[Blood-drenched Pirate Admiral of the Black Shark] – Spatial

The second class was significantly lower than the first one, and Iona was smelling a reset at some point in his history. This must be Lord Admiral Bloodpyre.

The two classes were giving her a moment's pause. The narrower a class was, the more powerful it tended to be. The pirate had gone all-in on his ship. If he didn't have his ship, he lost nearly all of his class skills, and would cripple his ability to level up.

Given that he was pushing 300, and had to have gotten them at 256 – he knew what he was doing.

Iona kept looking over the basics, not checking anything in-depth, and noted that the shark she'd punched was companion to the pirate. One line in particular caught her eye.

She couldn't help but laugh.

Lord Admiral Bloodpyre

[Name: Alfie]

Not even Alfred!
Iona still couldn't hear, but couldn't help saying something.

"Alfie? Seriously, your name is Alfie?"

She couldn't hear the pirate's response, but from how he was going all red and swinging a saber around Iona could make some guesses.

One last triple-check confirmed that the man, like all of the other magic-users Iona had encountered so far, was a sorcerer, not a wizard. Oh, sure the System still [Analyze]d both as mages, but the wizards – the "real" mages – were quite picky at the distinction, and bristled whenever people used the catch-all term "mage" for them.

It was a great way to distract them. Just start mentioning it to them mid-fight, and they'd get distracted as they started to rant about the differences, and how they were sooo much better than sorcerers who only used System-granted skills, and not whatever nonsense the "real mages" used.

Iona had never heard what the "real mages" used, she'd usually gotten an arrow through said wizard's head by that point.

Either way, Alfie didn't have any of the System skills that wizards usually had.

Iona grabbed her bow, and fired a few arrows at the pirate. The ship itself seemed to come alive, wooden planks rearranging themselves in small ways to get in the way of the arrows.

Bah. Blasted narrow classes, blasted narrow skills. Made Alfie unreasonably powerful on his ship, and simple arrows wouldn't do the trick.

Either way, she wasn't going to stand back and let the pirate warp knives into her face. Iona carefully eyed the stone the port was built on, the wooden docks, and the pirate's ship, tied up, quickly calculating material strengths and distances. Then she put her round shield up, covering her face entirely, and started to run.

She felt a number of weapons hit her shield, but she powered through them all, only staggering once as a "small" anchor hit her. Then she was far enough, fast enough, and she leapt, crossing the gap from the port to the deck of the ship in a single leap.

Then she was on the ship, gracefully moving from spot to spot as the ship itself seemed to rise up against her. The deck shifted and tried to open holes up for Iona to fall through, the planks twisted and tried to throw her balance off.

Iona had far, far too much dexterity to be concerned about that, as she rapidly ran over to where the pirate captain was. Alfie kept summoning weapons into his hands, then throwing them, only for them to promptly flicker out of existence –

And back into existence at a random angle at Iona, who twisted, dodged, and deflected the attacks.

She made it to the pirate, and with a savage grin, put her axe through his head.

Or would've, if he hadn't bloody teleported away!

Iona cursed, then a mace hit her on the small of the back, with enough speed to make her stumble forward. She whirled around, seeing Alfie on the other side of the ship, the planks twisting and turning into more defenses.

Iona realized she'd screwed up. The pirate admiral had two classes relating to his ship, and was lord and master of his domain. Iona had boosts and powerful gear, but it wasn't quite enough for this fight, not when she needed to brave a hail of steel and wood, only to turn around and need to do it again.

A new plan was needed. Iona fought her way to the front of the ship, then screamed in pain as a spear somehow managed to puncture her armor, her **[Celestial Armaments]** skill, her **[Stellar Body]** skill, and her vitality. She looked down at the spear, the tip blood, enchantments glowing along the length.

Iona gritted her teeth. This wasn't the time to deal with the spear running through her flank – and her brief lessons from the healer teaching the squires first aid once upon a time had told her not to. She just thanked Lunaris and Selene that it hadn't hit anything immediately vital, although it meant Iona was unfortunately due to find a healer next, instead of rushing to Julie.

Whining and wailing and gnashing her teeth would do Iona no good now. Deal with the threat here and now, stop herself bleeding out later.

Unlike the many squires and Valkyries, who never had a later to stop themselves bleeding out.

Iona shook her head, resetting herself, and continued her charge towards the pirate. She briefly debated trying to extract the spear from herself and throwing it at Alfie, but no. Even if it could break the planks, he'd just teleport out of range. She made it to him, faked an attack at Alfie, who just teleported away again. Iona twisted, and gracefully exited the ship, leaping back to dry land.

Alfie was back up in the crow's nest, waving his saber around and probably taunting her. Iona didn't care enough to try and read his lips, not that she had any skill in the matter.

[*ding!* You have learned the General Skill [Lip Reading]. Would you like to replace a skill with it?]

Iona dismissed the notification, instead studying Alfie and his skills in detail.

Disgustingly, he had almost all his mana… although one of his skills let him pull Arcanite from anywhere it was located on his ship. Which explained that, his skills weren't offering such a massive discount as to negate all his costs.

A mage that could go forever? A complete nightmare.

Attacking Iona from a distance was significantly harder than attacking her while she was on the ship, just due to the nature of his skills. It was easier to dodge the attacks, and Iona gracefully danced around the flurry of blades as they were conjured around her.

She continued to read his skills, and a piece of the puzzle clicked. He could re-use weapons on his ship – but once he conjured them off his ship, like he was doing now, Alfie couldn't re-use the weapon, not without leaving and gathering them back up.

Iona kept reading his skills, getting more and more frustrated. He seemed to be invincible while on his ship, and –

Wait.

That was it.

Iona checked, and felt a vicious smile overtake her face. The pirate captain had a skill for the ship's hull. Unlike **[Reinforced Hull]**, **[Eternally Regrowing Bulwark]** was an active skill, not a passive skill. The downside to a passive was it could be overwhelmed and broken, and since all of Alfie's power relied on him being on his ship, he'd gotten a powerful variant that could heal whatever damage was done.

At the cost of mana.

Iona looked at her axe as she cartwheeled to avoid a flurry of arrows.

She was not a lumberjack, but desperate times called for desperate measures.

So began the dance between Iona and Alfie. She'd hit the hull as hard as she could, with her axe, and with her gauntlets, having mentally reshaped the Mallium to form a row of spikes on her knuckles. When she punched through a plank, she'd grab it on the way out and flung it into the water.

Alfie wasn't taking this lying down, and continued his attacks. With more stable footing though, Iona was able to duck and weave – although she occasionally screwed up, the spear going through her stopping one twist or another.

Iona was bleeding though, painting the dock red even as she ripped and tore planks off the ship, keeping an eye on the captain's mana. She anticipated a trick, and even if the captain's mana was empty, she wasn't going back on the ship. Not with the ease that he could hide and pull more mana.

No, Iona was staying here until the ship was sunk, and Alfie's power was gone.

Distantly, she noted that the slaves seemed to be in the process of freeing themselves, aided by the slaves she'd freed in town. She just hoped it'd go smoothly over there – Iona didn't have the ability to fight off pirates interfering with the slaves, not while keeping Alfie here busy.

Her **[Vow]** demanded that she protect, but it allowed for judgment calls. It didn't demand the impossible. If she wasn't fighting Alfie, he'd be able to attack the prisoners. Iona leaving to fight remaining pirates would end up with a similar outcome.

As a result? She was allowed to choose how to interpret her [Vow] in the current situation.

Iona's world was narrowing. The edges of her vision went dark, as she tunneled and focused solely on the task in front of her. Right before her vision became a single point, focused on the ship, she noticed that the shark was back, and circling.

So much for the plan of going underwater to break open the last few holes to sink the ship. Iona didn't like the odds of her versus shark while underwater.

The shark didn't like his odds versus Iona above water. Neither would move into the other's domain.

Iona was getting frustrated though. It didn't feel like she was making progress, even though she knew she was. She also didn't know how she was going to finish sinking the ship – not until a pig ran past her, screaming and on fire.

Right.

Iona grabbed the pig with her left hand, ripped open a section of the hull with her right, and before [Eternally Regrowing Bulwark] could regrow that segment of the hull, shoved said scorching swine into the hull. Blood sprayed from her injury onto the hull, a bloody reminder of where she'd inserted the first pig.

Iona had no idea how well that would work, but even if Alfie instantly killed the pig, the fat and flesh would merrily burn. Iona hadn't seen an anti-fire skill, and she doubted that a pig would count as a weapon that Alfie could teleport.

As she shoved the 4th pig into the ship, Alfie suddenly started to target the remaining surviving pigs. Iona didn't see that though, she was wholly focused on her task. The dock was getting slick with Iona's blood, as her constant movements and dodging of attacks worked the spear inside of her, enlarging the wound, letting her life blood spill into the water.

Poor shark was going nuts – so much tasty blood, bleeding right above him, and nothing to do.

Finally – finally - the smell of burning wood met Iona's nostrils again, and she looked up, to see thick, black smoke rising from the ship. Alfie's mana was dropping fast, and not going back up. It could be a trap, but at this point, the fire was raging through the decks of the ship.

Iona staggered back to the rocky ground, not wanting to risk the shark trying one last stunt. She was slowing down though, which was bad as more attacks were able to solidly land, small cuts opening up on her face.

Something gave way, and the ship started to go down fast. Alfie continued to scream impotently at Iona, who couldn't care less.

Iona let out a curse as she saw Alfie jump from his ship into the water, and for him to emerge on the back of his shark, zooming to escape the cave and the sinking wreck of his ship. She was hurting, and hurting badly, and had hoped the ship sinking would've been enough.

Iona unslung her bow, letting **[Strength from the Stars]** continue to fuel her. Bless the skill for providing her with boundless energy, letting her fight and fight and fight.

The Dusk Valkyrie nocked an arrow, took an almost lazy aim, and let it loose, staggering as the normally unnoticed recoil caused the spear inside her to shake, falling to one knee as darkness threatened her vision.

[*ding!* You have slain a [Captain of the Black Shark - 311] (Wood)/ [Blood-drenched Pirate Admiral of the Black Shark - 270] (Spatial)]

With the notification, the confirmation of the kill, Iona couldn't hold on anymore. She pitched forward as darkness took her.

Chapter 49

Major Interlude – Iona

Julie d'Audrey III

Iona woke up on a cart, rattling around.

"Hey you! You're finally awake!" An all-too-cheerful cat beastkin man said, with a voice like sharp, rusty nails in Iona's ears. His voice instantly gave Iona a headache.

"You were amazing! Like the Valkyries in stories! I've started to write one about you!" He continued on, the words like the screaming of a tortured cat, digging into Iona's head and upgrading her headache.

Iona would pay any amount of money to hear him shut up.

"I was kinda nervous, you were touch and go for a while there. Fortunately, my skill worked!" He said, and Iona's eyes snapped open.

She could hear again! The entire fight being in utter silence had been a strange experience, and the man's – healer's? – voice wasn't nearly so irritating, as memories came flooding back.

With a thought, Iona had her Mallium armor withdraw, back into a neat little bundle on her back. The volume remained the same, just the location differed.

Iona could tell by the weight that she'd lost a small chunk of it, and Mallium wasn't cheap. Every gram was precious.

She sat up, and got her bearings.

She was in a cart, pulled along by a pair of cows – thanks to the pirate's pen – and there was a whole convoy of people walking along the road. Iona recognized a few faces here and there, and started to put the picture together, along with the bard Rory's help.

Being able to peek at names was awesome.

The slaves had broken free, and finished off a few pirate stragglers with a vengeance. Some had watched the end of Iona's fight with the pirate captain, and rushed over to help. Rory was a bard, and had a weak healing skill, which he'd used on Iona. Clearly, it had worked well enough for Iona to wake up again. The former slaves had organized, looted the remainder of the town to the bone, and were now walking to the nearest town.

Iona wondered if anyone had dived to the wreck, and tried to get at the treasure. It wasn't a deep dive, and from how much mana Alfie had pulled, it had to be loaded.

"Thank you." Iona said, after getting a few coughs out. She could've kissed him, if his voice wasn't so annoying.

"No worries!" Rory said, plucking a few strings of his lute.

Iona eyed it warily. How on Pallos had he managed to get a fully functional lute so fast?

Was he secretly a pirate who was turning coat as fast as possible? Or did the pirates like their entertainment, and their entertainment needed an instrument?

Iona took a quick moment to compose a prayer to Selene and Lunaris, while Rory was nattering on about something. How one slave had organized them all, etc. etc.

Lunaris. Selene. I survived! Smashed the pirates into pieces. They shouldn't be bothering people too much anymore. The shark escaped though, and it wouldn't surprise me if in a few years it's a problem again. Oh well.

I'm off to see Julie! Or get a new squire. We'll see!

Cheers!

Iona

"A song!" Rory declared, and a number of former slaves shuffled in closer, to better hear him. "Dedicated to our savior, The Dusk Valkyrie! I'm sure you'd like to hear it! Right?" He asked.

Bad bards, and songs on the spot. Iona didn't know which was worse.

"Hang on, hang on." Iona said, raising her hands. "Why not something more classic to warm us up? How about a song from The Bard?" She asked, plaintively, hopefully.

517

Anything to not hear about herself in bad song form. Iona almost wished Rory had left her deaf.

"A song from The Bard! Greatest of us all, songs passed down through untold millennia! Heroic in word, grand in stature! Yes! I will start with the song rumored to be The Bard's favorite!" He said, starting to strum his lute at speed.

"Rage! Sing, Goddess, of Artemis's rage!..."

Rory's singing voice was as good as his speaking voice was bad. Iona leaned back, and let the music wash over her.

Iona kept a careful eye out as they continued to travel. The Valkyries didn't really openly recruit, not in the way Iona thought they did. No, they waited for girls to do what Iona did – approach a Valkyrie and ask. A few minor hurdles, arranged by the individual Valkyrie, and boom! That was how they got new squires.

And while Iona was nice, polite, and paid extra attention to potential candidates – none of them seemed interested in becoming a Valkyrie. Oh, they hung onto her every word, hero-worship in their eyes, but asking to be one? They couldn't imagine it, even with Iona's gentle nudgings.

"I was talking with some of the travelers, one Thofur Krelur the 525th, and he had news. Wanna hear it?" Rory asked her, and Iona was surprised at just how awful his speaking voice was.

"Yeah sure!" Iona asked, wanting to know more.

"A healer in The Great Tang is past 256!" Rory practically exploded as he shared the news, licking his lips nervously. His ears were twitching in excitement though. "Oathbound to boot. Rumors have it that she can create Immortals!" He said, tail swishing at the thought.

Iona let out a fake-groan.

"Don't tell me. It's war?" She said.

Rory nodded.

"Yeah! Think of all the stories! The Great Tang has vowed to hunt her down, Rolland's getting an army together, and Nime is crawling out of their hole and also declaring war!"

"Poor healer is going to get assassinated." Iona said, frowning at the thought. "Nobody can allow an Immortal who bestows Immortality to live."

This is why Iona hated Immortals. One – just one – showed up, and three countries were at war. Thousands would die in fighting, and tens of thousands more would be a casualty of the war. Rolland shared a border with The Great Tang and Nime, and would get dragged in as well, just for the chance to capture or kill the healer. If they couldn't have her, nobody could.

For half of the nobles and sects on the border, the healer was just an excuse. A reason to fight each other, to try and capture a noble or elder for ransom, or extend the edges of their domain.

Of course, the thinking was short-sighted. If Rolland somehow got ahold of the healer, all of Rolland's neighbors would declare war. It was a giant game of "pass the buck", and it would continue until someone slipped a knife between the healer's ribs.

Well. Given that it was a healer, slipped many, many knives into her.

"Wonder if more Immortals will show up, and try to rescue her." Rory mused. "They do tend to stick together. Could be an elf. Oh! Or even one of the legendary vampires!" Rory said, dreaming of meeting one.

"Vampires almost never leave their country." Iona pointed out. "You'd need to travel to the Exterreri Empire to see one, and they're halfway around the world. Plus, any Immortal 'rescuing' her is just going to want her to make their friends and family Immortal as well. It's no different than a country grabbing her."

"The vampire Sentinels occasionally leave the border...." Rory whined, in his annoying, contradictory way.

Iona had enough of vampires and other immortals.

"So damn inconsiderate of the healer." Iona groused. "Setting off another round of Immortal wars."

"Is it really an Immortal war?" Rory asked. "There's only one after all."

"Right. One Immortal. Three nations at war – and the number will probably go up. That counts for me." Iona griped. "Good chance we're going to end up in it."

"You mean the Valkyries?" Rory said, practically salivating at the information.

"Yeah – wait no, don't tell people that." Iona said, cursing her mouth.

A bard? Keeping quiet?

It would never happen.

Iona and the rest of the former slaves made it to a local town soon enough, where Iona was able to get a healer to properly look after her injuries. A touch, a few coins begrudgingly changing hands, a map of the area, and Iona was off, to the Abbey of the Guiding Waves.

She was a little sad that none of the girls had asked to become a Valkyrie. This particular mission had been one of the best chances Iona had in ages to acquire a squire.

Iona shrugged her shoulders philosophically. Ah well. Next time. At least, the lack of a new squire let Iona see Julie, instead of heading back to the Valkyrie's base.

She whistled a merry tune as she walked alone over the roads. The nice thing about being [Analyze]ed as a level 350+ warrior – bandits didn't bother you at all. Nobody wanted to tangle with Iona, which was a huge pain when she needed to track them down, but great for traveling.

[Tracking] was great for tracking bandits down, but it didn't seem like they had a strong local presence… yet.

Either way, five days of easy travel at a pace that would outstrip most low and medium level couriers with explicit movement skills had Iona eyeing up the Abbey of the Guiding Waves.

The Abbey of the Guiding Waves was somewhat wealthy, given the obscene size and ornamentation of said building. It had gothic architecture on the front, which moved into flowing, wave-like walls and ceilings as the building moved towards the sea. The d'Audrey family was wealthy, and it wasn't too much of a surprise to Iona that they'd sent their daughter to this place.

Probably required a significant donation. The cynical part of Iona said.

Now, Iona could just walk in, ask to speak to Julie, and would probably be allowed to briefly chat with her. That was Iona's plan E. She wanted to have a long, erm, "conversation" with Julie instead, and there was no way the Abbess would allow that.

Disguising herself would be the easiest method, but of course Iona had taken a Vow, and part of it was never lying. Somehow, in Iona's mind, that extended to deceiving people via disguises, which caused no end of irritation and challenges for her.

Which left breaking in.

Iona first secured her weapons. They wouldn't be allowed in the Abbey, and for her plan to work, she couldn't have them hanging around the entrance. She built a small cairn of stone, put her bow, arrows, axe and shield inside, then sealed it up with more rocks and dirt.

A touch obvious, but Iona was willing to gamble that nobody in the next 12 hours or so would discover and disturb the cache she just built.

Iona kept her armor, because it stayed under her tunic until she needed it. It was hard to see, unless you knew what you were looking for. The benefit of loose shirts.

Iona walked out of the woods, down the path, and up to the front door, where one of the sisters was on door-duty. She was dressed in a simple blue robe.

"Hello Sister." Iona said politely, giving her a small bow of her head.

"Greetings. Do you wish to visit the humble abode of the goddess of the Wakacola sea?"

There was nothing humble about the gaudy Abbey, but Iona wasn't here to pick fights.

"I am. I was also recently saved from a brush with death, and I was wondering if there was an unaffiliated altar for me to give thanks to my patrons." Iona said.

Prayer could be done anywhere, but there was something special about praying at an altar. It was ok to pray to any deity from an "unaffiliated" altar, and it was considered more than a bit rude to pray to a different god at a particular god's consecrated altar.

"Of course! We have a small altar for you to give thanks to your deities. Ness would appreciate a small donation for the upkeep of the Abbey." The Sister said to Iona.

Iona didn't bat an eye, fishing out a few mid-sized coins from her satchel, with small flecks of rubies in the middle.

"Naturally, I'd want to help the good Sisters of the Abbey of the Guiding Waves." Iona turned up the charm. The amount should be more than enough to keep the Sisters happy, and off her back.

But not too much that Iona would suddenly be a VIP, to be buttered up in the hopes of getting more.

"Thank you! Do you mind if I check in your satchel? No weapons are permitted inside, nor are drugs and..."

She then recited a long, long list of contraband, which included a few oddities.

Who didn't like apples and vinegar in their Abbey?

This particular goddess, apparently.

Iona happily opened her satchel, showing coins, her drawing supplies, field rations, and miscellaneous supplies, like a rope.

Iona followed the Sister, keeping her eyes peeled for Julie, and hoping that they didn't bump into each other now. This was the riskiest part of the plan – if Julie saw her, the entire jig would be up. Iona was gambling that as a new initiate, Julie would be kept away from the paying guests until she learned how the abbey expected her to act.

Which would make finding her super hard.

Iona was led to the main room of worship, a grand chamber that had an altar and a large statue of Ness herself, missing a wall entirely. Instead of a wall, it opened up to the sea, and the breeze grabbed Iona's long hair and playfully whipped it about, as the smell of salt filled her nose.

Iona took a moment to kneel before the altar to Ness. It'd be rude to come all this way without saying hi to the goddess, as minor as she was.

Hi Ness! It's Iona.

We haven't chatted much, but I'd just like to say hello! It's nice to meet you.

Hey, so I'm not here for the purest of motives, but at the same time, I don't mean you or yours any harm. In fact, I wish them the best. I just want to say goodbye to my friend. I don't think I'll be able to visit frequently, and one way or another, our friendship is coming to an end.

Please don't take offense. I mean none.

Oh! There's a nasty shark that's now free and on the loose in your sea. You'll probably get some prayers about him. Heck, he might pray to you himself, I dunno how sharks think. Anyways! Take this first one from me – keep people safe from the shark.

Cheers,

Iona.

Iona had no idea how long she'd spent kneeling at the altar, but she felt just a hair stiff as she got back up. A different Sister was there.

[Magnetic Charm] was a great skill. While it didn't do something nearly as stupid as make people think something, or change their mind, it did help Iona read them. The way the Sister's gaze lingered on the view of the sea let Iona know that… she really liked looking at the sea. Gave her a little nudge.

"It's a wonderful view, isn't it?" Iona said, giving a raw, genuine smile. It was pretty.

A soft smile appeared on the Sister's face.

"Like none other in the world." She said.

Iona and the Sister made more small talk, while other nuns came in and out, and one or two other guests also came to pray. Both merchants, and Iona would bet they were asking for safe passage and favorable winds as they traded over the sea.

And with that, Iona was in her 'this is a decent person' books.

"I'm wondering where the unaffiliated altar is? I'd like to pray to my patrons." Iona asked.

"Follow me!" The Sister said. "Just don't touch any of the artwork."

As they walked through the Abbey, the Sister gave Iona a brief tour.

"Over there are the kitchens, the dining halls there, that's Mother Superior's room, those are the novice dorms..."

On and on it went, with Iona mentally marking the novice dorms. That was her target. She was careful not to touch any of the artwork. It was one of the rules here.

Nevermind that "sneaking around in the dead of night" was probably against the rules.

"... and here's the unaffiliated altar!" She said, finishing the tour.

It was a tiny room, out of the way, dusty, practically a closet, but that was fine with Iona.

"Let me know if you need anything!" The cheerful Sister told Iona.

"I'll probably be here awhile. I'll be able to find my way out on my own though?" Iona said, noticing how the Sister was somewhat fidgety, looking somewhat impatient. Good chance that –

"Yeah, ok!" She said, and turned and left.

Iona closed the door with a grin.

Unaffiliated altars were an afterthought in most temples and other religious buildings. The temple was to THE GREAT GODDESS, and, oh yeah, let's not offend the rest of the pantheon and include a secondary, minor altar for all of them.

But the acolytes of a religious building tended to be focused on their particular god or goddess, and benevolently neglected the unaffiliated one. Hence the dust, and general unused-ness of the altar.

This one was particularly bad, and Iona spent a few moments tidying it up, before kneeling to pray.

Selene! Lunaris!

*Found an altar! Going to work some mischief. Nothing too bad, but I don't think Ness would approve. Let me know if she's going to smite me or send some **[Paladin]** after me.*

Iona smiled as she heard the goddesses laughing, knowing the prank she was going to pull. She had their approval... which wasn't the same as having their protection.

Anyways, I wanted to talk more about the pirates. See, I first heard about them when....

Iona didn't know how long she'd been kneeling in prayer, just talking with the two goddesses. She'd also checked her level-up notifications while praying, it was just part of how she did things. It felt right for her, and joy of joys, she got a level in **[The Dusk Valkyrie]**, and three in **[Traveling Archer]**. When she got back up, it was dark.

Nighttime.

Perfect.

Iona creaked the door open a hair, and quickly looked around. Nobody was around, but that didn't mean a nun wouldn't turn the corner any minute now. It wouldn't surprise Iona if there were some younger acolytes who had been sent to the Abbey, who snuck around at night – and some of the Sisters patrolled the hallways, looking for wayward charges.

The moons were up, and half full, throwing red light around everywhere. More than enough to see and sneak around by.

Iona looked up, and briefly considered climbing up to the ceiling, and moving around up there. She had the stats for it... but she wasn't sure if the ceiling could hold her. It looked delicate, almost art-like.

And she had been told not to touch the art.

Fortunately, traps and alarms were unlikely. Who trapped their own home? Who risked waking everyone up when one of the younger nuns snuck around?

No, worse-case there was an alarm for one of the Sisters on-duty, but Iona imagined a perimeter alarm was much likelier than an internal one.

And Iona had made sure to brazenly walk in through the front door before nightfall.

Iona slunk around, silently padding through the hallways before reaching an intersection. She didn't have [Sneaking] or [Quiet Footsteps] or anything – but she did have soft shoes and over 10,000 points in dexterity. Sadly, there was no way to justify this as [Vow]-worthy.

Iona reached an intersection before the novice's dorms, only to freeze in panic as she heard footsteps.

She quickly determined that they were coming from the novice's dorms, and fled back down the hallway, making sure she restrained herself to move slowly enough to not create a breeze, to not have her clothes rustle against each other and give herself away.

Iona didn't have [Sneaking], but she and the other squires had totally done sneaking around the castle when they should've been in bed once upon a time. Iona was no stranger to this game – except nuns instead of Valkyries, and fleeing in embarrassment and not seeing Julie instead of a paddle and extra-hard training.

Iona allowed herself to shed a single tear for the friends that she'd lost, that she'd never see again, before refocusing.

She was losing another friend, but not to death, and this time, she'd say goodbye.

The Sister's footsteps receded down another hallway, and Iona seized the chance to blitz into the dorm.

Now was the hard part. Dozens of closed doors, and only one was right. There were three options when Iona checked on a door.

- It was empty. Try again.
- It had Julie! Success!
- It had someone else. Time to run away!

Iona thanked her lucky stars that she'd decided to pick up [Tracking]. Not only did it usually help with hunting down whatever monster was causing trouble, but it'd help now.

In theory.

Iona focused on her skill, her nose, and Julie, sniffing the air. She'd had her face buried in her soft fur often enough, smelling like a lively forest in spring, with a hint of sunshine and berries.

Iona was no beastkin, nor was she of a race that was blessed with an improved sense of smell. Almost 30,000 vitality together with [Tracking] somewhat made up for it.

Near each room she'd quietly sniff, seeing if the scent matched Julie's.

Weirdly, there was no smell from almost every room. Business wasn't doing well.

Eventually, Iona hit a room that smelled right enough. Not perfect... but Iona chalked that up to time and the new place.

Iona strained her ears to see if anyone else was around. Not hearing the menacing footfalls of one of the nuns patrolling the hallways, she softly rapped on the door.

"Julie! Psst, Julie!" Iona hissed at the door.

Nothing.

Iona knocked again, a bit louder.

"Julie!"

Nada.

Iona knocked one last time, a rapid staccato drumming on the door. She froze as she heard movement in two rooms.

The handle clicked, the door opened, and there she was, in all her tired glory – Julie.

"Huh? Iona? Wha-?" Julie said, at cursed normal volume, as Iona barged in, putting a finger on her lips and closing the door behind her.

"Shhhhhhhhhhhh!" Iona whisper-hissed. "Otherwise they'll find us!"

Having gone from "sleeping" to "someone's barging in my room", Julie was remarkably composed, not shouting – just getting that mischievous grin that kitsunes were so famous for, amusement dancing in her eyes.

The two of them said nothing, the only thing louder than their pounding heartbeats was the sound of the other acolyte asking questions of the hallway – then the patrolling nun finding her, and softly yelling at her.

Iona and Julie's face were both straining with restrained laughter, and at last, Iona couldn't take it anymore. She grabbed the pillow, shoved it over her face, and let peals of laughter break loose. Julie had better restraint, as she quietly laughed in that high, yipping way.

After a few minutes, they were able to compose themselves.

"What are you doing here!?" Julie hissed at Iona.

"I wanted to say goodbye." Iona said.

"You could've just asked to see me!" She retorted.

"Yes, but then how could I have..." Iona trailed off a moment as she patted herself for Julie's letter. She unfurled it, and started quoting from it.

"How could I have kissed your lips one last time? How could I rub your ears, run my hands through your fur, massaged your-"

Blushing, knowing the rest of the line, Julie snatched the letter back from Iona.

"I didn't expect you to sneak in!" She said.

Iona winked roguishly at her.

"Nobody does! You didn't expect it the first time either, did you?"

"I did too!"

Ok, fair point there.

"Well, look, I'm here now. Why don't we chat? Talk about old times before you become one of the stuffy nuns."

Julie snorted.

"I swear, the Mother Superior must have a **[Shove a Stick up your Arse]** skill. All the nuns get stodgier and stodgier as time goes on."

Iona grinned at her.

"See what I mean?"

Julie punched her in the shoulder.

"And what do you mean, 'old times'? We've only known each other for three years! We only spent like three weeks together, total!"

Iona's face went from smiling to sad. She tried to fight back tears.

"Julie... that makes you one of my oldest friends." Iona barely managed to get out.

Julie's face fell, as she hugged Iona.

Iona hugged her back, wrapping the smaller kitsune in her gigantic frame.

"I'm sorry." Julie said, after a moment or three passed. "I forgot."

Iona patted her on the back.

"It's ok."

They broke the embrace, and Julie hopped onto her bed.

"Hey Iona?" She asked.

"Yeah?"

"Do you still have [Drawing]?"

"Yeah, why?"

"Draw me. Get a picture of me as I am now, bring it with you."

The light played with the shadows to make an interesting portrait, but Iona had no trouble breaking out her drawing supplies, and starting to sketch Julie. Swift lines crossed the paper, drawing almost as fast as an experienced painter with classes and skills. Such was the tyranny of insane stats.

As Iona drew, the two idly chatted, catching up on what had happened since they'd last met. Julie told the mundane tale of the life of a trader, the discovery and subsequent ultimatum. Iona hung onto every word, hearing stories of a world not her own.

"Are you sure you want to be here?" Iona asked. "It'd be easy enough to walk out with you."

Julie nodded.

"What would I do? Where would I go? I'm not strong like you Iona. I can't forge my own path." She said.

Iona privately disagreed – anyone could forge their own path, especially with the System.

But maybe that was just it. Julie didn't have the drive, the resolve, the fire needed to do that – and hence, wasn't strong enough.

Iona shrugged.

"If you're happy, I won't stop you." She said.

Julie smiled, and settled back down further on the bed. Lounging on the bed, in a pose well-suited to being drawn.

Iona finished up, and showed Julie the portrait.

"Oooh! That's me! It's so good!" Julie cooed over the picture. "Do yourself!"

Iona rolled her eyes.

"With what mirror?" She asked.

Julie got a mischievous look on her face, and slipped the habit down over one shoulder, exposing a breast.

"Well... why don't you draw me like one of your Rolland girls then?" She asked with a sultry tone, waggling her eyebrows.

Iona's drawing was fast, and quickly discarded. She then made an attempt at filling Julie's entire wishlist of "things I regret not doing."

Except that one thing that needed a stuffed unicorn. Iona didn't count.

The bed did make a fine seesaw after some quick reconfigurations though.

They only stopped when the sun was starting to peek over the horizon, and both of them were covered in sweat and other fluids.

"You need to get out of here." Julie panted out, wrung out and exhausted. "The Sisters will be mad if they find you."

Iona agreed. She already heard footsteps in the hallways as people were getting up.

She gave Julie one last kiss.

"Hey. If you need anything – just write! I'll try to swing by." Iona said with a wink.

Julie laughed and threw a pillow at Iona.

"Shoo! Get out of here! If they catch you here with me, it's the birch stick for me."

Iona grinned.

The halls were filling up with nuns, and going out the normal way? Impossible not to get caught.

However…

"All the rooms are the same, right?" Iona asked

Julie nodded.

"Well. This is goodbye then." Iona said, giving her one last hug.

"Goodbye Iona." Julie said.

They broke apart, and Iona focused, seeing if her latest stunt would qualify as protecting Julie. She felt no boost come over her, and she mentally shrugged. It wasn't needed, it'd just be nice.

Iona cracked the door a hair, and seeing nobody in the hallway for a moment, burst out of the room, entered the room next to Julie's – to not implicate her – and launched herself feet-first out the window.

She ignored an alarmed shout as she landed on the grass outside the abbey, and was off in a sprint a moment later, off to her weapons cache, grinning all the way.

Crying all the way.

She made it back to her weapons, and as she slung them back on, considered what her next move was.

The pirate's treasure was still at the bottom of the bay, and with the stupid amount of mana Alfie had used, was probably more than a bit valuable. The Valkyries could use it.

There was the healer in the south, a flashpoint for a full-fledged Immortal war. Diving into the fray could be useful, although Iona would need to whisk the healer away somewhere nobody could find her – probably into the Immortal lands, where such people were welcomed.

Then again, Immortals brought the trouble on themselves, and for millions of others in multiple other countries. So thoughtless.

It was a healer that needed help though. Iona was indecisive.

In the other direction was getting back to the Valkyrie castle, and reporting back to Sigrun, and seeing what the next emergency that needed a Valkyrie was. Possibly getting a squire, expanding the order, demonstrating they still had value, etc.

Bonus – Randall was in the town around the castle, and it'd been a while since she'd visited him.

Finally, there was finally spending some time on working on acquiring and bonding with a companion. Iona was one of the oldest Valkyries who'd never tried to get one. Iona believed that she was good, that she'd bond with one – she'd just never had the time.

Choices, choices. She chewed on them – and some jerky – as she walked back through the forest.

Onto the next adventure.

[Name: Iona]

[Race: Human]

[Age: 21]

[Mana: 72880/72880]

[Mana Regen: 81,992]

Stats

[Free Stats: 0]

[Strength: 18,440 +(177,577)]

[Dexterity: 18,440 +(177,577)]

[Vitality: 33,286 +(65,074)]

[Speed: 20,415 +(196,596)]

[Mana: 7,288]

[Mana Regeneration: 21,782]

[Magic Power: 5,437]

[Magic Control: 5,437]

[Class 1: [The Dusk Valkyrie - Celestial: Lv 391]]

[Celestial Affinity: 391]

[New Moon's Dance: 391]

[Weapon Mastery: 376]

[Strength from the Stars: 377]

[Celestial Armaments: 375]

[Moon's Descent: 384]

[Stellar Body: 391]

[Gaze of the Galaxy: 383]

[Class 2: [Traveling Archer - Ice: Lv 314]]

[Ice Affinity: 314]

[Shortbow Skills: 299]

[Blizzard Shot: 271]

[Chilled Mind: 281]

[Trick Shot: 305]

[Ice Arrow Conjuration: 305]

[Glacial Slow: 265]

[Snowflake Drift: 261]

[Class 3: Locked]]

General Skills

[Drawing: 180]

[Valkyries Valor: 388]

[Adaptable: 202]

[Tracking: 210]

[Vow of Iona to Lux: 321]

[Magnetic Charm: 169]

[Comprehensive Education: 280]

[Dinosaur Husbandry: 280]

Other

Blessing of Selene and Lunaris

Printed in Great Britain
by Amazon

34675492R00297